THE ROSE WELL FILES

First Published in Great Britain 2021 by Mirador Publishing

A copy of this work is available through the British Library.

ISBN: 978-1-913833-97-8

Mirador Publishing
10 Greenbrook Terrace
Taunton
Somerset
UK
TA1 1UT

The Rose Well Files

By

David Luddington

Return of the Hippy
The Money That Never Was
Schrodinger's Cottage
Forever England
Whose Reality is this Anyway?
Camp Scoundrel
The Bank Of Goodliness

Rose Well Holiday Park

CARTER'S FIELD

Flat Foods Pizza

Codden Chips

Baquette 'n Go

Big Moo Burger

Main Dining Room

Admin

Car Park

Theatre

Pirates Bay

TICKET

Amusements

Kid's Playground

Swimming Pool

Laundry

Shops

Sunroom

RAGGEDY

Residential

Fixed Cabins

HAWAII

Variable quality Mostly residential

Grand Central Showers

BERMUDA

Mostly residential

Showers

YELLOW BRICK ROAD

MONTEGO BAY

Hippies & Preppers

CARTER'S FIELD

Old WW2 Airfield

ROUTE 67

BERMUDA

PARADISE BAY

Posh bit Holiday lets & residential

Chapter One

I TIDIED MY LITTLE DISPLAY of books and comics for the seventh time, not that I was counting. I just needed to make sure each item could be seen clearly when the visitors arrived. The clock above the entrance doors showed eight minutes to ten. The hands had moved on exactly two minutes since I'd last looked and now only eight minutes remained until the doors opened. With luck, today should get rid of the last of this batch of stock I'd been carting around, and after this I'd have to seriously consider what happened next. Do I go back home to pick up another load and simply carry on selling off my old stock until it's all gone? Or should I consider buying in more? It was a decision I'd successfully put off for a year, but which now loomed closer as each event further depleted the contents of my lockup back in London.

I pushed the last two copies of the Batman Vs Superman comics clear of the rest of the stack and studied them. They were the rarest items on the table and if I took a good price for those, they alone would cover the costs of this leg of my journey. Anything else would be a bonus.

"Your first Alt-Life Convention?" the girl at the next stand asked. She stood tall and willowy in front of her elaborate display of crystals and tarot cards. Her hair, black as the velvet covering her table, flashed with streaks of petrol blue.

"First time here," I said. "I mostly do the London ones, closer to home. Although, I did do Conspiracy-Con in Blackpool a few months ago. That was huge."

"Blackpool huh? That must have been awesome. I always wanted to go to Blackpool."

I nodded and looked around the room at the scattering of exhibitors. Ten or twelve stands. It wasn't a large hall by any standards, yet it still looked empty.

"I rather had the impression this would be bigger," I said.

"What, here?" Her voice traced the soft, rolling sound of the Cornish accent. "Little Didney doesn't really do alternative. More into home-made fudge and painted seashells. Their idea of alternative is to put the jam on *after* the cream on a scone."

She moved over to my stand and picked up one of my books. "The God Machines, Eric Scringle. Who's he then?"

"Ah, now there's a thing," I warmed instantly into my patter. "He used to work for the Ministry of Defence in their Special Projects Office, Cheltenham. S.P.O.C. Rather an unfortunate acronym I always thought."

"Why's that then?"

"Because…" I studied the girl in front of me and guessed her to be in her early twenties. "Oh, nothing. Anyway, the author, Scringle disappeared some years ago, shortly after he wrote this."

"Never heard of him."

I glanced at the clock again. Exactly ten o'clock. "We'd best get ready; they'll be coming in any minute." I took the book from her hand and squared the piles one last time.

She looked towards the doors. "Nah, Alfie's not here yet."

"Alfie?"

"He's got the keys. He'll be along dreckly." She poked at a few more books on my table. "You got any Buffy comics? I like those."

"No, just stuff about UFOs and so on. And a few collector's comics, rare ones mostly. I used to have a bookshop in London, these are my old stock. I'm just selling them round fairs and conventions now."

She picked up a copy of 'Secrets of Area 51' and riffled through the pages of the book like it was a deck of cards. "What's this one about then, Area 51?"

"It's an exposé about the alien creatures they're keeping there."

"Where?"

"Area 51. America. It's a top-secret military base."

"Not very secret though, is it?" She put the book down on top of the pile of Spiderman comics.

"What do you mean?" I took the book and returned it to its proper place and squared the pile.

"Well, *you* know about it, and now so do I. Not much of a secret." She chewed her bottom lip in thought. "And isn't it a bit stupid that they give their secret places numbers?"

"I don't think—"

"I mean, that lets on they've got another fifty secret bases. Doesn't it? They shouldn't number them if they want to keep them secret."

"I don't think they're *all* secret," I said. "Only that one. And possibly Area 52."

She picked up another book and idly flicked the pages without really looking at them. "If it was me, I wouldn't have numbered the secret ones." She flicked her head up as if a thought had just struck her. "Oh, but then I s'pose people would notice if they went from fifty to fifty-three. Somebody would spot that. Hmm... I see the problem."

"Do you think you should get ready?" I said and glanced towards the door. "We're going to be late."

"You're new to Cornwall, aren't you?"

I shrugged.

The girl continued, "Cornish timekeeping is a bit like a railway timetable. Much more to do with a sense of optimism than any basis in reality." She placed the book on the edge of the table and headed back to her stand.

Alfie eventually turned up at eleven minutes past ten, giving me just enough time to move my books from one side of my table to the other and then back again. He fiddled with the keys and the padlock as if it was the first time he'd ever seen such contraptions, before swinging the double doors wide open. I shifted to one side of my table to give the incoming wave of people a clear view of my display as they came in.

The wave turned out to be more of a trickle. That's if three people could be described as a trickle. One of the trickle, an elderly lady carrying two carrier bags stopped just inside the doorway and stared for a moment at the stands. She shook her head and muttered something before turning and shuffling back into the morning sunshine.

The two remaining visitors, a man in a baseball cap and a woman in white shorts and a Chanel T-shirt, wandered into the hall and drifted between the stalls. They each stopped briefly at my stand, picked up a few books and glanced at the covers before replacing them and wandering off again. Not so much as a word exchanged or even acknowledgement of my presence. The man looked at his watch and headed outside while the woman had a long conversation with the two guys selling hemp clothing.

I'd been there for nearly two hours before anybody actually spoke to me. A strange fellow with wild hair, a beard, and a permanently surprised face. He carried a cardboard box full of what looked like broken electronics. He pushed my books to one side with his box to clear space on which to park it. I had to snatch one before it fell to the floor.

"I only came in to buy a crossbow," he said, staring around the room.

I scanned the other stalls. "I don't think you'll get one here," I said. "The stall near the toilets has got some catapults."

He stared at me with eyes which seemed too big for the rest of his face and which, disturbingly, never blinked. "You can't kill a zombie with a catapult."

"Of course. Have you tried a sporting goods shop?"

"They won't sell me them. Haven't got an I.D. see." He picked up a copy of The Roswell Conspiracy. "Isn't that where the King of the Lizard People landed?"

I smiled nicely. Flogging these sorts of books around these events always made for strange conversations. "No, this one's more to do with the cover-up," I said.

He handed the book back to me then asked, "Do you want to buy some computer bits?" He dove into his box and came out with a little black box trailing dangly wires. "I got one of these."

"No thanks. I think I already have one of those."

He picked up his box. "I gotta go. Scooter will think I've been kidnapped again."

I watched him disappear out of the doors, then searched the room in the hope of seeing any likely prospects. A boy, sixteenish, drifted through the stalls. He headed in my direction and picked up a rare Thor comic, the 131 issue. I fought the desire to snatch it away from him.

"It's a very rare issue," I said. My fingers twitched, ready to catch it if he dropped it.

"Cool," he said. "Who's in it?"

"Um, Thor."

"Cool, same name as the geezer in the Avengers movie."

"Sort of. This is the original version. Would you like to buy one? I have some less expensive ones here."

"Nah, I read comics on my phone. Simpsons are best, Bart's my favourite but I like Otto too. He's cool." He tapped the comic on the table as he spoke.

"Sorry, I haven't got any Simpsons." I took the comic from his hand. I don't think he even noticed.

"My granddad's got a load of comics and magazines and stuff in his shed. Porn mostly, he don't know I know. Do you want to buy some? I can fetch you some, he'll never notice."

"No thank you, I'm trying to sell these."

He pushed a couple of books around the table as if playing draughts. "Didn't think nobody bought books no more. You should use Tap to Share." He left several books the wrong way round and wandered off to look at hemp T-shirts and banana leaf plates.

I waited by the side of my stand in the fading hope of the next wave of eager attendees. They never came, so I spent some time reorganising my display. When they still didn't come, I pulled out my folding garden chair and sat for a while beating myself up over the stupidity of spending my dwindling savings on this fiasco. Self-flagellation was a road previously well-trodden and took no more than a few minutes to do it all over again. I glanced at the door. It remained stubbornly devoid of people so, for the want of something to stare at other than an empty room, I pulled out my smartphone and looked up Tap to Share.

I tried several variants, Taptooshare, TapTwoShare, Tap-to-share, all with no results. At one point, my phone was overtaken by a particularly persistent, and very noisy, porn site. It took a good minute to get rid of the groans and oohs which emanated surprisingly loudly from my phone. For a moment, I was quite grateful for the absence of customers. In the end, I had to yank the battery from the phone in order to clear it.

Finally, I discovered it was spelt *Tap2Share*. Of course it was.

The website described it as '*A file sharing Micro-Market platform for the buying and selling of eBooks in a contact environment.*' I guessed that meant face to face. It looked like all I needed to do was put the text file of a book on my phone and then when somebody wanted to buy a copy, we each enter a code in our respective phones, and they get the book and I get paid. I stared at the pile of books on my table. How had all this moved on so quickly? It seemed like only weeks ago when I'd proudly opened my bookshop, lovingly choosing the books and displaying them to encourage book-lovers to browse and engage.

"Not quite up to Conspiracy-Con, huh?"

I looked up to see the girl from the tarot and crystal stall standing over me.

"No, but I can't afford that one anymore," I said.

"I sold a couple of packs of Mother Teresa Tarot Cards. They always go down well. Do you want to get some tea?" She nodded towards the temporary café at the far end of the room.

"Shouldn't we stay here? There might be more people any minute."

"No, it's afternoon nap time now. The locals will all be asleep soon, or in a bar." She thought for a moment and added, "Or asleep in a bar."

"What about the tourists?"

"Too early for them. Wait till the schools break up, then you won't be able to move."

I looked towards the door. The spring sunshine breaking the entrance only served to emphasise the stillness. "I suppose we can keep an eye out from there."

An elderly woman with a careless thatch of white hair smiled as we approached. Her eyes blazed unnaturally blue from the contours of a well-loved face. "Tea, loves?" she asked. "Got some lovely fudge-cake or a treacle tart if you'd rather. All home-made."

We took our tray of teas and sticky cakes and found a place where we could keep an eye on our stands. Our little fold-up table threatened to refold itself every time I moved my teacup, despite the wedges of folded serviettes under each leg. I sipped at my tea and kept a watching eye on the emptiness that surrounded our respective stands. The sugar rush of the treacle tart softened the edges of my frustration.

"I'm William, by the way." I held out my hand then realised it was sticky with treacle. I wiped it on a serviette. "William Fox."

"Cool, do I call you Bill or Billy?"

"Um, I prefer William, if that's okay? Bill, to me, is a Flowerpot Man and Billy is a wild west gunman."

"Huh?"

"Although, I also answer to Basil. That's what my school mates called me when Basil Brush was on the telly."

Her face distorted into a crumple of confusion. "Why?"

"Basil Brush, a puppet fox. Fox you see, my name? Boom-boom?"

"Dunno. I'm Rachel. My parents were watching Friends when I was conceived. Just glad they weren't into Pokemon. Can you imagine? Pikachu?"

My eyes drifted hopefully to the main doors again. "Do you think they'll all come after nap time?"

"They didn't last year."

I studied her for a moment. "So, why did you come back this year?"

She wrinkled her eyebrows as if trying to fathom a deeply stupid question. "I come every year. I have to, my dad runs this. What about you, why did you come here all the way from London?"

"How did you know I was from London?"

"Haven't you seen my stand? I'm psychic. I can read auras and talk secretly with your spirit animal while you're not looking."

I stared at her for a moment as I struggled through her explanation.

"And besides," she continued, "you left your London City Airport tag on your rucksack." She nodded towards my bag on the floor by my seat.

"Ah, yes. Well spotted."

"Flying to Cornwall, you must be well posh."

"No, far from it. Actually, it's cheaper than the train. And Icarus Airlines had a sale on."

"Still a bit out of the way for you though? Little Didney's hardly Oxford Street."

"I can't afford London rents. As I said, I'm just selling off stock from my old shop. Atlas World Store took all my customers, so I figured I'd do the one thing they could never compete with, face-to-face sales."

"Taking on Atlas World Store? Wow, respect." She made me fist bump. "What you gonna do when you've sold all your stock?"

"I really don't know," I said. "I hadn't planned further than selling off what I had."

A shadow fluttered through the glaring light of the door and a young man materialised. He stared around for a moment, then headed towards our stands. We both stiffened as we tried to anticipate which one he would make for. It looked like mine.

"Be back in a minute," I said and rushed to beat the man to my display.

He smiled and nodded at me as he picked up the Eric Scringle book 'The God Machines'. "I saw a TV documentary about this guy. Didn't he take off with a bit of a crashed UFO from the Rendlesham Incident?"

"So they say. He was in the MOD department responsible for investigating UFO sightings. Although, the MOD claimed he'd just run off with a bit of a space toilet from the European Space Agency. Would you like to buy it? I can do a discount."

He handed the book back to me. "No, I can download a video on him from Youtube, there's loads there, you should have a look. You don't know where the toilets are do you? That's all I popped in for really. I'm on these tablets you see."

I pointed to the far end of the room. "Over there, second door."

"Cheers, mate."

I watched him go, then headed back to the café.

"Toilets?" Rachel asked.

I just nodded and finished my tea. It had gone cold.

"Get a lot of that. They don't do public loos here, not like in Wolverhampton. They've got these magic boxes on street corners with a robot cleaner that come in after you've finished. I went there once, Wolverhampton. It rained."

The sunlight in the door shimmered briefly to announce the departure of the last visitor. I gathered the teacups and plates together. "I think I'll cut my losses and call it a day."

"You staying in the town?"

"No, I'm booked in at a Moto-Lodge out near Trekenwryth."

"You ought to come down The Smuggler's Arms tonight. They've got Elvis on. Not the *real* one."

"Sounds delightful but sadly I have some paperwork to do. I expect there'll be more people tomorrow."

"There wasn't last year."

~ * ~ * ~ * ~

I took a taxi up to the Trekenwryth Moto-Lodge and checked in.

"Have you stayed in a Moto-Lodge before?" asked the girl behind the counter.

"Yes, once or twice."

"Super. There's a TV in the room and a mini-bar. Would you like some bottled water brought to your room?" She pointed to a glass fronted fridge behind her counter. It was stacked with plastic bottles of water and proclaimed in a big sign across the top, 'Jejune - Nature's Own Water'.

"Is there something wrong with the tap water here?" I asked.

"Good heavens no, we just have a franchise with Jejune," she said, then added, "it's French," as if that explained everything.

"Why are we importing French water?" I caught her puzzled expression and finished, "Never mind, no. I'll stick with the tap water, thanks anyway."

I dropped my bags in the room and headed to the nearby pub for a pint and something to eat.

The man behind the bar in The Camelot welcomed me with a genuine smile and a cheery, "Evening, chief. What can I get you?"

I pointed at a pump on the bar with an ornate label proclaiming, 'Arthur's Courage'. "I'll try a pint of that, please."

"Good choice. Holidays?"

"No, I'm at the Alt-Life Convention down in Little Didney."

"What's that then?" He pulled at the lever and concentrated on the beer as it tumbled into the glass.

"It's a fair for alternative lifestyles but I'm selling books on alien encounters, ancient mysteries and ghosts and stuff."

"I saw a UFO one time." He pushed the pint across the bar towards me. "Name's Mike, by the way."

"Thanks, I'm William." I took the pint and sipped at the froth.

"It whizzed across the sky, then just disappeared. Real spooky it was."

"Might have been a meteor. Do you have a menu?"

Mike turned and nodded towards a chalk board behind the bar. "Got a special on tonight, Steak and Ale Pie with fettuccine. It's Italian."

I ordered the special and took my pint to a small table in the corner furthest away from the football pouring out of the television. Apart from a pair of young couples who sat at a table near the window staring at their phones, I had the place to myself. I relaxed into the seat and let the beer work its magic.

The meal came, and with it, another beer, unasked for. I could grow fond of this place. My natural nervousness of Steak and Ale Pie with fettuccine faded as soon as I started eating and wondered why nobody had thought of this combination before. I finished my meal and relaxed back for a moment while I gathered the necessary motivation to leave the comfortable surroundings in exchange for a cold but functional Moto-Lodge room.

Somebody had turned the television away from the football, and images of airport chaos filled the screen. Huge delays somewhere by the looks of it. The news reporter bounced from person to person, presumably asking how they felt at their impending delays but the sound was on mute so I could only guess. Probably French Air Traffic Control again. This was a Bank Holiday weekend after all, and that seemed to be their annual sport. I watched the unfolding drama with a slight sense of relieved detachment until the image of several grounded planes snagged my attention. They all bore the insignia of Icarus Airlines. That was a coincidence. That was the airline I'd flown down here with. More images of chaos. More images of Icarus planes. I moved closer so I could read the running newsfeed line across the bottom of the screen. 'Icarus Airline Collapse - Passengers Stranded.'

Chapter Two

I STARTED DAY TWO OF the Little Didney International Alternative Lifestyle Exhibition with a degree less optimism than I'd had on day one. My books and comics drifted somewhat more lazily across the table, and I settled in my chair immediately with the expectation of a long, boring day ahead.

Rachel busily fluffed peacock feathers, polished crystals and laid out tarot cards in some carefully designed way which clearly held deep significance for the universe. She glanced over at me. "You're Mister Cheerful this morning?"

"My airline's gone bust, so I'm stuck here." I tried not to make that sound sulky but failed.

"Stuck?" She stopped mid-polish and stared at me with duster in one hand and crystal in the other. "This is Cornwall, not Outer Moldovia. We have roads here now, you know. And railways."

"I know, but a rail ticket from here back to London is more expensive than a return flight to Barcelona. And takes longer. And I don't have a car so driving's out."

"You don't have a car?"

"I live in a flat in London. I can barely afford my own rent, let alone another thousand a month for a parking space."

"You could always hitchhike. I hitched all the way to Glastonbury last year. Easy."

I scanned her slender build, long legs and rush of thick jet hair. Briefly, I considered pointing out the obvious advantages she had over a middle-aged man when it came to hitching lifts with several large cases of books. I didn't. In the end I just said, "Maybe I'll get lucky today and make enough to pay the rail fare. Or hire a private jet, if that turns out to be cheaper. Which I suspect it might be."

"Here." She handed me the crystal she'd been polishing. "You can borrow her for the day. She's citrine, the merchants' stone. She'll bring you luck."

I took the crystal. It was about the size of a walnut and it transluced a soft honey colour. "Thank you, though, have you got a bigger one?"

"It's not the size that's important."

"Hmm, I—"

"Don't." She wagged a finger at me in mock scolding and went back to arranging a display of little twisty sticks.

The doors opened to an avalanche of morning sunshine but little in the way of people. I stroked the citrine crystal a few times for want of anything more constructive to do, but my luck remained stubbornly unturned.

I tried to find the phone number to Icarus Airlines, but my phone kept sending me to porn sites and I had to do another battery yanking restart to the phone before I could track down their number. I spent the next hour staring at my screen, trying to contact Icarus Airline's Emergency Customer Service number. Most of that time was filled with listening to a thirty second loop of Vivaldi's Four Seasons with occasional respites of a computer informing me how important my call was to them or being randomly disconnected.

Phoning Newquay Airport just produced even more frustration, as all calls concerning cancelled Icarus flights were simply rerouted back to

Vivaldi. I wondered how Vivaldi would react if he knew the strange infamy his masterwork had achieved. I gave up trying to find anybody to talk to me and watched the story unfold on the BBC news instead. After thirty minutes of interviews with unhappy passengers, knowledgeable pundits and third tier politicians blaming the other party, I decided I was screwed. No chance of a replacement flight or even a refund.

By lunchtime I'd had only a handful of visitors to my stand, and one of those had simply browsed the books before taking a photograph of the covers and heading off. Presumably to go online and order them from Atlas World Store. I counted my morning's takings and decided I could afford either a beer or a sandwich, but not both. The beer won the argument, and I left my stand under Rachel's watchful eye and went in search of a bar.

I didn't have to look very far. A sign outside The Smuggler's Arms caught my eye. "Real Ales, Genuine Home-made Cornish Pasties and Friendly Local Information'. Okay, so maybe a solely liquid lunch wouldn't be so clever. I decided I could probably push my budget into a deficit for the day and that a pasty might just do the job. I went inside.

At first sight, it looked like a caricature of an old English pub, a Disneyesque rendering, designed to appeal to foreign tourists. But as I scanned the ancient oak beams, the myriad horse brasses and the scattered wonky wooden tables, I realised this was all original.

The barman, however, clearly wasn't original. A soured looking youth, with a complexion which had clearly never seen either vegetables or sunlight, glanced up from his phone and muttered, "Yeah?"

"A half of that," I pointed at a pump declaring Smuggler's Best, "and one of your pasties."

"Where ya sittin?"

"Outside I think." I paid and took my beer outside and sat outside at a wooden bench table to watch the world drift about its business. The spring sunshine warmed the parts the beer hadn't reached, and I relaxed for a while and contemplated my options. That never took very long these days, as since the Inland Revenue had taken my house and shop, options were about as rare as seats on a Southern Railway's train.

On the other hand, I had no reason to hurry back to London. My dwindling original stock would need replenishing soon if I intended to continue this trail of the Comic Cons, Alt-Life Fairs and general Nerd Markets. Although, not the great life ambition with which I'd left school, but then, looking back, I'd never really had a great life ambition in the first place anyway.

And the sunshine was nice, so while I was here, I might seek out any local bookshops with whom I could do a deal. I looked up at the sign offering Local Information. There, I'd ask the barman if he knew of any.

A shadow appeared across the table and a plated pasty dropped in front of me with a, "Pasty."

I glanced up at the barman. "Thank you."

He grunted and turned to go back inside so I called, "Hang on."

He paused, sighed and turned.

I pointed at the sign. "Can I take advantage of your local information?"

He stared at me for a moment, then shrugged and said, "Well, for a start, I wouldn't eat the pasty if I was you." He turned and left.

I poked at the pasty then broke it open. It looked, and smelled, delicious so I decided to ignore the *Local Information* and took a bite. Every bit as good as it looked.

"You're William Fox?"

I turned to see the silhouette of a man standing against the sun. I squinted my eyes and the shape coalesced into a man with a straggly beard and baseball cap.

The silhouette didn't look much like a VAT man, so I said, "Yes."

"Rachel said you was here. Rachel, you know, with the crystals and wands? You're the guy with all those cool books about aliens and Deep State stuff. Rachel said you'd be here, she said, *'He'll be at The Smuggler's'*, that's what she said."

I squinted against the sun to make out the man's face and realised it was the man who'd come to my stand the day before looking for a crossbow. "Ah, we met yesterday. Did you find a crossbow?"

"Nah, got a samurai sword instead."

"Do they work on zombies?"

"Yeah, but not as good as a crossbow. You gotta get way too close for my liking."

"Of course. How did you know my name?"

"Rachel told me, and I was like, what? The *real* William Fox? And she was like, who? And I was like, how'd you not know?"

"I see. Well, I'm terribly flattered, but I'm only a bookseller. Are you sure you're not confusing me with somebody else?"

"You were kidnapped by the military and interrogated for a year at Mount Weather because you knew too much about aliens."

"Nope, not me." I sipped at my pint and studied the character across the table. He appeared to be mostly hair. Even his brown eyes seemed to blend in colour with the surrounding tangle.

"Are you sure? They framed you for murder?"

"I'm fairly sure. I think I would probably remember something like that. Though, I did once get the sack from my job as advertising sales executive for the Daily Sentinel."

"They activated the special DNA to read people's minds," he persisted.

The penny dropped. "Ah, you're not confusing me with Fox William Mulder, X-Files, by any chance?"

"Yes, that's you."

"No, that was a fictional character in a TV programme. I'm William Fox the bookseller, easy mistake."

"Oh." He looked disappointed. "Name's Wayne." He thrust a hand at me.

I took his hand and immediately regretted it when I noticed the caked-in dirt.

"Nice to meet you, Wayne."

"Scooter's going to be pissed off. I told him it was really you and he was like… wow. He didn't believe me. Are you really sure?"

"Yes, absolutely. Now, I really must be getting back, I have some books to sell." I finished my beer and stood to leave.

"I'll come with you." Wayne picked up his cap, flapped it against his arm as if shaking off dust, then planted it on top of his hair. "I want to buy another book. I've already got one you know."

"I never doubted it."

The hall seemed a bit livelier when we returned. Rachel stood by my stand and seemed in deep conversation with a couple of young men, one of whom was thumbing through a copy of Nick Pope's 'Open Skies, Closed Minds'.

I slid alongside Rachel and said, "It looks busy all of a sudden. What happened?"

"Coachload from Truro." She nodded towards my new best friend. "I see Wayne found you."

"Yes, thank you for that." I watched Wayne as he studied the back of a book on SAS survival techniques.

Rachel took payment from the man with the Nick Pope book and dropped it in my tin. "There you go." She handed me the tin. "I need to get back to my stand."

"Thanks, I owe you a drink."

Wayne waved the book at me. "How much?"

I took it from him and glanced at the back. "Five ninety-nine. Call it five."

He pulled a screwed-up note from his pocket and unfolded it carefully.

I took the note with fingertips and dropped it in my tin. "Thank you."

"You should come up to Rose Well Park. You'd sell a ton of books up there."

"Rose Well Park?"

Wayne slipped the book in his pocket. "Yeah, loads of cool people up there. Enlightened, know what I mean?"

"Sounds great, but sadly, I have to get back to London. Maybe next time."

"There might not be a next time." The hair surrounding his face took away any clues as to whether that strange statement was given in jest or as a dire prophecy.

I pondered it for the few seconds it took him to walk over to Rachel's stand. They exchanged a few words then he continued his way through the main doors where the sunshine swallowed him.

The rest of the day yielded a handful of sales and at least elevated the overall project from disaster to mediocre. Things were looking up. I gathered up my remaining stock, said my goodbyes to Rachel and took a taxi to the Trekenwryth Moto-Lodge.

I rang the Icarus Airline's help number but couldn't even get through to Vivaldi this time. I checked the prices of a train ticket back to London and provided I wanted to travel in three months' time then it would cost slightly less than a flight to Barbados but if I wanted to go tomorrow, it would be cheaper to buy the train and start my own railway. I attempted to find the website for a coach company to see if that might be cheaper, but my phone once more decided to present me with images of what could best be described as very intimate three-way naked yoga.

I gave up and headed to The Camelot under the self-delusion that it would be a good place to find somebody who might be driving back up to London.

Mike pushed a pint towards me as I approached the bar. That's always a bad sign when a barman starts to anticipate my needs.

"Evening, William. We've got a nice shepherd's pie with egg fried rice tonight. Cornish Asian Fusion, it's all the thing."

I ordered the special and asked Mike if he knew of anybody heading to London.

"Don't know many people who go up to London. We get lots of people coming *down* from London. Specially on a Bank Holiday weekend. That's probably not much help though."

I pulled my phone out. "Can I use Wifi here?"

"Sure." He pulled a little card from under the counter. "There's the code."

I looked at the card.

'*Wifi name = CIA Tracking Station 154*

Password = surrender.'

"That's different," I said.

"It keeps all the weirdos from Rose Well Park away. When they try to hook up to my wifi and see that come up, they run a mile." He gave a husky laugh which turned into a coughing fit.

I took my beer to a seat in the bay window and stared out at the road. The evening folded glowing red clouds across the hills and dusted the hedgerows with touches of orange. If I was going to be stuck somewhere for a few days, there were worse places. I remembered being snowed in on the M4 services at Membury one time. That hadn't been fun. Screaming kids everywhere and several coach parties of football hooligans who munched their way through the food concessions like an invading Pacman army.

I could afford a couple of days more in the Moto-Lodge, especially if I found somewhere to sell a few books. Maybe it was worth checking out that Rose Well Holiday Park place. Wayne had seemed to think it might be worth a punt. This could well be the turning point.

Mike turned up with my Cornish Asian Fusion and another beer, which I hadn't ordered.

"You mentioned Rose Well Holiday Park?" I asked.

"Yeah, you don't want to be going up there. All hippies and tinfoil hat wearing nutters. Their spring water's good though. Famous it is. Here, have a try." He picked up a square pottery jar with a picture of a rose entwined around a well and the words 'Rose Well Spring Water' hand-painted on it. He slopped some in a small glass and pushed it towards me.

I sipped, it tasted like water. I'd never been one for designer water. "It's okay," I said.

"Highest longevity in the UK in these parts. Locals say it's the water. What you be wanting up there anyway?"

"Oh, it's just that somebody mentioned it might be a good place to sell some books."

"Hmm, only if they're about space fairies or little green hobgoblins running the White House." He paused for thought. "On the other hand, you might do quite well." He gathered my empty glass and headed back to the bar.

Chapter Three

THE LOCAL BUS DROPPED ME at the end of a narrow lane. The driver assured me that Rose Well Holiday Park was "Just short hop 'n a step down yonder that way," and then continued on his way towards Penzance.

A short hop 'n a step turned out to be at least a mile, but the scenery, when it appeared through the gaps in the high banks and hedges, made up for the distance. Before I'd set out, I'd loaded my rucksack with books, unloaded it, reloaded with less, reloaded with more and eventually settled on just a handful. For that, I was grateful now, as even with my diminished selection, the straps were carving gouges in my shoulders. A moped hurtled past me as I stopped to adjust my straps for the third time. I couldn't see the rider as a thick, leafy bush, strapped to the pillion, completely obscured the top half. A cloud of smoke from the exhaust brought tears to my eyes and prevented any scent from the bush. Even so, I could take a fair guess at the species.

A few minutes later and the high banks and hedges ended, giving way to a wide expanse of green. The land was surprisingly flat here and only broken by a few drystone walls or ditches before breaking abruptly at the sea line. I paused to take in this sudden change, shrugging my bag to the ground. I guessed the sharp line between land and sea to be cliff tops, but it was impossible to judge how high from here.

In the distance, near the cliff edge, a gathering of grey shapes stood sharp with their geometric lines disturbing the gentle curves of the surrounding countryside. I guessed that was Rose Well Holiday Park. I re-saddled my rucksack and tried to persuade my feet we were just popping down Stanwell Street to the nearest Starbucks for coffee. They weren't convinced.

As I drew nearer, the grey shapes gave up their uniformity and the haphazard nature of the various structures caused me to stop and wonder how all this had come about. The area closest to the cliff edge retained the most uniformity. Rows of static caravans lined up like a game of dominoes at an OCD therapy meeting, each separated by a uniform patch of green. As the units spread backwards from the cliff edge, they became more anarchistic. Different shapes and sizes, different colours and increasingly haphazard parking. Gathered in a semi-circle around the chaotic end, stood several buildings of varying designs but all with a common theme of gentle dilapidation. I took a punt that if this strange site contained anything resembling an administrative area, it would probably be in one of these buildings. I selected what looked like the biggest and headed towards it.

The building turned out to be a onetime bingo hall. A fading poster behind a cracked plastic panel declared the opening hours of 10am to 10pm, except on Sunday. The bit detailing Sunday's opening hours had faded into obscurity, but as today was a Monday, it didn't concern me.

The doors, big grand affairs in crimson red and gold, seemed in remarkably good condition and when I pushed them, they swung inwards easily. I stepped cautiously inside, half expecting the doors to fall in on me. My feet crunched on bits of fallen plaster as I made my way across the huge foyer towards a smaller door at the far end. It had seemed like the best preserved door in the foyer, a modern pine affair, and so on the assumption that this represented some sort of functioning office, I knocked gently.

After receiving no response to a second knock, I pushed the door and it swung open. A woman sat behind an overcrowded desk in an otherwise empty room. She looked to be in her late fifties, shortish straight hair, unnaturally brown. She pulled a set of earphones from her head when she saw me.

"If you're looking for Scooter, he's not been here for weeks." She closed her laptop and pushed it to one side as if disowning it.

"Um, no. I was actually looking for the Concessions Manager."

"Concessions Manager is it? I don't think we have one of those. We have Charlie, the maintenance manager."

"Hmm, it's not really about maintenance. It's about setting up a stand here with some books."

"Ah, then you need to see our Book Stand Manager."

"Is he around?"

"Fixing a leaky pipe in the shower block at the moment."

"The Book Stand Manager? Oh, I see, that'll be Charlie?"

"Yes, there is only Charlie. Unless you're the Health and Safety Inspector, then you need to make an appointment to see James. But he doesn't really count."

"Why?"

"Because he doesn't exist."

"Okay, well Charlie then, can I book a meeting?"

She smiled and sat back in her chair. "Bless, aren't you a sweetie?" She pointed her hand to the door then indicated right. "Out the main entrance and you're in Downtown, then follow The Yellow Brick Road. You'll see the shower blocks on the left."

"The Yellow Brick Road?"

"Yes, yes, that way. Over there." She waved her hand again and opened her laptop as a sign the conversation was now over.

I headed through the door and turned right as indicated. Another, slightly less ornate, door took me out of the west side of the building. In the centre of a paved area, a tall mast, painted in a red and white spiral, held aloft a sign proclaiming, 'Downtown'. I assumed this to be the central area of the site. It was certainly quieter than any other 'downtown' I'd encountered before. There was also no sign of a Yellow Brick Road. A wide, paved path led past the door. To the right, it seemed just come to a dead end just beyond the buildings. So I turned left where it continued down in the direction of the cliff top disappearing in amongst the static caravan area. I followed it down and noticed a twee, but ageing wooden sign, announcing The Yellow Brick Road. Maybe it had once been a road and possibly even yellow, but today it was just a wide path with nature reasserting herself through ruptured tarmac at various points.

Downtown continued with a jumble of buildings which gathered around the road. A few fast-food outlets stood in line, Baguette & Go, a fish and chip shop called Codden Ships, a Big Moo Burger outlet and a Flat-Foods pizza parlour. The only one that showed any signs of life was the Big Moo Burger.

A small row of shops stood on the opposite side of The Yellow Brick Road, they all seemed empty apart from one which had a hand painted sign above the frontice announcing it to be, 'Dolly's Daily Shop'. Although this was currently closed. A closer look through the window suggested it offered a peculiarly eclectic selection of groceries, bread, camping equipment, alcohol, little pottery bottles of the local Rose Well Spring water, newspapers and camouflage clothing. I paused to check a small sign in the window outlining the opening hours, 'Mid-morning to lunch time, most days'. The next building down resembled a huge concrete block, square and grey. I wondered if this was the shower block and took a closer look. A couple of wooden-shuttered windows flanked a large double door, the brass handles of which were secured by an oversized chain and padlock. Above the door, a painted sign announced it to be 'Pirates Bay Pub' and a gaudy painting of a jolly pirate with an overflowing beer glass in his hand added confirmation. I felt an irrational urge to find some paint and add the possessive apostrophe to the word 'Pirates'.

I followed the path as it left Downtown and drifted between a few fixed cabin type structures then into the main area of static caravans. A lot of them looked dilapidated and empty, some dilapidated and occupied and others showing varying levels of care. Another path crossed my Yellow Brick Road at right angles, and just at that intersection stood another large concrete block. The Yellow Brick Road continued down beyond this crossing and into an area of seemingly well-kept caravans. I didn't follow any further as I noticed another wooden sign announcing Grand Central Showers.

I heard banging noises coming from an open door and ventured in.

"Hello?" I called, and the banging stopped.

"Shower block's closed. You'll have to use the ones in Bermuda."

I followed the sound of the voice. "Isn't that a bit far?" I stepped through an opening and felt water lapping at my shoes and took one step back to dry land.

A figure appeared from an open shower cubicle clutching an adjustable spanner. "You new?" she asked.

I studied the figure as she emerged into the dim light of the room. She wore oil-stained green overalls and short Wellington boots. Her tightly cropped, bleached hair clung to her forehead. Clearly the result of a recent encounter with a large amount of water.

"Not really new," I said. "Just visiting. Isn't Bermuda a bit far to go for a shower?"

She pulled a cloth from a pocket and wiped her face. "It's the east field, over there, love." She waved her cloth. "Bermuda. This is the west field, Hawaii. If you want a shower, then the block in the Bermuda field is still working."

"I see. No, I'm not after a shower, I'm looking for Charlie," I said.

"Well, it looks like you found me. What can I do for you, love?" She wrung out the cloth and stuffed it back in her pocket.

"The lady in reception sent me to see you. I'm thinking about setting up a book stand here. She said you'd be the person to talk to."

"She did, did she? Well, you can tell her to... No, never mind, I'll tell her myself." She tossed the spanner in a gentle somersault and it landed with a slap in her palm.

"Oh, I'm sure she never meant—" I started.

Charlie smiled and stepped forwards out of the puddle of water surrounding her. I flinched back as she approached.

"Don't worry, love," she said. "That lazy twonk is my wife, heaven help me." She tapped my shoulder and headed out through the door. "Come on then, a book stand you say?"

I followed her out of the shower block, and we set off back up The Yellow Brick Road.

I looked again at the fixed cabins as we passed them. Some showed signs of obvious neglect, but many seemed quite well maintained, although none seemed occupied.

"So, what *is* this place?" I asked.

She stopped and turned to face me. "Rose Well Park? Well, backalong aways, it was a holiday camp. Toplin's Camps?" She studied me for a moment. "No, probably not *your* childhood. All the thing in the fifties and sixties. They had all the big names. Tommy Handley, Morecambe and Wise, Billy Fury. They all played here. Even the Beatles one time. Before they were famous of course, the Quarrymen I think they called themselves then. Nowadays, it's mostly home to lots of folks. Some of 'em live here all the time, some of 'em come and go. This bit here f'rinstance," she waved her arm around the cabins on each side of The Yellow Brick Road, "these are mostly out-of-towners. Come down here bank holidays or summer weeks. Keep themselves to themselves mostly. Then down there, Hawaii and Bermuda and Montego Bay, that's where most of the full-timers live. Get some holidaymakers too, but not so many lately."

She led the way back to the main building and into the office.

"Laura," she called. "What you send this emmet down to me for?" She pointed at me without turning her head.

Laura looked up from her laptop. "I was busy."

"And how *is* Facebook?"

"I was checking the bookings schedule." The laptop gave a little toot-toot noise, and she shut the lid quickly.

"Well, this fella wants a book stand." Charlie pointed at me.

"I'm William," I said. "I'm a specialist book and comic dealer. Somebody told me this would be a good place to promote." I looked around the bare room with its peeling plaster and faded paintwork.

"Hmm, comics," said Laura. "That'll be about the mark for this lot here. Comics. Beano's about right."

"So, do you think I could have a stand somewhere?" I asked.

"Suit yourself," Laura said. "Shall we say a hundred quid a week?"

"Shall we say five percent on sales?" I said.

"Cash?"

"Of course."

"Deal, but say nothing to Jenna. Our little secret."

"Who's Jenna?"

"Never mind."

Chapter Four

THE FOLLOWING DAY, I HEADED back to Rose Well Holiday Park. Mike in The Camelot had offered me the loan of a little van he wasn't using. Nominal fee of course, but still easier and cheaper than the bus. I soon understood why he never used it. The steering was so loose it resembled a ship's wheel and was about as responsive. I had to anticipate each corner and start turning long before it seemed necessary, but with luck and good timing, I managed to drift round them and stay mostly on the road. And with Cornish lanes, that meant a lot of anticipating and drifting. By the time I reached Rose Well Park, I'd even managed several corners entirely on the right side of the road.

I parked in the gravelled area at the front of the main buildings and unloaded. Mike had also offered me free use of a stand he'd found in his shed. It was a wire-framed, revolving tower and had clearly once been used as a pork scratchings display. I'd worked that out by the fact that it had big lettering around the top proclaiming, 'Krunchee's Porky Scratchings'.

Laura showed me what she considered the best spot to set up, a glass fronted conservatory type construction next to the laundry room. She'd suggested that, as apparently, it was where everybody sat while they were either waiting for their laundry to finish or for the Pirates Bay pub to open. Often both. Either way, it wasn't altogether unpleasant. The sunlight powered through the glass and despite the early hour, the area warmed nicely.

I set up the pork scratching tower first. The wire pockets, each of which were designed to carry several packets of Krunchee's Scratchings, accommodated a paperback book perfectly. The rest of the books, along with the comics, I displayed on my folding table. Once I'd set everything and rearranged it all a few times, I settled in an overstuffed, and well-worn, armchair to enjoy the view over the bay.

My first potential customer was a woman, probably in her mid-forties. She wore dark charcoal jeans and a black shirt which accentuated her slim, almost masculine physique. Her one concession to femininity was a tumble of auburn hair flashed with dashes of gold. I couldn't make out if that was intentional or nature. She gave me a smile of acknowledgement, checked her watch and stood at my table.

"You're new," she said. "You set this up with Laura?"

"Yes, she was very helpful," I said.

"I'm sure she was."

"I'm having a sale. Two for the price of three and must finish Friday."

"I could never resist a sale," she said, picking up a Wonder Woman comic. "I used to love these as a kid. She was my hero. How much is it?"

"That's a really rare one." I stood and joined her by the table. "*The Kidnapped Dummy*, only a handful left. It's a bit tatty though, so you can have it for fifty?"

"Pence?"

"Quid."

"Fifty quid? I shouldn't have thrown all mine out." She placed the comic back on the table and turned her eye to the books. "You're into space aliens then?"

"Not just. I do conspiracies and general spooky stuff as well."

She picked up a book exposing how the CIA had a secret base underneath Stonehenge. "And you believe all this stuff?"

"Of course."

She turned and gave me a look which clearly said she didn't believe me. Her left eyebrow twitched upwards. "Really?" she challenged.

"Not a word of it," I admitted.

"Thought so." She tapped the book in her palm once then replaced it on the Krunchee stand. "I've been around here for long enough to spot bullshit a field-and-a-half away." She checked her watch again and settled in an armchair. She tapped and swiped at the screen of her phone.

"So, I can't talk you into a copy of 'King Arthur was a Martian'?"

She didn't glance up from her phone. "No thanks, I'm only here waiting for my tea-towels to finish their rinse cycle." She flicked her head in the direction of the launderette.

"Oh." I sat back down in the overstuffed chair. "You must have a lot of tea-towels."

She sighed and looked up at me from across the phone. "You're going to be a talker, aren't you?"

I waved my hand dismissively. "Sorry, no. Don't mind me."

She returned to her phone and I shifted my gaze to the sea beyond the cliff edge. At least the view was better here than in the Little Didney International Conference Centre. And the chair was comfy. The silence of the room allowed the soft whir of the laundry machines next door to hum through the wall. She must have a lot of tea-towels to need a laundrette run. Maybe she collected them up? I couldn't even think how long I would need to collect tea-towels for to necessitate a devoted laundry cycle. A month, at least. I wondered why she just didn't put them in with a normal wash.

"Um…" I started.

She gave a tst noise, planted her phone on the arm of the chair and said, "They're from the bar next door. The Pirates Bay? So today I'm doing the weekly tea-towel run. Tomorrow is the highlight of my week when I go to the frozen food wholesalers."

"Oh, I see. I didn't mean… Sorry. What time do you open? I might pop in when I finish up here."

"Twelve. Providing I get the tea-towels finished." She smiled. "Now, I need to concentrate, I'm trying to complete Piggy Farm."

"Piggy Farm?"

"Mmm. It's an Angry Birds level. I've been working on this for two months."

I returned to sea-gazing and relaxed in the warmth of the sun through the glass. At least I did for two minutes until a man entered and stood in the middle of the room, staring at me. He seemed familiar.

He turned to the woman. "You alright, Jenna?"

She looked up briefly from her phone. "Oh, hi, Wayne."

The name rang a bell. Wild tangly hair escaped a green woolly hat, and he wore a camouflage jacket and trousers. His appearance gave me a slight concern that I was about to be taken hostage. He seemed to be waiting for some sort of response from me.

Then I twigged. "You were at the Alternate Living thing? How're you getting on with your Samurai sword?"

"Nah, Scooter took it off me. But I bought a shirt made from garlic stems which they said vampires can't touch. Laura said you were here, I thought you'd gone back to London?"

"Airline went pop, and I seem to be stuck here for a few days. You looking for some more books? I've got a copy of The Zombie Survival Guide."

"No, we've already got that. You got any books on how to disarm bombs?"

"No, oddly enough, there's not a huge demand for those. I've got a book on reverse engineering the Roswell spacecraft." I picked up the book and showed it to him.

"Has that got anything about bombs?"

I flicked through the synopsis on the back cover. "No, just run-of-the-mill stuff about quantum drives and subspace wormholes."

"Oh." He looked disappointed. "How about something like one of those books they do for cars, you know, the ones which show diagrams with bits of the engine and arrows and stuff to where all the bits are supposed to go."

"You mean like a Haynes Manual?"

"Yeah. That's the one."

"I've actually got one of those here for the USS Enterprise. That's quite fun."

"No, that's no good. I'm looking for one on... um..." He shifted his feet around as if unsure whether he should speak or run.

"Bombs?" I suggested.

He nodded and the green bobble on his hat bounced a few times before settling on his forehead.

"Sorry," I said. "How about a book on how to release your Psychic Inner Self? It's very popular."

"Already got that," Wayne said.

"This one?" I picked up the book.

"No, not the book. The psychic inner self. I got that. I see stuff. One time I had this dream where these clouds turned into pigeons and swooped down to steal all the apples from the butcher's shop in Little Didney. One of the pigeons looked like Boris Johnson. Then, exactly three weeks and a bit later, Nathan falls off his bike and breaks his arm. What'ya think of that?"

"I heard Nathan was as high as a kite when he broke his arm," Jenna said, without breaking her concentration on her phone.

"I still had the dream though. You can't argue with that. Anyway, gotta go. Catch you later then." He turned and scuttled out.

I watched him go, then looked towards Jenna. "Odd fellow," I said.

She looked up from her phone. "Huh? Oh Wayne? Yeah, one of a kind, Wayne. But then they're all a bit odd down there, if you ask me." Her phone gave a blip-blip noise. "Damnit," she said. "Now look. I've got to do that level all over again."

"Down where?"

"Montego Bay. But they keep themselves to themselves." She snapped the case closed on her phone and stood. "I've got to collect my tea-towels then I need to have a little chat with Laura. How much did she say she was charging you for this?" She nodded to the bookstand.

"Five percent," I said.

"Hmm." She dropped the phone in her bag and slid out of the door.

~ * ~ * ~ * ~

After selling a few books through the rest of the morning, I packed up around one o'clock and headed for the Pirates Bay pub for lunch.

The main doors had been fastened back and the entrance now consisted of a pair of short, red-painted swing-doors reminiscent of a western movie. I pushed my way through them, trying to resist putting on a John Wayne swagger. I failed.

The size of the place caught me by surprise. It seemed so much larger inside than it looked from outside that I was tempted to step outside again to see if I'd come through the door of a Police Box. The bar itself was a huge wooden L shaped affair taking up the furthest corner from the door. Fake palm trees formed pillars holding up the ceiling and huge, polystyrene rocks clustered either side of a stage which took up the opposite corner from the bar. Above the stage, plastic palm fronds meshed with a bamboo canopy in a pastiche of a Hawaiian beach bar. The walls featured fading murals of seascapes with desert islands interspersed with posters for mojitos at half price or adverts for Donny 'Mr Elvis' Jones.

I weaved between the empty tables and chairs and headed to the only part of the bar which showed any sign of life.

Although she had her back to the room, I recognised Jenna by the black shirt and gold flashes in her hair. She flicked a feather duster over the rows of brightly coloured liqueur bottles behind the bar.

Her secret spidey sense picked up my approach, and she turned towards me. I noticed the shirt she wore was actually different, although still black.

"Ah, the famous Mister William Fox," she greeted. "How go the books?"

"Surprisingly well."

"Good. Just a tip, anything to do with renting a space here, or basically anything to do with money, check with me, not Laura."

"Oh, okay."

She smiled. "Now, what can I get you?"

I scanned the row of ornate beer pumps and pointed to one with a picture of a hedgehog on it. "I think I'll try a pint of Old Furze-pig."

"Oh, those are just for show. All people want in here is Stella, Tennents or Carlsberg. Although, we do have bottles." Jenna pointed to a chiller cabinet behind the bar.

I chose a bottle of San Miguel and she opened it and planted it on the bar.

"This place reminds me of something from the seventies." I scanned the room. "Is it some sort of theme pub?"

"No, it *is* from the seventies."

"It's very quiet." I sipped at the beer.

"It'll pick up later, but it's always quiet this time of year. Only the residents here at the moment." She opened a San Miguel for herself. "Cheers, I don't mind if I do."

"What? Oh, right. Would you like a drink?"

She smiled and waggled the bottle in acknowledgement before drinking.

"You're not from round here, are you?" she asked.

"No, London. Came down for the Little Didney Alt-Lifestyle Fair. I never realised this place was here."

"Well, at one time, it was a luxury family holiday park, and then along came the cheap Spanish package holiday and everybody buggered off to Benidorm. Now it's sort of part holiday park, part residential and part top secret base for a bunch of Hobbits."

"Hobbits?"

"Yes, that lot down in Montego Bay. Wayne's mates. Busy digging holes in the old airfield and preparing for the zombie apocalypse. Harmless, mostly. Apart from Scooter, that boy's got problems. Anyway, how come Wayne was so excited to meet you?"

"He had me confused with Fox Mulder from the X-Files TV programme."

"Oh, I see, William Fox, Fox Mulder. It's not difficult to confuse Wayne. So you're turning a profit then?"

"Enough to cover my costs and a beer or two."

"If it pays the bills these days, that's a win." She ran a polishing cloth across the fake beer pumps.

"Wasn't my first choice," I said. "I used to sell advertising space in a big newspaper until they dumped me, so I used the payoff to buy a bookshop in London."

"That was brave of you, buying a bookshop? I thought Atlas World Store was busy killing off all the small bookshops?"

"Yes, they did. The shop went pop, but the liquidators left me with a lock-up full of stock, so now I go round these shows and Comic-Cons selling them."

"And so you end up here," she said.

Before I could question what she meant by that, she moved further up the bar to serve a small, elderly man in a flat cap.

A menu behind the bar drew my eye. Basic fare, mostly variants of eggs, sausages, burgers and chips. The special of the day, chicken curry with rice or chips, was drawn on a small chalkboard, along with a childish sketch of a chicken.

I heard a click and a pop from the stage area and a man in a brightly coloured shirt tapped at a microphone. "This one's for my gorgeous missus." He waved a hand loosely towards a very large woman sat at a table in front of the stage. "Love ya', babes."

Babes opened her arms wide in an air-hug for her hero as the opening riff of 'Can't get no Satisfaction' drifted across the room.

Jenna returned and finished off the last of her beer. "The curry's okay, if you're hungry."

"No thanks. I think I'm going to take a wander. I need some air." I paid for the drinks and tried to shut my ears to the mangling noises coming from the stage. I tried not to look at the stage as I passed by, but the human compulsion to see if reality measures up to one's worst imaginings was too strong. The man, for all his size, bounced into his Mick Jagger impersonation with the enthusiasm of a Labrador on a sugar rush. His vocal ambitions however, fell somewhat short, and he managed to miss most of the notes he aimed for by a good five feet.

I slid out of the double swing doors and blinked into the sunlight. I took a moment to decide where to explore and settled on heading towards the cliff top. I followed The Yellow Brick Road until it met a staggered crossroads where I took Route 67 and continued towards the bottom end of the site. The further I travelled from the Downtown area, the more random the static homes became. The idea of neat lines and little white fences had been abandoned in favour of creating what looked like small enclaves of several homes with higher fencing between them. Some looked quite new and well kept, but others showed distinct signs of clumsy repairs and modifications. One had even been covered in military style camouflage netting, which, as it stood amongst a group of rectangular static caravans, made it stand out like a Humvee at a Greta Thunberg rally. A small wooden sign announced, 'Welcome to Montego Bay', to which somebody had added, '*Keep Out*' in red spray paint. Walking between these static homes proved trickier than the other sections as paths had been closed or diverted, creating a labyrinthine confusion of twists and turns. Behind the Montego Bay area lay a large open area, and I threaded my way towards it. Here the ground seemed unusually flat with grassy patches and several huge symmetrical mounds arranged in groups of three. The whole area was encircled by a high chain link fence which, although badly rusted, still stood firm.

I skirted the fence until it broke away at the edge of the cliff. Had I felt the need, I could have clambered round it at this point, but the fall to the beach below was vertiginous. And probably final. I moved eastward along the cliff path until I came to a cut which weaved its way down to the beach. That would be for another day. I sat on the cliff top and watched the sea washing into a small sandy bay some fifty metres below. I couldn't see any easy access from either side of the little bay, at least at the moment, but there might be when the tide went out. Despite the fine day and gentle sea, the beach was deserted which supported my feeling that perhaps access was difficult. I stretched my knees out and started back. As I came to the high fence, I noticed some movement near some bushes which pressed against the fence from either side. Despite the fact I was on a public footpath, I still froze in a moment of slight panic at being caught out.

A human shape pushed through the bushes and appeared in front of me.

"Oh," said the shape. "It's not what it looks like." As he cleared the bush, I saw it was Wayne.

"So you're *not* coming through a hole in the fence then?" I asked.

"No. Yes. Not really. I was just looking."

Another shape pushed out of the bush. This shape held a spade over his shoulder.

"For Nathan," Wayne added, pointing at the new shape.

"That's all good then," I said. "So what is that place?" I nodded towards the huge flat area.

"What place?" asked Wayne. He saw the look and quickly added, "Oh, you mean *that* place?" He turned to follow my gaze. "Dunno." He shrugged.

"Well, I must be off, I have some books to sell." I gave a short wave and continued on up the path.

The afternoon saw a few more sales. Just enough to warrant being there but not enough to celebrate. As the sun started to close the day, I packed up and decided to have a quick drink in the Pirates Bay before heading back to the Moto Lodge.

The place was much busier now and there appeared to be activity on the stage. A red-faced man in a purple suit held the hand of a smiling little girl as he announced her the winner of the Rose Well Holiday Park New Stars

Under Twelve competition for her rendition of Britney Spears' '*Hit Me Baby One More Time*'. The applause from the small audience of parents near the stage crackled half-heartedly from those whose little darlings didn't win. The purple clad man handed the little girl a certificate and told her that entitled her to a lovely Chicken Dinner for two from the bar.

Jenna was still busy behind the bar serving drinks and periodically diving to a table with plates of food. I waited for a gap in her flights and grabbed a San Miguel which went away far too quickly so I decided it was probably time to go.

Another wobbly drive through the lanes in Mike's drifting van brought me back to the Moto Lodge, where I unloaded my books and headed to The Camelot for a nightcap and a quick bite before bed.

Chapter Five

I SAT OVER A FULL English Breakfast and coffee while trying once more to find somebody to talk with at Icarus Airlines. This had become more of a ritual than any real hope of getting my money back, but it allowed me to put off making any real decisions about what to do next. I'd give it another day at Rose Well Park to see if I could pick up a few more sales and then maybe work out a way of getting home without draining the small profit I'd made.

I finished up breakfast and took the tray back to the bar.

"So how goes the Happy Farm?" Mike asked as he cleared the tray.

"Happy Farm? Oh, you mean Rose Well Holiday Park? Yes, I sold a few books, so I thought I'd give it one more day."

"Well you wanna' double check what they pay you with. Rumour 'as it they've got their own money printing machine down there somewhere."

"Thanks, I'll keep that in mind."

I drifted the little van back along the roads to Rose Well Park and set up my stand in the Sun Lounge. Everywhere appeared quiet still, so I went in search of a coffee. I found the Big Moo Burger Bar which offered a large sized coffee-to-go and a pink doughnut for two quid. It seemed like a reasonable deal even though it necessitated wading through a kid's party to get to the counter.

"Would you like to upscale your coffee to a Megasize?" asked the girl behind the counter.

I looked up at the menu behind her. "But it says it's already large." I pointed at the menu.

"Yes, but that's the smallest we do. We do Large, Extra Large and Megasize."

"What if I wanted small?"

"We don't do small," she said. "Only Large, Extra Large and Megasize."

"But large is a comparative word," I said "A thing can only be large as a comparison to something smaller. You can't have a large as your smallest option. That just doesn't make sense."

She stared at me for a moment then said, "But we don't do small."

I could see me spending the rest of the day on this conversation, so I gave up. "Just your Special Deal please, the Large coffee and pink doughnut."

"Would you like the King Size pink doughnut or the Presidential?"

"What's the one in that deal?" I pointed at the menu offering again.

"That's the Jumbo Size."

The girl eventually packed my Large coffee and Jumbo Size pink doughnut in a Big Moo Burger bag along with a surprise toy and a pink serviette. By the time I came out, I was also wearing a paper hat with a smiling burger on it and plastic straw in my mouth, none of which I'd asked for.

As both hands were occupied, I needed to go find somewhere to put things down. A small park area offered a handful of trees and some wooden tables, and I was just untangling myself from hat and straw when a voice from a nearby table caught me.

"Oh, hello. William, isn't it? The book man?"

I looked round to see Jenna. She sat at a nearby table and wore her ubiquitous charcoal jeans and black shirt. I noticed her shirts always seemed to struggle a bit across the well-defined muscles in her shoulders.

"That's me." I tipped my Big Moo Burger hat in salute. "Day off?"

"No, I've got cover until lunchtime. Just grabbing five while I can." She waved a hand indicating I should join her, so I gathered up my party kit and moved opposite her.

She scanned my collection with a puzzled look.

"I got mugged by a kid's party," I said. "I only wanted a coffee."

"Ah, that can happen."

"Are the other food places not opening?"

She looked up at the little row of food outlets. "Codden Ships and Flat Foods only open in the evenings, off-season. As for Baguette and Go, I haven't the faintest idea what they're up to."

I took my doughnut and serviette from the bag, then retrieved the surprise toy. A garish plastic ring with a small red ball pretending to be a ruby. An odd compulsion drove me to try it on, but of course it wouldn't fit. I held it out to Jenna. "Not my size."

"Shame, I think it would have suited you." She slipped it on her little finger. "You're going to be well pissed off when I discover this is magic and I find a pot of gold under my bed."

"You have to share. It's the way it works."

She stroked the ring and smiled. "My preciousss."

I fought my way through a layer of froth and found my coffee. It tasted more of the cardboard cup than coffee, but I really only needed the caffeine. "I had a wander yesterday," I said. "Went down to the cliff. What's that big fenced off area down there?"

"What, Hobbiton?"

"Hobbiton?"

"Sorry, that's what I call it. It's where all the Hobbits are busy digging their tunnels and hiding underground. Its real name is Carter's Field. Back in the war it was an airfield, but when the Americans came, the generals all wanted to live in Devon, rather than Cornwall, so it was abandoned. That part was never developed."

"Ah, that would explain it. The humps then, they were shelters?"

"Yes. After the war, my grandfather, Tommy Toplin, bought up several of these places over the south west and turned them into holiday camps."

"Your grandfather? So this is yours?" I waved my arm around, indicating the site.

"My name is on the top of the Final Demand letters, if that's what you mean."

"Hmm, I know that one. I think my grandparents took me to one of these camps near Bournemouth when I was a kid."

I tore my doughnut in two and offered her half. She shook her head. "I'm on a diet, I'm only allowed pink food on alternate days. Bournemouth, huh? Lucky you, my grandfather just used to dump me outside the camp pub with a can of Coke and a bag of cheese and onion crisps. Tight git."

I thought about the big flat area for a moment and the tunnels. "That will explain why I saw Wayne coming out of there with a spade, I guess."

"Goodness knows what they're doing down there. Bonkers, the lot of them. But they keep themselves to themselves and they're far less trouble than the stag parties we get, so who's to worry?" She finished her coffee and tossed the cardboard cup in a nearby bin with practised ease. "I have to go. The chickens aren't going to cook themselves."

She swung her legs free of the bench and headed towards the Pirates Bay. I couldn't help but let my eye follow.

I finished my coffee but abandoned the rest of my doughnut. The sugar rush from the small portion I'd already eaten made me feel light-headed. As I tossed it in the bin, I felt a slight tinge of guilt and wondered if rats could get type two diabetes.

I returned to the Sun Lounge and the rest of the morning yielded a few sales but certainly not enough to consider this a positive upturn in my fortunes. As I waited for the clock to approach something I could loosely call beer time, I pondered this strange place in which I seemed to have ended up.

Half the place appeared to be stuck in a sixties' time warp and the rest of it in some strange futuristic dystopia where zombies hunted the last survivors of mankind. Either way, it was a place which existed outside the norm. An island of otherness which had looked at the twenty-first century and said, '*No thanks*'. My erstwhile advertising salesman's mind toyed with that concept for a moment. I could spin that up into a good publicity feature. Maybe Jenna might even give me a job as Promotions Manager or something. I could do something with this.

Come and enjoy a break in a place where tranquillity is the new adventure and harmony is the menu of the day. Not bad for an impromptu tagline, I still had my touch.

Maybe I should approach my old paper? If I could persuade Jenna into some advertorial deal, it might be a way back in. I could offer a grovelling apology to Lucas Schonberg, and maybe he'd take me back on a freelance basis? Reality invaded my brief flight of fantasy. No, I'd well and truly burnt those bridges when I'd upended the recycling bin over Lucas' desk. However, that didn't stop me hawking it out to other media outlets. Maybe I could set up as an independent advertising creative consultant? Now, there was an idea.

The door burst open, and a man rushed in. He pressed the door closed behind him before slipping behind my stand. He grabbed a book and pretended to be reading it. The door swung open a second time, and a woman rushed in. She paused and her eyes scraped the room until she spotted the hiding man.

"There you are, you little weasel." She held a set of what looked like car battery jump leads in her hand and waved them towards the now terrified man.

The man stepped backwards and fell over my empty cardboard boxes. She took advantage of his tumble and closed in, swinging the leads like a set of nunchucks. I wondered if I should intervene.

"It wasn't me, honest." The man held out a hand towards her.

"Then what's this?" She waved the leads in his face as he cowered further into my boxes. "Bleedin' fairy lights put there by lepre-soddin'-chauns? No wonder my electric bill's bigger than Oxford Street's on Christmas Eve when you lot are busy tapping into my meter to power your grow-farms. Next time, I'm wiring these into your testicles and using you as a porch light." She threw the cables in his face and stomped out of the room.

The man clambered out of my now flattened box, paused at the door to check all was clear, then slipped out. It took a moment to realise that he'd taken my book with him.

Maybe I'd drop the word 'harmony' from the tagline. And 'tranquillity'. Maybe I'd drop that idea completely.

I gathered up my stock in the remains of my boxes, locked them in the storage cupboard and went off to explore. I headed down to the cliff top. I paused when I reached the bush which concealed the gap in the wire fence. I scanned the field again, now with a better understanding of at least part of its history. The humps in the ground revealed themselves more clearly as air-raid shelters and reinforced storage buildings. Several small, square, concrete constructions struggled against the reach of nature, fighting clear of the grasping greenery. A couple of areas of the field were still devoid of grass where the remains of concrete tracks still survived.

My eyes followed the flat field and grassy humps beyond the fence and into the main area of the static caravan parks. It now became easier to see how the airfield had once covered this whole area of the holiday park. It was just that the caravans, cabins and other assorted constructions concealed parts of the land. I looked back up towards the Downtown area. The strange, smaller construction on the top of the theatre building now showed its origins as part of the original control tower. I wondered how much of the building remained underneath the multiple extensions and modifications.

I poked at the bush which concealed the gap in the fence. A well-trodden path led through a neatly cut access in the rusted chain link. I looked around, already feeling the mild paranoia of guilt at the very thought of what I was contemplating. I had an overpowering urge to pull my collar up high and hunch forwards to disguise my face, just in case I wasn't giving off enough guilty signals already.

No, I was doing nothing wrong. Composure. I forced myself to straighten up and slipped through the gap with a well-constructed display of confidence. I pushed through the bush with the self-assurance of somebody who had every right to be doing this and looked around the field with the absolute authority of one who has nothing to hide. A flicker of movement near one of the humps snagged my attention, and I pushed myself back into the bush, crouching on the ground to make myself as small as possible.

Risking a peep, the movement coalesced into three human shapes who seemed to be moving in and out of one of the humps. It was probably some sort of bunker or storage unit which had been covered in earth and now resembled a Neolithic long barrow. I watched for a while, fascinated by the activity which seemed utterly pointless. Repeatedly, they appeared out of the mound, flopped down on the ground, lay there for a moment, then jumped up as if something had bitten them before disappearing back into the mound. This seemed to repeat about once a minute and looked like going on for quite a while.

Feeling braver, I pushed my way back through bush and fence and continued along the path. I reached the point where the path gave way to the cut down to the beach. Feeling more adventurous now, I negotiated the gravelly path downward. On two occasions, the gravel slipped away under my feet and threatened to send me to the beach the fast way, so I slowed my descent from cautious scrambling to timid creeping.

The beach welcomed me with soft yellow sand, which stayed reassuringly underfoot. The small bay extended for about a hundred metres to each side from where I stood, curving gently towards the sea at the furthest points. High rocky faces controlled each end of the bay and, from my position, seemed impassable. Near the westernmost end, a lone figure stood knee deep in the water, making strange movements with what looked like a long stick. Curiosity pulled, and I ambled towards the figure. As I approached, I realised it was a young woman and she appeared to be jabbing a spear into the water. She wore jeans rolled up over her calves to keep them clear of the water and a T-shirt with what looked like a picture of a heavy metal band. She made another jab at the water, followed by a short squeal. I closed quicker in case she needed help.

She turned and froze as she spotted me. Her spear held high with a flapping fish on the end of it.

"I'm not doing nothing wrong," she said. "It's just fishing. Fishing's allowed, it's in the Magna Carta. It says so, the right of the citizenry to take fish."

"I'm sure it does," I said. "It says a lot of stuff about all sorts of things." I pointed to the fish on the end of the spear. "That was clever."

She turned to study the fish. "It's a fish, they're not especially clever. Not like crows."

"No, I meant, it was clever catching it like that. With a spear. Most people use fishing rods."

She shrugged. "How you gonna fish with rods when there's nobody left making fishing line?"

"That's not something I'd considered."

"Nobody has." She pulled the fish from the spear and dropped it in a bag on her hip. "They'll see." She turned her attention back to the swirling water near her feet, spear poised.

I watched for a while, but despite a couple of empty jabs, no more fish turned up. I continued on towards the end of the little bay where the rocks piled straight into the sea. My knowledge of the sea extended to the fact that I generally tried to stay out of it, or off it, as much as I could, therefore I had no idea if the tide was in or out. If the tide was high at the moment, then there might be some way of walking round the rocks when it went out. I looked towards the girl with the spear and thought about asking her, but she looked frozen, like a Greek statue of an Olympic athlete preparing to launch a javelin. I thought she might not welcome another interruption and walked on back to the cut and fought my way up the scree covered path. I could always come back later and see if the tide had moved in or out. I stopped and looked back down the path while I tried to regain my breath. Or I could always ask Jenna, she'd know.

As it happened, on the way back up The Yellow Brick Road, I bumped into Charlie. Or rather, she hijacked me.

"Ah, just who I need," she said as I neared. She held a screwdriver in one hand and had one foot braced against the bottom rung of a ladder. "Brace yerself against this, will you? Bulb's gone again." She pointed to the top of the lamppost against which the ladder balanced.

I looked at the old wooden ladder and the lamppost. "Okay, but isn't that a bit dangerous? Shouldn't you be using some sort of platform, or at least a step ladder?"

She looked at me as if I'd just spoken in Klingon. "What?" she asked after a pause.

"Well, the ladder is wider than the width of the lamppost." I pointed at the lamppost. "It will wobble."

She shook her head. "Just plant your foot on the bottom and hang on. Step ladders, tsk."

I did as instructed and she took the screwdriver in her teeth and shot up the ladder like a pirate up a mainbrace. Despite my best attempts, the ladder wobbled as I'd feared it would. But Charlie seemed either not to notice or not to care. To make matters worse, the ladder wasn't quite long enough for the job and she had to balance on the last-but-one rung and stretch to reach the light. I held my body tight against the ladder and stopped looking.

After a few grunts, scrapes and colourful swear words from up top, a piece of metal hurtled past my ear and clattered on the ground.

"Sod it," came the voice from ten feet above my head. "Chuck that back up here will you?"

I forced my eyes to the ground. A metal grill lay at my feet. I stretched out a foot to try to hook it closer but couldn't reach. "I can't get it without letting go," I said.

"Well let go then," the voice from above said. "I'm alright up here."

I stretched towards the grill as far as I could while maintaining at least some contact with the ladder, but still couldn't reach it.

"Will you just grab a hold of it and chuck it up here," she called again. "I'm not up here for the view, you know."

I let go of the ladder for the briefest second, snatched the grill and lunged back at the ladder. "Got it. Ready?"

"No, not yet, I'm just finishing my cup of tea. Will you just get *on* with it."

"Coming up." I tossed the grill upwards and it somersaulted lazily in the air a good five feet from Charlie, then clattered to the ground again.

"For goodness' sake," she yelled. "You throw like a girl. Throw it, man."

I threw again and watched as she reached out and calmly took it out of the air. I pressed into the ladder once more.

After a few more minutes, I heard shuffling and looked up to see her descending.

"All okay?" I asked.

"No, don't know what's wrong with it. Bulb's okay." She sat on the ground at the foot of the lamppost and set about unscrewing a panel in the base.

"Do you know what time the tide goes out?"

She looked at her watch. "About six, I think. You thinking of going for a swim?" She eased the metal panel free and took a torch from her pocket.

"I was just wondering if it was possible to walk further along the beach when the tide's out."

"Usually, but you might get your feet wet. Don't know why you'd want to, though. Perfectly good path down from West Field. So, that's what's going on." She wiggled her torch beam into the gap and poked at some wires with a screwdriver. "Gotcha." She pulled a wire free and held up the bare ends. "Little sods."

"What's that?"

"Damned hippies, tapping into the wiring." She fiddled with something I couldn't see, and the light overhead flickered into life. "That's got it," she said with an air of satisfaction and switched it off again before screwing the cover back in place.

"West Field path?"

"Yeah, over there." She pointed beyond the flat airfield area. "There's a path goes down to Rocky Bottom Cove. Easier than paddling along the beach. Bugger all there though." She closed her tool bag and set off down Route 67.

I looked at the lamppost again, then down to the Montego Bay field. The park homes and caravans there scattered the area, some in strange grouping, some in twos and threes and others standing alone. Certainly not the tidy, regimented layout of the Bermuda field on the other side of Route 67. This was certainly a strange hotch-potch of people. I turned and continued up The Yellow Brick Road. Time for a lunchtime drink.

Chapter Six

THE PIRATES BAY SEEMED PARTICULARLY quiet. Jenna sat at one of the tables, coffee poised in one hand and the other stabbing at the numbers on an oversized calculator.

She looked up as I approached. "You'll have to wait a minute."

I settled at the next table. "No hurry. Doing the accounts?"

"Yes, shush. Concentrating."

I scanned the room. Apart from one family down near the stage, the place was empty. Most of the tables still had the chairs upturned on them from the morning's clean through. Unusually, all of the overhead lights were on, giving the place a much more industrial feel than the normal relaxed ambiance of the concealed feature lights.

The sound of buttons being stabbed from the next table built to a sudden crescendo, and I turned just in time to see the calculator being slammed on to the top of the pile of papers.

Jenna turned to me and painted a forced smile over her lips. "Now, what can I get you?"

"Is it too early for a beer?" I asked.

She glanced at the clock. "Only if you're planning on drinking it alone."

"In that case, would you care to join me?"

"I thought you'd never ask." She headed to the bar and returned with two bottles.

I took mine from her hand as she slumped back in her chair. "You look a tad stressed," I offered.

"Only in the way the captain of the Titanic was a tad stressed. I'm waiting for the band to start playing *Abide with me*."

"Ah, those sorts of accounts. I had some of those not so long ago."

She sipped from her beer. "What did *you* do?"

"I gathered what I could of my stock before the bailiffs arrived and ran away to… where is this place?"

"Cornwall."

"Cornwall then."

"Cornwall's about as far as it goes. Nowhere to run from here." She took another pull, closed her eyes and let out a long sigh.

I looked around the nearly empty bar again. "Surely it picks up a bit in the season?"

She waved a dismissive hand towards the room. "This? Oh, this is normal this time of day. I'm talking about the whole place."

"The site? Rose Well Holiday Park?"

"Yes, the whole place has been running on dream breezes and pixie shit for the last twenty years."

"You said before that this is all yours?" I asked.

"It was left to me by my grandfather, Tommy Toplin. Sort of an heirloom. To be honest, I'd rather have had his clock, but his third wife got that." She realised her bottle was empty. "You want another?" She stood and headed for the bar.

"Thanks," I said. "I had a wander round earlier. It looks busy enough, even for off-season. Not that I know anything about this sort of place."

"Most of the good park homes are privately owned. I just lease the plots to them." She planted a fresh bottle in front of me and sat down. "Apart from that lot down in Montego Bay, where all the Hobbits live, they're rentals. Not that I make any money on them. Half of them don't pay anything and they keep stealing my electricity."

"These Hobbits, what's the story with them? Are they hippies or nutters?"

"You say that like those terms are mutually exclusive." She smiled. "But they're a strange bunch for sure. Busy digging holes and stocking up on toilet paper and baked beans. They're convinced the aliens or zombies are coming, or something."

The glimmer of an idea formed. "You know, this place is unique, it's quirky. You should exploit that, people love quirky."

"Quirky? That's one word for it."

"Have you ever thought of an advertising feature in a big paper? I'm sure you'd get good results."

"Advertising in a national paper? Where would I get money to do that? I can't afford a card in the local newsagent's window."

"No, they don't have to be expensive. You see, the idea is, you pay for an advert and the newspaper do a feature on you as well. I used to work for the Daily Sentinel, it's what I did. I could help."

"A newspaper man, huh? You don't look much like a journalist."

"No, not as a journalist. I sold advertising space."

"And you think you could get me a cheap advert in the Daily Sentinel?"

"Mmm, well maybe not the Sentinel, I sort of fell out with them."

"You fell out with them?"

"Yes, I sold a four-page advertising feature to Green Socialist Coalition, 'How to Live Without Capitalism in the New World'. Great success for them, I was really pleased with it."

Her eyebrow tilted. "So how come you fell out with them?"

"I forgot the paper was owned by Sir Robert Green, and he's a major contributor to the Tory Party funds."

"You forgot?"

"I got carried away with the idea," I said. "I wasn't really paying attention as to who was who, just following my salesman's nose."

"So, they sacked you and that's when you came up with the idea to go head-to-head with Atlas World Store and bought yourself a bookshop?"

"Yes, not one of my better ideas."

Jenna lifted an eyebrow. "You think? So, just where do you suggest we place this advertising feature?"

"I'm sure I cold punt it around a bit, somebody would be interested." I sipped at my beer while mentally trawling through my contacts in the business. "Somebody," I repeated.

"So, your plan, if I may call it that." She pressed her beer bottle against her forehead as if trying to ward off a headache. "Your plan is to write an advertising feature promoting a bunch of tinfoil-hat wearing numbskulls as 'quirky' and punt it around to see if anybody fancies printing it for my five-quid budget and thereby making both of us pots of money?"

"Well, I wouldn't have put it exactly like that. But it's got to be worth a try."

"Well, as long as you don't go costing me any money, I suppose you can look into it. As they say, any publicity is good publicity. What have I got to lose?"

"Erm, just a caravan for a few days?" I scanned her eyes for a reaction, but she kept a face that Doc Holliday would have been proud of. "I'll need somewhere to stay, you see."

"And you'll pay me back when you get yourself a plum job in the Guardian off the back of this?"

I shrugged and smiled.

"Oh, sod it," she said. "Okay, but you're paying for your electricity." She lifted her bottle and wobbled it to see if there was any beer left. Clearly there wasn't. "And it's your round."

Two beers at lunchtime was normally my absolute limit, and I was already feeling a bit fuzzy round the edges. But anxious not to upset my host, I said, "Excellent, we'll raise a glass to this new enderever... endevoory... plan."

~ * ~ * ~ * ~

I left the Pirates Bay, wobbled my way back to collect my stock and dumped it in the park home Jenna had said I could use for a few days. The cabin was located in the higher of the two Bermuda sections and usually a family rental unit. It consisted of two bedrooms, a lounge which blended into the kitchen and a small bathroom. I allocated the smaller of the bedrooms as my stockroom lay back on the bed for a moment to gather my thoughts and woke about four o'clock. Rule One, no more lunchtime drinks. Rule Two, don't try to keep up with Jenna.

I headed to Big Moo Burger and force-fed myself coffee until the fug cleared and then wrestled the little van back to the Moto Lodge to collect the rest of my possessions and check out.

"Going back to London then, sir?" asked the girl at the desk as I paid my bill.

"Actually, I'm spending a few days up at Rose Well Holiday Park. I'm a freelance Advertising Creative Consultant." I wanted to try out how that sounded.

She noticeably paused between keystrokes, then swiftly regained her composure. "That will be... erm... very brave you. Did you take anything from the mini bar?"

I shook my head. "Huh uh."

"Here we are then, sir." She pushed a printed sheet towards me. "Will that be card or cash?"

I handed her my card. "You said, brave?"

"Hmm? Oh, sorry. I should have said... interesting. Yes, interesting." She waved the card at the terminal, then turned it to me to enter my PIN.

I tapped the numbers. "What did you mean, brave?"

"I don't know. They're all very strange up there. We had one guest, not so long ago, he was going to write a book or something. He went up there and was never heard of again. Scringle his name was, Eric Scringle. Nice gentleman. Said he was something to do with the ministry of something or other. Even had the police round here looking for him." She tore the receipt from the machine and handed it to me with my card. "Enjoy the rest of your holiday, Mr Fox."

I slipped the card away, picked up my bag and returned to the little van. Eric Scringle? Where did I know that name from?

I stopped by The Camelot to ask Mike if I could rent the van a few more days then headed back to my new home of the moment.

The car park lay a good ten-minute walk from the cabin, or Bermuda 248, as the little wooden sign near the door announced, so by the time I'd lugged my bag there, the step up to the cabin looked more like a seat than a step, so I sat for a moment and surveyed my new neighbourhood. Ageing beech trees provided shade between some of the cabins and little patches of gardens fought against nature and neglect with varying degrees of success. My cabin had a fairly well tended little lawn and small flower bed. I guessed this was down to the fact this one was used as a rental regularly. The ones directly adjacent also seemed well kept, but many others looked like they'd given up all hope a long time ago.

"Hi-de-hi, good neighbour," a voice called to my left.

I turned to see a man leaning out of the door of the next cabin. He was a small, roundish looking man wearing an unnecessarily bright, multi-coloured shirt and a yellow baseball cap.

I waved back and said, "Hello," rather hoping this minimal response would forestall more conversation, at least until I'd caught my breath.

"You've chosen the best neighbourhood." The man descended the two steps from his cabin and came over to the miniature picket fence which divided us. "Bermuda North, we won the Crazy Golf Cup *and* the Country & Western karaoke Challenge last month. First time *that's* ever happened."

I worked hard at creating what I hoped was a smile across my face. "I'm sorry I missed that."

"We're drumming up a team for the Boules tournament at the end of the month. Can I put your name down? We've been a man down since Mrs Pengelly had her hip operation."

"Sadly, I'm only here for a few days otherwise I'd have loved to."

"Oh, that's such a shame. I'm Brian by the way, and the little lady..." he pointed in to his cabin. "She's Brianna. Funny story, when we—"

"Sorry," I interrupted, "That's my phone. Catch up later." I scrambled up the step into my cabin and pressed the door closed behind me.

I put the kettle on for tea and hung my clothes up as I waited for it to boil. I didn't have much of a collection of clothes with me as I'd only planned to be here a couple of nights for the Alternative Living Fair, but what few items I did have, filled the little wardrobe. I found my little supply of teabags in the bottom of my bag, then realised I didn't have any milk. I pulled the plug on the kettle and slumped onto the L-shaped sofa in defeat. I contemplated asking Brian and Brianna for milk, but the pain-benefit threshold was not in my favour on that one. I remembered the little shop.

I peeped through the pink floral curtains on the back window to check my escape route was clear of Brians then slipped out and headed up The Yellow Brick Road towards Downtown.

Dolly's Daily Shop was open, and several people squashed into the compact interior. The woman behind the counter was trying to measure off several metres of camouflage netting for one customer while explaining to another how to fill a pressure lantern lamp with paraffin.

I pottered around the shop gathering a few essentials, milk, bread, chocolate biscuits and an SAS type survival pack which was the size of a cigarette packet but contained everything necessary to survive a plane crash in the Andes and invade a small country.

"You're new here," the woman greeted as she took my money.

"I'm an Advertising Creative Consultant, just here researching for a publicity campaign." The bustle of noise in the shop stopped as though I'd just hit the mute button.

I glanced around and everybody was looking at me. I paid for my items in silence then threaded my way through the human statues and into the sunlight. I glanced back into the shop where everybody remained frozen, so I walked away slowly. I'd seen enough episodes of Dr Who to know this could go wrong very quickly.

I scuttled back to my cabin and once more sank into its protection. Maybe I'd best not mention anything about publicity anymore.

After eventually managing to make my cup of tea, I settled with my scribble-pad to prepare notes for my project. As I started, I became more optimistic of the idea. If I could produce an interesting advertising feature, full of human interest, it would be the start of a portfolio. Then I could get more clients and I might just land myself a job back in the newspaper industry. And who knows where that might lead? I might even set up my own agency and get a nice new office in Holborn.

I jotted down my thoughts on who I should feature. Certainly Jenna, she had a good overview of all the different people here. The Hobbits would be key of course, although, going by the reaction in the shop, they may prove tricky. I'd have to tread carefully there, as without them, I'd have no real hook to the piece.

I turned the page on my pad and headed up the next sheet as potential people to contact who might run it on a budget. That page didn't go quite so well. After twenty minutes of staring at the blank sheet, writing a few names then crossing them out, I closed my pad and went on an explore.

Once off the main paths of The Yellow Brick Road and Route 67, the paths became more tangly and random. A tiny chapel nestled behind a trio of beech trees, looking slightly confused by its own presence. I took a walk around it, which I accomplished in around twenty steps, and came to the conclusion that this place hadn't seen a service in a long time. Just round a corner from the chapel, a small water spout set in a rock trickled water into an ornamental basin. The basin appeared to be carved from stone, but could have been cast concrete, and bore raised images of water cherubs along the front. A small, and heavily oxidised, brass plate above the spout bore the legend, 'Rose Well Spring - c1665'. I guessed this was how the place got its name. I cupped my hands and drank a few sips. It was water. Possibly, to connoisseurs of such things, it was an exquisite tasting water. To me, it was water. I dried my hands on my trousers and made my way up to the Pirates Bay for supper.

~ * ~ * ~ * ~

A man I hadn't seen before stood behind the bar. He wore his sun-bleached hair tied back in a ponytail and the five day's growth on his face displayed a distinctly natural look, as opposed to the neatly trimmed of the hipster set.

"What can I get you, mate?" he asked. His accent spoke of Bondi Beach, surfing and shrimp barbies.

"A San Miguel," I pointed to the chiller cabinet behind the bar. "And what's on the menu tonight?"

He stood to one side so I could see the chalkboard behind him. "Usual stuff, or the special of the day is Chicken and Mushroom Pie with peas and chips."

"I'll have that then. Jenna's night off?"

"It's her karate night."

"She's learning karate?"

"No, she teaches at the Little Didney church hall." He glanced at the novelty pirate-face clock behind the bar. "She'll be back in about half an hour." He pushed the bottle towards me and gave me a wooden spoon with the number twenty-three burned into its bowl.

I took the spoon and beer and scanned the sea of empty tables. Spoilt for choice. I settled on a secluded table as far away from the stage as was possible. I'd just pulled out my notebook to scribble down a couple of ideas when Wayne sat himself down opposite me.

"Oh, hi," I said. "Wayne, isn't it?"

"Yeah." He quickly scanned the room to see if anyone was listening. Satisfied, he said, "But everybody here calls me Batman."

"Batman?"

"Yeah, on account of my name, see, Wayne. Bruce Wayne? Batman?"

"Okay, Batman it is."

He grinned. "You writing your publicity thingy? Everybody's talking about it."

"It's just notes," I said, closing the book and forcing a smile.

"How much you gonna pay me?"

"For what?"

"For my story."

"I haven't got any money to buy any stories," I said. "I'm planning on selling an advertising feature. Or trying to."

"I can help, we can do a deal. Fifty-fifty."

"Why do I need your help?"

"'Cause nobody'll talk to you. You're an emmet, an outsider. And anyways, I know where the bodies are buried."

"Bodies?"

He looked uncomfortable for a moment. "Well, not the *real* bodies. Nobody knows where they are, that would be illegal. And not sayin' there *are* real bodies anyway. Just the metaphysical bodies."

"Metaphorical."

"See, that's why we're a team. I got the info, you know the words."

I was just about to protest again when the guy from the bar turned up with a tray and asked, "You number thirty-two? Chicken and mushroom pie?"

I looked at my spoon. "I'm twenty-three, but I did order the chicken and mushroom pie, so it's probably me."

He looked at his little ticket. "No, it says thirty-two." He stared around the virtually empty bar.

"Probably just a slip of the pen," I said. "You took the order only a few minutes ago."

I reached for the tray and he flinched back.

"No, definitely says thirty-two." He looked slightly forlorn and cast around the room again. "They must have gone."

"Who?"

"Number thirty-two. They must have buggered off. People do this all the time; it really pisses me off." He shrugged and pushed the tray to me. "You might as well have this then, if it's the same. No point in wasting it."

I took the tray. "That makes sense."

As the barman left, Wayne said, "You gonna eat all that?"

"It's my plan, but if he comes back in a minute with number twenty-three, it's all yours." I poked my knife into the puff-pastry and let the steam of the microwave escape. White sauce oozed from the wound and puddled around my chips.

"So, how do we start then? I can give you a tour and introduce you to the movers and shakers."

"Oh, hello, what are you two plotting?"

I looked up from my pie investigations as Jenna sat down at my table. I wondered if she had anything in her wardrobe other than jeans and black shirts. She planted a bottle in front of her. This was getting busy.

"Ah, hi, Jenna," I said. "Batman was telling me—"

"Who?"

"Batman." I pointed to Wayne. "He says that's what everybody calls him."

"No they don't," Jenna said flatly.

"My old nan used to," protested Wayne. "She called me Batman."

"Anyway," said Jenna, ignoring Wayne. "Moving on, I've had an idea as to who might be interested in your advert."

"Advertising feature," I said.

"Whatever. I know this chap in television, he stayed here once when they were doing a programme."

I brightened but tried not to let it show. "Who was that?"

"Chap called Martin Springborn. Charming man. He was doing a programme about ghosts in the old mine down Bottalack way."

My brightening turned to gloom. "Martin Springborn?" I took a fork of chicken pie and rolled it around my mouth until the heat became bearable.

"You've heard of him?" asked Jenna.

"He's that idiot who takes fading celebrities and humiliates them for the entertainment of morons."

"That's him. I take it you don't like him then?"

I spread the pie around my plate. "Where do you get microwaves which can take chicken to a thousand degrees and leave mushrooms cold?"

"I'll have a word with Ray, he's not supposed to microwave that at all. Martin Springborn?"

"When I worked for the Sentinel, I placed a double page advert for his latest celebrity massacre, but I didn't realise the paper was running a feature on reality TV and its effects on social cohesion. I forgot to check. I was supposed to always talk to the editors before I placed any big adverts for anybody in the public eye. You know, just in case they clashed. Anyway, I'd just had a run-in with my landlord, and I wasn't really paying attention when I negotiated the advert with Springborn." I ignored eye contact and focused on my chips. "They featured his programme as a bad example and mentioned him by name in the article."

"I see." She took a drink from the bottle. "I'm guessing it didn't go down too well."

"The advert bombed, and he sued the paper."

"I'm beginning to see a pattern to your career."

"I can't help it if my tolerance threshold for ego politics is low."

"Well, that still leaves us at a dead end for your publicity ideas," Jenna said. "Do you know anybody else?"

I shook my head. "We really need somebody who embodies alternative lifestyles."

"Like Bear Grylls," suggested Wayne. "He could do a survival thing with us about prepping. That would be well cool."

"Prepping?" I queried.

"It's what the Hobbits call themselves. Preppers. They seem to think the term Hobbit is derogatory."

"I see," I said. "I think Bear Grylls might be a bit out my contact circle."

"I could have a word with him," said Wayne. "He gets down The Smuggler's Arms of an evening,"

Jenna sighed. "You're thinking of Ben Grays. He's hardly a survival expert, the Coast Guard have had to bring him back in twice when he went out on an old crocodile inflatable airbed to lay his lobster pots."

"Oh yeah, well what about Steve Irwin, you know, the Crocodile Hunter. He's a mate of mine."

"He's dead."

"I didn't even know he was ill."

"Stingray got him."

"Okay then, Crocodile Dundee. I met him on the bus to Truro."

"Fictional." Jenna picked up her bottle and waved it towards Ray at the bar.

Wayne stared at the ceiling for a moment, then, "I could get Wilderness Jack."

"The ex-SAS survival man who writes all those books?" I asked.

"Yeah, I went to school with him." Wayne pointed at Jenna's bottle. "You gonna get me one of those?"

Jenna waved the bottle towards Ray once more and held up her other hand with three fingers upright. "You know the only thing more outrageous than your claim that you know Wilderness Jack?"

"What?"

"You claiming you actually went to school."

I finished my meal, during which time Wayne had successfully harangued me into letting him be my guide to the Prepper Community, then I headed back to my cabin.

Feeling the weariness of a busy day and the mental exhaustion of trying to fend off Wayne, I completely failed to notice the activity outside number 247, home of Brian and Brianna. I rounded the corner and froze. A group of people gathered around several small tables which each held a selection of bottles, glasses and snacks. Novelty candles positioned on each table pushed bravely against the darkening evening while the music of Abba whined from a little Bluetooth speaker.

I thought of running back into the darkness, but Brian's voice called from the halo of light, "Hi de hi, good neighbour." A waving arm from the furthest table identified one of the silhouettes as Brian. He turned to another person on his left. "This is William, our new neighbour. He sells books."

"Come and join us," called Brianna from an adjacent table. "Do you like Elderberry Wine?"

"No thanks," I said. "I've had a long day."

"I've got just the thing to help you unwind," Brian said. "I've got this lovely bottle of Galliano we brought back from our little trip to Tuscany last year."

"You're just in time for a game of Garden Jenga," called another voice from the gloom.

"Isn't that a bit tricky in the dark?" I asked as I doggedly continued to my cabin door.

"That's the fun of it," said Brianna. "Come and join us, we have cheesy puffs."

"Normally, I'd love to, but I've got a headache coming on. Maybe another night." I fumbled with the key in the lock and slipped inside to sounds of, "Never mind," and "Sleep tight."

I shut the door and collapsed onto the sofa. When I awoke, it was velvet dark and as silent as the moon, so I felt my way to the bed and continued my sleep from there.

Chapter Seven

I MET WAYNE OUTSIDE BIG Moo Burger at ten in the morning as arranged. He was tucking in to a Mega-sized Breakfast-in-a-Bun by the time I arrived.

He waved when he saw me and mumbled something I couldn't understand but which resulted in a spray of breadcrumbs in my direction.

"Morning, Wayne," I acknowledged. "So what's the agenda?"

"Gonna take you down to the headquarters. That's a place where everybody goes and gets together, and we plan stuff."

"I *am* familiar with the concept of a headquarters."

Wayne stuffed the remains of his Breakfast-in-a-Bun into his mouth, lobbed the packaging into a nearby bin and said something which sounded like, "Cool, it's this way."

We headed down The Yellow Brick Road with Wayne pointing out various features as we went. "That's where I broke my wrist practising rope climbing." He pointed to a large beech tree overhanging a children's play area. "And over on the shower blocks, I knocked myself unconscious when I fell off the roof."

I stayed quiet as long as I could, but then I had to ask, "What were you doing on the roof of the showers?"

"I was rigging up a zip wire from there to the boating lake in case we needed to make a quick getaway."

"To a boating lake?"

"Zombies can't swim," he said, as if that was a perfectly reasonable explanation.

We walked on down and took the dogleg onto Route 67. He showed me a fence where he gashed his arm open and needed sixteen stitches and pointed out some little cherry-like berries which I must never eat because they make you throw up and then your ears go numb and you can't leave the toilet for two days.

We followed a track which led between the top of the old airfield at Carter's Field and the Montego Bay area. Towards the westernmost end of the track, it deteriorated into a dirt path between encroaching bushes and brambles before opening into a large meadow. At the southern edge of the meadow, backing on to Carter's Field, stood a barn-like structure with a corrugated iron roof and what looked like prefabricated concrete walls. A few windows still held glass, but many had boards nailed across them. I guessed it to be about fifty-years old, but my knowledge of building design lacked any substance so I could easily have been out by a hundred years either way. The graffiti gave clues to its more recent history with suggestions to 'Resist the Poll Tax', 'Thatcher Out' and 'No to Iraq War'.

Wayne pushed at the door and it swung open easily. We stepped inside. As headquarters go, this one certainly positioned itself at the more casual end. Apart from the far wall covered in whiteboards, pin boards, posters and maps, it could have easily passed as a second-hand furniture shop. At least a dozen sofas littered the open space. Leather, cloth, plastic, all styles and configurations. Some in good condition and others leaking their stuffing over the concrete floor. A random scattering of armchairs added to the general feeling of casual abandon. A few tables interspersed between the soft furnishings provided landing places for bits of paper, pizza boxes, ash trays and a variety of cups, mugs and empty beer cans.

A tall, well-built looking man pushed himself out of a once pink and white armchair when he spotted our entrance. "What ya got, Wayne?"

Wayne shuffled when he saw the man. "Oh, hi, Scooter. Didn't know you'd be here. You alright?"

"Who's this?" Scooter pointed in my direction and approached a bit closer. He stood quite a bit taller than me, maybe six-two or six three even, and from the shape of his face and shoulders, he was probably quite keen on steroids and lifting heavy things. He wore camouflage trousers, which looked original, and a green sleeveless T-shirt which strained across his chest.

I wanted to step back but held my ground and smiled. "I'm William. I'm a friend of Jenna's, Wayne was just showing me around."

"You're that advertising guy, ain't ya?"

"I used to be," I said, trying to deflect any potential problems.

"He's writing a publicity thing about us here," said Wayne, unhelpfully.

"You can't do that," Scooter said. "It's against human privacy."

"We're going to be on the telly," Wayne said.

I glared at Wayne and telepathically transmitted a message telling him to stop talking now. It failed.

"We're getting that guy who does the programme about celebrities and ghosts. Martin Springborn," he continued.

"It's just an advertorial, featuring different lifestyles and people." I tried to read his face, but all I saw was suspicion. "It'll probably never get taken up anyway."

"Wayne said you worked for that newspaper, the Sentinel?"

"Yes." I wondered where this was going.

"Did you have anything to do with that big advert for the Green Coalition, 'How to Live Without Capitalism in the New World'?"

"Yes." I had to force the word out. "How…?"

Scooter pointed to a corkboard on the wall to which was pinned a fading copy of my advertising feature. My great triumph and the final nail in the coffin of my career with the Daily Sentinel, my vocational suicide note.

"You did that?" Scooter asked.

"Um, yes." I desperately tried to work out which way this was going and how quickly I could cover the distance from where I stood to the door. "It wasn't my finest moment. I got the sack over that. I forgot that the owner of the paper was a major donor to the Conservative Party."

Scooter walked towards me and I flinched as his arm reached for me. My fight-or-flight system fled and left me standing rooted to the spot.

His left hand folded around my upper arm and he took my hand in his right and shook it as if trying to extract the last of the ketchup from the bottle. "Good stuff," he said. "I read that. Spot on and kudos to you, standing up to the capitalists in their own land" He guided me to an armchair facing a pallet on bricks which served as a table and motioned me to sit.

I sat.

"Have you read Silicon States by Lucie Greene?" he asked. "Of course you have." He took a six-pack of beers from an ageing and rust-spotted fridge and dropped them on the makeshift table. "Help yourself," he said as he slumped into the remains of a two-seater sofa opposite me.

"Bit early for me," I said, but then caught his eye. "But as it's a special occasion…" I pulled open the can and held it up. "Cheers."

"Hundred years on from Das Kapital and still nothing changes, huh?" He took what looked like most of the can in one.

Wayne shuffled into an armchair to my right and took a beer as unobtrusively as he could manage.

"You've read Marx?" I tried to keep the surprise from my face.

"Don't look so surprised," he said. "Just because I was a professional thug for Her Majesty doesn't mean I'm illiterate."

"I didn't mean—"

"Just ribbing you. So what's this about being on the telly?"

"I think Wayne's probably being very optimistic there," I said. "To be honest, I'm so far out of the loop now, and after the mess with the Sentinel, it's unlikely I'd even be able to get an advert in the local free rag, let alone a national."

"That's alright then." Scooter seemed to relax. "We don't want no prying eyes round here, if you get my drift?"

"Totally."

"Good. Do you know how to defuse a bomb?"

"Oddly, no."

"Oh, never mind." He stood and beckoned me to follow him. "Have a gander at this." He pointed to a chart on the wall. "This is our schedule of upcoming exercises."

I ran my eyes down the schedule. Hostage rescue. Rapid exit strategies. Foraging in an urban environment. Impromptu weapons in your larder. Mantraps for beginners. "I see you keep busy," I said.

"The enemy won't wait until we're ready," he said.

"Um," I hesitated. "Who *is* the enemy?"

Scooter looked genuinely shocked, and I wondered if I'd overstepped the mark. "Anybody who isn't in our unit."

"You mean… er… No, I'm not sure what you mean."

"Everybody not in our unit," He waved his arms around to indicate the building. "They are the enemy. They just haven't been activated yet."

"I'm sorry, I'm still not sure I understand. You mean everybody outside of this group is the enemy?"

"There you go. When it all goes tits up and people realise we have the means to survive and they don't, what are they going to do? They'll panic. That's how they get activated. That's when they realise we are their enemy, 'cause we have what they want. Ipso facto, they are *our* enemy." He tapped the side of his nose. "It's just that we knew it before they did, so we're ready for them. Rule one, know it before they do."

"So, what is it that's going to go… tits up?" I asked.

"Really? Don't you watch the National Geographic channel? Anything. Aliens, pandemic, nuclear reactor meltdown, the Americans, famine, polar shift—"

"The Americans?"

"Global warming, world war three, Godzilla, banking collapse, zombies, religious nutters, anti-religious nutters, the Illuminati, You Tube influencers, mutant squirrels…" He paused for breath and I took the opportunity.

"You said, Americans?"

"What? Yes, of course Americans. Have you ever known them to actually improve *any* crisis by getting involved? Whatever it is that's going to happen, you can guarantee that as soon as they get involved they're going to make it ten times worse than it needs to be." He stalked the room like King Kong in search of his favourite aeroplane, his eyes staring out from under his heavy brow.

"I see," I said, hoping bland statements would calm him down.

"We've got to be ready, we don't have much time." He froze. "What was that?"

"I never heard nothing," said Wayne, looking around.

"Because you're not tuned." He patted his own head. "See?"

Wayne and I nodded in agreement.

Scooter prowled to the little window and pushed aside a corner of the cardboard which served as a curtain. "Can't see anything. They must be hiding. Shh, don't say anything."

"Right," said Wayne.

Scooter glared at him, then returned his attention to the window. "See if you can call in a drone," he said, across his shoulder.

I looked at Wayne with an expression which I hoped conveyed, 'What's he on about?'

"He gets like this, it's his PMS."

"PMS? You mean PTSD?"

"Yeah, one of those." He turned to Scooter. "It's alright, the chickens are here."

Scooter turned. His eyes held a glazed look as he stared vacantly at Wayne and repeated very slowly, "Chickens."

"Chickens?" I whispered to Wayne.

He waved me to be quiet, then pointed to the door. I took the cue and slipped out.

I waited outside the door for a moment, then Wayne appeared. "C'mon," he said. "I'll show you the training centre."

He led the way back down Route 67.

I tried again, "What is it with the chickens?"

"It's his calming word, supposed to make him feel all peaceful and relaxed."

"Chickens?"

"He said when he came up for leaving the army, the brain doctors told him he had STD... SMS... what did you say?"

"PTSD."

"Oh yeah, that one. I can't ever remember that. Too many letters, I've got dyspepsia."

"Dyslexia?"

"There you go. Anyway, part of the therapy is to have a calming word. S'posed to be something all soft and fluffy like a meadow or tree or flowers. But when they asked him, all he could come up with was chickens. I don't know."

"Chickens never seem very calm to me."

"I don't like chickens, you can never trust them. It's the way their heads move, like they're pretending to agree with you but not really," Wayne said. "Alright with chips though."

"So, how come you know about this? He seems very... um, difficult to me."

"He's my mate. I look out for him. It's what mates do, right?"

"And he looks out for you?"

"Not so much. Mostly he shouts at me and calls me stupid and stuff."

We stopped by the bush against the fence and Wayne pushed some brambles aside with his foot. "Through here."

I scrambled through the gap, picking brambles from my skin as I went. Once inside the fence, a strange feeling of paranoia closed over me. I glanced round, eyes not really focusing, but half expected a squad of guards to descend on us. "You sure it's okay to be here?"

"Of course. It's still part of Rose Well Park. Jenna doesn't mind."

"Then why the big fences and warning signs?"

"Just Health and Safety Nazis. There's old buildings and holes and stuff and somebody might break a fingernail and sue for a million quid. Like that woman who asked for a hot coffee then sued because it was too hot or something. It was on Facebook." He marched off across the grass with the purpose of an invading army.

I scanned the ground in front of me. With no apparent sign of any holes or hot coffee, I followed his lead.

We came to a black-roofed Nissen hut, half concealed under earth and foliage. I couldn't decide if the camouflage was deliberate or nature. Two window shaped holes flanked a door shaped hole through which Wayne disappeared into the gloom. I followed, more cautiously, picking my steps through ageing bits of wood and fallen masonry.

Wayne flicked the switch on a battery powered storm lamp hanging from the ceiling and the gloom retreated reluctantly into the corners. A children's merry-go-round occupied the centre of the space. A galloping horse, a stage coach, a London bus, a motorbike and a tractor all chased each other round the wooden platform. At the far end of the room an old rowing boat stood on end, propped against the wall and next to it, a rickshaw bike with a Toplin's Holiday Camp sign on the canopy.

Wayne noticed me taking all this in and said, "It used to be a store shed for equipment from the camp until we did it up."

"I can see." I nodded towards a mattress laying in one corner, a pile of blankets and pillows were neatly folded at the end. "And that?"

"It's for the night watch."

"Night watch?" I asked. "What are they watching for?"

"Aliens, of course." Wayne looked thoughtful for a moment. Then added, "And maybe the Chinese, I think they would come at night if they wanted to invade. But mostly aliens. That's when they do their crop circles, at night."

"How can you be sure it's aliens if they do it at night?"

"Have you ever seen anybody else doing it?"

"Well, no but—"

"There you go then, that's why, 'cos they do them at night. Stands to reason. Look." His eyes searched the room as if afraid of being seen. "I shouldn't really show you this." He opened a 1930s oak wardrobe. "This is the armoury."

The wardrobe bristled with home-made weapons. A stack of broom handles with knives tied on their ends stood under the hanger rails, which in turn were strung with about a dozen sets of Ninja Nunchucks. On the shelf above, several plastic boxes bore labels announcing, Throwing Stars, Catapults, Wooden Stakes, UV Torches and Garrotes. A clear gallon tank on the bottom shelf was filled with what the label called Holy Water and next to it, a large sack of rock salt.

"Ready for anything then," I said.

"Only what we know about. We don't know about knowns we don't know… which are unknown knowns… Knowns unknown… no, I can't remember. Made sense when Scooter explained it."

"You mean unknown unknowns?"

"Unknown unknowns? That doesn't make any sense. How can you not know something you don't know you know, if you don't know it?"

"I don't know," I said.

He squinted at me as if trying to decide if I was taking the mickey. "We gotta be ready, see?"

"This training centre." I cast my eyes round the space again. "What do you actually do here?"

Wayne glanced at his watch. "If you hang around a bit, you'll see. We're having a surprise training session. But you'll have to swear an oath of silence."

"To be expected," I said. "How do you know people are going to be here for the surprise session?"

"We do it every Thursday."

"Not so much of a surprise then?"

"I know, but if we don't tell everybody, nobody'll come then it would be a waste of time." He shook his head.

I noticed a boarded section on the floor just behind the merry-go-round. "What's that?"

"Nothing," Wayne said, far too quickly. The look of innocence even more of a worry than the covered hole.

"Looks like a trapdoor of sorts."

"Dunno, just some wood. Somebody put it there I expect."

The sound of approaching voices interrupted further conversation about the trapdoor that wasn't, and Wayne took the opportunity to slip out. I followed and found two men and a woman approaching. Wayne greeted them as they neared and introduced them as Katie, Simon and Jeremy. Katie and Simon were both probably in their mid-twenties, but Jeremy looked closer to fifty. They all wore some sort of attempt at military type clothing, although most of it was a bit random. Even *I* could see that Katie's camouflage pattern Lycra leggings and clingy T-shirt were probably not NATO standard issue. And Jeremy's hat looked more like it belonged on the head of a French onion seller rather than a member of Her Majesty's Parachute Regiment.

"I heard about you," Jeremy said as Wayne introduced me. "You're that chap who's making a TV documentary about this place."

"Yeah," said Wayne. "We're getting Wilderness Jack and everything."

"Oh, cool," said Simon. "Can I be in it? I always wanted to be a Reality TV person."

"No television, no Wilderness Jack," I said. "I'm planning an advertising feature to promote this place. If I can find a newspaper who will still talk to me."

"Oh," said Jeremy. "Have you tried the Daily Sentinel? That rag will print anything. Did you know that a couple of years ago they ran some propaganda pull-out for the Green Socialist Coalition? I ask you, in a right-wing crap-sheet like that?"

"I'll bear that in mind," I said.

"Down on the ground, nobody move." The shout was authoritative and forceful, but oddly controlled.

I turned towards the door we had just exited to see a figure in black combat gear. A black balaclava and goggles covered his head, and his hands held some sort of machine gun looking thing.

My body helpfully turned to lead encased in cement, rendering movement impossible. The gun spat five times in rapid succession, and I felt a thud in the centre of my chest. My hand instinctively went to the source of the pain and liquid oozed between my fingers. Not quite how I'd expected to meet my end. I looked towards the others and each of them had a splatter of green blood in the centre of their chests.

Green blood? I looked at my fingers. Green blood.

"You're all dead." Scooter pulled the balaclava from his head and let the paintball gun swing free on its harness. "None of you did what you were ordered, so now you're all dead."

"Sorry," said Wayne. "I got confused, you said nobody move then get down on the ground. I didn't know which you wanted."

"No I didn't," said Scooter. "I said, down on the ground first and *then* nobody move."

"Are you sure?"

"Of course I'm sure. Why would I say nobody move then get on the ground? That would be stupid."

"He did," said Jeremy. "I heard him."

"Then why didn't *you* get down on the ground?" Scooter's face reddened as his frustration built.

"Sos," said Jeremy. "I didn't think you meant me. Shall we try again?"

The gun appeared in Scooter's hands and spat once. A new splodge of green landed neatly in the centre of Jeremy's chest, perfectly obliterating the original.

"Ow," Jeremy said. "That's not fair. I wasn't ready."

"Why weren't you ready?" yelled Scooter. "You asked me to do it again. You can't ask an invading zombie army to wait till you're ready."

"How did he sneak up behind us?" I whispered to Wayne.

"Secret trapdoor in the hut. There's tunnels underneath."

"Ah, thought that might be a trapdoor."

The gun popped again, and Wayne yelped in pain. "What was that for?"

"Telling outsiders about the tunnels. Rule one, you don't tell nobody about our tunnels." Scooter waggled the gun skywards. Listen up, we're not doing Hostage Escape today, 'cause none of you are ready. So we're going to do Hijacking the Food Lorry instead."

"This one's good," said Wayne as we followed Scooter inside the Nissen Hut.

Scooter crouched next to the children's merry-go-round and pulled a cable out from underneath. He threw the end towards Wayne. "Here, hook that up."

Wayne took the lead and plugged it in to a museum piece of an electric switch-box. Old style ceramic breaker switches sprouted random coloured cables in all directions. I couldn't help flinching as Wayne threw one of the breakers, but nothing exploded. Instead, the merry-go-round creaked into life with dust tumbling from the canopy as the overhead lights flickered and buzzed. Wurlitzer music wound its way laboriously up to speed as the revolving platform gathered pace. The horse bobbed up, the tractor seat wobbled and the bell on the London Bus tinkled as they all began their futile pursuit of each other.

"Right," said Scooter. "Simon, you're driving the food lorry."

"Can't somebody else do that?" Simon asked. "I did it last time. And besides, I can't get my feet in the driver's seat of the stagecoach."

"Doesn't matter," said Scooter. "We're using the tractor this time."

"But we always use the stagecoach as the food lorry," complained Wayne.

"Well, this time it's the tractor. 'Cause you never know what they'll use, see?" Scooter waved at Simon. "On you get."

Simon hopped onto the revolving platform and edged his way to the tractor. He eased into the tiny seat and grabbed hold of the steering wheel.

Scooter took a blue holdall and dumped it on the backplate of the tractor. "Katie and Jeremy, you're Alpha Team. Wayne and newspaper man, you're Bravo Team. Positions."

"C'mon," Wayne tapped my arm and pointed to a large wooden crate. "We're over here."

I followed Wayne's lead, and we crouched into hiding behind the crate. Katie and Jeremy squashed themselves behind a similar crate on the opposite side of the merry-go-round.

"What do we do now?" I asked Wayne.

"We hijack the food lorry. Here, have this." He passed me a thirty-centimetre wooden spike.

"What am I supposed to do with this?"

"The food lorry driver might be a zombie."

I puzzled over that for a moment and then said, "I thought wooden stakes were for vampires, not zombies? And... what would a zombie want with a food lorry anyway?"

Wayne looked at me as if I'd just suggested Batman was a Kryptonian. "You're not taking this seriously, are you?"

"Sorry, I'll try." I smiled.

"Here comes the lorry," called Scooter as the merry-go-round completed another circle, bringing the tractor round again.

Wayne tugged at my sleeve. "Here we go." He leapt from behind the crate, ran for a moment to pace himself with the turning platform then hopped on.

I followed and lost my footing as I landed then had to hug the horse to stop myself being thrown off. It bobbed up and down with my arms wrapped round its neck and I watched as Wayne and the others converged on the tractor, prodded at Simon with their wooden sticks, then dragged him out of his seat.

Katie grabbed the holdall and held it up in the air. "I have the food."

"One minute twenty-two," said Scooter, looking at his watch. "Far too slow."

We went through the same exercise a couple more times and failed to improve on the time, so we moved on to Stealing Weapons from the Enemy. Which was pretty much like Hijacking the Food Lorry, except this time it was the London bus we attacked instead of the tractor and we had to grab a sack of kindling sticks. Oddly, we all did a lot better that time.

Scooter called a halt to the day's training around one and I headed back to my cabin to change out of my paint spattered clothes. Brian and Brianna were lying in wait and pounced before I spotted them.

"Hi-de-hi, good neighbour," Brian called. "Just in time, we were about to open a nice bottle of Elderberry Champagne to celebrate."

I jerked to a halt, angry with myself for failing to anticipate this. "I need to change." I pulled my shirt away from my body slightly so they could see the reason.

"Ah, you look like you've been on one of Scooter's little shindigs. He's quite a card, isn't he?"

"Yes, a real character. What are you celebrating?"

"We're all going to be on the telly, haven't you heard?"

"I think it's a mistake," I said.

"No, it's true. Got that chap Martin Springborn and Bear Grylls. We were nearly on the telly once before." He turned to Brianna. "Weren't we, dearest?"

"Yes, we went—" Brianna started.

Brian cut across her. "It was that show where you have a rich person for dinner and you can only spend twenty quid. Anyway, funny story—"

"Sorry," I interrupted. "I really must get this shirt into soak before this paint sets."

"Well, do come and help us with this bottle, won't you? If Brianna has more than half a glass, you never know what's going to happen."

Brianna giggled and nudged Brian's arm. "Shush, you'll embarrass him."

I slid into my cabin and pressed the door firmly shut, then tested it again just to make sure the catch had caught.

Chapter Eight

I DODGED THE RANDOM PORN on my phone and scrolled through the names in my contact list until Lucas Schonberg's number appeared. I stabbed 'Call' then panicked and immediately pressed 'End' and dropped the phone back on the little coffee table.

I peeped out of the curtain to see the Brians fiddling outside like a couple of Flowerpot Men. They seemed to be setting up a barbecue. Either I was going to have to crack and go outside or I was in here for the rest of the day. I scanned the inside of my cabin and chic eighties bijou stared back at me.

I pulled out my notebook and scribbled down a few notes on the morning's adventure with the Preppers. If I could keep in with them long enough, I might just get enough of a hook for the feature point of an advertorial. I just needed some forward-thinking newspaper to cut a good deal, maybe even on a pay-by-results basis?

I picked up the phone again and stared at Lucas' number. He'd only reject my idea out of hand, I knew that. And then I'd come away feeling deflated and angry, and I'd sworn that I'd already left all that behind.

I pressed 'Call'.

I let the ring-tone cycle twice this time before hitting 'End'. No, I couldn't put up with earache he'd give me. And even if he did think it was a good idea, he'd make me grovel. I put the phone down only for it to start ringing. I stared at the caller display. Lucas Schonberg. Damn.

I waited as long as I could bear and then picked up the call. "Hello?"

"You do realise that your number comes up when you prank call me, don't you?" Lucas asked.

"Sorry, no." And there, I was on the back foot already. That was why I didn't like talking to him. "I got interrupted. I've told my secretary to hold my calls now."

"Your secretary? You must be doing well. Tell me, how is the bookshop business going?"

"You know, up and down."

"I'd heard that you sold up?"

"Somebody made me an offer I couldn't refuse." I wasn't going to tell him it was the Inland Revenue who'd made the offer.

"So, assuming you had a purpose to this call other than to wind me up with hang-up calls, to what do I owe this pleasure?"

"I'm working on an advertorial feature you might be interested in, and I thought I'd give you first option. Old time's sake."

"I didn't know you were in the business again?" The sneer in his voice oozed through the phone.

"Just a bit of occasional freelancing."

"Go on then, what's this one about?"

"It's an advertorial for a holiday camp—"

"I thought they'd all gone years ago?" Lucas interrupted.

"This one's a bit different. It's the last of the Toplin's chain and it's got some really unusual elements. I thought we could do it as a Pay-by-results deal. You'd end up getting more that way, I know you would. There's even a group of Preppers here who—"

"Preppers?"

"Yes, people who think the end of the world is coming and they're preparing."

"Well, William, I think that all sounds absolutely fascinating. But apart from the fact your last advertising feature for us, the Green Socialist Coalition fiasco, not only cost our owner, Sir Robert Green, his peerage but very nearly killed the paper and almost lost me my job… putting that to one side for a moment, what in the world gave you the idea that a national daily would be in the remotest bit interested in running a pay-by-results advertising feature for a run-down holiday camp and a bunch of tin-foil hat wearing nutcases? I mean… really?"

"I just thought I'd give you first option, you know, a favour. But if you don't want it, that's fine, I'll offer it to the Guardian. They were all over it when I told them, but I thought I owed you so there we go."

"I'm sure they'll do well with it. Oh, and please, no more prank calls."

"I told you they…" But I was talking into dead air, he'd hung up.

I held the phone in my hand, I so wanted to throw it through the window. But the thought of the hours I'd spent re-adding all my contacts the last time I did that held my hand just long enough to resist. That and the realisation that I couldn't afford to lose another phone.

I slumped into the sofa and dropped my head into my hands. A tap tap on the door forestalled my dive into self-pity.

"I say, William? You there? How do you like your burgers?"

"Left in the deep freeze," I muttered into my hands.

"Sorry, didn't quite catch that," he called.

"Erm… lettuce and cheese," I said, a bit more loudly.

"Jolly good."

I leaned back in the sofa and drew a deep breath. Okay, so just because Schonberg didn't want it, doesn't mean that nobody will want it. Maybe a glossy weekly, a Sunday supplement perhaps. Or maybe even one of those chat magazines they have in hairdressers. No, I haven't sunk to that yet.

"I say, William," called Brian. "We haven't got any lettuce. Thought we had, but it's gone all curly and slightly brown. Do you like cucumber?"

I pulled myself out of the sofa and took the two steps necessary to reach the door. Everything in this cabin was only two steps away.

I opened the door and stepped down. "I was just finishing off my day's notes. Yes, cucumber is good. In fact, I think I actually prefer cucumber in a burger."

"Jolly good. They're home-made burgers. Brianna got the recipe from the BBC cookery website. Of course, she's added her own secret ingredient." Brian gave an exaggerated wink.

He led the way round the back of his cabin to reveal a strange oasis hidden from obvious view. A small, paved patio hosted a brick-built barbecue and pizza oven, and beyond, a large vegetable garden weaved between the trees. My knowledge of vegetables extended only as far as the frozen section in Sainsburys, so the assorted foliage gave few clues. Some bamboo sticks in one patch supported a tangle of green which could have been tomatoes or peas. I had a vague recollection from my grandfather's garden that peas and tomatoes needed sticks.

"Elderberry champagne?" Brianna thrust a glass into my hand.

"Uh? Oh, thank you." I took a sip. "That's not bad. Not bad at all."

"It was only supposed to be elderberry wine," explained Brian. "But for some reason it carried on fermenting in the bottle. Most of them exploded, but a couple survived and came out fizzy. Excuse me, I must tend the burgers." He waggled a set of tongs and headed for the barbecue.

"Would you like one of my home-made canapés?" Brianna hovered a selection of miniature toasts on a wooden board under my nose. "These are pickled elderberries and this one's elderberry jam. Ooh, and those are my own invention, elderflower jelly and goat's cheese."

I took one of the elderberry jelly and goat's cheese offerings. "You like elderberries?"

"We had a very good harvest last year."

I nibbled at the canapé, it was far too sweet for my taste, but I said, "Lovely!" and her already rosy cheeks rosied up a bit more.

"From your own garden?" I scanned the garden, but the absence of any labels announcing elderberries didn't help.

"Oh no. We forage as much as we can. Our garden is just for things which don't grow wild. No point in competing with nature, as Wilderness Jack says."

"Wilderness Jack?"

"Yes, in his book, *How to Outlive the End of the World*."

"Cooee!" a voice behind me caught my attention.

I turned. A small, balding man in a multi-pocketed khaki jacket and matching trousers approached. He carried a Lidl's carrier bag.

"I brought some of my Special Malt Ale."

Brianna took the bag. "Thank you, how sweet." She nodded towards me. "This is William. He's our new neighbour."

The man held a hand to me and we shook. "Gordon," he said. "Like Gekko, only not quite as rich." He laughed.

"Gekko?" I asked.

"Wall Street, Gordon Gekko, Money never sleeps."

"Ah, yes, the movie." I studied Gordon. He looked like everything that a Wall Street tycoon wasn't.

Brianna said, "Gordon is a technical wizard. Anything technical you want, Gordon's your man. I'll just pop these down here." She removed the bottles and planted them on a small folding table.

"Burgers are ready." Brian flopped a burger into a bun, topped it with cucumber and cheese, then passed it to me.

"Have a beer." Gordon twisted the lid free from a bottle and placed it on the table in front of me. It fizzed and frothed like a slow-moving volcano.

I took the beer and drank sufficient to stem the overflow and mopped at the surplus with a serviette. There was no doubt about the malt origins. It tasted full and probably quite lethal.

"Thanks," I said. "It's a bit on the lively side."

"Still experimenting. You're my guinea pig. How are you doing? Can you still feel your feet?"

"Um, yes."

"That's good." He caught the worry my voice betrayed. "Only kidding." He laughed. Then, "But I suggest you don't drive anywhere for a while."

"Oh good." I took a bite of the burger, regretting the fact I hadn't eaten before drinking.

"What do you think?" asked Brianna. "Doesn't Brian cook a wonderful burger? You can't say no." She slipped her arm around Brian's waist.

"Yes, lovely," I said. "Certainly better than the ones at Big Moo Burger."

"Oh, you don't want to eat there," said Gordon. "Even the mice are on repeat prescriptions for Gaviscon."

"You're the man for tech problems then?" I asked Gordon.

"I like to tinker, why?"

"My phone keeps sending me to porn sites."

"You've probably picked up a virus, I can have a look if you like?"

"Thanks."

"Drop it round tomorrow. I'm 476 Montego Bay. Two rows down from West shower block. It's painted in a camouflage pattern. You can't miss it."

"William's been with Scooter today," Brian said to Gordon, then turned to me. "What was it today? Attacking the Government Nuclear Bunker? That's my favourite."

"No, we did Hijacking a Food Lorry. I think. Or it might have been a food tractor. It was all a bit chaotic and I got confused."

"We did Defences against Zombie Chickens one time," Gordon said. "That was fun. Although, we did end up having to pay compensation to old Tom Pengelly, the farmer. He says his hens never laid again."

"Zombie chickens?" I said. "Surely that's a bit out there even by Rose Well Park standards?"

"Don't you believe it," Gordon said. "The Pentagon have a contingency plan for it, so if they think it's a potential threat, we have to prepare for it."

"Seriously?"

"Mate of mine hacked their servers. It's all in their Contingency Plan, Conplan 8888."

"Chickens?"

"Chickens. And ordinary zombies, of course."

"Oh, of course," I said. "I can't believe we've overlooked the ordinary zombies." I noticed everybody had stopped and they were all watching me. I picked up the bottle and said, "This stuff's quite strong, isn't it? My teeth feel funny."

~ * ~ * ~ * ~

After what was intended to be a five-minute nap turned into a two-hour coma, I jet-washed myself in a cold shower, found the last of my fresh clothes and headed to the laundry room with everything I wasn't currently wearing. If I was going to stay here more than a couple more days, I was going to need to augment my wardrobe.

I dumped my clothes in the washer and headed to the Sun Lounge with a book.

"Interesting look," Jenna greeted as I entered.

I glanced down at my attire. Brightly coloured Bermuda shorts, packed only for the remote possibility of a beach trip, and a white dress-shirt, intended for any dinner engagement to which I might have been invited.

"All I've got left. I thought your tea-towel day was Tuesday?"

"It is, but a girl has other interests in her life apart from just tea-towels. Today is now my emergency bedding day. My cat brought me a rat and dismembered it on my duvet, then threw it up again on the pillow."

"I don't trust cats," I said.

"Very wise." She looked at her watch. "Your timing is perfect, mine should be done now, you can give me a hand to fold it. Saves me struggling."

I followed her back to the laundry room, and she pulled her laundry into a waiting basket then gave me a corner to hold.

"Well, don't just stand there," she said. "Hold it up, move back a bit. No, not like that. For goodness' sake, have you never folded a duvet cover?"

"If I said no, would you think any less of me?"

"Just hold that up and stand still."

I looked at the duvet cover and it took a moment to work out what was on it. "Is that She-ra? Princess of Power?"

She narrowed her eyes. "Are you about to judge me?"

"No."

"Good. I was never allowed one as a girl, too childish, my mum said. So now, I have a She-Ra duvet and I also have every episode of Star Trek Next Generation on DVD." She pursed her lips and gave a short nod to underline the finality of her statement.

"I preferred the original Kirk," I said, and handed her my duvet corner.

She paused and studied me as if deciding whether to have me executed for heresy. Finally, she gave a short grunt and shrugged. "That was okay. For a practise run." A twitch of a smile flashed across her lips.

I took a look at the timer on my machine. Still about fifteen minutes to go.

"Is that your stuff in there?" she asked.

"Yes, why?"

"Hope there's nothing in there you wanted to keep. You've set it at ninety degrees." She picked up her basket and headed out through the door.

I poked at the buttons on the machine, but nothing would respond. Why don't they have 'Abort' buttons?

It took another twenty minutes until I was able to retrieve my washing. Apart from a grey sheen to my once light blue shirt and a new streaky pattern to my jeans, I seemed to have got off lightly.

I took my clothes back to my cabin and attempted to pull on my newly repatterned jeans. They stalled at my thighs and finally came to a full halt at my hips. Either I'd gone up two sizes since my burger and homebrew or they'd shrunk. The shirt had fared a bit better, although I could no longer do up the top button. With fifty percent of my wardrobe now out of commission and the remainder a hotch-potch of randomised chaos, a visit to a clothes shop moved up the urgent list. I remembered Dolly's Daily Shop sold some clothing that might get me through.

~ * ~ * ~ * ~

If I'd wanted to get a table in the Dorchester, then the clothing selection in Dolly's was not going to help. Unless of course I was an eccentric rock star or a visiting general from the Bulgarian armed forces, as that seemed to be a source of most of the clothes on offer. On the other hand, I *would* fit right in with those who sat on the pavement *outside* the Dorchester. All I needed to complete the ensemble would be a tin mug and a dog. I chose the least military looking trousers I could find, although they were still khaki in colour and sported more pockets than even the most acquisitive Boy Scout would be able to fill. Shirts were easier as the Bulgarian Navy seemed to like white and blue and mostly, they looked quite un-navy like. I also chose some basic camouflage pattern trousers and T-shirts, as they were ridiculously cheap and good for knocking about in. While I was there, I couldn't resist a jungle hat complete with a mesh on top into which I could insert twigs so I wouldn't be visible when hiding in trees.

I took my new wardrobe back to my cabin, made myself a cup of tea and watched Countdown on the tiny LCD television on the wall above the electric log-effect fire. Once I'd completely humiliated myself by failing to get more than a five-letter word for the whole programme, I searched the cupboards and fridge for supper. It didn't take very long, partly because the cupboards and fridge were too small to warrant much of a search, and secondly, I hadn't bought any food yet other than teabags, milk, biscuits and a bar of chocolate.

I headed up the Pirates Bay and checked out the special of the day. Chicken Supreme with a choice of rice or mashed potato. I chose potato, took my bottle of San Miguel and numbered wooden spoon and found myself a table in the furthest corner from the stage. That still didn't stop the squorgling noises from the children's talent contest reaching me, but at least they were muted by the country and western music which, inexplicably, still dribbled out of the overhead speakers.

Ray brought my food far too quickly, and the plate was too hot to touch. I pushed the sauce around a bit to cool it to sun-temperature before attempting to taste. I leaned back and picked at a bread roll while marvelling at the vocal contortions of a five-year-old belting out the Spice Girls' song, '*Do It*'.

"It didn't take *you* long to go native," I heard from behind me and turned just as Jenna set two beers on the table and sat down. She pushed one towards me.

"Thanks," I said. I realised she was talking about the camouflage clothes I was wearing. "I needed an emergency re-supply in the wardrobe department. Mishap with the washing beast."

"I thought that might be the case. How goes your assault on the Pulitzer Prize?"

"My advertising feature? Not so good. And it's the Effie Awards for advertising, the Pulitzer is for journalists."

"By '*not so good*' you mean as in struggling to put it together or finding somebody who will run it for nothing?"

"At this present moment, both." I decided the Chicken Supreme had cooled enough to try. I was wrong and had to take a quick splash of beer to preserve at least some of the roof of my mouth. "You need to have your microwave looked at," I said. "I think it needs a smaller reactor."

"I'll have a word with Ray. He struggles a bit with anything mechanical which isn't actually part of a boat. But he works for board and tips so I can't be too hard. I take it nobody wants to publicise our little community here?"

I thought about how to spin this into a more optimistic version, but in the end, I just said, "That's about the sum of it. Sorry."

"Not your fault. Do you want to buy a holiday camp?"

"Not especially. Do you want to buy an empty bookshop? The liquidators are quite keen to get shot of it."

"I don't think I could raise enough to buy a book." Jenna sighed.

I scanned the room with its air of fine eighties chic. The feature lighting and bright murals concealed the tiredness which lurked in the shadows, patiently waiting for the right moment to take over completely. On the stage, the little Spice Girl was sitting on the floor in tears while an irate, heavily tattooed woman berated the judge. To the side, a small boy in a magician's cape and top hat had clearly failed to contain his magic rabbit which now hopped around the stage with a red silk handkerchief tangled around one foot and pursued by a man with a set of headphones over his head.

"I can see this place must cost a fortune to keep up," I said.

"It used to tickle along okay. Nothing great, but it paid its way. But now, when airlines are subsidised to the point where it's cheaper to fly to Lanzarote than get a train to Penzance, who wants to spend their two weeks here?"

"Have you thought about selling up?"

"Funny, that's what my personal business manager in the bank keeps saying to me." She took a long drink and stared unseeing towards the unfolding chaos on the stage. "But it was granddad's dream. His life. He trusted me with it." She finished the bottle and planted it back on the table. "Besides, who in their right mind would buy this?" She waved her arms expansively. "Although, I do have an offer from Jejune, the bottled water people. I have natural spring here and they want it so they can build a factory on the site."

"A factory? For water?"

"No, the water will need a pumping plant, the factory is to make plastic the bottles. They plan on making it a worldwide operation. Apparently, the Americans go mad for English spring water."

"They'll never get that past the planning people, surely?"

Her eyebrows wrinkled in a look of puzzlement. "It'll fly through. They'll just shout about all the jobs they'll create, bung a few bribes, and pay for a new bypass. Atlas World Store are sniffing around too, they want to build a regional fulfilment centre."

"They're the reason my bookshop went down," I said. "It came to the end when they introduced an app where people could come into any bookstore, browse, then scan the barcode of a book they want on my shelves and have Atlas World Store to deliver it to their door at a guaranteed discount off my price. Sometimes, before they'd even got home." I felt the weight of that trauma settle over me once more.

Jenna waved a bottle towards Ray as he passed with a tray and he brought two more beers. We sat in deflated silence. I wondered if this was how the Delaware Indians of Manhattan Island felt when they stood there with their bag of beads as they watched the Dutch builders unpack their cement mixers.

"Hey, what's up?" I heard Wayne's voice call. "You two look like someone's just dropped your birthday cake."

I twisted in my chair to face the voice. Wayne stood with a big grin on his face. Alongside him stood a man in his forties with a shaved head and a neatly curated three-day growth on his face. He stood a good three or four inches taller than Wayne, so I guessed around six two, and although not overtly muscular, he certainly wouldn't get out of breath running up the cliff path.

"Who's your friend?" asked Jenna.

"It's Jack," Wayne said, with a degree of surprise in his voice, as if we should have realised this straightaway. "Wilderness Jack. I told you he was my mate."

Chapter Nine

THE NEXT MORNING, ON MY way for my morning Breakfast-in-a-Bun at Big Moo Burger, I found myself once more hijacked by Wayne.

"Where you going?" he asked.

"Just breakfast, why?"

He slipped into step alongside me. "Scooter's running a bugout training session today. You should come?"

We reached the counter in Big Moo Burger, and I ordered my breakfast, declining the opportunity to mega-size it or add fries, then turned to Wayne. "What's a bugout?"

"It's getting your shit together real quick and heading to your bugout location when the world ends. Or it might not end, it might just be aliens or the French invading again. You gotta be ready."

"I see." I paid for my breakfast and took my little paper bag from the assistant and headed for the door.

Wayne skipped along at my side. "We got Katie and Simon, you met them when we did the food lorry hijacking."

"Oh yes, Katie and Simon. The girl in the jungle-coloured Lycra get-up, how could I forget?"

I aimed for the wooden benches in the little park area opposite Big Moo Burger but Wayne interposed himself, keeping me heading down The Yellow Brick Road.

"You'll have to eat that as we go," he said. "Be late otherwise. Scooter doesn't like people being late."

I thought about protesting but decided it wasn't worth the effort and started on my breakfast bun as I walked.

"How often does he run things like this?" I asked.

"Depends, sometimes he don't do none for months. Then others, he's at it a couple a times a week. He's well known in the circles, people come to find 'im."

"And that's how he makes his living? Running these sessions? People pay him? Actual money?"

"Yeah, money ain't everything. What good's money when a zombie's busy eating your brains?"

"I don't think I'd ever thought of it that way," I said.

We took a shortcut across the field and found Scooter standing in front of the door of his headquarters. Katie and Simon squatted on matching logs on each side of the door like a pair of surreal Foo Dogs. Katie had changed her outfit since the last outing, and although still vaguely following the camouflage theme, she wore an arctic pattern Lycra strappy T-shirt and calf length matching leggings.

"Jeremy's not coming," announced Scooter. "He's having a Skype meeting with his Tibetan monk spiritual guide. So, if you lot are ready, we're good to go." He observed our inactivity for a few seconds then said, "Well don't just stand there like spare pricks in an orgy, grab one of those sacks. We have a job to do." He pointed to a pile of hessian sacks on the ground.

We did as instructed and stood in a semi-circle, close enough to hear, but just out of reach of the stick that had suddenly appeared in his hand.

Scooter pointed his stick at an arrangement of four logs placed in a square about a hundred metres up the slight incline in front of the building.

"That is your bugout vehicle," he said. "It's fuelled and ready, but that's all. Now, follow me."

He led the way into the building, and we all stood expectantly until he was satisfied we were ready, then he pointed his stick at a pile of cardboard boxes piled against the wall.

"That's your kit, but you can only take what you can carry in one hit."

I studied the boxes. There must have been fifty or so, all shapes and sizes. Each was marked in felt-tip pen with their apparent contents. Medicine, toilet rolls, batteries, baked beans, bottled water, books, ammunition and so on.

"It's teotwawki time and you've just heard that the enemy is coming and you got three minutes to take what you can and load it into your bugout vehicle."

Nobody else asked, so I felt it was down to me. "Teotwawki?" I asked.

Scooter looked at me and shook his head as if he couldn't believe somebody could be that ignorant. "The End Of The World As We Know It, numbskull. Who let the sheeple in?"

"Ah, okay, thanks."

He pointed his stick at Simon. "Right, you're up first." He fiddled with his watch then shouted, "Go!"

Simon stared at Scooter for a moment, looked at the pile of boxes, then back at Scooter. "What now?"

Scooter said flatly, "Yes."

"But aren't you going to give me a get ready, go? Or at least a three, two, one?"

"You think the hordes of hell are going to give you a three, two, one before they come swarming over the hill with their flesh-eating wolves?"

Simon started to speak, but Scooter hadn't finished. "Three, two, one is for kids when Mummy is coming to tickle chase. Do I look like your mummy coming to tickle chase?"

"Er, no. Sorry, Scooter."

"Well, sorry don't cut it neither." He glanced at his watch. "And now you're too late anyway. Your sack is empty, the hordes have taken your bugout vehicle and your 'ead is sticking on the end of a pole decorating some barbarian's cave."

Simon looked decidedly sulky. "That's not really fair," he complained. "I wasn't ready. Can we do it again?"

"No." Scooter turned to Katie. "You're next. Go!"

"What, now?"

"Yes, now."

Katie picked up her sack and skittered over to the pile of boxes. She chose one marked, 'Salt' and dumped it to one side. "That's heavy," she said.

She pushed a box marked 'Pasta' into her sack, tested the weight, then added one marked 'Tinned Mushrooms' and another of kitchen towels, tested the weight on her back then ran up the slope. She just managed to drop the sack into the log square representing the bugout vehicle when Scooter yelled, "Stop."

We followed Scooter up the hill.

"Why'd ya choose this stuff?" Scooter asked.

Katie smiled the confident smile of somebody anticipating high praise. "Pasta's good, it keeps and so do the tinned mushrooms. My nan's got a tin of those from back before I was born and she said they're still good. The kitchen towel, I thought clever here, I doubled-up you see. You can use kitchen towel as kitchen towel but also as toilet tissue." She certainly seemed pleased with her choices.

Scooter walked in a little circle as if trying to corral his thoughts. "Pasta's okay, but you'd 'ave been better with the flour. You can make pasta out of flour and other stuff. Tinned mushrooms are a waste of time. Mushrooms are fungi and fungi grows faster than a politician's expense account. As for the kitchen roll, absolute waste of space. Plenty of leaves and hay around."

Katie's posture sank.

"And you didn't keep an eye on your six. I told you they was coming from that way."

"What way? Where's six?"

"Behind you, like on your watch," Scooter said. "Twelve is in front, three to the right, nine on yer left and six is behind you."

Katie studied her watch. "Mine just says 9:45. It's digital."

Scooter stared at her for a moment, then turned to me. "You're up."

I had a definite advantage in being third, as I'd had time to eye up the boxes. I rushed to them and grabbed the one marked 'Ammunition', and another which said, 'Canned vegetables'. I ran up to the wooden vehicle and threw them in, then realised that because I'd wasted no time choosing, I had time for another run. I grabbed a tent and a couple of five-litre water bottles. I stumbled back to the headquarters and leant against the wall while my breathing stabilised.

"And what the hell are you planning on doing with that lot?" Scooter asked.

I managed to catch enough breath to puff, "What's wrong with it?"

"Well, ammunition for a start. What weapon you got?"

"I thought... wheeff... huff... I thought... I might have one."

"You ain't got nothin' you didn't pick up. So that's just dead weight. Even if you did have a gun, you got any idea how many types of ammunition there are? And why are you lugging water around? You picked up ten kilos of water and left behind a half-kilo water filtration set? Then there's your canned vegetables, more water. Get dried food, not shit loaded with water you don't need."

I managed to regain control of my lungs. "But the tent's good, huh?"

"Waste of time. A tent is extra heavy 'cause you're lugging around poles which you could make on site, and anyway, it's a single option item. Far better off with the tarp and some rope. Much more useful in lots more situations."

"So what are you doing with all this stuff, if it's no good?" asked Simon.

"Lesson two," said Scooter. "Don't believe nothing just 'cause it's written on a box. None of you numpties even bothered to check what was in the boxes. If you had done, you'd 'ave seen it was just house bricks. So unless it's the Big Bad Wolf comin' over the hill to huff and puff yer 'ouse down, you lot are cannibal food."

Scooter made us cart all the boxes of bricks back then he gave us a guided tour of his perfect bugout kit. which included items I'd have never considered such as air filtration masks and a stack of reference books. Apparently books would be the new currency once the internet died.

Feeling suitably castigated, I slipped away explaining I needed to see Gordon about my phone.

~ * ~ * ~ * ~

Gordon's static caravan tried to hide in amongst the herd of white caravans surrounding it. Had it been painted white, or sun-peeled yellowy white, like the rest of the herd, it might well have blended in to the point of invisibility. However, as it was the only one painted in jungle green disruptive pattern, it stood like a luminous beacon in a desert. Even the camouflage netting draped over sections of it only accentuated its inability to be ignored.

Gordon opened the door as I approached and glanced side to side as if checking for secret agents tailing me, then motioned me inside. The caravan would have been crowded had it been empty, but as it strained with every piece of electrical equipment imaginable, it felt like being in the back of a supercomputer.

I noticed a large flat screen on the wall showing segmented images of the view outside. Obviously the security cameras had picked up my approach some way back.

Gordon moved a pile of magazines to reveal a chair. "Sit, sit." He turned in circles as he struggled to find a new home for the pile and eventually balanced them on top of a half-dismantled computer tower. "I don't get many guests."

I scanned the room. "You certainly keep busy."

"Modern equipment is designed to break. It's built into the infrastructure of Big Tech. Why would somebody want to buy a new phone just because the latest one has a processor which is one ten billionth of a second faster than your old one? You don't." He answered his own question before I could think and went on, "But if the thing one day suddenly turns into a plastic doorstop for no apparent reason, then off you go and shell out five hundred quid for a new one."

"And you can get them working again?"

"Mostly."

I pulled my phone from my pocket. "Here you go."

Gordon turned it in his hand. "Not seen one of these in a while. You've done well keeping it going this long."

"Needs must," I said. "I had lots of motivational letters from my bank encouraging me to not upgrade anything."

He flicked through various screens and menus. "Ah, here we go. You've got a Universal Cross-Site Scripting virus." He plugged a wire from the phone to what looked like a half-dismantled desk top computer and brought a nearby screen to life. The screen instantly filled with dense, nonsensical text.

"Would that be why I can't play music on this anymore?" I asked.

"No, that would be because you've assigned all your music files to open in your heart-rate monitor app."

"Oh, I wonder how that happened?"

"I really don't know," he said. "I didn't think that was actually possible, and yet, here we are."

"Can you fix it?"

"Probably. I'm just resetting your email."

"My email?"

"This virus looks like it's also taken over your email and sent porn to all your contacts. You might want to send some apologies to your contact list."

"Probably not worth it," I said. "Half the numbers are dead now anyway and most of the others are various Inland Revenue departments."

"In that case, would you like me to pass this little virus on to them? Easily done."

I thought for almost a full second then said, "I think they would appreciate that."

He tapped a few more keys. "There we go, that should keep them busy for a while. Now let's see what we can do about your music."

I watched as he whizzed through screen after screen at a lightning pace. "Oh, dear," he said. "Oh, this is bad."

"What is it?" I felt a tinge of panic.

"Abba?" he asked.

"Ah, yes. My dirty secret. Can you fix it?"

"What? The phone or your addiction with eighties dance anthems?"

"The phone."

He pulled the lead out and slapped the phone in my hand. "All done, but I can't help you with Abba, you're on your own with that one."

"How much do I owe you?" I fished around in my pocket for some notes.

"We'll work something out at some point, sometime."

"Huh?"

"You haven't got the hang of this place yet, have you?"

"You noticed."

"Money is the yoke of the oppressed. Only when we release ourselves from that reliance can we be truly free. We work together here, I make beer, somebody else makes a burger, we have a barbecue. I fix your phone, you get rid of my ex for me."

"Okay, I see, sort of a barter… What? Get rid of your ex? Hang on…"

"Just kidding. Although, if you fancy having a go…?"

"No," I said flatly, then just to change the subject completely away from assassination of ex-spouses, "is all this stuff here for repair?"

Gordon looked around the stacks of electronics. "Some," he said. "Most of it I use for listening in to Deep State communications or alien broadcasts."

"Alien broadcasts? You mean the SETI Home project? I thought they'd stopped that now?"

"They have, but that was just to keep the sheeple occupied while they got on with the real work of planning the takeover."

"Who are the sheeple?" I asked.

He threw his arms wide to encompass the whole world. "Everybody." His hand bumped a microphone boom which swung away in a large arc. "All the people who are sleepwalking through what the Deep State is feeding them while they busy themselves with the latest upgrade offer on their iPhone or trying to work out what bit of rubbish goes in which bin."

"But alien broadcasts? Really?"

"Have you not heard of the Black Knight?" His hand blindly fumbled at the boom as it made a second pass over his head.

"Black Night?" I queried. "You mean the Black Sabbath song in the eighties? What's that got to do with aliens?"

"Well, apart from the fact I was talking about Black *Knight*, as in swords and stuff, not night-time, and the fact that the song was by Deep Purple, not Black Sabbath and in the seventies not the eighties, apart from all that, you were pretty much on the money there."

"So what is this Black Knight then?"

He stabbed a button on one of the numerous electronic gadgets and it at once lit up like a diorama of a Santa's Grotto and filled the small room with a crackling fizz of static noises. "There," he announced, as if that explained everything.

"I don't hear anything. It's just static."

"That's what they want you to think, but it's really coming from the Black Knight satellite which has been orbiting Earth for 13,000 years. It's communicating with the Deep State, that's what you're listening to. Encoded transmissions between secret bunkers on Earth and a 13,000-year-old alien space probe. Mind blowing or what?"

"Well, yes. But how do you know?"

"Everybody knows. Nikola Tesla discovered it over a hundred years ago, but they've only been doing two-way communication recently. I think they were waiting until we were woken enough to understand."

I listened again to the noise, but it still just sounded like standing under a waterfall. "Still can't hear anything."

"That's because it's encoded." He tutted and shook his head in despair at my lack of understanding of the basics of human-alien communication. "How about this?" He twiddled a dial on Santa's diorama and the static was replaced by a tinny-sounding child's xylophone playing four bars of Happy Birthday repeatedly.

"What on Earth's that?" I asked.

"Hang on, listen."

I listened. The tune stopped and was replaced by a synthesised female voice reading out a string of numbers. She repeated the sequence several times, then Happy Birthday came back.

"I don't understand," I said. "What is it?"

"It's called a Numbers Station. It's a way for secret agents to communicate."

"I've heard of them, but I thought they were just used in the Cold War. Never actually heard one though."

"Still around. They're very simple, effective and impossible to crack unless you have the key. Now listen to this." He pushed a cassette tape into a machine and pressed play. "I haven't got round to converting a lot of this stuff yet."

The machine hissed in a comforting nostalgic way then a crackly voice said, "Say again, Houston."

"That's off the Apollo missions," I said.

"Apollo Eleven. What you're hearing is Neil Armstrong talking to Mission Control on the secret medical channel. The open broadcast transmission cut out for two minutes during this period. Listen."

Neil Armstrong's voice was clearly agitated. *"Those are giant things. No, no, no, this is not an optical illusion. No one is going to believe this."*

The conversation continued with Armstrong explaining they could see what looked like flying saucers on the rim of a crater.

Gordon pressed stop after the conversation ended. "And in a remarkable coincidence, NASA also misplaced a chunk of the video from the same time." He did air-quotes with his fingers at the word 'misplaced'.

"That has to be a fake," I said.

"There were several copies of the same recording circulating from different sources within twenty minutes of it happening. I thought you'd know all about this, what with all your books."

"I just sell them; it doesn't mean I believe them. But I've never heard of this or your Black Knight."

"You really should start reading some of those books instead of just selling them. Start with Eric Scringle's The God Machines. That'll open your eyes. You know he comes here from time to time?"

"Who? Eric Scringle?" I now remembered the receptionist in the Moto Lodge. She'd mentioned Eric Scringle, and I hadn't twigged that he was the author at the time.

"Yes," said Gordon. "He comes here when he needs to hide. He's got a cabin down Lower Bermuda way. Not been here for a while though."

"You mean the guy who worked for SPOC and ran off with a bit of a space toilet from the European Space Agency?"

"Spock?"

"Special Projects Office, Cheltenham."

"But there's no K?"

"I know, SPOC."

Gordon stared at me for a moment, then shrugged. "I don't know about that. Anyway, Eric's just the tip of what's going on." He pointed to a high shelf of box files which stretched wall to wall. "Anytime you need a little more material for your publicity campaign, let me know."

"Ah, yes. That's not quite working out the way I hoped."

"So which way is it working out?"

"To be honest, it's not. Nobody will talk to me. On the upside, it turns out that Wayne *did* know Wilderness Jack after all. Although of course, that doesn't help much now."

"Hmm, that's a pity." Gordon slumped noticeably in his seat. "We thought the publicity might just be enough to save the place. If Jenna is forced to sell out to Jejune, they'll force us all out in no time. I don't fancy moving all this lot though."

~ * ~ * ~ * ~

I headed back to my cabin with the idea of seeing if I could find a cheap way of getting back to London. This place was clearly not working out and, pleasant as it was, the longer I stayed here the smaller my diminishing resources became.

I put my hand on the door to my cabin and heard the dreaded, "Hi-de-hi, good neighbour," from the adjacent cabin.

I breathed deep to stem my frustration, fixed a smile which I hoped would look passably realistic, and turned. "Oh, hello, Brian. Didn't see you there."

"Did you get your phone fixed?"

"Yes, it was a virus."

"He's a bit of a whizz is Gordon. He rescued all our photographs from when we went on a caravan holiday to Newport Pagnell. Our computer crashed and we thought we'd lost them all. Brianna was very upset as we had a special one of us together in front of the Office for National Statistics. Long story, we were just—"

"Sorry," I said. "I've got a Skype call coming in a moment. About a book show." I fumbled at the lock.

"Oh, never mind. Another time, perhaps. We can show you the photographs over a glass of Fennel gin one evening."

"Yes, that would be lovely." The door finally yielded under my desperate fingers and I slid in, closing the door on the opportunity of an afternoon viewing of the attractions of Newport Pagnell.

I found enough in the food cupboard to make a cheese sandwich and a cup of tea, and I took them to the sofa. The television sprang to life without me realising I'd pressed the button on the remote control to make that happen. I changed channel when an orange Kardashian appeared on the screen only to find some more orange celebrities. This time they were cooking what looked like string and twigs for each other and painting them in Day-Glo colours. More Playschool than Michelin. I flicked again, and I was presented with a pair of minor celebrities trying various Activity Holidays and generally bigging themselves up by making snidey remarks to camera about everyone and everything. I tuned my mind to neutral and munched at my sandwich.

After a few minutes, I realised the moving wallpaper had changed without me noticing and I was now watching a fly-on-the-wall documentary about a family trying to live off-grid on a remote island off the Scottish coast. Their dog had just eaten their only laying chicken.

I took my plate to the sink and let my gaze wander outside while I rinsed it off. The Brians looked like they were off on a mission. Sensible clothing, a couple of canvas bags and a set of those extendable tongs which old folk use to pick up their socks with. I guessed they were going for a forage somewhere.

For a moment, the world went away while the fragments of an idea started to come together. Not quite together enough yet to make a plan, but a possible precursor to a plan. A plan towards a plan. My feet were wet. I stared down and realised the sink was overflowing and I was still washing my plate. Me and Archimedes. Eureka. I needed to find Jenna.

Chapter Ten

I BUMPED INTO JENNA ON my way to the Pirates Bay.

"Ah, just the person I was looking for," I said.

"I hate conversations which start like that," she replied.

"No, this is good. I've had an idea."

She stopped and faced me square on. "An idea? Haven't you used up your idea allowance for the week?"

"No, this one could work. Really. Just give me five minutes, trust me, you'll love it."

"That sounds exactly like the line used on me ten minutes before I lost my virginity."

"What? No, nothing like that. I would never... I mean, not that I wouldn't if... Um... Shall I stop talking now?"

A fleeting grin broke free of her lips and she nodded. "Okay, but I haven't got time to stand here and talk, you'll have to explain as we go. I've got World War Three about to kick off down in Montego Bay." She turned and continued in the way she'd been heading.

"You see, I didn't actually believe that Wayne really knew Wilderness Jack. But when he turned up, well, that started me thinking."

"One of the things I've learned over the years is that people have this constant ability to surprise. And Wayne, more than most."

We turned right off The Yellow Brick Road and threaded between some interestingly personalised caravans, one of which hid behind a two-metre fence topped with razor wire.

"They're not very keen on visitors," I commented.

"They claim it keeps away the Jehovah's Witnesses," Jenna said. "So, this idea of yours?"

"Yes, sorry." I skipped a couple of steps to keep up with her. "I was watching this documentary last night, about this family living on an island off Scotland. Faskoul, I think. I'm not sure, one of the Shetlands anyway."

She stopped without warning and my feet slipped on the gravel as I managed to stop before colliding with her.

"Can we flip through to the last page of this?" she asked. "I know it spoils the build-up, but I do have rather a lot to do today."

"You could do activity breaks," I said. "I can draw up an advertising campaign for you. They're all the thing now. I can negotiate a deal for you with some of the places like Tripadvisor or even TV slots in those holiday programmes. You would offer Experience Holidays. Have a break, learn a new skill."

"That's it? People come here for a holiday and your idea is to give them pottery classes or send them out on bicycles and somehow that's going to magic up more customers?"

"No, that's not it. What I was thinking…" But I was talking to her retreating back as she was already marching down Route 67.

I caught up with her once more. "The world is changing. People are worried and they feel they no longer have any control over their lives. So what do they do? They try to prepare for some unknown threat. They learn to grow tomatoes or bake bread and watch Wilderness Jack on telly as he catches a snake with a stick and turns it into supper and a pair of sandals."

She stopped again, but this time I was ready for her.

"I know it may be a bit impertinent to ask," she said "But, are you *actually* a crazy person?"

"No. At least not that crazy. Look, you have a unique group here. This place is full of people who know stuff, how to prepare against a zombie attack, how to grow elderberry gin, make beer. Gordon knows how to listen to aliens and fix stuff. All sorts. People are really into alien stuff, UFOs and so on, I sold loads of books on it. You could do a holiday where people learn about alien spotting. Gordon can help, he knows all about that stuff. Look how many people trek all the way out to Roswell in America every year. And that's just a village in the desert and it's even nearly the same name."

"How many?" asked Jenna.

"What?"

"You said, '*look how many people go to Roswell every year*'. I just asked how many?"

"Um, I don't know. Not actual numbers. But it's a 'Must See' thing for people visiting New Mexico."

"Just to visit a village in a desert?"

"Yes, there's a whole tourist industry there, completely built up over the rumour of a UFO in nineteen forty-something. There's even a UFO museum there now."

I waited for the argument, or at least a sarcastic comment or two, but none came. Jenna just stood silently, seemingly contemplating the clouds. After a long moment, she said, "Okay, let's talk about it. But not now, now I have to stop two of my tenants killing each other. Or at least, help the victor hide the body."

I followed her through the tangle of caravans and static homes until we came to what looked like a bad day on the set of a Jeremy Kyle shoot. Two women circled each other like a pair of tigers weighing each other up, looking for a weak spot on which to pounce.

Charlie hovered in the background. She held a huge adjustable spanner in one hand and I couldn't work out if she was getting ready to intervene or settling down to watch the match.

Jenna called, "Debbie, Willow, enough. What is it *this* time? You're not still arguing about the bamboo, are you?"

"No," said Debbie. "But I still don't see why I have to put up with it invading my broccoli when I didn't plant it."

"You should thank me, not complain," said Willow. "It's a natural barrier, much nicer than your wire fence here." She kicked a foot at the wire fence around Debbie's garden.

"You kick that again and I'll kick your bony arse right off your scrawny, vegan legs."

"Well, at least they're not bloated with cellulite. If you didn't eat so many dead animals—"

"Enough," repeated Jenna. "What's going on?"

They both started shouting at once, and Jenna held a hand up. "Stop!" She turned to Charlie. "Well?"

"Don't ask me," Charlie said. "Willow called me down saying her water had stopped and when I get here to have a look, these two are trying to tear chunks out of each other. I'm just here for the entertainment now."

Jenna sighed then said, "Willow, you first, what's this all about."

"Little Miss Perfect here thinks it's okay to tap into my spring water. My water tank is empty, and my tomatoes are wilting."

"That's because you don't eat properly," Debbie yelled.

Willow lurched forwards but Jenna's hand slipped between the pair of them. "Firstly, Willow, I've told you before, it's not the Rose Well Spring, that doesn't run this way. This is South-West Water's main supply and you're illegally hooked up to it."

"I did try to tell them that," offered Charlie.

"See!" yelled Debbie. "I told you it wasn't your private water. We're all entitled to that."

"No, you're not," Jenna said. "Nobody is. You're supposed to get your water from the metered supply. Both of you."

"I'm not buying water," said Willow. "It's a fascist control, everybody has the right to free water. It's a natural resource."

Debbie pointed to Willow. "What she said."

"You," Jenna addressed Willow. "If you're going to steal water, you're going to have to put up with other people tapping in as well. And, Debbie, you didn't need to divert it from Willow. If you must steal the water as well, at least have the decency to put in a divert so you can both use it. And if you can't agree, I'll turn off this pipe completely."

"You can't do that," said Willow. "We have rights."

"Not here you don't. I can't risk you two getting me taken to court. I don't have the money for the bus fare to get there, let alone enough to pay any fines. Unless you two are going to pay them?"

"Why've I got to share my water with her?" Willow complained.

"Because, like I said, if you don't, I'll get Charlie to cut it off completely," Jenna said. "Now, do we have a deal?"

They both mumbled grudging assent and Jenna said, "Charlie, you think you can take it from here?"

Charlie tossed the adjustable spanner in a lazy arc and caught it perfectly. "No problem."

Jenna turned to me. "Come on, there's someone I think you should meet."

We followed a labyrinthine path back through Montego Bay.

"Is it a regular problem, stealing?" I asked.

"Not really, but I have to keep on top of it. The Hobbits are the worst, they'll have anything which isn't nailed down, *and* much that is. Lost a couple of swan pedalos off the boating lake a while back." She stopped and looked at me. "Swan pedalos, I ask you, what the hell would they want with those?"

She didn't wait for me to answer and set off at a brisk pace.

At points, the path seemed to recoil on itself to avoid a random fence or vegetable plot where the original path once lay. We broke free of the tangle and crossed Route 67 then into an enclave of high-end static homes. Each unit sat in perfect symmetry and within a regimented white picket fence.

"I've not been to this bit," I said.

"This is Paradise Bay," Jenna said. "This is where we once made ninety percent of our takings over the summer season. Families used to come from all over, often booking a year ahead."

Despite the pristine condition of each unit and the immaculate, miniature gardens, which surrounded each one, there was a strange feel of desolation.

"What happened?" I asked.

"Tax-payer funded airline subsidies. Started in 2000 or so. Didn't take long before people realised it was cheaper to fly to Benidorm than drive down here and they just stopped coming."

We stopped outside one unit which looked identical to all the others apart from the number on the door and the fact there was a family of gnomes in the small front garden. Jenna opened the little white gate then knocked on a goblin faced door knocker.

A white net curtain moved inside an adjacent window, then a few seconds later, the door cracked open a couple of inches.

"Nathan? It's me, Jenna."

"Who's that with you?" asked the voice behind the door.

"This is William, he's a friend of mine. He's okay."

The door briefly closed again as Nathan fiddled with the chain lock. He opened the door wide and looked around as if expecting to see an invading army hiding in the bushes. Finding no immediate threat, he beckoned us inside with a waving hand and a, "Come on then, quickly."

The smell of cannabis hit me immediately. Not smoke, but the smell of the fresh plant. I glanced around the room. The far end had been strung with multiple washing lines running from wall to wall. Each line held dozens of little cannabis branches in various states of drying. I felt my brain going away just by being in the room.

Nathan was a tall, wiry man and probably a fair bit younger than his well-worn face pretended. He watched me with a slight furrow in his brow, clearly not sure of my intent.

"Drying time," he said, nodding towards the plants. "Can't leave it down the tunnels, too damp, it'll never dry there."

Jenna noticed my confusion and said, "I'll explain later." She patted my shoulder like I was a little boy who'd just discovered his first porn picture. "Nathan saw a UFO over here a few years ago, I thought you two should meet."

Nathan looked as confused as I felt.

"A UFO?" I queried. "When?"

Nathan pondered for a moment then said, "Ooh, must be a couple of years now."

"More like twenty plus," said Jenna.

"Really? You sure?"

"It was not long after the Blair-Git Project got in."

"Whoa, where did all that go? Did I miss much?"

"A couple of wars, a pandemic and Game of Thrones. Not so much."

"Tell me about the UFO," I asked.

Nathan waved us to sit on the sofa. "Well, I'd got a couple of nice fat spliffs in me pocket and was cycling down to The Smuggler's in town for a quiet pint and a smoke, when I get a phone call from Wayne warning me the Old Bill were sat in the car-park of the Shepherd's Rest on the Little Didney road. Now I didn't want to take the chance of them pullin' me over, so I did the only thing I could. I stopped off and smoked the spliffs."

"And what happened?"

"It was a good thing I done that, 'cause I was just cycling along minding me own business when these coloured lights appeared in the sky and then... bang." He held both hands in front of his face with fingers outstretched to show me what 'Bang', looked like.

"The lights exploded?" I asked.

"No, I'd cycled straight into the back of a police car."

"The one in the pub car-park?"

"Yeah, I'd got a bit lost. Anyway, I told them about the light, but they were only interested in searching me. Right miffed they were when they found nothing. Lucky I'd smoked it all earlier or they'd have busted me sure enough."

"And the coloured lights?"

"I'm gettin' to that. So there I was, feeling all woozy after my tumble, and the Old Bill were busy trying to pick fish and chips out of their uniforms and then... whoosh, there it was again. Only this time it was just white, pure white like an angel's wings, only round, so it must have changed. Weird or what?"

"You said, whoosh?" I asked.

"Well, not in as many words. It was silent. Probably 'cause it was in space where there's no sound, but it looked like it was going whoosh." Nathan threw a hand into the air to illustrate the sound of a silent whoosh. "Or zoom." His hand swept left to right, then stopped suddenly while he stared at it as though seeing it for the first time. His eyes widened.

"What did it look like?"

"Huh? Oh, sort of like a light. Only moving."

"A bit like a moving light then," I suggested.

"Yeah, did you see it as well?"

"Just a lucky guess."

"You should try Three-card Monte," Nathan said. "There's this bloke gets down The Smuggler's. I had a go once, but I'm not much cop at guessing. Lost me Jobseeker's Allowance."

"The light," I reminded him. "You were telling me about the light."

"Yeah, so it moved across the sky and disappeared."

"And then?" I prompted.

"It went back up to the Mother Ship and vortexed into a different universe."

"You saw that?"

"That's what it looked like. It sort of faded away as it moved across the sky, so what else could it have been?"

"Well, that certainly appears to be a nice piece of unassailable logic," I said.

"Yeah, what you said. Want a beer? I've got some of Gordon's special." He pulled open the fridge and handed beers to Jenna and me. "I saw a goblin once as well. Do you want to hear about that?"

"I haven't really got time today," I said.

"I was coming back from a bit of a session down at Wayne's place over Montego Bay, and on the way back I fell down a rabbit hole. Not all the way like Mary Poppins did, I just tripped into it and landed in a prickle bush. I was sat there, getting me breath back, and there it was. All green and hiding in the bush with these twinkly eyes, laughing at me. Well weird it was."

"I can see how that would have been disturbing." I finished my beer and put the bottle on the draining board. "Well, thanks for—"

Nathan put his hand on my arm as I rose. "Another time, we'd been on an all-nighter in the field with the twelve stones... or was it Old Man Pengelly's farm?... No, it was—"

Jenna stood and said, "We really must go, Nathan, but thanks." She nudged me out of the door.

I took deep breaths of cannabis-free air as we headed back up the path.

"Tunnels?" I asked.

"What?"

"You said you'd explain the tunnels." I had to walk fast to keep pace with Jenna as she marched.

"Oh, yes. There's a load of tunnels under Carter's Field, where the old airfield was. They were used in the war as bunkers or something. Some of the Hobbits have been opening them up a bit, don't know what they're doing, probably best I don't. Anyway, Nathan's got a cannabis farm down in there with special lights and stuff so he can grow all year."

"And you don't mind?"

"Mind? Nathan is one of the few people living here who pays his rent each month without fail. *And* he's in one of the most expensive units, of course I don't mind. Give me a dozen Nathans." She stopped walking suddenly. "Look, I've got to check back with Charlie and make sure those two don't spring a major leak and flood the site again. I'll catch up with you in the Pirates Bay this evening and you can tell me how your idea of making this place into another Roswell is going to work."

"Um, okay, but that wasn't exactly…"

But I was talking to her disappearing rear again. I paused for a moment, watching her go. Her ubiquitous jeans and simple shirts emphasising her androgynous figure. I felt slightly guilty at enjoying the view and turned and headed back to my cabin.

~ * ~ * ~ * ~

I'd arranged to meet Gordon at the Pirates Bay early that evening. I'd thought early, with a view to avoiding the karaoke. A children's birthday party was in full apocalypse overdrive, with balloons everywhere and tables plastered in what had probably once been cakes but were now sticky splodges of coloured goo. A tired-looking clown attempted to wrest control, but he was completely outnumbered and outgunned.

Gordon was nowhere to be seen, so I positioned myself at the bar as far from the ensuing cake melee as I could and ordered a beer from Ray.

"You eating?" he asked as he pushed the bottle towards me.

"What's on?" I squinted at the chalkboard behind the bar.

Ray saw me struggling with the scrawly writing and dim light and lifted the menu to the bar. "We've got Chicken Tagliatelle, that's French, or Chicken nuggets, that's not. That was really only cooked for the party but they only wanted crisps and cake so we've got a lot left over." He froze in thought for a moment, then said, "I wasn't supposed to say that. Don't tell Jenna I said, huh?"

"Your secret's safe with me. Which is the cheapest?"

"The nuggets, we need to get rid of them. Bugger, I wasn't supposed to say that either."

"I'll have the nuggets."

"Good choice."

I took my numbered spoon and settled at a table in the quietest bit of the room I could find. I'd only been there a few minutes when Jenna arrived and sat opposite me.

"Ah," I said. "I meant to ask you something earlier."

"I haven't got any," she said.

"What?"

"Whatever it is you want. I haven't got any."

"No, nothing like that. I was talking with Gordon the other day, and he mentioned a chap called Eric Scringle stays here from time to time."

I noticed her stiffen slightly at the name.

"Never heard of him," she replied, a little too quickly. "Why do you ask?"

"Coincidence really, he wrote one of the books I have in stock. He used to work for the Ministry of Defence in their Special Projects Department. He went missing some time ago."

"Well, he didn't come here. How's the big plan coming on?" she asked, changing the subject.

"Do you mean my original life plan to a be a Doctor Who companion, or my more recent one of trying to survive to the end of the week?"

"Neither, I meant your plan to turn this place into the next epicentre of UFO tourism with added macrame workshops."

"Ah, yes. That's still in the planning stage."

"Your plan is in the planning stage?"

"Yes, but I have completed the preliminary study stage."

Ray arrived with the nuggets and chips and also a small paper plate with a piece of cake, some cheesy puffs and a Little Mermaid serviette. I looked at the cake and cheesy puffs, then I looked at Ray.

"It's how they come." He shrugged and wandered off.

"Hey, he's cheap." Jenna held her hands up as a pre-emptive strike against any possible complaint.

"I never said anything."

"Good, then don't. You were telling me your plan."

"Was I? I thought I was telling you about the death of my dreams."

"You were, but I wasn't listening."

"You're a bar owner, I have one of your beers in my hand, so you have to listen to my tales of woe. It's the rules."

"No, it's not. I only have to give the *appearance* of listening. That's what it says in the Bar Owner's Manual." She took a nugget from my plate and popped it into her mouth. "What did you think of Nathan?"

"He's a nutjob. He got stoned and saw... I don't know what he saw. Probably a plane or the ISS or even pixies, who knows?"

"Piskies," Jenna said flatly.

"Piskies?"

"We have piskies in Cornwall, not pixies. Or pigsies."

I studied Jenna for a moment. "Really? Pigsies?"

She nodded.

I shook my head briefly to get rid of the idea of pigsies and said, "Well, whatever. He was clearly as high as a kite and the police didn't want to do the paperwork, or the problem of explaining what they were doing in a pub car-park with a bag of fish and chips, so nobody challenged his story."

"I know, but it made the papers. It's a start."

"A start? How do you mean?"

"For your plan to make this the new Rosewall. It's already made the papers once."

"Roswell," I corrected. "Anyway, how on Earth did something like that ever make the papers in the first place?"

"You ought to know, I thought you were a newspaper man."

"No, I keep saying, I just sold advertising space. I wrote snappy catch lines and extended truths. I never paid much attention to the news end of things. That was all a bit too frantic for me."

Jenna thought for a moment, then, "Well, it was August 1997, a particularly quiet time for the news. Parliament was on holiday, so nothing much was happening. The biggest news of the month, as I remember it, was the new Oasis album and Manchester United beating Chelsea 4-2 at

Wembley." She took a chip from my plate and dipped it into my little pot of ketchup. "Do you mind? Only I'm starving, haven't had time to stop."

"Help yourself. Do you like pink cake?"

"Not especially." She sucked the ketchup from the chip and my brain went off to all the wrong places.

She finished the chip and continued, "Well, I guess the papers had pages to fill and a flying saucer made a change from flower shows, so Nathan got his moment of glory. Then before anybody got time to look too closely, Princess Diana's personal driver rolled out of a Paris pub late one night, three sheets to the wind, and suddenly, nobody wanted to know about Nathan's flying saucer anymore. Poor Nathan, his fame disappeared faster than a paparazzi motorbike in a Paris Tunnel. Probably just as well though, it wouldn't have stood up to too much scrutiny."

"I think even *my* old paper would have thought twice about printing that one."

"They ran it," she said.

"Really? Well there you go, I told you I wasn't paying attention."

"It even made the 'And Finally' slot on the local BBC television news."

I paused to think, a forked chip held frozen halfway from plate to mouth. Jenna took my hand and guided the chip to her own mouth and grinned as she ate it.

"Okay," I said. "So if we stir things up a bit, hopefully people will pull out the old reports and it will all look like the same thing. What we need is another sighting."

"Can we mock up a video?" Jenna asked. "I've got a nephew who made a video of a dancing kitten on his phone. It looked very realistic."

"No, people are wise to hooky videos, we need credible witnesses. We need to create a real UFO that people can actually see."

"Oh, okay. And there was me worrying you were going to come up with something ridiculous."

"No really, I have an idea." I looked at my watch. "I was waiting for Gordon, he said he'd be here by now."

"Gordon?" Jenna asked. "Techy Gordon? The guy who fixes computers and stuff?"

"Yes."

Jenna tried to intercept another chip by again redirecting my hand mid journey. But I was wise to that now and simply removed the chip from the fork with my other hand and popped it in my mouth.

"Do you want me to order you a plate of chips?" I asked.

"No, I'm staying off carbs for a few days." She patted her non-existent tummy.

I felt somebody approaching from behind and turned, expecting to see Gordon but it was Wayne.

"Hey, Jenna, just who I was looking for," he said, sitting next to me and helping himself to a chip. "Have you got a mini digger we could borrow for a couple of days?"

Jenna's eyes narrowed as she fixed Wayne with a stare which made me uncomfortable even as an observer. "Why would you think I have a mini digger? And what's more, even if I had one, why do you think I would lend it to you lot after what you did with my leaf blower?"

"That wasn't my fault, we were trying to get rid of a wasps' nest."

"But you set fire to my leaf blower," Jenna said.

"That was an accident," Wayne protested. "YouTube said we had to blow smoke at them."

"By filling my leaf blower with burning cardboard?"

"That was Scooter's idea."

"Sorry I'm late." Gordon arrived and sat opposite Wayne. "I picked up some strange signals from a NASA asteroid tracking station. They think Apophis has shifted slightly. It's all a bit of a worry."

We looked at Gordon in varying degrees of puzzlement.

"What's Apophis?" Jenna asked.

"It's a Near Earth Object, coming very close to Earth in 2029. They now think it might have shifted a bit, enough to put it through the keyhole."

"Keyhole?" I asked.

Gordon looked irritated by my lack of basic astrophysics. "It's a region of space, close to Earth, where if Apophis goes through that, then a collision is a certainty."

"Have you got a mini digger?" Wayne asked.

"I never heard anything on the BBC," I said.

"They're not going to put out anything public," Gordon said. "It would create a global panic. We need to move up our preparations."

"In the meantime, William has a plan to save our site here from being snatched by Jejune Water and turned into a plastic bottle factory." Jenna nodded in my direction.

"I need to make a fake UFO," I said.

"You can't actually make a fake UFO," said Gordon. "By definition, all UFOs are real, because the term means 'unidentified'. At the point where they're identified as either fake or real, they are therefore no longer *Unidentified* Flying Objects."

"You got a mini digger?" persisted Wayne.

"No, Wayne, sorry." Gordon looked at me. "So what is it you're after?"

"I was thinking about some helium balloons with little lights inside that would float around and, at night, would look like UFOs."

"Hmm, that could work. At night, without a point of reference to scale, they could look huge to an observer."

"Yes, that's exactly what I thought," I lied.

I caught Jenna's look which said, '*Yeah, right.*'

"And miniature lights and batteries are easy," Gordon continued. "I could certainly fit some inside a helium balloon. Leave it with me."

"How about bombs?" asked Wayne.

Gordon studied Wayne for a moment, then, "No, sorry, I don't think we'll get any bombs in them."

"No. I didn't mean that. I don't want a bomb, I've already... no, just thinking like... about if you know how to disarm one. Not a real one, just asking." Wayne seemed to go off in thought for a moment, then added, "For a friend."

"Not my field of expertise, I'm afraid," Gordon said. He pointed at my chips. "You finished with those?"

I pushed the plate at him. "Help yourself. I've lost my appetite."

Chapter Eleven

I WOKE WITH A REMINDING nag from my stomach that I hadn't eaten much the night before. Feeling brave, I decided to risk the breakfast buffet in the Pirates Bay.

Half of the room still had chairs on the tables, restricting breakfasters to the lower end of the room. I took a selection of the usual breakfast items from the buffet along with two cups of coffee and settled down with a copy of the Daily Sentinel from the paper rack.

More shops closing on the High Streets, internet social media giant in data breach, new iPhone released and the Prime Minister has a new haircut. All normal in the outside world. On page seven, I found an article about Icarus Airlines saying that the Administrators had basically decided there was no money in the pot and that all customers had to file claims with their card companies. There goes another three months of my life holding on a telephone to talk to somebody in Mumbai about twenty quid.

"Oh, hi, William."

I looked up from the paper to see Wayne hovering by my table.

"Morning, Wayne. You're up bright and early."

"Still trying to find a mini digger." He thrust his hands in his pockets and looked slowly round the room as if, by hope, somebody had left a mini digger lying around.

"I don't think you'll find one here." I shook the mustard bottle and eased a line along the length of my sausages.

"I know, but you never know who you'll find here. Had a guy in here once who used to sell horse sperm to the Saudis."

I paused with mustard bottle in midair while I studied my sausages and the yellow streaks which now decorated them. "So what are you needing a digger for?"

"Gotta dig something." Wayne looked at the floor and shuffled his feet.

"Have you asked the local farmer? They often have digging machinery?"

"I asked Old Tom Pengelly, but he's only got a shovel thing what goes on the front of his tractor."

"And that won't do it?"

"Too big to go down the tunnel."

"I'll tell you what." I pushed my uneaten breakfast to one side and stood. "Let's go have a look, maybe there's a different way." I folded up the paper and stuffed it in my pocket.

Wayne pointed at my sausages. "You gonna leave those?"

"Help yourself, I've rather gone off them."

~ * ~ * ~ * ~

I followed Wayne down to Route 67, then through the fence into Carter's Field. He led me into the building which served as the Preppers' headquarters where I'd first met Scooter.

Wayne grabbed one end of the huge failing sofa which dominated the centre of the room. "Give us a hand with this, will you?"

We dragged the sofa a couple of metres from its position to reveal a large wooden trapdoor in the floor. He grabbed the metal ring and heaved the door open. It crashed to the floor, exposing a wooden ladder reaching into the darkness below.

"Tunnels?" I asked.

"Yeah, but it's a secret." He put his forefinger to his lips.

"You were certainly right about one thing," I said.

"What's that?"

"You weren't ever going to get Tom Pengelly's tractor down there."

"Told ya'." Wayne descended two steps down the ladder then reached for a switch and light flooded the space below. He continued to the bottom then waved at me to follow.

The ladder creaked with each step I took. "What's down here?"

"It's our bunker, you'll see. But don't tell Scooter."

I heard a voice from above. "Don't tell Scooter what?"

"Oh, hi, Scooter," said Wayne. "Didn't know you were there."

I looked up and saw Scooter's face peering into the trapdoor.

"What are you up to?" Scooter asked.

"William said he might be able to help with a digger. He was just having a look."

Scooter looked at me. "You got a digger?"

"No, but I just thought maybe, you know, another pair of eyes on the problem…" I clung to the ladder wondering whether I should go back up or continue down. I opted for holding on tightly where I was.

"What've you told 'im, Wayne?"

"Nothing, Scooter, honest. Just asking about a mini digger."

"But he ain't got a digger, he just said."

"Sorry," Wayne yelled back up.

"Sorry don't cut nothin'. Too late, he's seen this. What we gonna do wiv 'im now?"

"I haven't seen anything. Just a ladder." My fingers were starting to complain about the severity of the grip I was employing. "I haven't even looked down yet."

"I never look down from a ladder," said Wayne. "I'm afraid of heights. They say you shouldn't look down if you're afraid of heights."

"I'm not actually afraid of heights." I eased one hand at a time to flex my fingers. I had visions of Scooter, knife between teeth, shinning down to me any second.

"And clowns," continued Wayne. "I *really* don't like clowns. Clowns in high places, now that's the worst. You ever seen the Cirque du Soleil? They get clowns up on trapezes. They should put warnings on before the programme, like they do with porn."

"I'm not interested in clowns on ladders, or porn," said Scooter. "Well, maybe porn sometimes, but definitely not clowns. But what are we going to do with him?" He leaned over the hole, his eyes flaring with the orange glow of the light, giving him a decidedly satanic appearance.

The metal rungs of the ladder felt fused to my hands as I waited for Scooter to reach down and drag me out by the scruff of the throat.

"Scooter," Wayne called. "You gotta mind your chickens. They're getting out. All over the place they are, the chickens."

"The chickens?" Scooter said, quietly.

"Yeah, they're getting all worried. You gotta keep calm or they'll be everywhere."

"Oh, yeah. Watch the chickens."

"You remember William, the book man? He's alright, you remember? You met him a couple of days back. He did the hostage training with you," Wayne yelled back up.

"Oh, yeah. You're that bloke with all the books, you did that thing in the newspaper about the fall of capitalism, yeah got ya' now. Sorry, got a bit... wotsit there for a moment. It happens."

"No worries," I said. "Although, it wasn't me that wrote it, it was the Green Coalition. I just did the advert and... Should I come back up?"

"No, you go down. I'll come down with you," Scooter said. "What do you know about bombs?"

"What is it with bombs?" I took the last step off the ladder and breathed.

Scooter slid down the ladder and landed beside me. "Just a hypothetical, so to speak."

Within the range of the light from above, I noticed a wall behind me and to my left. Beyond that, the light reached a few metres into the dark, then faded. I heard another click and my eyes flinched at the new brightness. I squinted into the glare and the two walls I'd noticed came into better view. I'd expected a rough-hewn tunnel, instead, aged brick facing showed that this had been built a long time ago. In places, the bricks bulged threateningly, but given their age, they'd probably survive a while longer. At least until I could get back out, anyway.

The area in which we stood appeared to be about the same size as the room I'd just left above. A metal desk, piled high with cardboard boxes, stood against the left wall and was flanked either side by several racks of metal shelves, each jammed with more boxes. A couple of large grey metal cupboards stood against the wall behind me, their doors closed and secured with padlocked chains.

"This way." Scooter pointed into the tunnel in front of me. The row of overhead lights showed a short passage which seemed to open into something much larger. Wayne was already disappearing into the distance.

"Wayne's not quite in this world," Scooter continued as we walked through the tunnel. "Generally, he's about as much use as a lawnmower in a helicopter, but he's got a good soul, know what I mean?"

"I think so."

"But he ain't got nobody, so I look out for him. It's what mates do, ain't it?"

I nodded and made a noise of agreement, and as we walked on, I scanned the boxes on the shelves lining the tunnel. Baked beans and other tinned vegetables, tinned fruits, tinned meats, pasta, pulses and cases upon cases of beer.

The short passageway ended in a larger space with a domed ceiling propped at various points by original brick pillars and more recently applied scaffolding poles. What looked like a large generator stood at one side with a jungle of cables running from it in all directions. It reminded me of a stage rig I'd seen when I'd worked the beer tent at a local free rock music festival for the Chipping Sodbury Real Ale Society. That had eventually needed three fire engines and field electrician from the nearby Army base.

Another large machine stood near the generator and resembled a monster vacuum cleaner. Tubes extended from it and ran up to the ceiling, then continued on into another passageway.

Scooter noticed me studying the contraption. "It's our air re-gen unit," he explained. "We rigged it up from a bunch of old industrial vacuum cleaners we got from the Wylfa Magnox Plant when it closed."

"Wylfa? The Welsh nuclear power station?"

"Yeah, got loads of good stuff, they were just throwing it out."

"And this?" I pointed at a massive copper tank with curly copper pipes looping around it.

"Yeah, got that from an old hotel in Padstow and turned it into a water purifier. You'll never guess what it was originally."

"A hot water tank?"

"Oh." Scooter's face fell. "Lucky guess. But we rigged it up into a still and now it turns piss into fresh water." He glanced around and picked a pint beer mug from a table. "I'll pour you a glass, see how good it is."

"Um, no thanks. I only drink mineral water. It's for the... er... minerals. And beer, I can drink beer."

"For the minerals?"

"Yes."

Scooter went to one of the metal shelving units and pulled a cardboard box free. He took three beer bottles from the box and gave one each to Wayne and me, then twisted the top off the third.

"Is this Gordon's beer?" I looked at the bottle.

"Yes, he brews it down here, he's got a full-on brewery down in Harry."

"Harry?" I queried.

"Tunnel Harry." He pointed off into the tunnel. "We called the tunnels

Tom, Dick and Harry, like in the Great Escape. This one's called Tom and Gordon's brewery is in a room just off Harry. Stable climate down here, he says."

"It's a bit early," I said as I twisted off the top. "But one has to support local artisans." I sipped at the beer and failed to suppress the sigh that always seems to accompany my first beer of the day. "So, where's Dick?"

"Dick? Oh, tunnel Dick." Scooter pointed down a dark gap in the wall. "Down that way. We've not done much with that, there's too much clutter down there."

"Clutter?"

"Yeah, loads of old bits of old planes and stuff. It was probably the workshop stores during the war or something. Could be worth a few bob to a collector but we don't want nobody pokin' around down here so we just leave it there and use odd bits when they come useful."

"What sort of planes?" I asked.

"I dunno, World War Two stuff. I don't know what's there, but there's probably enough spare parts down there to build another plane."

I studied the beer bottle in my hand. "This goes down way too easily."

"He does make a good brew. It's his magic ingredient that does it."

"Magic ingredient?"

Scooter tipped his bottle towards the huge copper tank. "It's our water, he claims it gives it that slight floral taste."

I stared at the copper tank, then at my beer bottle. "Your water? The recycled stuff?"

"Swears by it." He finished his beer and tossed the bottle into a black bin. "C'mon, I'll show you the War Room."

I put my beer on a nearby shelf with the intention of abandoning it, paused, changed my mind and picked it up again. *What the hell, I'm sure I've drunk worse.*

We followed the tunnel about ten metres where it opened up once more into a room, this time slightly smaller than the first.

More metal shelves lined the walls, interspersed with odd cabinets, several old arcade games, a couple of pin tables, a 1950s juke box, and a vending machine stocked with packets of sweets. Wayne had his back to us and was concentrating on hooking a cuddly toy in a brightly lit crane machine. A Tardis stood in the far corner.

"Is that real?" I asked then realised what I'd just said and explained, "I meant, is that a real old Police Box, not is it a real Tardis. I know there's no such thing as a real Tardis."

"It's a leftover from the Dr Who Show the Entertainment Team used to put on in the Pirates Bay," Wayne said without turning. "We just use it as our Marmite cupboard, it's full of the stuff at the moment. Well, I say full, but it's a bit odd, we can never seem to *actually* fill it. There always seems to be room for a few more jars."

I headed for one of the arcade game cabinets. "I used to love these. My favourite was Asteroids." I played with the control stick.

"That one's a Polybius machine," Scooter said. "You don't want to mess with that."

"I've never heard of Polybius."

"Few have, they were all rounded up by the FBI. They were part of a mind control experiment. Loads of them there were, at one time. They could programme gamer's brains as they played. But they got sussed in the end, and the Spooks had to secretly get rid of them. That one's probably the last one left."

Alongside the Polybius cabinet stood another three metal racks, jammed with cases of tea and coffee.

"That lot'll keep you going for a while," I said.

"That will be the new currency, post apocalypse, you mark my words," Scooter said. "Nobody wants to be dealing with the end of civilisation on a caffeine come-down. That wouldn't be nice."

A crackly voice snagged my attention. It came from an overly complicated radio sat on another grey metal desk. "Utah Eighty-Three calling Station Corn Wall One, come in, good buddy," a languorous American voice drawled.

"Gotta get that," Scooter said to me. "Could be mission critical." He fiddled with some controls on the radio, which squealed back at him like a terrified owl. He picked up the over-sized microphone. "Cornwall One here, on station, reading you at ten-ten what's happening?"

"Reporting on the latest status from Utah Station Eighty-Three at condition Defcon Five, repeat, Defcon Five. Over."

"Roger that," replied Scooter. "Reading you at Defcon Five. Local situation here logged as Defcon Five, repeat Defcon Five."

"Roger that, Corn Wall. Good catching up with you."

"Nice talking with you guys too, Utah Eighty-Three. Talk again. Signing out." Scooter flicked a switch and all the lights on the radio died.

"Defcon Five? That sounds a bit serious," I said. "What's happening?"

"Nothing. Absolutely nothing." Scooter picked up a torch from a hook on the wall and flicked it on to test it was working. "Defcon Five is the lowest."

"So who is Utah Eighty-Three?"

"Some of our fellow Preppers from over the pond. We're all over the world, apart from Belgium. No units in Belgium, don't know why. But mind you, if I lived there, I think I'd probably be lookin' forward to the end of the world." Scooter unlocked a metal door in the wall. "Mind your step in here, this is new and we ain't got no lights yet." He switched on the torch and aimed it into a narrow, roughly dug tunnel.

I followed him through the narrow opening, stumbling on the uneven floor. "Why are you making new tunnels? You seem to have plenty of room here already?"

"These are the access routes, we're joining up places so when the balloon goes up, we can get to key locations without coming up. Did you know the Viet Cong had a 150 miles of tunnels under the jungles? Kept the Yanks running in circles for years."

"150 miles? I doubt you'll need that much here. That would take you to..." I trawled my mental map. It wasn't a very good map. As I hadn't owned a car for many years, I was well out of practice with mental maps. "… somewhere near Bristol, I suppose."

"We don't want to be going to Bristol. It's a local network. We've already linked up the bunker here to the pump room at the boating lake and the windmill feature on the crazy golf course. And now we've reopened the old caves through to Rocky Bottom Cove."

"That's the next bay along, the one round the headland?" I asked.

"Yeah, once we join up the tunnels here with the caves, we'll be able to get access to the sea right from here all underground and safe from whatever's kicking off up there." He pointed at the ceiling. "That means we can get to and from mainland Europe."

I struggled to keep up with Scooter as he slipped easily through the narrow tunnel. "Have you got a boat?" I asked.

"Of course, we've got a couple of those old swan pedalos Jenna threw out from the boating lake. Needed a bit of doing up, but they're okay now. Gordon's rigged up a satnav and we've even managed to put a gun mount on the bow of one of 'em. Just need to find a fifty-cal now and we're good to go."

Following Scooter was proving increasingly difficult. It was alright for him, he had the torch but I was following in his shadow and kept tripping or bumping my head on the low ceiling. I decided not to ask any more about his idea of a swan shaped pedal-powered battleship in favour of concentrating on not injuring myself in this place. After what seemed like an hour, but was probably only two minutes, the tunnel opened a bit and Scooter stopped.

"There's our problem." Scooter aimed the torch at a pile of fresh earth and a dark shape in the wall.

"What is it?" I struggled to make out the black shape in a black hole in the dancing light of a torch.

"Hang on, I'll change the beam." He clicked the torch button a few times and the weak beam turned into a flashing strobe light which had clearly been designed to alert a mountain rescue team from five miles away.

The scene in front of me danced like an old movie in a rave party, and I hoped I didn't have any latent epileptic tendencies I didn't know about. I tried closing my eyes, but the strobing broke through anyway and only increased the disorientation.

"Hang on," I heard Scooter say. "I can't find the right setting." There was a clatter, a curse from Scooter, and now the light came from floor level, dancing as it tumbled along the ground. "I got this, don't go anywhere."

"I promise."

The light stabilised and turned to full beam. "There you go." He aimed the light at the dark shape again, which materialised into a black symmetrical shape, about the shape of a scuba-diving tank, only larger. Disconcertingly larger.

"Why's somebody buried a scuba diving tank down here?" I asked, hopefully.

"That's not a scuba diving tank," Scooter said, destroying my last hope of wilful ignorance. "It's a bomb, innit?"

"I was rather hoping you weren't going to say that," I said. "Why has somebody buried a bomb down here, then?"

Even though I couldn't see Scooter's expression, his tone of voice told me exactly what it looked like. Disbelief tinged with resignation. "I don't think anybody actually set about burying a bomb here," he said. "I expect it got left over from when this place was an RAF base in the war."

"Yes, that makes sense. And you plan on getting it out of here with a mini-digger?"

"Hell no," Scooter said. "That was just Wayne's mad idea. I let him run with it 'cause there's no switching him off once he gets an idea in his head. Besides, I thought it might be a giggle to watch him try to get a Bobcat down here."

"Ah, thank goodness for that. Getting it out of here would be really dangerous, I would have thought. Best leave it here, huh? That's what you're going to do, isn't it? Leave it here? Maybe block it all up with rocks

~ 129 ~

and stuff? You could concrete it in?" I stared into the darkness which held Scooter's face, hoping to see some clue.

"Are you mad? We've got to get it out. We can't leave it here, it might go off one day. You know, maybe we're doing a bit of hammering up top some time and boom... there you go, and your insides are decorating the walls. You ever seen that?"

"Erm, no."

"Well, I have. It's not pretty. Although there was this one time... No, probably not the right time, you're sober, you probably wouldn't find it half as funny. You had to be there."

"We have to tell the authorities. They have people to deal with this stuff."

"We can't do that. They'll close the place down, then where would Jenna be? They'd have to dig up the whole place in case there's more of the buggers under here somewhere."

"More? There could be more of them?"

"Yeah, well maybe. Who knows? That could be the only one, you know, some Flyboy couldn't count when they was loading up the trucks. Or maybe they just couldn't be arsed and left a shitload of them down here when they all pissed off."

I shuffled backwards. "Well. It's been interesting seeing your bomb, but I really have to be somewhere else right now." I looked at my watch but couldn't see anything in the dark. "Oh, is that the time? Why don't we all meet later? Somewhere... oh, I don't know... somewhere without bombs, perhaps? Just a thought."

Chapter Twelve

THE POST-LUNCHTIME LULL IN the Pirates Bay proved to be the perfect place and time for the inaugural meeting of the Resistance. Not a perfect name, but Wayne had suggested it and nobody else could come up with a better one, so it stuck.

We sat at two tables pushed together at the top end of the Pirates Bay. Far away from a family birthday party going on at the other end. Wayne and Scooter were already there by the time I arrived, and Jenna turned up shortly after.

"Sorry I'm late," she said. "Had some new arrivals, Italians. My knowledge of Italian extends about as far as a pizza menu, so I had to find Charlie, she's half Italian. They kept asking me if there was somewhere they could eat local ostriches."

"Ostriches?" I queried.

"Yes, but it turns out all they wanted was oysters. That's what they call them in Italian apparently, ostriches."

"I can see how that could go wrong in a Cornish restaurant," I said.

"I lost a lot of good people in Italy," said Wayne. "Rome, it was."

"I'm sorry, man," said Scooter. "Respect." He fist-bumped Wayne.

"When were you in the army?" Jenna asked. "You never told me."

"What? No, it wasn't anything to do with the army," said Wayne. "I was a tour guide. Only for a week, I kept losing my customers. I didn't speak the lingo, see. I always told everybody to meet at the Trippy Mountain if they got lost."

"Trippy Mountain?" I asked. "You mean the Trevi Fountain?"

"Yeah, well, I know that *now*. But back then, that was what the local hippies called it, Trippy Mountain. We'd eat a load of happy mushrooms and sit there watching the bubbles all night."

"Bubbles?" Jenna queried. "I don't remember bubbles when I visited the Trevi Fountain."

"Yeah, well you need a box of washing powder, or if you want a good show, a bottle of Matey's the best."

Fortunately, the arrival of Gordon curtailed the conversation. He carried a large cardboard box under one arm and held the string of a helium balloon in the other. The pink balloon bobbed along a foot above his head, proclaiming 'Happy Birthday Becky'.

"Party's down the other end." Jenna nodded her head towards the gathering at the far end of the room.

"Very funny." Gordon dropped the box on the table and sighed into his seat. "I've been experimenting." He pulled a wooden board from the box. It looked like a breadboard and had a small metal eyelet attached to one end. He delved back into the box and came out with a toy fire engine and a length of thread one end of which he tied to the fire engine and passed the other end through the eyelet.

"You see, the problem was, not only how to make a mysterious light in the sky, but to also make it behave like something other-worldly." He tied the end of the thread to the string of the balloon as he spoke. He reached into his pocket and pulled out what looked like a remote key fob for a car alarm. He pressed the button and a bright light appeared inside the balloon.

"Wow," I said. "That's impressive."

"Easy, really. Miniature LED light with a button battery and remote sensor. Took a bit of squeezing to get the sensor in the balloon, but for the real thing, we'll probably use bigger balloons anyway."

"Balloons?" I asked. "Plural?"

"Yes, one mystery light in the sky... meh. Three, four, five? All acting in unison? Now it's something special." He moved the fire engine to-and-fro along the breadboard and the string, threaded through the fixed eyelet, pulled the balloon up and down as it moved, rising and falling in time with the movement of the toy.

"That's clever," said Jenna.

"That's a bit like the way they used to get the blimps up and down during the blitz," said Scooter.

"It's where I got the idea."

"But where are we going to get a fire engine from?" asked Wayne.

"It's only for..." Gordon started, then added, "we'll have to make do with a car or something, Wayne."

We all watched for a moment as the balloon bobbed up and down in unison with the little fire engine's movements.

"That's brilliant," said Jenna. "All we need now is to make sure we get a reporter here at the right time." She looked straight at me. "William? That looks like your department?"

"That shouldn't be too difficult," I said.

A few days later, phase one of the Grand Plan struggled into the light. Or, more accurately, the darkness. Wayne had managed to talk Wilderness Jack into coming up for a drink and a chat with the Brians, as representatives of the modern face of survivalism. Jack had needed little persuading. The two things I knew most about Jack were his liking for whisky and the fact that his public profile was dipping in the rise of the young, ruggedly handsome, new-age TV outdoor adventurers.

I headed straight for the bar when I arrived at the Pirates Bay for our meeting. I collected a beer from Ray behind the bar and handed him a bottle of whisky.

"What's this?" he asked.

"Can you keep it behind the bar and when I ask for my special whisky, pour me one of these?" I caught the puzzled look and added, "Jenna knows about this, it's okay."

He studied the bottle. "Lagavulin? Never heard of it. Is it any good?"

"I hope so, cost me nearly a hundred quid."

I took my beer and joined Jenna and the Brians while waiting for Wayne to arrive with Jack.

They each briefly acknowledged my arrival and continued their conversation.

"We've never been on the telly," said Brianna.

"Yes we have," said Brian. "Don't you remember? We were filmed in the studio audience for Countdown once."

"Oh yes, I'd forgotten that. I'm sure that was only because you wore your Countdown pullover."

"You're not *really* going to be on the telly," Jenna said. "It's only to get Wilderness Jack here."

"Well, they might be," I said. "He might decide to feature them in a programme about urban foraging, or something."

Jenna took my hand and looked me in the eye. For a moment, I felt a strange electric fuzz ripple up my arm.

Then she patted the back of my hand and said, "That's what I love about you, your relentless optimism. You'd have been the guy on the Titanic with the mop and bucket." She slipped her hand free and turned to the Brians. "Just don't get your hopes up," she said. "We only need him to be a credible witness."

"Shh," I said as I noticed Wayne and Jack enter and scan the room. "Here they are."

I waved my arm and Wayne noticed. I finished my beer quickly and called Ray over just as they sat down.

"Hi, Wayne, Jack," I said. "Just in time, I was just about to have my early evening Scotch. Care to join me?"

"Cool," said Wayne.

I glared at Wayne and narrowed my eyes in an expression intended to convey the message that we'd discussed this earlier, and it hadn't involved him drinking my £100 a bottle Scotch.

"I didn't know you liked Scotch, Wayne?" My eyes hardened.

"Yeah, did a bong full of Bell's once. That was a night."

I grimaced. "That must have been." I turned to Jack. "They always keep a bottle of Lagavulin behind the bar for me here. Fancy a drop?"

"Lagavulin? I don't think I've tried that," Jack said.

"It's an Islay. From the island of Islay." I tried to recall the website blurb. "Brewed in sherry casks for sixteen years to give it that sherry undertone."

He looked a bit puzzled but said, "Well, I live for new experiences. It's what keeps us alive, don't mind if I do."

I looked up at Ray. "Two…" I felt Wayne's stare and corrected, *"three* of my special whiskies please, Ray."

"What?"

I gave him my special stare. "The one you keep behind the bar for me. The special one? You know, the Lagavulin?"

"Oh, yeah. Do you want me to give you the bottle back?"

"No, Ray," interrupted Jenna. "It's William's special, we keep it in for him, remember? Just pour three and bring them over. I'll have another San Mig."

"No wuckas." Ray shrugged and strode back to the bar.

Jenna smiled at Jack. "He's Australian," she said, as if that explained everything.

"So, you guys are Urban Foragers, Wayne tells me?" Jack asked the Brians.

"Yes," said Brian. "When it all comes down, we have to find food from whatever the remains of civilisation leave us."

"When I was on deep Special Ops in Kabul, I survived for three weeks on the food left out by a local granny for the stray cats."

"We're a bit more inclined to wild growing food," said Brian. "Have you ever tried sea beet? We get a lot of that round here."

"And stinging nettles, of course," added Brianna.

"Just have to watch out for the dog truffles," Brian said. "Lot of those as well."

"Dog Truffles? Oh, yes, I see. I had to survive for a week in the Serengeti just on stinging nettles." Jack paused to watch Ray as he set three wine glasses on the table. "What's this, son?" he asked.

"It's your whisky, like what he asked for." Ray nodded in my direction.

"Ray, come with me." Jenna gathered the glasses and led Ray back to the bar.

We watched as a short, but vigorous, conversation took place, culminating in Ray returning to the table with three whisky glasses. Jenna fixed a smile to her face and sat.

Jack took a cautious sip. "That's not bad, that one. What did you say it was?"

"Lagavulin," I said. "I especially like the undertones."

"Do they have stinging nettles in the Serengeti?" Brianna asked.

"Oh, yes." Jack emptied his glass. "The Maasai just call them stingers. They make baskets out of them too, you know. I wrote about them in my book, Breakfast in the Serengeti. It's on special offer in the Atlas World Store."

"Would you like another whisky, Jack?" I asked.

"Well, as you've not finished yours, it would be rude of me to make you drink alone, so, yes." He held his glass up for Ray to see.

Wayne quickly finished his whisky and held his up as well. "That's okay, that is. Not as good as Bells, though. But that might have been the weed smoke which gave it them... what ya call it... undertones?"

"Are you going to make a television show?" asked Brianna.

"I've had lots of offers," said Jack. "But I like to keep my options open.

I've got this idea about doing a special about trying to survive in the Atlantis Hotel in Dubai after a global pandemic."

"I've heard of that place," said Jenna. "Isn't that about ten grand a night?"

"Don't know, but what I *do* know, is that nobody has done a survival show set there yet, not even Bear Grylls has done that. Think about it, how do you survive in a place like that when all the staff have been killed by some plague? Huh? Just trying to find a production company with enough vision. Where's that boy with my whisky?"

"I think Brianna was meaning more in terms of a television show here," said Brian. "About this place and the Preppers here. We have quite a community thing going."

"This place?" Jack cast his eyes around the room. "I'm not sure I could do that, I've got a big contract coming up with the Discovery Channel, they might not want me doing anything else. Shame, it sounds fascinating."

We chatted for a while, or listened rather, as Jack trotted out his stories with seasoned skill. Most of them seemed to start with the words, 'When I was in...' and the majority ended with '... and we all got very drunk'.

By nine-thirty, he and Wayne had managed to destroy my bottle of Lagavulin and were now busy going along the top row of liqueurs behind the bar.

"You should try Brian's blackberry gin," I suggested, our prearranged code.

"Jolly good idea," Brian said. "I have a special bottle in the fridge. It does have a bit of a kick though. You're not planning on driving anywhere, Jack, are you?"

Jack peered into his empty glass and said, "Blackberry gin, huh? Perhaps I should investigate, in the interests of research of course."

"Of course," Brian said.

"Can I try some?" asked Wayne. "Never had blackberry gin."

I glared at Wayne and shook my head slightly. '*That's not the plan,*

Wayne,' I transmitted telepathically. *'It's your cue to go find Scooter and tell him we're on our way.'*

Wayne stared back at me. I could see the puzzle pieces moving and I held his gaze while hoping they would make the right pattern.

After an awkward silence where I realised the others had noticed the two of us staring into each other's eyes, Wayne eventually said, "Nooo... I don't go with you. I have to go see... um... Scooter! I have to go see Scooter."

"Never mind," I said. "I'm sure Brian will keep some back for you."

"Yeah..." Wayne's face sagged in disappointment. "I'd better be going then."

I watched Wayne thread his way between the tables and to the door, then checked Jack. He seemed to be dissolving slowly in his seat, so it looked like he hadn't noticed anything out of place.

I nodded at Brian and he stood and said, "Right we are then. To the Brian Cave."

We left the bright lights of the Pirates Bay and headed for The Yellow Brick Road. I used my phone as a torch and kept a hand guiding Jack's shoulder. "Mind the track, there used to be a miniature railway running down here and the track's a bit high in places."

"Yes, sorry about the lack of light," said Jenna. "We're having some work done and the path lights are all out at the moment."

In reality, Charlie had switched them all off about an hour ago, leaving this side of the site in almost pitch dark.

I kept an eye towards the Carter's Field where the old airstrip was, but nothing showed. If they didn't get on with it, we would be at Brian's lodge and we'd have lost our moment.

I stopped the group. "I love the way the Pole Star shines across the sea in the evenings here." I pointed at a bright light to the south.

Jack squinted at the sky. "Fat lot of use you'd be in the desert," he grumbled. "That's Venus. The Pole star's north." He turned and aimed a finger straight at another bright point somewhere over St Ives.

"Are you sure?" I asked.

"Of course I'm sure. When I was in the Arctic, that was all I had to go on for three weeks. Just me and my dog team through the endless night and our only friend, a clean bright pointer in the heavens leading the way to safety. I tell you, I raised a glass or two to that fine lady when we finally reached Camp Barneo. Now, the Russians, they can drink. Have you ever tried to outdrink a Russian arctic soldier?"

"No," I admitted.

"Best you don't try it."

I caught a glimpse of a new light over Carter's Field. There we were. "So, what's that one?" I pointed at the light, which had now been joined by three others. "Is that Orion?"

"Orion? Not that way, this time of year." He followed my pointing finger. "And Orion is not that shape." He squinted at the lights. "And it doesn't move. What the hell is that?"

The four lights rose in the sky and moved north before swooping in unison low over the distant trees, disappearing briefly then climbing once more.

We stood silent and still, watching the dance in the sky. Even though I knew the mechanics, and I could even visualise the little van running up and down the field with the balloons trailing high, I still marvelled at the illusion. As we had guessed, the lack of perspective made them seem much larger than they really were. The lights blinked off one at a time, then came back and seemed to fall into a pattern of blinking and fading. We hadn't planned that. It must be a setting in the LED lights, like those on a Christmas tree. I was just pleased we weren't close enough to hear, as they may well have been tinkling out God Rest Ye Merry Gentlemen.

"Is it an aeroplane?" I asked.

"An aeroplane?" Jack said. "That's not just one thing, there's four of 'em up there and no aeroplane moves like that."

"What do you think it is?" asked Brianna.

"Probably the Space Station," offered Brian.

"Don't be daft, man," Jack snapped. "The ISS is a single dot, and it doesn't move like that."

"I tell you what it reminds me of," said Jenna. "It's exactly the way that Nathan described the UFOs he saw twenty years ago."

"UFOs?" I prompted.

"Yes, made all the papers and the BBC. Nobody could explain it."

Jack turned and stared at Jenna but said nothing. He slowly turned back and continued to watch the dancing lights.

"Oh, yes, I remember now," said Brian. "The papers wouldn't leave poor Nathan alone. He couldn't even go for a quiet pint without hordes of reporters hassling him."

Jack looked at Brian. "Reporters, you say?"

"Damned nuisance they were too. We don't want that all over again."

Jack's face stalled as he worked through the information we'd carefully fed him. He said nothing and turned back to watch the show. For a while they continued their aerial ballet, silently swooping and climbing in little formations. Then, in the middle of a long sweep, they stopped. All four of the lights came to a dead stop and bunched together. I heard a faint bang and then the sound of a car horn. The lights bobbed slightly, then stopped again. Something was wrong.

"That's bloody odd," said Jack.

The air stilled, and we waited for Jack to round on us. But he didn't.

"There's no aircraft I've ever seen can do that," he said. "And I've seen stuff even the generals don't know about."

"What do you think it is?" I asked.

"When I was in Alaska, training a bunch of Navy Seals in mountain survival, the American Air Force had some secret hybrid Heli-planes. Of course, I can't talk about it or they'll have me in an orange suit, upside down with a bucket of water on my head. But I can tell you, even they couldn't do that shit."

"So...?"

"So they're not from here," Jack said.

The lights disappeared. I guessed that whatever was going on over Carter's Field, Gordon had now switched them off.

We stared at the empty sky for a moment longer, then Jack said, "Did somebody mention blackberry gin?"

Chapter Thirteen

I LISTENED TO THE PHONE ring, promising myself that if nobody answered within three rings, I would hang up. The call was answered after two.

"Good Morning, Daily Sentinel News Desk, how may I direct your call?"

"Oh, hello, is Keeley Trevellick available please?"

"Trying to connect you." The phone went silent, and I promised myself thirty seconds before disconnecting and started counting.

"Keeley Trevellick," a voice said after twenty-two seconds.

"Hi, Keeley, it's William, William Fox."

"That's a voice from the past, Lucas told me you'd rung him a while ago. Weren't you trying to punt a story about some hippies living in an old holiday camp?"

"Preppers, actually. But yes, it was just a silly idea, but I thought he might be interested."

"So, how're are you keeping? I heard your bookshop went pop, what happened?"

"Atlas World Store. People used to come in, browse the books then order from them at prices cheaper than I paid the wholesalers. I ended up owing more in back tax than that lot pay on their twenty billion turnover. Go figure."

"They're doing the same all over. Though I guess that's no comfort. What can I do for you?"

"It's what I can do for *you*," I said. "I have a story you might be interested in."

"And how much is this going to cost me?"

"Nothing, really. Just a favour for old time's sake."

"You're long enough in the tooth to know that nobody does a favour for a journalist without motive, so don't try and pull that one on me." I heard the smile in her voice.

"No really, although—"

"Here we go," she said.

"If it comes to anything, you can slip me a drink from petty cash. How's that?"

"Okay, what have you got?"

"Wilderness Jack, you know, the adventurer and—"

"I know Wilderness Jack," she cut in. "Misogynistic loudmouth with a passion for young women, hard liquor and killing small furry creatures and eating them. Go on."

"Yes, well, last night he witnessed some UFOs flying around down in Cornwall. One of the most credible UK sightings ever, he says."

"Was he drunk?"

"No," I lied. "He may be a bit... erm... old-school, but he is respected and certainly knows his stuff when it comes to military hardware. And he said this is nothing like anything any military has, anywhere. I think he's a bit freaked by it."

"I should ask what your angle is in this, but I won't. You probably wouldn't tell me anyway. So what's he after? Publicity for a new book?"

"No, nothing like that. He hasn't even thought about going to the press yet, so you could jump the pack here. If you're interested, that is?"

"Hmm, okay, I'll talk to him. No promises and the moment I get a sniff you're up to something, I'm out. Okay?"

"Of course. He's staying in The Smuggler's Arms in Little Didney. You'll be able to reach him there."

"Okay, I'm not far from there at the moment. I'll drop by."

"No, I didn't mean... I thought you'd just ring him, don't want you to go to any trouble."

"Now I *am* intrigued. You're up to something, I can smell it."

I clicked the phone off and headed over to Carter's Field to catch up with Scooter and Wayne. I found them in the middle of the field, standing by Gordon's little red Fiat Uno. I noticed a pair of legs protruding from under the car and guessed they belonged to Gordon.

"Problem?" I asked.

The legs slid out and Gordon blinked into the morning sunlight. "Somebody," he said, pointedly towards Wayne, "somebody drove over the ground hook and now it's all tangled in the rear axle with the balloon cable."

"I couldn't see. It was dark," protested Wayne.

"Of course it was, that was the idea. That's why I put the stakes in the ground, so you were just supposed to go to-and-fro between them."

"I got distracted."

"By what?"

"By the lights in the sky."

Gordon stared at Wayne for a moment. He looked like he was building to an explosion, but then he just let go of his breath and slid back under the car.

"That explains the strange movements we saw then," I said.

"Yeah, it got all stuck. I had to shoot the balloons with my air rifle in the end or they'd have been up there all night."

"I said we should have used a fire engine," Wayne said.

I ignored Wayne and said to Gordon, "Ah, what are we going to do about tonight? We're supposed to be doing it again."

"I'll be alright," came the voice from under the car. "Just got to…" The sound of hammer on metal was followed by some interesting expletives and then, "That's got it." Gordon slid out with a tangle of nylon string and a bent piece of metal. "We're going to need some new rope and a ground-hook though."

"What about the balloons?" I asked.

"I've got some spares." Gordon straightened up and brushed the mud from his clothes. "The lights are still okay, so we'll be good to go by this evening. But he's going nowhere near Betty." Gordon pointed to Wayne.

"Betty?" I asked.

Scooter nodded at the little red Fiat. "He calls it Betty."

"Oh."

~ * ~ * ~ * ~

I caught up with Jenna in the Sun Lounge next to the Laundry room. I remembered, Tuesday, tea-towel day.

"Ah, my oasis of peace and tranquillity is about to be shattered." Jenna looked up from her magazine as I entered.

"We need to talk about tonight." I sat on the ageing sofa opposite Jenna.

"What's happening tonight?"

"Part two of the UFO project. You remember, we talked about how we needed to do this over several nights, you know, to keep the interest up."

She folded her magazine in half and placed it on the little table. "Hmm, I may have zoned out at that point, remind me."

"We thought that doing it each night for a few nights at the same time would spread the word a bit. People would turn up to see if it happened again, hoping to see it for themselves."

"Isn't there a danger they will spot what you're doing if they're more prepared? What's to stop them turning up with video cameras and stuff?"

"It's a risk," I said. "But everybody's got a video camera in their pocket these days, anyway. If we can get more people, and perhaps even a reporter, we stand more chance of this spreading."

"I'd have thought it was a bit dangerous involving a reporter," Jenna said.

"Yes, about that…" Her eyes seemed to shift from brown to green as she looked at me, and I winced as I continued. "I may have sort of arranged a reporter."

"Sort of arranged?"

"Yes, well, I was setting something up for Jack, for an interview, and I think she got the idea to come down herself. I thought she was in London, but it turns out she's in Cornwall at the moment anyway. Coincidence or what?"

"You invited a national press reporter to come down here to have a look at our balloon alien mothership tied to the rear bumper of Gordon's Fiat Panda?"

"Not exactly how I would have put it, how about we look on this as an opportunity for some extra publicity we weren't expecting?"

"You know, when I took this on from my grandfather, I really thought this was either going to go pop in a spectacular fashion very quickly, or it was going to pick up and I could stick a manager in, then sod off to Marbella and live on a yacht with Johnny Depp. But no, it's just going to dribble on until it gradually dissolves into dust and me along with it. And Johnny Depp has clearly got fed up with waiting for me as he went and got married."

"I think they've split up now, so that might be back on."

"Look, do you really think this insane plan has any chance of working?" Jenna asked.

"Roswell in America has built a seventy-year, million-dollar industry on nothing more than a drunk farmer and a handful of tinfoil. It's a Woozle."

"A Woozle?"

"From Winnie the Pooh. Pooh and Piglet went Woozle hunting, but were actually following their own footsteps around in a circle. A Woozle is something which only appears to exist because there are lots of circular references to it. My whole bookshop was really all about Woozles, things which only exist in the books written about them and the only evidence being references to other books written about them."

"So we're building a Woozle. You pull this off and I'll join you on *your* yacht."

"Might be able to run to a fishing boat in Little Didney harbour."

"You're not really selling this." Her eyes flashed sparkles of mischief. "But hey-ho, Johnny Depp's blown his chance so you're in luck. What's your plan?"

~ * ~ * ~ * ~

The Smuggler's Arms bubbled with lunchtime conversations. Little Didney's early tourists and regulars mingled loosely and noisily with the sounds of chinking glasses and calls from the bar announcing meals.

As Wilderness Jack was staying there, I guessed he would probably be in the bar over lunchtime. I guessed right. He sat at a table tucked in a corner nursing what looked like a large whisky. Opposite him sat Keeley Trevellick, notebook in hand. Despite her relative youth, she'd always preferred Old School pen and paper when interviewing. I slid into a crowd before they noticed me and made myself as invisible as possible. Jack nodded to the odd passer-by, but didn't engage in any conversations beyond his intent engagement with Keeley. I kept a watching eye on the steadily reducing level in his glass and as soon as he drained the last drop, I headed to the bar and waited. I didn't have to wait long.

Jack elbowed his way to the bar and planted the empty glass on the counter. "Another one of those," he said to the barman.

I pushed my way to arrive next to him and slid my glass next to his. "I'll get these," I said loudly.

Jack turned towards me. "That's very kind of you."

"It's nothing. After seeing those strange objects in the sky last night I think we could both use something to settle the nerves." I noticed one or two ears tipping in our direction and continued. "Do you think they really were alien spaceships?" I asked, keeping my voice raised.

"Well, it's certainly odd." Jack seemed unusually surprised by the attention gathering around him.

Somebody said, "Hey, did you really see a UFO?"

"Well..." started Jack, but he was caught by another voice cutting across him.

"Told you there was UFOs round here," Nathan said, right on cue. "Twenty years ago I saw 'em. Even on the Beeb I was."

Jack scanned the growing cluster around him, and I could almost see the calculations going on behind his eyes.

His ego finally took control. He stretched his arms out and waggled his fingers as if drawing the eager ears closer. "If I hadn't seen 'em with my own eyes, I'd never have believed it." His gaze raked the group, years of experience in weighing up just how to play to an audience. The light shone brighter in his eyes as he continued, "I tell you, the things I've seen... of course, I can't say half of it, but this, this was something else."

I eased myself away from the clamouring group and Jack's words. "When I was in Tunguska, Siberia..." faded away under the babble of awe surrounding him as I headed for the door. I risked a glance towards the table where Keeley sat but she didn't seem to have spotted me, so I slid out.

I headed back to Rose Well Holiday Park in search of Gordon and eventually found him along with Scooter and Wayne, in West Field. Scooter was hammering a post into the ground next to the hook for the balloon line.

He noticed my puzzled expression. "Gonna put a flag on it so as this idiot," he flicked his head in Wayne's direction, "can see where *not* to drive over the hook this time.

"I'll drive next time." Gordon gave the roof of the little Fiat an affectionate pat.

"But you're our tech support guy, you're needed to twiddle with all the clever electronic stuff," Scooter said. "You can't do that and drive at the same time. I'll drive."

"But you can't drive, you haven't even got a licence," said Gordon.

"I *can* drive," Scooter corrected. "It's just that the magistrates asked me *not* to drive."

"I think we're going to have a bigger audience tonight," I said. "Wilderness Jack was gathering quite a crowd in The Smuggler's when I left. We might even have a reporter there."

"A reporter?" Gordon queried. "A real reporter? Is that altogether wise?"

"I didn't actually arrange it. I was just expecting her to talk to Jack on the phone, not turn up here. But I've got an idea."

"Oh good. I was beginning to worry there for a moment."

"No, listen." I followed Gordon as he began laying out the nylon cable on the ground behind the Fiat Panda. "We start exactly an hour later than last night. That way, there's a chance she'll get bored and give up, but the locals will hang around. At least enough of them."

Gordon stopped and looked at me. "You think?"

I shrugged. "My guess is she'll be thinking it's all nonsense anyway and just be looking for an excuse to pack up and go home."

"Well, you're the Newspaper Man, I just fix electronics and make beer." He returned to laying out the cable.

Scooter appeared next to me. His way of doing that was quite unnerving. "We could always kidnap her," he suggested.

"No kidnapping reporters. That never ends well. She'll soon get bored standing in a muddy field listening to Jack's stories."

Chapter Fourteen

AS THE EVENING SUN PAINTED its last splash across the sky before sliding behind the horizon, I scanned the gathered crowd once more. Any hope I'd had about people getting bored with waiting, melted away faster than a snowman in a desert. Small clutches of people stood around jabbering and pointing at random stars or birds in the hope of them being the first signs of alien visitors. One or two had binoculars and one couple even had a large telescope on a stand. I just hoped they wouldn't be able to focus on a moving object or we were in trouble.

Big Moo Burgers had set up a mobile stand and looked like they were doing a steady business. One family set up chairs and a picnic table and looked more geared for a day on the beach rather than a chilly evening field and nearby, a bunch of teens with a boom-box and beer cooler looked ready for a night of partying.

I stood in a small group along with the Brians, Jenna and Nathan. Wayne, who'd been furloughed from his role as UFO Ground Pilot, chatted with Wilderness Jack in the centre of a growing clutch of admirers. He seemed to be enjoying the reflected attention.

I kept a watching eye out for Keeley while hoping she'd opted for a cosy evening in front of the telly rather than out here hunting aliens. So far, so good. A glance at my watch showed ten, about fifteen minutes to the time we'd launched the previous night's display. The general hubbub of anticipatory conversation quietened to one of hushed expectation as eyes strained at the darkness.

Brian tapped my shoulder. "What time is it starting?"

I put my finger to my mouth. "Shush, not so loud. In about an hour."

"Oh, yes sorry, I forgot," he said in a stage whisper which was actually louder than his original question.

I looked around wondering if we'd been overheard, but everybody seemed focused on the night sky. "If people are too alert, they might see how it works. Need them to get a bit bored first."

A rise in the chattering from the group surrounding Jack caught my ear, and I turned to investigate. Keeley had just arrived. That was annoying. I slid behind the Brians as Keeley studied the gathered people. I didn't know if she was looking for me in particular or it was just her reporter's eye. Either way, I didn't want the inevitable conversation. She engaged with Jack between glances at the sky and surrounding people. I pulled up the collar on my jacket like every good spy and turned away from her view.

After half an hour, several people drifted away and the music from the party crew grew louder in inverse proportion to the diminishing stocks in the beer cooler. I checked my watch again and squinted into the dark over West Field. No sign of anything happening yet.

"I thought it was you," I heard from behind my shoulder.

I turned to find Keeley standing next to me. "Oh, hi, Keeley, I didn't know you were here."

"Didn't you see me in the pub earlier? I was sure you'd seen me." Her eyes searched the inside of my head, burrowing for all my secrets.

"Oh, really? Sorry, I didn't notice, it was just a flying visit." I pretended to squint at the sky. "You come to see if E.T. turns up?"

"I came to see what was happening, certainly, but as far as E.T. is concerned... Hmm, not so convinced."

"Me neither." I kept my gaze at the sky to stop her Spidey powers getting in my head.

"That's odd," she said. "Jack said he was with you when he saw them?"

I turned to her. "Ah, yes, of course. What I meant was, I wasn't convinced they were aliens. Just some lights, you know, could have been anything." I searched her face for clues, but she did her reporter's impassive expression. "Jenna was there too." I turned to indicate Jenna. "Have you met? Jenna runs this place."

Jenna gave me a quick, '*I'm going to kill you later*' glance then said to Keeley, "No we've not met." She smiled sweetly as they shook hands. "William tells me you were colleagues?"

"Sort of, he was in the advertising department and I did the foot-slogging. We didn't cross paths much. So you run this place? That must be fun?"

"You'd think, wouldn't you? It probably would be if it made any money. But at the moment I'd make more money selling your papers on a street corner for you, and it would probably be a whole lot less hassle. Do you want to buy my story? A tale of one woman's struggle to maintain the last of a great British holiday tradition against the odds?"

"I'd love to, but sadly, my editor thinks I should spend his money talking to Crime Scene Officers or politicians who've been caught with their pants down. Anyway, if you'll excuse me, I missed supper and I'm famished, and those burgers smell so good." She headed over to the Big Moo Burger stand.

We all stared silently at the night sky for a while, as if expecting the imminent arrival of E.T.'s Mothership.

When I was sure Keeley was well out of earshot, I said, "They should have started by now. Can anybody see anything?"

"I thought I heard a car engine," said Brianna. "But it's difficult to tell with that party going on over there."

Just as another family gathered up their children and headed for the car park, the air hummed with oohs and aahs and I raked the darkness in the direction of West Field. A light drew a gentle path across the sky, then appeared to retreat rapidly before disappearing. That was impressive. I threw a quick glance around the people and all eyes were now locked to the sky. Looking back, I saw another light, or it may have been the same one, appear to rush forwards towards us before lifting high into the sky then vanishing into the dark. I remembered Gordon saying how he'd been fiddling with settings on the lights and that by bundling several of the tiny LEDs together, he could increase or decrease the brightness, giving an illusion of the lights approaching or retreating. It was certainly convincing.

"My, my," said Brian. "That's very clever, I wonder how he did that?"

I turned and shushed at Brian then scanned the nearest people to find any clues that he'd been overheard. All looked okay.

"Oh, whoops," Brian said. "Odd how you never know how your own voice sounds. Funny story, we were visiting the Vatican once and Brianna realised she'd forgotten to put her underwear back on after we'd been—"

I waved my hand frantically in front of him and whispered, "Can you save that one for later?" I pointed to West Field. "E.T.?"

"Oh yes. I blame Gordon's beer." He studied the bottle in his hand. "Not for the Vatican incident, you understand. That was more—"

Brianna touched Brian's arm. "Perhaps you should just watch the pretty lights, dear. And let's say no more beer for a while?" She took the bottle from his hand.

"If you say so, sweetest."

I turned back to the lights and nudged Jenna in her side to silence the giggle which was building.

The lights ducked and swooped across the night and I tried to visualise how Gordon was achieving the effect. I guessed he, or somebody, was controlling the brightness as the car drove to-and-fro, raising and lowering them. The overall illusion was one of separate lights, not only moving up and down but approaching and retreating. Sometimes together in formation, sometimes separately. Finally, they all zoomed off in the distance together, although I guessed he had simply turned the brightness down. There was a moment's silence across the gathered people, then, as if on some cue, everybody started talking at once.

I turned to watch the response. No mobs with pitchforks heading our way, so that looked like a win. I noticed Keeley in conversation with Wilderness Jack, but I couldn't begin to guess the context. Jack certainly looked animated though.

"Do you think they bought it?" Jenna asked.

"Mostly. Hard to tell. I guess we'll find out tomorrow when social media comes alive."

As it happened, we weren't going to have to wait that long.

I started back to my cabin, but Jenna stopped at the point our paths diverged.

"Fancy a quiet drink?" she asked. "I'm a bit to keyed up to settle just yet. And a bit weirded out by all this, to be honest."

I studied her face. Her eyes danced, refusing to settle and her lips flashed between forced smile and frown.

"Sure, I was going to suggest it myself," I lied. "But I thought my cabin might not be quite ready for visitors." I realised what I'd said and started digging. "Sorry, I didn't mean anything against your cabins, they're very nice. Great, in fact. It's just that I might not have been quite as tidy as I should be. Not that I'm a naturally untidy person, far from it."

She touched my arm. "You can stop now. My place is just down here." She nodded to a little path that drifted between the main office block and the boating lake.

We followed the path for about a hundred metres until it ended in front of a chalet style house set in a small overgrown field which had probably once been lawn.

She pushed open the door and led me through a small hallway and into a small and very functional lounge. I wasn't sure whether the minimalistic look was by design or just a lack of personal possessions, but it gave the impression of only being slightly lived in. An Ikea style sofa faced a brick-fronted fireplace next to which a television sat on a smoked glass stand. A glass cabinet with a music centre balanced the other side of the fireplace and a huge print of an icy landscape with a lone reindeer in the distance.

"Have a seat." She indicated the sofa. "I haven't got any whisky, but I've got a bottle of gin somewhere." She disappeared through a doorway momentarily and returned with a ruby red bottle and a couple of mismatched glasses. "A brewery rep gave it to me as a sample. It's Chinese." She sloshed a random amount in each glass and handed me one.

I took the glass. "Thanks, I didn't know the Chinese made gin." I took a sip, and it bit the back of my throat.

"Oh, did you want something with it?" she asked. "I haven't got any tonic here, but I think I've got some lemonade."

"No thanks, this is fine."

She sat in a small rocking chair facing me. "To be honest, I had a bit of an ulterior motive inviting you here." She sipped at her glass and winced, then held up the glass to study it. "It's a bit full on, isn't it?"

"Very Chinese," I said. I settled back into the sofa and it shifted under me. I realised it was a convertible and appeared to be getting ready to convert underneath me. I sat forward a bit to ease the pressure on the back. I wasn't sure what her ulterior motive was, but having a bed suddenly manifest itself underneath me would probably be jumping the gun a bit.

"Make yourself comfortable," she said and shrugged herself out of her jacket and wriggled her boots from her feet. "It's surprisingly chilly outside still."

I unzipped my jacket and tried easing back again. The sofa held. I took another sip of the Chinese gin. "It gets smoother as it goes on," I said.

"Clever people, the Chinese." She took another sip, then reached to set her glass on the TV table. Her thin shirt slid over the muscles in her back and arms as she moved. "I don't spend much time here, apart from sleeping, so I don't keep in much to eat or drink. Are you warm enough? Take your jacket off, you look like you're about to go."

I took my jacket off and draped it over the back of the sofa. "You said you had an ulterior motive?"

"Down, boy." She smiled. "I've noticed you don't seem in much of a hurry to head back to the big city?"

"I'm behind on the rent to my flat, ditto my lockup with all my stock in it. I was rather hoping my trip down here would generate enough to catch up, but that little dream has been dashed on the rocks of lost hopes. So, yes, no hurry." A thought struck me. "Are you throwing me out?"

"No, far from it. Look, I know it's a longshot, but if this ridiculous project does work and we get enough bookings to scrape through another year, how do you fancy staying on to be my Promotions Manager? You can keep the cabin and food and stuff. I can't pay anything yet, but I'm no good at this PR stuff. To be honest, I'm not actually very good with people."

"Bit of a handicap in this business?"

"You think? My grandfather, Tommy Toplin, could get a conga line going at a funeral. Me? As a child, I used to come up with excuses to not attend my own birthday parties."

"And what makes you think I can make this work?"

"You worked in the newspaper business; you know how publicity works. At least better than me. What do you say?"

My phone made its warbling sound to indicate a message. I pulled it out and glanced at the screen with the full intent of switching it off. But the message made me pause. It was a message from Wayne with a link to a social media site. 'Mysterious lights over Cornwall. Witnessed by hundreds'. A string of images followed with pictures of Gordon's show from barely thirty minutes ago.

"You need to see—" I started, but Jenna's phone started bleeping and she swiped at her screen.

"It's everywhere," she said, her eyes wide. "What are we going to do?"

"I don't know. Hide?" I suggested.

"Is that the official line from my newly appointed Head of Publicity?"

I thought for a moment, then smiled. "We call it thinking outside the box. Head of Publicity, huh? Okay, what can possibly go wrong?"

Jenna held up the bottle of Chinese gin. "Top up? We should have a toast."

I reached forwards to hold my glass towards her and the convertible sofa chose that moment to convert itself into a bed. I slipped off the edge and landed sitting on the floor as it collapsed under me.

Jenna leaned forwards a bit further and filled my glass. "Ah, forgot to warn you about that. I don't get many visitors." She slid out of her chair and settled beside me on the floor, bottle in one hand, glass in the other.

"You do realise that my business acumen is not quite as sharp as you might think. Let's say..." I studied my glass for a moment. "More Del Trotter than Richard Branson. I'm the person who thought that taking my redundancy cheque and starting a bookshop, just when Atlas World Store was forcing them all out of business, was a good idea."

"Ah, yes, the omnipresent omnivores that hunt for easy prey and drag it back to their-tax free caves to divide up among their chums."

"That's very lyrical," I said.

Jenna studied me for a moment, then shrugged. "The buggers are everywhere. Did you know that Jejune Water bought West Field? The field where Gordon is flying his UFOs?"

"Why did they want that?"

"That was years ago, when this place was doing okay. I wouldn't sell Rose Well Holiday Park to them, so they thought they could get access to the spring water from there. A local diviner told them the spring ran under West Field."

"And does it?" I asked.

"Does it hell. The diviner is the brother-in-law of the farmer who sold the field to them. They went digging and burst the local water main."

"Have you never been tempted to sell?"

"Sure, but since then, leisure businesses here have collapsed and their offer is now way less than what I owe the bank. But even if it wasn't, there's no way I'd be giving in to them." She drained her glass and topped it up again. "It's my personal stand against unfettered toxic capitalism."

I held up my glass. "To unfettered toxic capitalism." I emptied my glass and paused for a moment. "No, what I meant was, *death* to unfettered toxic capitals... ist...isms. I'm not very good at rousing speeches."

"You're not really selling yourself at this interview." She giggled and stared at her empty glass.

"Hmm, that's another area I don't do so well in. Interviews. You know that question when they ask you... *and what you'll bring to the company?*"

"Yes."

"Well, apparently, your own coffee machine is not what they have in mind."

She poked my arm. "Idiot." She tried to pour more Chinese gin in our glasses, but most of it missed. I don't think I've ever had a job interview in my life."

"Just as well, you'd never have got a job working in a bar, that's for sure."

She wiped at the gin on my sleeve with her fingers. "I don't think it will stain."

"I'm not worried about it staining, I'm more worried about it burning a hole in my shirt."

"I'll give you a complimentary token for the washing machines." Her head lolled to one side and came to rest on my shoulder.

"And there was me hoping for a company car."

The room seemed warmer now, or maybe it was just the warmth of Jenna's body against mine. Either way, I found it comforting. That, added to the numbing effects of the gin, settled like a warm blanket around me.

"I probably need to make a move before I fall asleep," I said. Hearing no answer, I looked at Jenna slumped against me. She was already asleep. I decided to give it five minutes, then I'd slip away.

Chapter Fifteen

MY EYES OPENED BUT REFUSED to focus beyond informing me that daylight existed in some part of my world. I was also cold. I must have lost my duvet in the night. I reached and patted for it but found nothing. There was also a large crease down the centre of the bed.

I blinked my eyes a few more times to clear them. The first thing I noticed was this wasn't my bedroom. I realised that because I couldn't reach the bedroom doorhandle from the bed. I forced myself up onto one elbow and waited for my eyes to focus. I seemed to be on the sofa bed in the lounge of Jenna's house. I also appeared to be alone and still in my clothes, so at least whatever apologies were going to be needed were likely to be controllable. I'd woken up in worse states.

I swung my feet to the floor and sat for a moment on the edge of the bed while I sorted out which bits hurt. My head felt like an over-inflated tyre and my teeth itched, but apart from that, I'd probably live.

"Coffee?" I heard from behind the kitchen door.

I formed the words, 'Yes please,' but what I actually said was, "Yurm bleable."

"Milk?"

"Bleable."

A moment later Jenna appeared, wearing a denim shirt and clearly little else. "Morning, Sleepy Head. Good coma?"

"Hmm, what time is it?" I looked at my watch, but the hands pulsed in time with the vein in my temple, making them difficult to read.

"Eight thirty."

"That's okay then." I took the coffee from her. "Do I need to apologise for anything?"

"Don't worry, my virtue is unassailed." She sat on the edge of the sofa bed next to me, cupping her own coffee with both hands. "Although, on the other hand, I could of course take offence at that."

"Huh? Oh… um, I thought it might not be wise to make a pass at my new boss on my first day."

She smiled and her eyes studied mine. "Good answer."

"I should make a move. I guess you need to get to work and I should try to find out how last night went down and whether we're likely to be getting a visit from the local police anytime soon."

I finished my coffee and headed back to my cabin for a shower and change of clothes, then set off in search of Gordon.

I eventually tracked him down in the headquarters hut in Carter's Field. He looked lost in the huge ancient sofa which dominated the far end of the room. Scooter sat at a table with piles of paper in front of him and Wayne perched on an old wooden chair, staring at his phone.

Scooter looked up at me as I settled on one of the other sofas. A large, fading chintz affair which bled stuffing from various wounds.

"We ain't gonna be able to do tonight's gig in West Field," Scooter said. "Place has been swarming in alien hunters all morning. We'll 'ave to do it somewhere different."

"Tonight's gig?" I questioned. "I thought we'd done. Bit dangerous to go again, surely?"

"Nah, cement it in. Once is a happening, twice is coincidence, the third time, the enemy's up to something."

"Is that an army thing?"

"James Bond, Auric Goldfinger."

"So we're basing our strategy on a fictional baddie?"

Scooter stared at me as if I'd just suggested he take up knitting as a hobby. "Not just a baddie, the greatest baddie *ever*."

"Dr Evil," muttered Wayne, without removing his gaze from his phone. "He's the greatest baddie."

"But he's not real," said Scooter. "He was just a spoof of baddies."

"But Goldfinger's not really real. You can't be more not real or less not real. It's like saying Schrodinger wasn't really a real cat."

"Actually, Schrodinger was…" I started, then gave up when I realised where *that* was going. "Never mind, can we get back to the bit about another UFO outing tonight and why that idea is completely insane?"

Scooter swung in the chair to face me. "If we leave it at two times, people will say it's just a coincidence, or that the people what watched it second time wanted to see it, so they did." He flapped his hand at me. "Come and 'ave a look at this." He pointed at the papers on his table.

Several hand-drawn maps lay scattered, each detailed with arrows and various symbols which bore no meaning for me.

"Where is this?" I asked.

"Well, it's not Helmand or Baghdad is it?" He shook his head. "It's here, look, 'ere's Carter's Field, the airfield."

"That squiggle?"

"That's the NATO standard sign for an airfield. What you going to do when it all kicks off and satnav dies? How you going to find the tofu aisle in Sainsbury's then? Look, 'ere's where we flew the balloons, and this is where people watch, night one, night two. See?" He stabbed at the map twice.

"Second night was closer?" I asked, waiting for more insults.

"Right."

I breathed. "So, doesn't that just prove my point that if we do a third night they'll be even closer? Maybe they'll even come into West Field and then we're screwed."

"Exactly, that's why we set our new FP in the oggin, here." He stabbed the map again.

I studied the point where his finger sat. "But isn't that the sea?"

"What I said, in the oggin. They won't be expectin' that, see? And they can't get no closer to 'ave a look."

"But we can't use Gordon's car in the sea, we'd need a boat. Where do we find a boat?"

"We got two," said Scooter. "That pair of boats Jenna threw out and we recommissioned them."

"You mean that pair of swan shaped pedalos?" I asked.

"Yeah, well, that's what they were once. But now they're battle-ready marine warfare vehicles."

"I think it's a five-hundred pounder," announced Wayne, looking up from his phone. "There's one on Wikipedia looks just the same."

"What is?" I asked, worried that I actually knew the answer to that, but rather hoping I was wrong.

"The bomb. It's a five-hundred pounder GP. They got pictures of how they work here. Probably be able to work out how to disarm it too. Wikipedia's so cool."

"Don't even think about it," snapped Scooter. "I'm meetin' an old pal of mine from Iraq later. He was an ATO, till the stress got him."

"ATO?" I asked.

"Ammunition Technical Officer, bomb disposal. He'll know what to do with it."

"Are you sure you can't just fill in the hole again and pretend it's not there?"

"What? And have it go off in some poor sod's face in ten years' time when he's just trying to plant his potatoes? No, we gotta get rid of it."

"I had a horrible feeling you were going to say that."

~ * ~ * ~ * ~

"Are they mad?" Jenna said when I told her about the Pedalo Battle Fleet. I wasn't going to tell her about the bomb yet. Or ever.

She pushed a coffee across the bar to me.

"I think Scooter has a letter from the army Medical Officer to confirm that." I sipped at the coffee, my sixth of the day, and it wasn't even lunchtime yet. Over on the stage, Donny 'Mr Elvis' Jones was setting up his gear for tonight's show.

"Hmm, well, at least I know what happened to my pedalos. Battle Pedalos? And there was me worried that somebody had done something stupid with them."

"I've got to go into Little Didney this afternoon," I said. "Scooter wants me there; he's meeting up with some old army buddy of his."

"What does he need you for?"

"Apparently, I have to be his 'Sanity Companion'. He says his mate won't believe him unless someone sane is there to back him up."

"And you qualify?" She raised an eyebrow and grinned. "Well, I suggest you keep an eye on him and make sure he stays off the Absinthe. It wasn't pretty last time. And they're serious about another show tonight?"

"Yes, I couldn't talk them out of it. Both he and Gordon are convinced that if we do another one, it'll go viral."

"And what about your mate, that reporter, what was her name?"

"Keeley?"

"Yes, I take it that never made the paper?"

"It did." I pulled a copy of the Daily Sentinel from my back pocket. It was already folded open to page seven, Fun Tidbits from the Regions. "There." I pointed to the one inch of column halfway down the page, 'Mysterious Lights in Cornish Sky'.

She read the piece, then, "Is that it? All that work and planning and half a dozen lines with a quote from Wilderness Jack saying he's never seen anything like it?" She folded the paper over and pushed it back at me. "We're wasting our time."

"That's why they think we need this other go. Push it out there more."

"You do realise you're only on a trial as my Promotions Manager? I can always get Saatchi and Saatchi, you know."

"You said Head of Publicity last night," I protested.

"Did I? I must have been drunk, that doesn't count. Now, I've got a delivery arriving, so you'd better go and make us famous. And *not* by getting Scooter drunk and letting him take all his clothes off and climb the tower of St Mary's church again."

"He did that?"

"Yes, they've only just recently fixed the spire. Nobody wanted to touch it." She seemed to go away in thought for a moment, then added, "Although, I have to say, that boy does keep himself in shape."

~ * ~ * ~ * ~

The Smuggler's Arms bristled with late lunchtime customers. The warm day had woven its somniferous charms, and nobody seemed to be in a hurry to be anywhere else.

Scooter spotted his mate as soon as we entered. To be fair, I'd have spotted him even without Scooter yelling across the room, "Hey, Bangy, you ugly git."

Bangy stood at the call. Or about as stood as he was able, given his height in the low beamed bar. I was a shade under six foot and I cleared the beams easily, so I guessed he must be six-four at least. And just in case I was in any doubt, he wore a T-shirt which read, *'Bomb Disposal Technician - If you see me running, try to keep up'.*

"Scooter, you muppet," he yelled across the bar. "Thought they'd got you in the Happy Factory?"

"You know me, they can't keep me in nowhere."

The two shook hands and slapped backs, and Scooter pulled me forwards. "This is William, he's alright."

Alright. All my life people have described me as *'alright'*. Just once, I'd like to be introduced as *'This is William, he's dangerous'*, or *'Radical'* or even perhaps just, *'Creative'*. But no, it's always, *'This is William, he's alright'*.

Bangy took my hand and shook with surprising gentleness; I'd expected a hand crunching. "Lee Bangrove, but everybody calls me Bangy," he said.

"Scooter tells me you're a Bomb Disposal man?" I asked.

"ATO, but yes."

"That must be scary. Not sure I could do that."

"Just training," he said. "Be surprised what you can do with the right training." He gave Scooter a camaradic punch on the shoulder. "Apart from this twat here. They couldn't even train him to use the latrines properly."

"Me and Bangy were muckers in Helmand together."

"Actually, it was Basra, Iraq," Bangy corrected. "But none of us ever reckoned you were fully there, anyway. Way too much of the local waccy baccy." He settled back in his seat. "You wanted my help? Always there for you, mate, you know that. What is it? A woman? Debt collectors?"

"I've got this bomb—"

"Are you fucking mad?" Bangy stood suddenly and bumped his head on a beam. "You're on your own with that one, pal. I'm out of here." He rubbed at his head.

"Why do people keep calling me that," Scooter protested. "I'm not supposed to listen to those words. Chickens, chickens." He gripped Bangy's arm.

"Oh, I don't know, let's have a think... Perhaps you just should stop doing crazy shit like telling people you've got yourself a bomb."

"No, wait. It's not mine, I didn't get it. I want rid of it."

Bangy slumped back in his seat. "How did you manage to accidentally end up with a bomb?"

"You know that Rose Well Park where I live is half on that old airfield?"

Bangy nodded and drank from his pint. "Uh-huh."

"Well, we been extending our headquarters, underground like, loads of tunnels down there, and we opened up this one bit, and there it was.

Stickin' out of this dirt wall, bold as yer hat." He pulled out his phone and flicked at the screen. "There, that's the beastie."

Bangy took the phone and studied the screen. "That's a World War Two, early, British. Probably a five-hundred pounder. There should be two yellow bands further up. You need to call in the EOD. If that bugger goes off, it'll take most of the camp with it."

"No, can't do that. Can't have the Old Bill finding out what we're doing. They'll close us down for sure."

"So what do you want from me?"

"I want you to disarm it, then we can chuck it in the sea."

"You need to get your Smarties back in line, mate. I can't do that. For a start, I'd need the truck with all the gear, the support tech team, and not to mention my EOD suit. If you think I'm sticking my unprotected bonce anywhere near that thing you're so far out of your tree, I don't think you're even in the right forest."

"I'm sure you can do something. It's eighty years old, it can't be that complicated. You do this stuff all day."

"I know, but it's not like being a mechanic, we don't usually get much call for private jobs on the side. In fact, I think the Army actually discourages their ATOs from doing homers."

"We need to rethink this," I said to Scooter. "Perhaps we should listen to Bangy and get the right people in to deal with this?"

Scooter stretched back in the seat and looked to the ceiling in search of inspiration. "What if you just gave me some pointers? You know, how to get the lid off and which wire to cut? Green or red, that sort of stuff."

"You're not listening, are you, Scooter? Same old, same old. That's how come you got yourself stuck on that roof with half an ISIS battalion snapping at you. What if it's armed? What if the detonator's come loose? What if there's a load more down there? If that was a store room, there's a good chance there's more of them in there somewhere. You go dicking around with that one, and it sets off the others, you're going to take out half of Cornwall. Not to mention ruining *your* day."

"All these negative vibes. I need some positivity. What if I just move it? We could move it somewhere else and then get the Bomb Squad in."

"I'm not going to help you move it, Scooter. Something that age is probably well unstable."

"Not askin' you to. But just as a hypothetical like, if you wanted to move it, how would you do it?"

Bangy shook his head slowly. "There's no stopping you once you get an idea, is there? Show me that picture again."

Scooter flicked at the screen of his phone a couple of times, then slid it across the table.

Bangy picked it up and looked at the screen. "That's a picture of your ear."

Scooter took the phone back. "Oh, yeah, that keeps happening." He flicked again. "There you go."

Bangy studied the picture. "That's not good. The tailpiece is attached. That means it was ready to be boarded, so the detonator will likely be in place. You knock it, off it goes. You want my opinion? Keep about three miles away from it. But knowing you, you're not going to listen so, everything very slowly and whatever you do, don't bump the nose or tail. That's it. That's all you're getting from me."

"You don't fancy—"

"No, I don't. You're on your own with this one." Bangy stood. "Keep in touch. No doubt I'll hear how it goes." He smiled. "One way or the other."

Chapter Sixteen

WE GATHERED AT ROCKY BOTTOM Cove to prepare for the evening's display. Scooter, Wayne and Gordon had been there for a while and the pair of little swan-headed pedalos bobbed on the waves of the shoreline. Each had been painted in a two-tone grey camouflage pattern with what looked like a camera tripod duck-taped to the swans' necks. At the rear, a short piece of scaffolding pole had been bolted to a wooden board which reached into the water at the stern.

Scooter noticed me studying the contraption. "It's a rudder," he explained. "Better for high-speed manoeuvres than trying to steer using the pedals."

"High-speed manoeuvres?" I asked. "In a pedal-powered swan boat?"

"Yeah, well, we're still working on that bit. Nathan's got an old Vespa, which he totalled after a night on his special harvest. Engine's okay though, so we reckon we can fix it to one of these."

"But that's no good for tonight, these can't move fast enough to give the same effects as towing it with a car?"

"All sorted," said Gordon. "I've got a pulley system set up between the two boats with an electric winch. Easy really."

"You do know those are my boats, don't you?" said Jenna. "How are we going to do the Pirate's Parade for the kid's Flotilla Party?"

"I thought you'd thrown them out," said Scooter.

"What, just because they weren't actually bolted to the ground with titanium padlocks and patrolled by armed guards?"

"We can fix 'em up again afterwards, like?"

She stared at the swans and shook her head. "No, you're never going to get those back to a condition where any sane parent is going to want to see their precious sat in one. You owe me." She glared at Scooter. "And if this doesn't work, I'm going to sell your kidneys to a Russian organ market. While you're still wearing them." She turned and marched off up the rocky track which led up to West Field.

"Right we are then," said Gordon. "Time to give this a trial run. Scooter, you take Gloria and I'll take Penelope. Wayne, you can feed out the line. Make sure it doesn't tangle."

They clambered on board their respective swans and started pedalling. After a minute or so of much water churning, little headway had been made.

"We've got the tide against us," said Scooter. "Be easier later. Wayne, you're gonna have to push us off, for a head start."

Wayne dropped the roll of cable and paddled into the water. He put his shoulder against the backside of Gloria and heaved. Gloria bobbed into the little breakers which lapped at the beach and then Scooter's pedalling finally took purchase, and the swan swam, none too gracefully, into the sea. He repeated the same with Penelope then stood back satisfied, watching them as they caught the inshore current and started heading off in the general direction of Europe.

"They seem to be getting a good speed out of those," he said, just as the cable he'd dropped earlier finished taking up the slack, wrapped itself around his leg and pulled him off balance and dragged him into the water.

I rushed into the shallow surf and managed to untangle the cable before it pulled him out to sea. We stood dripping, knee deep in the English Channel, watching a pair of battle-ready swan pedalos setting off to invade France.

"Do you think we should call the Coastguard?" I asked.

"Probably. But Scooter's going to be well pissed off. Maybe we should let him calm down first."

Jenna glared at me. "Tell me, how do you think your first day as my Head of Publicity is going?"

"I don't think you can blame me for that one," I said. "And besides, it did *actually* get us some publicity."

At four in the afternoon, the Pirates Bay was enjoying its pre-evening quiet time. We sat at the far end, around a double table. Scooter and Gordon seemed none the worse for their adventure, but Wayne was still keeping as much distance between him and Scooter as he could. The Brians had brought some home-baked elderberry biscuits to share, and Ray kept us in tea and coffee. Apart from Scooter, who was already three lagers in and getting ready for his fourth.

"Well, we can't go ahead with the show tonight," Jenna said. "People are bound to put two and two together."

"With all due respect," said Brian, "I don't see why. A couple of holidaymakers drift out to sea on pedalos. Happens all the time. Funny story, one time we were in Benidorm and these young British lads were playing pirates on a giant inflatable penis—"

Jenna cut across Brian's story, "Can we jump to the part where this starts to have any relevance to our current problem?"

Brian's expression fell, and he gave a barely audible, "Hrumph."

"No, he's right," I said. "Nobody would have any reason to associate a couple of stranded leisure-boaters with alien spaceships. If anything, the extra bit of focus from the rescue won't hurt."

"Like the Mary Celeste," offered Wayne. "That was aliens what took them. Only it wasn't a giant penis."

"A bit of extra focus?" Jenna ignored Wayne's offering and gave some secret signal to Ray, which resulted in a beer appearing in front of her instantly. "That focus was a local news crew filming my bastardised swans, with you idiots on board, being towed in by the Inshore Rescue Boat."

"All to the good." Brian picked up the plate of elderberry biscuits and offered it round. "Do help yourself. We have far more than we could ever eat. As I was saying, Rose Well Holiday Park has been noticed. It's making tweeting, as they say these days."

Brianna tapped his arm. "Trending, dear. They say trending. Tweeting is the other one."

"Are you sure, dearest? I thought that was twittering?"

"Twatting," muttered Scooter. "It's all twatting bollocks. Social media's just full of conspiracy nuts anyway." He emptied the rest of his pint and stood. "I've gotta go and find some more cable."

"I'll come with you," said Gordon. "We need to rethink the tethering system." He followed Scooter out of the Pirates Bay.

Jenna watched them go, then turned to me. "They're ignoring me, aren't they? They're just going to go ahead and do it anyway, doesn't matter what I say."

I nodded slowly. "In the short time I've been here, I've learned that trying to come between Scooter and an idea is about as futile as asking a herd of stampeding elephants to mind the flowers."

"They're going to get me closed down." She pushed back in her chair and stared at the ceiling.

"Only if the plan doesn't work."

She closed her eyes and sighed. "That's what I meant, they're going to get me closed down."

~ * ~ * ~ * ~

As the sun commenced its final dive towards the smouldering horizon, we gathered at the shoreline of Rocky Bottom Cove to ready the launch of the Swan Battle Fleet towards its Trafalgar.

Gordon and Scooter had driven a large stake into the beach to anchor the cable, therefore not relying on Wayne to hold the pulley system in check. Gordon was busy trying to placate Jenna by explaining in great detail how the system worked.

"You see, this pulley system goes between the two boats so that it leverages the movement of the electric winch on my boat. A short spin on this, and the balloons go up and at a gearing of ten to one."

"Ten to one." Jenna nodded.

"And on Scooter's boat, he controls the lateral movement."

"Lateral movement."

"To-and-fro. That means we can zoom them up and down as we want and really quickly." Gordon stood back to let Jenna study the set-up.

She gazed at the boats and the cat's cradle of cables, then turned to Gordon. "Is there any chance this side of fairyland that this will actually work?"

"It's foolproof," said Gordon.

Jenna studied Scooter and Wayne then said, "That didn't actually answer my question."

"We've even got this." Gordon pulled a huge, deflated balloon from his bag. "It doesn't look much like this, but when it's inflated and with the lights in, it will blow your mind." He held the balloon up and stretched it open to show the pattern printed on it.

I studied the balloon. It looked familiar. "Isn't that the Death Star from Star Wars?"

"Yes, but nobody'll notice that from a distance," Gordon said. "Not when the lights are going as well. It'll be spectacular, you wait."

She turned to me. "You're supposed to be my Head of Publicity, you deal with this, I've got a karate class to teach." Jenna turned and set off back to Downtown.

I watched her go, then turned to Gordon. "What now?"

"Now, we do a trial run."

We pushed the swan pedalos into the gentle surf and I played out the cable as they chugged away from the shore. We'd agreed to keep the boats close in for the test to avoid risking another incident, so when they reached about twenty metres, I locked the cable to the stake. It held fast. Scooter and Gordon now moved apart with the secondary line between them. For this test, we only had one small balloon in flight, and they kept it low to avoid being seen. After a few minutes of fiddling with cables and pulleys, the balloon bobbed in the air just a couple of metres from the sea. Gordon put it through a series of jumps, dives and rapid lateral movements and all seemed smooth. How it would look at night and illuminated was a whole different thing, though. All we could do now was hope.

From somewhere, Scooter had got hold of a roll of Police Line tape and he strung it across the bottom of the track. We didn't really expect anybody to venture down here, but that would deter the casual walker. We dragged the swans clear of the water, threw a plastic tarpaulin over them, then I left Scooter and Gordon with them while Wayne and I headed back up to Downtown.

Already, the Pirates Bay was busier than normal. The usual pre-dinner tipplers chatted in bunches and Donny 'Mr Elvis' Jones was busy setting his rig up on the little stage while Ray shuffled tables and chairs from their lunchtime functional layout to evening convivial. Around the room, I noticed clutches of newcomers, conspicuous by their obvious fascination with the setting and decor. Several carried cameras, some alarmingly sophisticated looking beasts. I wonder just how close up those things were going to be able to zoom. And what if they had night vision lenses? Or were they just in spy movies? One particular group looked highly professional and carried what seemed to be a TV camera and fluffy-headed microphones. Milling around in between these were a collection of individuals who looked like they'd drifted off from a twitcher's convention with their many-pocketed khaki jackets and binoculars strung around their necks.

Most odd were a number of people wearing T-shirts with an image of a little green alien and the words, 'Earth welcomes you to Little Didney' printed on them. Somebody had been busy.

Wayne and I collected a couple of pints from the bar and found a quiet corner in which to sit.

"This is all a bit worrying," I said.

"Good though, innit?" said Wayne. "Gordon got it right, he said there'd be lots more turn up for the third go."

"Just need to keep them looking the right way."

A commotion near the main doors caught my attention. I stood briefly to catch a glimpse of Wilderness Jack weaving his way through a froth of people all keen to engage him in conversation. He slipped most of them with the skill born of years dealing with this, but eventually, he found himself ensnared by the professionalism of the TV film crew. I guessed they had probably honed their capture tactics on slippery politicians.

Their camera lights sprang into life and a fluffy-headed microphone swooped overhead. I couldn't hear what was being said, but Jack seemed totally at ease, so it was unlikely he was being challenged too much about his previous sighting. That was all to the good.

As the place gradually became busier, and the regulars started to collide with the UFO spotters, we ducked out and headed for West Field. As expected, people were gathering here rather than closer to the Downtown area where they'd been the previous night. This had been the place where the lights had appeared the last two nights, so the spectators clearly anticipated being right on Ground Zero tonight. Even at this early hour, the field hummed with activity and excited chatter. Big Moo Burger had their stand up already but were now in competition with Big Boy Hotdogs and Codden Ships. Several barbecues were already sacrificing a selection of dead animals and music mingled with the sounds of chatter to add to the general party mood.

As ten o'clock approached, the time of our first display, a general hush spread around the field and binoculars scraped at the darkened skies. The TV film crew gathered, and somebody did a 'Piece to Camera', although I couldn't hear what was being said. Occasional excited pointing caused pockets of activity, but each subsided again as the objects of their attention turned into aeroplanes or stars. Each time this happened, the excitement levels dampened, and a feeling of pause descended as everybody waited for the clock to close on the time of last night's show. They were going to have to wait a little longer.

"What's happening?" Jenna's voice said from behind me.

"Oh hi." I turned. "Not much, how was karate?"

"Violent and noisy. Just what I needed. There's a lot of people here."

"I know. Great, isn't it?"

"I'm not so sure." She scanned the field. "Some of the people have some serious kit. If they point it in the right direction, they're going to see what we're doing."

"It's alright. Gordon and Scooter are ready. They know what they're doing."

"Hmm. And why am I not getting a franchise fee off these food stands? What sort of Marketing Manager are you?"

"Well, firstly, I thought I was Head of Publicity, not Marketing, and secondly, this isn't your field. Doesn't this one belong to Jejune Water?"

"Picky, picky. They'd never know. At the very least we should have had a beer tent here."

"That would make it look like you're cashing in and could even be seen as motivation for a scam."

She studied me for a moment, then, "Hmm, nice save." She checked her watch. "What time are they doing it?"

"About twelve. An hour later than last time."

"Well, I'm going to find something warmer to wear and grab a bite to eat." She headed off across the field and disappeared into the darkening crowds.

As ten o'clock came and went, so did the hubbub surrounding us. A few people drifted off, but most stayed. Clearly the consensus was that, if the aliens were going to put in an appearance, it wouldn't be until the same time as last night.

For a while, the party atmosphere reappeared as expectation grew for an eleven o'clock happening, but as that too came and went with no sign of E.T., a feeling of disappointment settled.

A significant number packed up and went, but enough remained to still make me feel nervous. Jenna returned just before midnight and thrust a can of beer into my hand.

"Thought you might be in need of this," she said.

Another hush of anticipation settled across the field as midnight approached. The TV film crew pulled themselves out of their camping chairs and fixed their eyes to the night sky. Around the rest of the field, people gathered in clutches with a few setting up tripods for cameras or telescopes, but the majority seemed more casual about the whole thing and spent most of their time picking at their phones while casting an occasional glance at the sky.

Just after twelve, a bright light appeared over the sea and a murmur of excitement trickled across the field. A few shouts and fingers pointing turned the attention of the less alert from overhead to the sea.

My ears strained to pick up snatches of words. Several grumbly voices complaining they were in the wrong place gave a slight sense of satisfaction that we'd done the right thing. Although more worryingly, one or two were asking around how they could get down to the beach to be closer. Mostly, people babbled incoherently in excitement.

The bright light shot straight up into the air, giving the impression of having emerged from the sea. With the lack of anything with which to gain a sense of scale, one could easily imagine this was a large object some miles out rather than just a party balloon a hundred metres from the shore. Two more lights shot up and sat fixed in the sky close to the original, then after a few seconds, all three swooped low before splitting in different directions. If these had truly been large objects, a long way off, then the speed would translate as almost impossible. They continued upwards, fading quickly then disappearing. The effect being that of massive acceleration out into the atmosphere.

Cameras swung in wild arcs, trying to track the objects and hopefully, just recording blurs of light. The TV film crew were more worrying though. The measured skill of the cameraman followed his targets smoothly, and no doubt, the powerful lens was pulling in sharp images which would later be subject to intense scrutiny.

A few shadowy figures headed to the cliff edge, obviously hoping to find a way down for a closer view. I couldn't see what they were doing, so I just hoped the combination of darkness, a slippery descent and Scooter's Police Line tape would deter them. At least for the next fifteen minutes.

A new light pulsed into being high above the sea. This one was much bigger than the others, and even with unaided eyes, I could just make out some patterning. I guessed that with the assistance of zoom lenses, the detail would be more apparent. The level of chatter increased and pointing fingers joined the telescopes and cameras as they raked across the darkness, trying to keep up with the erratic aerobatics of the Mothership.

Brian sidled up to me and, in a very bad stage whisper, said, "That's jolly good, isn't it? Almost looks real."

I shushed him and looked round quickly to see if anybody had overheard, but fortunately, everybody seemed focused on the display.

"That's the Dalek's Death Star, yes?" asked Jenna.

"Star Wars," I corrected.

"What's the other thing?"

I strained my eyes to see. At this distance I could only make out a rough shape to the right of the Death Star. I squinted more. A silvery disk wobbled and although it wasn't emitting any light of its own, it glinted light from the neighbouring Death Star. "Looks like a proper flying saucer," I said.

"It looks like the hubcap off my Clio," Jenna said. "I was wondering where that had gone."

As the display continued, I couldn't help keeping a watching eye on the TV film crew and I became increasingly worried about material they were recording. Wobbly amateur footage from a smartphone was one thing, but these guys knew what they were doing.

After another couple of fly-bys, all but one of the lights stopped. The last one remained frozen in the sky. We knew it was the end of the show of course and that Scooter and Gordon were probably already ashore with swans now hidden in the cave. The last light had been set to be fixed on a single line in order to keep focus there while they did their exfil, as Scooter called it. When that light blinked out, I knew they were now clear of the beach.

As yet, nobody seemed interested in leaving. Telescopes still probed at the sky and cameras waved randomly, shooting off digital film at anything which glinted.

"Alright then?" I heard a voice behind me and turned. Scooter grinned at me. He was clearly out of breath from his rapid exfil from the beach. But considering it would have taken me half an hour, I was seriously impressed.

"How'd it look?" he asked. "D'ya like the flying saucer? Wayne's idea that."

"Thought he'd be behind it," Jenna said. "He owes me a hubcap."

"It seemed to go well," I said. "I'm just a bit concerned about these guys..." I nodded in the direction of the film crew. "Not sure who they are, but they've got some hi-tech kit there and I'm worried about what they've actually managed to film."

Scooter studied the film crew, who were still scanning the dark horizon in the hope of spotting any more visitors.

"You're right," he said. "They could be a problem. Leave it to me."

"No. Don't do anything—" But I was talking to fresh air, Scooter had gone. I scanned the area with no sign of him. *How does he do that?* I looked towards the film crew who were starting to pack up. At least he hadn't gone straight over to them to trash their equipment. Small comforts.

We waited until the field had mostly cleared, then I said to Jenna, "I'm heading back now. I'm drained."

Her eyes widened slightly, and she gave me a lopsided look. "I'm a bit too wired. Can you stay awake for a quick drink? I could do with a nightcap."

"You're not getting me on the Chinese gin again," I said.

"No? Oh well, I've got some Korean Schnapps somewhere."

"Any Scottish whisky? From Scotland as opposed to Taiwan?"

She slipped her arm through mine. "Come and help me look for some."

Chapter Seventeen

FOR THE SECOND MORNING IN a row, I awoke not in my own bed. I realised that as my bedroom didn't have a full-sized poster of Wonder Woman on the back of the door.

This also wasn't the self-collapsing sofa-bed on which I'd spent the previous night. I flopped my left arm to the side and made contact with a warm body. The warm body said, "Uh, what?"

I froze. It always amazes me how quickly a brain can work things out when needs press. In the space between two heartbeats, I'd flashed through '*How did I get here?*' onto '*Did I disgrace myself?*' and finally arrived at '*It's okay, it was all sober and consensual*'.

I caressed the warm body gently and guessed that the particular part with which I was in contact was probably an arm.

The warm body gave another, this time even less intelligible, grunt.

"Are you awake?" I asked, realising as I did so, that this was probably the most pointless question ever asked of another except, '*Can I ask you a question?*'

"What time is it?"

I brought my watch to my eyes and forced them to focus. "Coming on seven."

"Then I'm not awake. Try me again in an hour."

I stroked her arm a little more persistently. "We should find out how last night went down."

"Oh, hell." She shrugged my hand away and pushed herself into a sitting position. "I forgot. They'll be coming with the burning pitchforks any minute. How did I let you talk me into this?"

She eased herself free of the bed and padded off to the bathroom. I allowed myself a brief moment to enjoy the view and a warm memory of last night before dragging myself out of bed and heading off in search of my clothes.

"I hope you've got your official denial ready," Jenna called from the bathroom. "You're my Public Relations Manager, start relating. Here's your chance to prove your worth."

"I thought I was your Marketing Manager..." I gave up as the sound of a power shower drowned any chance of her hearing my protest.

I slipped my clothes on and pulled up the local social media feed on my phone. Instantly, my screen flooded with images of last night. Mostly blurry lights against a black background and pictures of the crowds. There were also plenty of selfies of people, each making their own special selfie face to prove they were actually there. A few captured some quite sharp images and several caught clear pictures of the Mother Ship which, although Gordon had painted on other details, still looked like Darth Vader's spaceship to me. I scanned the comments attached to the pictures. Lots of WOWs and OMGs with a few WTFs thrown in. Mostly the comments were enthusiastic, and although a few posited theories of a hoax, these were mostly directed at a Deep State conspiracy to divert us from the real issue of the Lizard People.

"You need to see this," I called, but my words disappeared under the buzzing of an electric toothbrush.

I gathered my courage and checked the Daily Sentinel site. After a lot of searching through stories about High Street closures, philandering politicians and either a housing market crash or boom, I didn't read long enough to find out which, I found a small piece commenting on some strange goings on in Cornwall. It was a slightly whimsical, filler piece, which referenced Cornish Legends and folk tales as background to reportings of UFOs buzzing the night skies over the peninsular. Quotes from local celebrity, Wilderness Jack, confirmed the veracity of the sightings, but the whole thing had a slight tongue-in-cheek feel.

"So, what's the verdict?" Jenna emerged in a cloud of steam and towels. "Local council closing me down for inciting panic or Fraud Squad want me for questioning?"

"No, all looks good. I think we've got away with it. There's a couple of people suggesting a possible hoax, but nothing levelled at you. Mostly they think it's the government covering something up."

"Hmm. Well, we'll see what happens when the local papers come out." She shrugged herself into a pair of black jeans and a black shirt. "Help yourself to coffee if you like. Just drop the catch when you leave."

I watched her hurry out of the door and pondered the fact that I'd probably had *less* romantic first encounters, but I couldn't quite recall when. I slipped the catch as instructed and headed back to my cabin.

I'd never been one for morning television, but this morning, I made an exception. I settled down with a black coffee and bowl of dry Sugar Puffs, I'd forgotten to get milk again, and tuned in to the local morning show, Greet the Day, with Patsy Kimbrell, or Cornish Patsy, as she was more commonly known. The weatherman was wrapping up his summary, apparently it was going to be a day of scattered sunshine and localised showers. Exactly three minutes of adverts for life insurance, stair lifts and online bingo and we were back to the morning sofa to be introduced to her new guest.

"So, this morning, I have the unusual honour of interviewing one of our own team, Robbie Clemthorpe." Patsy turned and smiled at the man occupying the sofa opposite her. "Robbie is one of our field cameramen and last night he had a quite disturbing experience while filming those strange lights which everybody is talking about this morning. Would you like to tell our viewers what happened, Robbie?"

Robbie shuffled in his seat, clearly not comfortable being at the pointy end of a camera. "Well, we'd spent the evening over at a field near Rose Well Holiday Park, you know, where people say they've been seeing flying saucers…"

He went on to recount his version of the lights and how strange they'd been. I listened carefully for any hints that he thought they might be faked, but like the good newsman he obviously was, he focused on the facts.

Even when Patsy pushed for an opinion, he simply replied, "I'm a cameraman. It's my job to record images, it's somebody else's job to interpret them."

I relaxed back in my seat and dug into my Sugar Puffs. It looked like we'd got away with it. My fear that everybody would immediately scream fake and sue us for emotional hurt or wasted digital film seemed unfounded. We may or may not get anything positive out of this, but at least it didn't look like we were going to end up in court.

My sense of relief, however, was short-lived.

"But it was when you were leaving that it all started to turn sinister," Patsy said. "Tell our viewers what happened."

I'd just gathered the last Sugar Puffs onto my spoon, but they never made it to my mouth as I recalled my last conversation with Scooter.

"Well, we'd just packed everything up and were on our way back to the van when these two men stopped us," Robbie said.

"Can you describe them?" Patsy did her special concerned face.

"One of them was in some sort of army gear, but he stayed back in the shadows so a bit difficult to say. But he looked important and never said anything. The other guy, he was the scary one. All in black with a balaclava and a machine gun."

"A machine gun?" Patsy said. "That must have been terrifying. Go on."

"I think he must have been SAS or MI6 or something. Anyway, he demanded the film from the camera. Said it was a matter of national security and we'd be… banged up, that's what he said, banged up for breaking the Official Secrets Act if we didn't hand it over."

"So what did you do?"

"We gave him the memory card, of course. It was a bit odd though, because he didn't believe that was it, he seemed to think we should have a reel of film I think. Anyway, I explained it was digital, and he accepted it. Then they just sort of disappeared."

Patsy turned to the camera. "Well, there you have it, strange lights in the sky and our very own Men in Black. Whatever next? Coming up after the break, we talk to Mrs Miggins from Treluggen whose dog can woof Dancing Queen. Don't go away."

I went away.

~ * ~ * ~ * ~

"A machine gun? He said you had a machine gun."

"A nerd like that wouldn't know a machine gun if it shot 'im up the arse." Scooter went over to the wall cupboard of his headquarters and pulled out an evil looking gun. "There you go, does that look like a machine gun to you?"

"Well, to be honest…" I started.

Scooter shook his head. "No wonder the world's heading for the toilet. How much use are you going to be in a foxhole when it all kicks off if you can't tell the difference between a Splatmaster Magfed Paintball gun and an MP5?"

"Well… Anyway, who was the other guy? They said there was somebody official looking with you in military gear?"

"Official looking? Oh, that'd be Wayne. He was just wearing his usual camo gear. I tried to tell him not to wear it, his camo is East German DPM instead of British army DPM, but would he listen?"

"Wayne?"

"I wanted to get Gordon 'cause he's got a suit and can talk posh, but we didn't have time." Scooter put his Splatmaster back in the cupboard. "You'll never guess what we done, come'n have a look-see." He beckoned me and headed for the open trapdoor.

I let him climb to the bottom, then followed him down. He led the way to the hole where the bomb was lodged. Or had been lodged. The thing now lay on the floor in the middle of a pile of freshly dug earth.

I froze. "You moved it?"

"Yup." Scooter looked pleased with himself.

"And it didn't go off?"

"Apparently not."

"Is it safe?"

"Dunno," Scooter said. "But then these things were never really designed with safety in mind, so my guess is, not very."

"And what are you planning on doing with it now?" I took a couple of steps backwards.

"Haven't really thought that bit through yet."

"Oh, good. When you do, let me know, I'll be doing something a long way away, I expect."

I made my way to Downtown and settled in the Pirates Bay with the first of what I intended to be a steady flow of coffees. The place was busier than normal and on a closer look, I noticed that Wilderness Jack was holding court amongst a group of millennial types waving copies of his book for autographing and phones for selfies with their new hero.

I sensed, rather than saw, a movement next to me. I turned to see Jenna settling down with a coffee.

"I saw the news," she said. "I assume that was Scooter terrifying members of the public?"

"At least it wasn't a real machine gun," I said.

"Even *he* knows better than that."

I wondered whether now would be a good time to mention the bomb, probably best not. "I see Jack's lapping up the attention."

"I think his agent is pushing him, I heard he's got a new book coming out. *Surviving Climate Armageddon*, or something." She shook her head as if trying to clear a memory. "He tried to tell me all about it, but he was drunk and I think he'd been eating garlic sandwiches."

I studied the throng surrounding him for a moment. "I've got an idea," I said.

"Haven't you used up your idea allowance for the week?" She patted my arm. "You can tell me all about it later, I've got a suit from Jejune Water coming out to see me and I've spent the last twenty minutes helping Charlie unblock a drain, I should probably change into some clean jeans. Always pays to make an impression." She picked up her cup and headed off out the back.

"Give them my love," I called as she disappeared.

I watched the hubbub surrounding Jack and at the point it seemed to be quietening, so I headed over.

"Ah, William," Jack boomed as he spotted me weaving through the people. He wrapped his arm around my shoulder and herded me into the middle of the group. "This is William, he's alright. He writes books about alien visitors."

"Not exactly," I said. "I only sell books written by other people."

"When I was in Mexico, working with the Fuerzas Especiales, we had a chap there writing a book about how the Aztecs were really spacemen. You probably know him? Jimmy, I think his name was. Nice chap, got bitten by a Fer-de-lance. Have you ever seen anybody die from a Fer-de-lance bite? Not pretty. We killed the bugger and fricasseed it with some cactus leaves as a sort of tribute. Not Jimmy, the snake, of course. Mind you, those Fuerzas Especiales can drink. Never try to keep up with a Mexican soldier, that's my advice. Where was I?"

"We were talking about books," I said. "When's your new one coming out?"

Jack paused. "This week. Maybe next week. They did tell me."

"Have you thought about doing a sort of promo event? If you did one here, where you saw the UFOs, you'd get masses of people."

"Masses?"

"Hundreds, probably. What with your sighting being in the papers and everything."

"It was?"

"Yes. Look, I know there's a group of…" I struggled for the right word, "… survivalists here who would love it if you did a thing with them as part of a promotion for your book. Think of the publicity."

"Publicity. Hmm. Perhaps I could do a little something to help. I could show them how I make a treetop bivouac to keep away from snakes."

"This is Cornwall," I said. "Maybe something about surviving overnight in a snow-bound traffic jam on the A30 might be a bit more relevant?"

"Good thinking. Urban survival, all the thing these days. How to catch and skin rats with just a machete and a piece of string, that sort of thing."

"Yes, that general direction. We can iron out the details later."

That evening brought renewed activity in the Pirates Bay. Both Ray and Jenna worked hard behind the bar and every table was occupied and despite the chill of the evening, people spilled out onto the tables on the patio. Magical Mervyn looked totally bewildered as he set up his gear on the small stage. This was probably the largest audience he'd ever had, and he obsessively checked and rechecked the position of every item on the stage. He gave little convulsive grins every so often, which indicated he was either about to break into a happy dance any second or collapse in a complete nervous breakdown.

I nuzzled my way into the crowd at the bar and hoped either Jenna or Ray would spot my presence and bring me a much-needed beer. Conversations babbled around me in a jumble of noise, but I caught snippets occasionally.

"Of course they won't appear till one o'clock tonight."

"That's what I heard. Something to do with them being on a twenty-five-hour planetary time."

"Yes, that's why they're an hour later each time…"

"Did you see the Mother Ship? Didn't it look like the Death Star?"

"I'll bet that's where George Lucas got the idea."

"I heard they abducted somebody on a pedalo and dumped him out to sea."

A beer landed in front of me while I wasn't looking. I turned to see Jenna moving up the bar and engaging with a forest of thrusting arms, waving paper money.

"Thanks," I called, but I knew she hadn't heard.

By ten, the crowds had started to reduce as those who didn't fully understand the implications of the twenty-five-hour planetary cycle of the alien homeworld wandered outside in the hope of another visitation. By eleven, the place was virtually empty.

Jenna instructed Ray to clear up, then came round and joined me at my table.

"Okay, so you can have that one," she said. "But one night does not a business make."

"Was that a compliment?"

"Yes, I read how to do those in my Bar Owner's Manual." She grinned. "How did I do?"

"Not bad. How did your meeting with the suit from Jejune Water go?"

"They've upped their offer." She cast her gaze around the chaos left behind in the bar. "I have to say, it's very tempting."

"Then why not?"

"Because they'll do the same here as they've done in other places. They'll suck the spring dry, build a sodding great factory to produce yet more plastic bottles, then ship the bottles to trendy America while transferring their tax liability to the Cayman Islands. Besides..." She supped thoughtfully at her beer. "... the offer still wouldn't cover what I owe the bank."

"But things are looking up," I said. "Just wait till we start with part B of the plan."

Her eyes narrowed in suspicion. "What's part B?"

"Ah, I haven't quite worked that out yet."

Chapter Eighteen

OVER THE NEXT FEW DAYS, the interest in Rose Well Holiday Park increased, then levelled off. Jenna's bookings picked up, more than she expected but less than I'd hoped. The two of us had slipped into a sort of relationship, although probably the word 'relationship' was too defining. We just seemed to be two people following similar trajectories, and strangely comfortable in each other's company.

Jack's agent had leapt at the chance to do a promotion video at Rose Well Park for Jack's new book, and the event was rushed into rapid planning before he had a chance to either change his mind or pull one of his famous disappearing tricks.

Scooter, on the other hand, was proving to be a bit more worrying, deciding, as he had, to take on a personal mission to protect Rose Well Park from some unnamed impending global disaster.

The bomb sat in the middle of the floor of Scooter's headquarters.

"How on Earth did you get it up the ladder?" I asked, not really wanting to know the answer.

"Several mattresses, a couple of pillows, some pulleys and a very long rope in case the pillows didn't work out." He looked thoroughly pleased with himself.

"Now what?" I asked. "You can't leave it there. Haven't you got your first group of Trainee Preppers coming today?"

"Who? Oh, yeah, the sheeple."

"Are you sure you should keep calling them sheeple?" I said. "We've discussed this, these people are paying to learn prepping stuff. That's why they've come here. Jenna's spent a fortune on advertising this."

"They can't just come here for a weekend and expect to be fully trained survivalists. You know, I saw one of them buggers wearing their camo gear in Sainsbury's yesterday. And she was buying sushi. Their idea of the end of civilisation is not being able to get the latest iPhone on the day it's launched."

"I know, you explained this before. But Jenna needs these customers, and she's letting you do your... whatever it is you're doing here without charge, so... Can't you just be nice to them for a couple of days?"

Scooter shrugged. "As long as they don't go banging on about Jamie Oliver and his bleedin' tofu wraps when I'm trying to skin a rabbit."

"I'll add it to the pre-course Information Pack. Now, what are you going to do with this?" I pointed at the bomb in the middle of the floor.

"I've got a plan. It's full of explosives, you see. If we can get that out, we have a good supply for making our own bullets for when it all kicks off. First thing to run out, ammunition. So this'll keep us going."

"How do you propose opening the thing without it going bang?" I asked.

"Still working on that bit. Wayne's looking for a YouTube video."

"And actually making the bullets?"

"Yeah, still working on that bit as well."

"Do you have any different plans so that we could perhaps have a vote on the one we like the best?"

Scooter shook his head.

"Are you sure we couldn't just go with calling in the bomb squad and getting rid of it?"

"They'd want to go poking around all over the place here, then where would we be? We gotta deal with it ourselves. Plus, it's a resource. You don't go handing over a resource to the enemy."

I gave up. I'd learned that arguing with Scooter was always a bit like trying to nail porridge to the ceiling. "Okay, but until you've figured out how to dismantle a seventy-year-old unstable bomb, what are you going to do with it when these people come?"

"Don't worry. I've got a plan."

~ * ~ * ~ * ~

I headed back to my cabin, stopping off at Dolly's Daily Shop on the way. I'd recently transferred my book stands in there on a profit share basis with them instead of the original setup. It meant I didn't need to be doing the day-to-day sales. The local interest in all things UFO-like had caused a minor run on my books, and my stand was beginning to look a bit sparse. I had a few more boxes in my lockup back in London, but as the complications of getting them here outweighed any potential financial gains, I'd hold fire on doing that for the moment.

I picked up some essentials and settled at my little kitchen table with a cup of tea, a packet of hobnobs and the morning news on the TV.

My moment of peace didn't last long.

"Hi-de-hi, good neighbour," Brian's voice called, accompanied by a gentle, but somehow very intrusive, tapping on the door.

"Come on in," I called. "Door's open."

Brian squeezed his way through the door and occupied the centre of the room. "Just wondered if you'd seen Jenna?" His eyes scraped the room as if expecting to find her hiding in a corner.

"No, I haven't seen her today."

"It's just she was supposed to be bringing these Weekend Preppers down for us to take out foraging this morning."

"What time did she say?"

"Nine-thirty."

I glanced up at the clock over the fireplace. "Well, it's only nine-forty. I'd give her another ten minutes or so. They might have got stuck in traffic."

"Oh, no. They've been staying here."

"Still, I guess they think they're on holiday so a bit lax. I shouldn't worry."

Brian's face drooped like he'd just broken his favourite mug. "But she said nine-thirty."

I heard the sound of voices outside. "There you go," I said. "That sounds like them now." I got up to encourage Brian to go out and look.

We stepped down out of the cabin to see Jenna with two women and one man approaching. One of the women I vaguely recognised from one of Scooter's sessions.

"Sorry we're a bit late," Jenna said. "Madison cut her hand on an easy-open olive jar and Grayson's taken her to casualty."

"Olives? For breakfast?" Brian queried.

"Yes, they go well with a tomato tostada," said the man in full camouflage and with a vicious looking machete hanging from a utility belt of which Batman would have been proud.

"Well, there you go," said Jenna. "You're all set, I have to go and open up the Pirates Bay."

"Hang on," said Brian. "I thought there were supposed to be six?"

"Yes, said the man. Madison and Grayson have gone off to A & E, and Roman had a panic attack when he saw the blood and then a nosebleed, so he's resting for the morning. I think it's his detox regime, he always overdoes these things."

I wondered how Scooter was going to take the news that fifty percent of his contingent had been wiped out by a jar of olives.

"So, you're just three now?" Brian said.

The man turned to look at the two women as if having a quick headcount. "Yes, just three."

"Well, that's no good," said Brian. "That will be uneven. We can't do this with an uneven number. That won't do at all."

I started for the door of my cabin as it dawned on me where this was going.

"William," Brian called in my direction. "How do you fancy a nice morning on the forage trail?"

"How about Brianna?" I asked.

"No, she'd love to of course, but she has to feed the scoby plant today."

"Scabby? What's that?"

"Scoby, it's a symbiotic yeast plant. You can't make kimchi without it."

I looked around, hoping to see some alternative victim strolling by, but none appeared.

I deflated as I realised my quiet morning had just disappeared. "Okay, be right there."

I slipped inside to change my shoes while I tried to think of an escape plan. Short of climbing out of the rear window, I had no options so gave in to the inevitable and re-emerged with the best smile I could muster.

"William, you can partner up with Tabatha." Brian indicated one of the women. She wore sensible shorts, shirt and a safari hat and looked like an escapee from an Enid Blyton book.

I smiled acknowledgement to Tabatha, and she smiled back.

"And, Theo..." Brian indicated the man with the machete, "... you're with Pandora, of course."

I guessed by the introduction, and matching, neatly pressed camouflage outfits, that Theo and Pandora were a couple.

Brian stood on a big rock and held up a wicker trug. "Have we all got something to gather in?"

Pandora held up canvas tote bag proclaiming 'I love trees' and Tabatha showed off her Waitrose Bag For Life.

"Jolly good." He stepped off his rock. "This way." He thrust his arm forwards as if commanding the Queen's Cavalry.

We followed him out of the bottom of the Bermuda area and along a winding path until it descended into a small wood in a dip between Rose

Well and the cliff tops. We had to stop a couple of times while Pandora untangled her hair from overhanging brambles.

Brian stopped in front of a tree. It looked like a brown tree with green leaves, but Brian explained it was a beech tree and pointed out the colour of the bark and shape of the leaves. Tabatha took out an oversized tablet computer and typed notes while Pandora took a selfie with the trees in the background.

"These little weird-shaped nut things are known as beech nuts," Brian said. "These are edible, so we're going to gather some of these and take them back. They are from last autumn but are still good."

I heard a spitting, spluttering sound and turned to see Theo making a face like a Pug chewing a wasp. He puckered his lips and spat again.

"Of course," Brian continued, "we wouldn't want to eat these raw, especially when they are still in their case. They often have a bitter tannin taste. Not nice at all." He looked at Theo. "You alright, son?"

Theo nodded but continued to try to expel the last of the beech fuzz from his mouth.

"Jolly good. Well, on we go." Brian marched off again.

A bit deeper into the wood, we stopped again by a smaller tree covered in a sprinkling of little berries.

"This is the Elderberry." Brian pulled a small white cluster of flowers towards us and held it under his nose. "These make delicious wine and jams. They're also jolly good for keeping evil spirits at bay. We'll gather a few of these and when we get back, Brianna will show you how to prepare them. Best if one of you holds the branch steady while your partner cuts the berries. Don't forget to leave some for the fairies."

My world had changed so much I didn't even think about commenting on the fairies. We worked in our pairings and picked a few handfuls of the little berries and dropped them in the bags.

"Moving on." Brian set off down the little path before stopping suddenly. "Gather round."

When we'd gathered round, he pointed to some other white flowers on the ground. "Now, this is a special treat, wild garlic. Delicious." He uprooted one of the plants to show a bulb and dropped it in his trug. "But you must pay attention and not confuse it with Lily of the Valley. Wild garlic is lovely with a nice bit of roast rabbit, while Lily of the Valley is quite dangerous. This is what Walter used in that TV show Breaking Bad to poison that child."

That information caused a few oohs and another flurry of selfies.

We carried on like this for a while, dropping more plants and stuff into tote bags or bags-for-life and of course the endless selfies and note taking.

At one point, Brian glanced at Theo and said, "You have purple fingers."

Theo looked at his hand. He looked like he'd been to finger-painting classes. "Yeah, those little purply berries. You said they were nice but rather too bitter for my liking."

"The Elderberries?" Brian asked.

Theo nodded.

"Ah." Brian paused while he searched for the right words. "We don't usually eat those raw either," he said finally. "How are you feeling? All tickety-boo?"

Theo looked puzzled. "Yes, fine. Why?"

"Oh, nothing." Brian shook his head. "Well, I think we should be heading back now before... before it starts to rain." He glanced again at Theo.

I looked up at the perfectly clear blue sky and wondered what he was on about but just went with the flow, grateful that this brief contact with nature was coming to an end and I might still get my cup of tea and hobnobs before I had to help organise Scooter's session.

Brian's pace back seemed somewhat more rushed than the outward journey. At least until I heard a moaning noise behind me. I turned to see Theo leaning against a tree. Even through his spray tan, he looked pale and drained.

"You alright?" I asked, approaching with some apprehension. "You're looking a bit—"

I jumped back as Theo doubled over and emptied his breakfast around the base of the tree.

I waited as he straightened again, gave a weak smile and said, "That's better. I might have overdone the Chianti last night. Sorry, okay now though so—"

He lurched again, and I stepped even further back.

"I feared that might happen," Brian said.

"Is he going to be alright?" I asked.

"Oh, yes. Upset tummy for a while, but no lasting damage. It's normally only children who do this. I didn't think to explain to an adult to not eat random berries."

"He probably thinks he's at the salad counter in Pret a Manger."

Brian shook his head.

Theo heaved once more and Pandora hovered around him, making little chirruping noises. At least the selfies had stopped for a moment.

We made our way back to the cabins, with frequent pauses, where Brianna came out and administered ginger and fennel tea to Theo.

"Who's a silly Billy?" she clucked as she nudged the bottom of the cup to keep him drinking. "Drink this all up, you'll soon be feeling right as a pudding."

"I just need to…" I pointed vaguely in the direction of Downtown, "… be up there. Sorry to rush off."

I slipped away before I had to give any more explanation and only when I was clear, did I actually give any thought to where I was going. For the loss of anywhere else to be, I headed for the Pirates Bay.

The usual pre-lunchtime quiet proved a calming retreat, and I was the only person at the bar.

"Morning, mate," greeted Ray. "What can I get you?"

"Just a coffee, please. Jenna not here?" I looked around the bar.

"No, she had to go out. Milk?"

I nodded. "I thought she said she was opening this morning?"

"No, she was all poshed up and hurried out. Wearing a skirt and everything. I think she even had a bra on." He slid the coffee to me. "There you go."

"A skirt? Jenna?"

"Yeah, I know. First the flying saucers, and now Jenna in a skirt. Strange times." He slid off to the other end of the bar to serve a couple of kids waiting by the ice cream machine.

I supped at my coffee and tried to imagine Jenna in a skirt. It didn't work.

Chapter Nineteen

I TURNED UP AT SCOOTER'S headquarters early in the afternoon, hoping to arrive before his trainee survivalists.

Scooter lounged in his favourite sofa with a beer in one hand and a joint in the other.

"You know they're turning up any minute?" I said.

"Who?"

"Your trainees, the sheeple, as you call them."

"Oh, yeah. All cool."

The bomb still sat in the middle of the room, only now, a sheet of glass lay balanced across the top of it half supported by a stack of house bricks and draped with a couple of pieces of old curtain material.

"Why's this still here?" I asked. "I thought you were getting rid of it."

"It's disguised," Scooter said.

"As what? A surreal house clearance sale?"

"A coffee table," he protested.

"I don't want to shatter your illusion, but I can still see that it's a bomb."

"Yeah, but that's only 'cause you *know* what it is." He placed his beer on the glass sheet and I winced involuntarily. "If you didn't know, you'd probably just think, '*Oh, that's a nice piece of modern furniture, I must get one like that for my posh house*'."

"I don't think I would."

The sound of approaching voices outside indicated the arrival of Scooter's victims. He stubbed the joint out with his fingers, stuffed it in his shirt pocket and flapped his hand at the air in a vain attempt to clear the smoke.

Two female faces appeared in the doorway.

"Theo's having trouble getting off the toilet," explained Pandora.

"Come in. You know Scooter?" I said. "He's your Team Leader for the survival session."

The women stepped cautiously inside.

"Wow, sick coffee table," said Tabatha.

"OMG, that's so rad," said Pandora. "It looks totes real. Did you get it at Baudelaire's? They're really deck these days."

Scooter gave me a '*Told-you-so*' smile, then peered out of the door. "Where's the others?"

I explained about easy-open jars of olives, extreme detox regimes and strange berries, and Scooter's gaze flicked between me and the two women, his eyes widening as my explanation unfolded.

"Well, that's bolloxed it," he said. "How we gonna run a training session with just a pair of—"

I touched his arm to cut the flow.

"What?" he said. "I was gonna say a pair of... um... ladies."

"I know, but we just need to think it through, you know, sometimes we have to adapt to changing circumstances. Didn't Wellington say no plan survives first contact with the enemy?"

"Von Moltke, actually. And I'm sure he wasn't talking about no jar of olives either when he said it. How we gonna do Capture the Flag with only one person in a team? I mean, you need at least two, one to guard yer own and one to go off and get the enemy's flag. S.O.P."

"Can't we do something different?" Pandora asked.

He picked up the pair of coloured cloths from the table. "No, I've got the flags all ready now."

"There must be somebody…" I suddenly realised that I was about to dig myself a nice hole here. "No, you're going to have to think of something else. How about escape and evasion?"

Scooter sat forwards. "I know, you and me can be on one team, the birds…" He caught my look. "The girls on the other. That'll do it."

"That doesn't seem very fair," Tabatha said.

Scooter paused. "Yeah, okay. You and me on one team and you two," he pointed at me and Pandora, "you're on the other."

With a sinking feeling, I realised what had just happened. Exactly where I didn't want to be.

"I've got to be…" I couldn't come up with anywhere I had to be and gave in. "Oh, okay. What do we do?"

He threw the blue cloth at me. "That's your flag." He held up the red cloth, "And this is ours. Blue Base is the copse over at the top of West Field, Red Base is the store shed behind the old hangar. First team to get the other's flag wins."

"What are the rules?" I asked.

He visibly winced and gave a slight shake of his head as if in disgust at my question. "This is survival, first rule of survival, there ain't no rules." He picked up his red flag and stuffed it into the top of his backpack. "When it all kicks off, you gotta do what you gotta do." He stood and turned to Tabatha. "Right then, look lively."

As the pair started for the door, I noticed the corner of his red flag protruding from the top of his pack. I reached forward and grabbed it just as they headed out of the door. It slipped easily from his pack and I shoved it into my pocket.

Scooter paused and turned to face me. I thought he'd noticed, but he just said, "You two best get a move on 'cause once we got our flag up, I'm coming for yours." He gave a brief confirmatory nod, and they headed off.

Pandora looked at me. "That was sneaky."

"No rules, he said." I grinned.

We set out uphill towards the little copse.

Despite Pandora's slight build, and far from sensible shoes, I had to work to keep up with her.

"Do you work here then?" she asked.

I scurried a few steps to bring us within talking distance. "No, well sort of, I suppose."

She stopped and turned to face me. "You don't seem very sure?"

I paused, grateful of the moment's rest to catch my breath. "I came here to sell books but stayed on to help a bit with marketing. Bit of a stop-gap, really."

"Must be fun, doing different stuff like this all the time?"

I considered. "I guess. Hadn't really stopped to think about it. What do you do?"

"I'm a Customer Outreach Experience Manager for a Media Consultancy Agency."

"Sounds important." I thought for a moment and then just had to ask, "What does that mean?"

"When a customer reaches out to contact the agency, it's my job to oversee their experience and to ensure it meets deliverable service expectations."

"I see," I lied.

"It can be really stressful, and Tabatha's job is even more stressful than mine, she's a Social Media Influencer, I don't know how she copes with the pressure. That's why we have to get away on weekends like this to re-ground ourselves."

"I can imagine." I drew a breath and pointed upwards. "We'd best get on, Scooter will be on his way as soon as he opens his bag and sees his flag missing."

We puffed on up the hill and found a semi-concealed spot. I hung both flags on the same tree, and we settled on a granite outcrop to wait.

"So what's the story with Scooter?" Pandora asked.

"He doesn't talk about it, but he was in Basra. I think he was invalided out with PTSD. He's convinced there's some sort of apocalypse coming and trying to get ready for it. Basically, he's a really nice chap, but he just has a few problems."

"Hey, you pair of dickwads," a voice yelled from down the slope.

Scooter marched up the hill with ferocious efficiency. "Where's my flag?"

I pointed at the tree where the two flags fluttered in the gentle breeze.

"What's it doing there?" He pulled it free in the same step with which he arrived.

"I took it," I said. "Does that mean we won?"

"What? No, you didn't win, you cheated." He closed on me and I shuffled backwards.

"But you said there were no rules. If there aren't any rules, you can't cheat."

"What?"

"First rule of survival, you said, there aren't any rules."

Scooter glared at me as he snatched our blue flag from the tree and waved it in my face. "Well, there you go, second game, I win. Right?"

"But that wasn't a game," I said. "You didn't say we were doing another game."

"There's always another game. When it all kicks off, their ain't nobody gonna tell you when it starts. You gotta be ready all the time."

"Okay, so it's one all," I said.

"No, it's two to one. 'Cause I got both flags now so you can't win game three, which just started and I just won again. Now I'm bored with this, you lot ain't no competition." He set off down the hill, waving both flags as he went.

Pandora looked at me. "You were saying?"

We followed Scooter, at some distance, down the hill and back to his headquarters. By the time we arrived, Scooter was back in his armchair, fresh beer in hand and feet up on the bomb table.

"What next?" asked Pandora.

"That's enough for today," Scooter said. "Want you fighting fit for tomorrow and I expect a full squad. Don't want no nonsense about injuries sustained by vegetables either. This is war you're training for, not a day out in Tesco."

"Olives are fruit," said Tabatha, "not vegetables. And it wasn't her fault. She's been advised to put in a claim for injuries from the makers."

A storm gathered over Scooter's face and I felt an urgent need to separate the women from his vicinity before it broke.

"I think we'd best go now," I said. "Scooter, haven't you got some chickens to attend to?"

He turned to face me. "Huh? Chickens?"

"Yes, you know, the chickens. *The* chickens. The peaceful chickens." I was aware of the strange looks I was getting from the women, but ignored them and focused on Scooter.

He stared at me the way a cat studies a mouse before leaping for its throat. I glanced at the door, wondering how fast I could make it, when he said, "Oh, yeah. Chickens." His eyes relaxed, and he settled back in his seat and repeated, "Chickens."

I flapped my hand at the women, indicating they should leave. "Come on, time for a quick refresher in the Pirates Bay? On the house?"

By the time we arrived in the Pirates Bay, Madison, Grayson and Roman were already there. Apparently Theo was still wedded to the toilet. The friends all gathered around a table and began talking at each other in a verbal torrent that would make a Casablancan street market sound like a nunnery.

I asked Ray to send them some drinks and tried to persuade him they should be on the house.

"You got authorisation for that? Only she really cracked the shits on me when I divvied out some cold ones for the local five-side-team after a match here once."

"It'll be alright, Jenna will okay it. Talking of which, is she back yet?"

"Yeah, she came back earlier. Looked like somebody had murdered her Barbie Doll." The sound of the food service bell snatched his attention. "I'd stay well clear, mate," he said as he turned and headed for the service hatch.

Ignoring Ray's advice, I cut through Downtown and headed to Jenna's house. I found her sitting on a bench on the track to her house. She didn't notice me until I sat down next to her.

"Oh, hi," she said.

"Nice view," I said.

I stared across West Field and out over the sea. The late afternoon sun rippled across the water like a golden path to the sky.

"I grew up with this view. Granddad used to bring me up here as a kid and we'd eat fish and chips and he'd tell me stories about all the famous people he'd met. I think he was bullshitting most of the time, but as a kid, I was in awe."

I reached and took her hand. "My grandfather used to tell me about all his exotic trips to far-away places. Turns out he never went further than Romford and all the times he'd been away, he'd been in the nick."

She flopped her head onto my shoulder. "I've got to sell the place," she said quietly. "Had a meeting with the bank today. They're not going to continue to support this."

"Ah." I squeezed her hand. "Hence the posh clothes."

"Didn't do much good. I even wore a bra."

"I noticed."

We sat silently for a while, listening to the sound of the breeze as it kissed the trees on its way inland.

"He's twelve, you know. Thirteen at a push," Jenna said. "My Account Executive. What does somebody his age know about running a seventy-year-old business? He's only just learned to dress himself."

"What did he say?"

"He said that the bank could no longer justify covering the outgoings on a business which was clearly in decline."

"I see. Did he make any suggestions? Like restructuring the financing or something?"

"No, he just started talking about the general decline of the Hospitality Sector and other stuff. To be honest, I sort of zoned out after that point. I was busy working out if his mother would notice he'd gone if I strangled him with my bra."

"But essentially, he was saying you couldn't carry on as you are? Yes?"

She looked at me with tired, but slightly puzzled eyes. "I suppose."

"Then perhaps they might be more accommodating if they saw a change? A different direction?"

Her look of confusion increased. "Huh?" she said.

"Sometimes, doing something left-field can work. Like asking for a loan to expand into a new area instead. If nothing else, it will confuse the hell out of them and buy time while they go through the paperwork."

She shook her head slowly, as if seeing me for the first time. "How do you do it? You just don't give up, do you? How do you keep so obnoxiously optimistic all the time?"

"Our species can only survive if we have obstacles to overcome. Without them, we weaken and die."

"That sounds like Darwin or somebody."

"James T. Kirk," I said.

"Of course, it would have to be. Come on, let's boldly go back to mine, I'll phone in for a pizza."

Chapter Twenty

"READY FOR THE NEXT EXERCISE?" Scooter greeted, rubbing his hands together.

He seemed more enthusiastic this morning as we'd managed to gather a full complement of attendees. I'd learned that an enthusiastic Scooter though is always something of a mixed blessing and depends to a large extent, as to which side of his enthusiasm one sits.

Madison's hand was wrapped in a bandage and cosseted in a sling and Theo, although now free of the toilet, still looked quite pale.

They nodded and mumbled assent to Scooter's question.

"Right, gather round." He stood in front of a large map on the wall. "This is where we are," he poked at a point on the map with a stick.

Six faces flicked their gazes between their smartphones and the map on the wall.

"What, this little green dot?" Tabatha asked.

Roman peered over at her screen. "That's where we are now."

Tabatha looked up at Scooter's map. "It doesn't look like it does here."

"That's because your GPS settings aren't set to re-orient to north automatically. Here, let me." Roman took Tabatha's phone and tapped a few times on the screen. "Easy. There you go."

"Oh." Tabatha rotated her phone a few times. "That's cool. I didn't know it did that."

"Are we ready?" Scooter said. "Only the apocalypse is waiting."

"Sos," said Tabatha. "It's a bit different to the one in my car. And… there's no road names here, so it's hard to see where we are."

Scooter closed his eyes and drew a deep breath. "So, as I said, this is our HQ," he stabbed at the map again. "And we're going to rapid tab up to here," he tapped the stick further up the map. "That's where we set up our FOB."

"FOB?" asked Theo.

"Forward Operating Base," Scooter said. "Doesn't anybody speak English anymore?"

"Big yikes, totes my bad," said Theo.

Scooter stared at Theo and looked ready to launch at him when Grayson asked, "Do you have the GPS for that point?"

"It's up there, look." He poked at the map again. "You don't need no GPS, you just follow the map."

Grayson squinted at the map. "And where did you say we were again? Maybe I could find it on street search."

"What are you nuggets gonna do when it all kicks off and their ain't no GPS no more and when you can't even find yer own arses with both hands?"

They fell silent for a moment, then Roman offered, "We could always ask somebody?"

"Right, that's it," Scooter snapped. "We'll do it this way. You'll follow me." He started for the door and pointed to several spades propped up in the corner. "One of those each and get a move on, we've wasted too much time yapping already."

Scooter threw his paintball gun over his shoulder, strode out of the door, seemingly uninterested as to whether anybody actually followed him.

After a moment's confusion, they each picked up a spade and trailed behind Scooter on his march up the slope. By the time we crested the brow,

Scooter was already in the dip which lay between two gentle slopes. He stood, waiting for us to catch him up.

"You've just escaped a horde of zombies over that hill." He waved his paintball gun in the direction we'd just come from. "And on the other side," he waved his gun again at the opposite slope, "there's a whole bunch more coming in. You're caught in a classic flanking manoeuvre. You've got reinforcements approaching from the east, but they ain't gonna get here before the enemy come down these hills at you." He strutted between the group, eyeing each one in turn. "What ya gonna do?"

"Erm, zombies aren't real," said Theo.

"Are you going to wait to discuss it with them?" Scooter asked. "Too late to find out if they're real or not when they're chewin' on your brains."

Heavy breathing to my left caught my attention, and I turned to see Roman walking in little circles and flapping his hands at his face.

"What's up with him?" Scooter asked.

"He's hyperventilating," said Tabatha. "Has anybody got a paper bag?"

Roman crumpled onto the ground and Tabatha helped him lay out straight. "Put your feet up on this." She stuffed her little North Face rucksack under his feet.

"I've got a plastic bag," Grayson said. "I'll just empty my emergency toiletries out." He fumbled a packet of wet-wipes and a wad of tissue paper from bag to pocket and handed the bag to Tabatha. "There you go, it might smell a bit of tea tree but it's clean."

Tabatha took the bag and placed it over Roman's mouth. "There you are, just breath slowly."

"You've got to find cover," Scooter pressed. "Just because you got a man down, it's no excuse for the rest of you to stand around like a selection box of zombie biscuits. What you gonna do?"

"Run?" suggested Madison. "Zombies don't run very fast." She did an impression of a zombie staggering slowly as she growled.

"You dig," Scooter yelled. "That's what you do, you dig a defensive foxhole you can hide in until the reinforcements arrive."

"Okay," said Grayson. "Understood, but we don't *actually* have to dig, do we? I mean…" He looked around for his companions. "We get the idea, in a real zombie attack we would of course dig, but as this is just make-believe, we don't need to *actually* do it? Not for real?"

"Of course you need to dig," Scooter said, expression deadpan. "You have to feel it. First rule of survival, commit basic strategy to muscle memory."

"Oh." Grayson looked at the spade he held. "Right, well, digging then." He speared the spade at the ground and it sank into the soft earth.

The others watched him for a moment, then picked up their spades and started digging random holes about the area until Scooter, not so gently, suggested they all dig closer together.

I slid over to where Scooter stood, a few steps away from the hole digging. "A zombie foxhole?" I asked.

"Yeah, shush."

"But why—" I felt something dig me in the ribs, but Scooter seemed not to have moved.

We watched for a few minutes as they puffed and mumbled and the hole grew very slowly.

"Is that enough?" Theo leaned against his spade.

"Dunno," said Scooter. "Let's find out. All of you hide in the hole."

"What?"

"Hide in the hole, lie down so I can't see you."

"But it's muddy," protested Tabatha.

"One of the features of foxholes," said Scooter. "Another one is you lose any part of your anatomy stickin' out the top of one."

They bundled themselves together and squatted in the hole, trying to keep as much of themselves out of the mud as possible.

Scooter walked up the slope a bit. "I can still see you," he yelled.

They dug a bit more and repeated the exercise. Once more Scooter strode up the hill and turned, only this time, he aimed his paintball gun at them and took a couple of shots. Despite the squeals of protest, the paint pellets exploded harmlessly in the hole, but still close enough that the next phase of digging was a little more productive.

Eventually, Scooter seemed content with the hole. Persuading them all to duck low once more, he ran to various positions and fired shots at the hole. Although I could see quite clearly that he was aiming wide, the group became quite elated with what they'd achieved, and even more so when Scooter congratulated them.

"Pretty good," he said. "Especially for a bunch of sprogs. Couldn't get a clear shot at any of ya'."

Nobody queried why zombies would be shooting at them from a safe distance, and I didn't want to disturb the general feeling of success by pointing this out. We left the hole and Scooter led the way back to his headquarters while stopping every so often with orders to hide quickly. The group seemed to enjoy this.

"It's like hide-and-seek we used to play as children," said Madison. "Only without the creepy uncle who always used to hide in the wardrobe with us."

They ducked behind old walls, into bushes and under some old sheets of corrugated iron. By the time we arrived back at Scooter's headquarters, they were all fairly exhausted and, for the main part, covered in mud. More importantly, they seemed in great humour. Scooter had heaped praise on them, and they'd responded with enthusiasm each time.

When they eventually left, I asked Scooter, "Okay, just what was that all about?"

"Dunno what you mean." He started dismantling his paintball gun, meticulously wiping each part as he went.

"I mean the hole. Hiding from zombies in a hole?"

"Hmm, it's possible." He took an oily cloth and pushed it through the barrel with a thin probe. "And anyway, they seemed up for it."

"Come on," I pushed. "What are you up to?"

He shrugged. "I needed a big hole to drop that in." He nodded towards the bomb. "It's beginning to give me the willies havin' it around here."

After a quick lunch of baked beans and a fishcake in a burger bun, I decided I really needed to get to a proper supermarket. I was heading to the car park when I bumped into Wayne.

"You seen Jack?" he asked.

"No, is he here today?"

"He was here earlier. Jenna sent me to find him 'cause the TV guys are starting to do some filming for his book promo."

"I didn't know that was happening yet," I said.

"Yeah, they wanted to set up something with him making a camp in the woods. Or it might have been building a boat out of banana leaves…" He stopped in thought. "No, it was definitely a tree house. It might have been *in* a banana tree though, or made out of banana leaves. Anyway, he's gone walkabout, and I gotta find him."

"Have you looked in the Pirates Bay?" I asked.

"Why would he be there?"

"Because that's where the whisky is."

"Yeah, I can see where you're thinking. We'll give it a look."

"We? But I was going…" I was talking to air. I shrugged and followed him.

The Pirates Bay was hosting its Wednesday afternoon bingo session and teemed with people. I guessed a coach outing may well have been responsible. A man in a brown cardigan turned the ball jumbling machine and yelled out to be heard across the babble, "All the twos, two little ducks."

"Twenty-two," somebody nearby translated for him.

I picked my way between tables of white-haired ladies, pots of tea and plates of egg and tomato sandwiches. I spotted Jack quickly as his was the only singly occupied table and set some way back from the bingo-goers.

"Hi, Jack," I greeted as I sat down opposite him.

He looked up at me through slightly bleary eyes. "Oh, hello, erm... I want to say Ian?" He tilted his head in anticipation of my reply.

"Close, it's William," I said.

"Ah, yes." He swirled the last drop of whisky in his glass before emptying it. "You're the newspaper man."

"Not really. I used to sell advertising space for a newspaper until I upset the owner, Sir Robert Green, by running a four-page advert promoting the Green Socialist Coalition."

"Ah, Sir Robert Green, one of the New Kings, he gives greed a bad rap. I shared a few drinks with him one night."

"Yup, he lost his chance at a peerage and I lost my job. Now I sell books."

"Ah, but the tide of good fortune beckons, I write books. We should get together over a drink sometime." He looked into his empty glass. "Apparently, I'm bringing out a new one."

"What's it about?" I asked.

"I'm not really sure, I haven't read it yet. Join me in a quick one?" He waved his empty glass towards the bar and Ray noticed and nodded. Jack waved at the two of us, then held up three fingers. Ray nodded again.

"No," I said. "I need to get into town before the shops close."

"You know, when I was in Iraq, that was before it got popular with the Americans, I lived with the Jubur people. Special adviser, I was. I helped them create small raiding units, using modern weapons, and they taught me how to survive in God's ashpan where everything which moves wants to kill you. They also taught me how to drink arak. You ever tried arak?"

I shook my head.

"Good decision. It means sweat, in Arabic. Looks like milk and tastes like a mix of anise and jet fuel. Pretty much has the same effect too. Ah, here's the man." He looked up and smiled as Ray arrived.

Ray set a whisky in front of each of us and a plate of egg and tomato sandwiches in the centre of the table. "There ya' go," he said. "Sandwiches are on the house. We did too many for the bingo group and they only seem to want cake."

"Good health." Jack waved his glass at Ray and sank half of it, then turned back to me. "So, after years working in the most hostile environments on Earth, what do I do? I do encounter groups showing Life Coaches and Nail Technicians how to survive three days without an iPhone."

"Jenna's looking for you," said Wayne.

Jack cast his eyes around the bar. "She's not looking very hard, I've been here for…" He picked up his glass and studied it. "One or two."

"She's in the Sun Lounge with some bloke from the telly. She says to get your arse down there now."

"How does one resist an invitation like that?" Jack drained his glass.

Wayne drank his whisky quickly and winced as it bit him. I pushed mine to one side, hoping Jack wouldn't notice. I needn't have worried, Jack seemed to be having trouble standing and his attention was mostly focused on bringing his feet into line.

"You okay with him, Wayne?" I asked. "Only I've got to get to a supermarket."

Wayne looked at Jack, then turned to me. "To be honest, I could use a hand." He made sad panda eyes at me.

I sighed. "Okay, I'll just help to see he gets there, then I've got to go."

"Cool."

We walked slowly down The Yellow Brick Road, pausing every so often to nudge Jack back onto the correct path.

As we walked, I explained to Wayne the importance of this event to the survival of Rose Well Holiday Park.

"So what you're saying," Wayne reflected, "is that even with all the flying saucer stuff we did, Jenna's still going to have to sell the land?" he asked.

"Looks that way," I said.

"That's like heavy shit. There must be something. I really don't fancy trying to find somewhere new to live." He stopped dead as a thought struck him. "I'd have to pay rent."

"We have to up our game," I said, encouraging him to continue walking. If Jack stopped, there was a good chance we wouldn't get him moving again.

"What do you mean?" Wayne asked.

"We need to think of something bigger. Something that makes more of a bang. The initial interest will drop off soon, but if we give it a big boost, it will create its own momentum. Like a self-feeding machine."

"More of a bang, huh?"

I didn't like the look which caught in Wayne's expression but didn't have the chance to pursue it as we'd just arrived at the Sun Lounge and Jack was struggling to push the door open. I guided him out of the way and pulled it open for him.

"Ah, so glad you could finally join us," greeted Jenna. "Jack, this is Lionel, he's the producer for Ersatz Television Productions. He wants to film the introduction."

Lionel shook hands with Jack. "I'd like to see the place where you plan on building the erm, how do you call it, Bug Out Shelter? That is the term?"

"Bug Out Shelter?" Jack queried. "Oh, I can do that. When I was in—"

"Wayne," Jenna interrupted, "can you take Lionel and Jack down to Tinker's Wood?"

Wayne's face slipped into panic. "I gotta go. Scooter, I gotta see Scooter. Important stuff and things." He headed for the door.

"It won't take long, just show them onto the path, please? It's nearly on your way."

"Really love to, but urgent business, big sorry. William knows the way, he was there yesterday with Brian's lot." He dashed out of the door.

Jenna turned to me.

"No," I said. "I'm just on my way to the supermarket."

"Well. That's not really urgent, is it?"

"If you'd seen the state of my food cupboard, you wouldn't say that."

"Well, if you do this for me, I'll get supper for you later. Save you the trip into town. Deal?" She didn't wait for an answer and just slipped out of the door with a departing, "Now, I've got a bingo party to see to."

Lionel and Jack stared at me like a pair of lost puppies.

"This way," I said, reluctantly.

I followed the track down which Brian had taken us on his ill-fated foraging expedition. Jack stopped several times, mostly in search of a location for his Bug Out Shelter and once to relieve himself behind a bush. Eventually, he settled on a location he declared suitable, although I couldn't see it carried any differences to a dozen other locations we'd passed through.

Lionel set his portable camera rig on its stand and asked, "This is the location you've chosen for your Bug Out Shelter. Can you tell us why this particular spot?"

Jack stuffed his hands in his pockets and appeared to be looking for something. He came up empty and gave a slight scowl. "Well, you look here," he pointed to a dribble of a stream. "We've got water. The most important thing. Now we build uphill of the water, of course, just there on the flat bit. And the sun, that comes up over there so bringing warmth early. And you see there?" He pointed at some trees. "We can cut and weave those branches to form a canopy without having to create a structure. And then through there," he pointed at a trail leading down towards the cliffs, "if my calculations are correct, that track would eventually lead to The Smuggler's Arms in the village."

Lionel looked at the track and then at Jack. "How do you know that? You said you hadn't been here before."

Jack grinned. "It's my superpower."

Lionel did a couple of panning shots and some stills of Jack in the middle of the designated spot then we made our way back up to Rose Well Park. When we reached the top of The Yellow Brick Road, I peeled off towards Jenna's house and left them heading for the Pirates Bay.

Jenna must have heard me arrive as she yelled, "Door's open. Come on in."

I found her sat at the table at the end of the lounge. Random piles of papers scattered the table, and she peered at the screen of her laptop.

"Sorry, didn't realise you were busy. Do you want me to come back later?"

"No." She closed the laptop. "I was going through some numbers, I've been thinking about what you said."

"Which particular thing? Only I say lots of things and most of them, you probably shouldn't be paying any attention to."

"Your idea of doing something crazy like asking the bank for money to expand."

"That wasn't quite what I said, but okay."

She swung her chair round to face me. "Water. If Jejune think that selling Rose Well Spring water is a viable business, maybe I should be doing that. Cut them out and take it for myself. After all, the main spring is on my land."

"Your idea of getting yourself out of the financial soup is to take on a billion-pound multinational and steal their business idea?"

"Isn't that exactly what you did when you invested all your redundancy money in a bookshop in the middle of Atlas World Store's global domination phase?"

"Well, yes. But did I ever share with you how that worked out?"

"You might have mentioned it. But didn't you say we can only survive if we have obstacles to overcome?"

"Captain Kirk, actually." I settled on the sofa to ponder. "Okay, but you have no experience in selling water. Banks like experience, or at least some sort of track record in a similar field."

"Ah, but you see, in reality Jejune's business is not about selling water, they're actually in the business of selling plastic bottles. That's what they're *really* selling, water is just the excuse. That's why they wanted West Field, to build their bottle factory on. I won't be doing that. I'm thinking about tourism and I do have experience in tourism. The idea would be not to ship water all over the world in plastic bottles the way Jejune planned, but to get visitors to come here. Like a spa. This area has the highest longevity in the UK, you know?"

"I'd heard," I said. "Water tourism? There's a new concept."

"The locals put the longevity down to taking a little of the Rose Well Spring water each day. I've never paid too much attention to it, you know, local legends and so on. I've basically given the water away, people come and fill up their own bottles and I sell some nice pottery bottles to the tourists. But your idea—"

"Hang on, don't set me up for this."

"No, really, your idea to stop thinking about fixing the holes in what I've got, and instead to branch out into something different, really got me thinking. I could remarket Rose Well Holiday Park as a health resort. We could even have a Jacuzzi filled with Rose Well Spring water."

Her eyes seemed more alive than I'd seen her before. I studied this new side for a moment, then asked, "This is a change for you. What brought this on?"

"It was you. Watching your totally misguided confidence in your own plans time after time, and yet, you keep at it. I thought, maybe I need a bit more of that."

"Was that a compliment? Only I got a bit confused there."

She smiled. "Yes, let's go with that."

"Thank you, I think. Now, didn't you say something about doing supper?"

"I did indeed."

She disappeared into the kitchen and returned with a huge plate of egg and tomato sandwiches. "That'll keep you going, sorry, there's no cake though."

Chapter Twenty-One

STAYING OVER AT JENNA'S SEEMED to have become a bit of a regular thing. We drifted through shower, coffee and out of the door in a smooth ballet of movement that felt as if we'd been doing it for years.

I left Jenna on her way to the main office and then slipped away to find Scooter. Wayne's eagerness to hunt him down the day before had me worried. He looked like he had a plan, and I'd come to learn that Wayne with a plan was always something to be worried about. Even more so if that plan included Scooter.

I knocked on the door of Scooter's headquarters and breezed in. Four faces looked up at me in silence. Scooter was sprawled on his usual sofa with Wayne sitting opposite. Brian sat in the armchair and Gordon was perched on a wooden trunk.

"Hi, guys," I said. "Did I miss an invite?"

Scooter narrowed his eyes at me, Brian smiled but said nothing, Gordon turned his glance away and Wayne looked guilty, like a child who'd just been caught with his dad's porn collection.

I waited.

Wayne broke first. "We didn't think you'd go for it," he said.

"Go for what?" I asked, scanning the faces. Then I noticed the bomb-feature coffee table had gone. "And where's that gone?" I pointed at the empty space.

"We buried it," said Scooter. "In the hole those numpties of yours dug for me."

"I've said before, they're not my numpties, they're Jenna's numpties."

"And now we're going to explode it," said Wayne. "Like what you said."

"I said nothing of the kind," I said. "How is any of this down to me?"

"You said we needed a bigger bang," said Wayne.

"No, I didn't. Well… not in that context. I didn't mean a literal bang, as in exploding a World War Two bomb in the middle of a residential holiday home park. I was thinking more in terms of a publicity boost. A metaphorical bang. And why do I feel that if… sorry, *when* this all goes horribly wrong that, somehow, it will all be my fault?"

"What sort of publicity did you have in mind?" asked Brian.

"I don't know." I looked at the ceiling for inspiration. "Maybe something similar to what we did before, but just making sure that somebody important is there to witness it. Somebody credible, you know, like the mayor of Little Didney. I don't know."

"So we kidnap the mayor and then blow up the bomb in front of him?" asked Wayne.

"What? When did you hear me say anything about kidnapping the mayor? Do *not* kidnap the mayor."

Brian looked like a sad bloodhound. "But if we don't do something, Jenna will have to sell to that French water company and we'll all have to move out. We're too old to be starting out again. And all our friends…" He opened his arms, indicating the group.

I settled into an old fold-up director's chair. "Okay, but what made you think that exploding an old bomb would create enough interest to increase customers? Even supposing it could be exploded safely?"

"We rather thought that we might convince people it was a crashed UFO," said Gordon. "We were going to go round a few scrapyards to find any weird looking things and put them in with the bomb then set it off."

I thought about that for a moment. "So, leaving aside for a moment that you've just perfectly described a nail bomb, nobody's going to be fooled by that. Any engineer will spot it in five minutes, let alone a police forensic team, or whatever they'll send to look at it. We would need something unknown. Like the crash site at Roswell, New Mexico, it left some silvery material that nobody knew what it was."

The room fell silent and all the faces watched me. A slow dawning occurred. I'd been set up.

"So, what do you suggest?" Scooter asked.

"No, not me. I'm having nothing to do with bombs and fake spaceships. This is a different world now, it's not 1948 back-of-beyond yahoo country. We've got half a dozen universities with state-of-the-art science departments, all within a couple of hours' drive. This is going to take more than a couple of hubcaps and a sheet of tinfoil."

The room returned to silence, and all eyes watched me.

"What?" I asked. "What do you want me to say?"

"There must be something in one of your books," said Gordon. "People keep buying them because they present mysteries. Even with today's science, there are still mysteries out there which fascinate people. We need a mystery."

"They're not my books, I didn't write them. I haven't even read them, well most of them. I just sell them."

"But you're still the one best placed to come up with something convincing," Gordon said. "You have a pile of books full of stuff that's been puzzling people for years. This is our best bet, our only bet. We can make an explosion, but as you've pointed out, that doesn't make a mystery. We need a mystery to go with an explosion."

I looked round the room. The feeling of deflation sagged in the air like a blanket of mud.

"Okay," I said. "I'm not promising anything, but I'll go through some books and see if I can come up with an idea."

"Jolly good," said Brian. "I think that calls for a toast. Wayne, bring on the Elderberry Champagne, we're going to celebrate."

I sat at one of the wooden tables at the outside seating area of Big Moo Burger. My second coffee was starting to do the trick, but I was still not convinced I should tackle the burger just yet. I lifted the lid on it. Hungry as I was, the dripping cheese and tortured lettuce leaf which graced the burger inside, still brought a curl to my stomach. I replaced the lid and sank the rest of the coffee, with yet another silent oath to stay away from Brian's Elderberry Champagne. Especially before lunch.

Jenna appeared on the bench opposite me. "Early lunch?"

"I thought so." I poked the burger a few more inches away from me. "Not so sure now."

"There's still some egg and tomato sandwiches back at the house."

"I'm sure there are."

"You know you asked about a chap called Eric Scringle some while ago?"

"Yes, and you said you'd never heard of him."

"I lied," she said.

"There's a thing now." I gave her my special Roger Moore look. The one with the single eyebrow lift.

"I promised him not to tell anybody."

"So, what's changed?"

"Well, he's back. He arrived late last night. I spoke to him this morning, and he said it was okay to talk to you. As we're... sort of... you know, friends."

"Sort of friends?" I smiled. "I was wondering where we were in our relationship. Glad you've cleared that up."

"Don't be mean." She rabbit punched my arm. "I'm not very good at... you know..."

"Sort of friends stuff?"

"Whatever, anyway, he said I could tell you. So now you know. You going to eat that burger?"

"Not in this universe."

She grabbed the burger and took a bite. "I'm starving. Haven't stopped all morning."

"I'd like to meet him," I said. "You know he worked for the Ministry of Defence? He was their researcher into UFO stuff. Special Projects Office, Cheltenham, SPOC."

She thought for a moment, then, "But there's no K?"

"I know, SPOC."

"But that doesn't work?" she said. "Never mind, anyway, if you want to meet him, I'll see if I can fix it up. Bit of a fanboy, huh?"

"Not at all. I just think he'd be a really interesting person to talk to."

"Hmm, he is that alright, interesting." She pushed the burger back at me. "That's disgusting. I'll talk to Eric and get back to you." She disappeared off back into the main admin block.

I tossed the remains of the burger in a nearby bin and made my way back to my cabin for an afternoon of reading.

I awoke in the dark and for a moment, I thought I'd slept through the afternoon and into the night. It was only when the darkness slid off my face as I rose, that I realised I'd nodded off with a book on my face. A quick glance at the clock showed three, and my stomach reminded me I'd not eaten anything since breakfast.

I nipped out to Dolly's Daily Shop and treated myself to some Pot Noodles and a packet of cheese and onion crisps. I brought them back to the cabin to enjoy with a cup of tea and some chocolate digestives I found in the back of the cupboard. Not exactly cordon bleu, but infinitely better than the Big Moo Burger. As I ate, I went over the scrappy notes I'd made while reading. Alien abductions, flying saucers over the White House, impossible metals, crystal skulls, strange craft buzzing military jets, carvings of spacemen in ancient temples, pyramids on the moon, Sphinx on Mars, alien autopsy. It was all way beyond anything we could replicate. The only evidence that was any way close to something we could achieve were crop circles. I thought about that as I munched my crisps. No, that would never work. Most people thought they were fakes now anyway, they'd been so overdone. I even saw a picture of one with Homer Simpson in it.

I closed my notebook. This was hopeless. If I couldn't come up with an alternative plan, then Scooter was going to explode a pile of scrap metal and Wayne was going to kidnap the mayor.

That left Wilderness Jack and the Activity Holidays as the only viable lifeline to save Rose Well Holiday Park from bankruptcy and falling into the hands of Jejune Water. And me from having to return to London to find a proper job.

I needed to talk with Jenna and needed to tell her about the bomb. It was only fair. She'd trusted me with the revelation about Eric Scringle. I wasn't looking forward to that conversation. I steeled my fortitude and made my way to the Pirates Bay.

As it happened, my fortitude steeling was in vain as she was nowhere to be seen. Ray told me she'd gone down to Tinker's Wood to watch Wilderness Jack doing a segment for his promo film. I snatched a quick beer to re-steel everything and took to The Yellow Brick Road again.

The area Jack had identified previously now resembled a filmmaker's parody of itself. Bright lights and reflective shields surrounded the grove, making the branches and leaves somehow look like plastic imitations. The ground had been levelled and then spread with a sprinkling of leaves to disguise the earthworks. A pile of freshly cut branches lay in several piles to one side and arranged by size and bushiness. Lionel hovered in the background, watching as a technician carefully laid cables under the leaves while another tweaked the angles of reflective shields.

I spotted Jenna and sidled over to her.

"Oh, hiya," she greeted. "Come to watch?"

"Yes, this looks more complicated than I thought."

"Yes, I know. Apparently they have to do this because real life doesn't look good on TV. Who'd've thought?"

"Reality's over-rated, anyway. Where's Jack?"

She glanced around. "Dunno, Wayne's gone to look for him. I thought he'd be back by now."

"He's not in the Pirates Bay, I've just come from there."

"Whose idea was this?"

"Sorry, look," I braced myself. "I need to talk to you about something."

She turned to face me square on. "If you're going to drop another problem on me, now is probably not the best time."

"Hmm, it's not really a problem, as such. It's just something I thought you ought to be aware of. In fact, you could view it as sort of amusing, if you looked at it that way."

She narrowed her eyes. "Amusing as in the way that Last of the Summer Wine is sort of amusing or the way that little Korean dictator is?"

I nipped at my top lip. "The second one."

She folded her arms and set her jaw. "Go on."

"Well, it's about Scooter. They were digging under the old airfield and he discovered a bomb and—"

A crashing of branches of twigs and raised voices cut me off.

Jenna snapped round to see what was going on then looked back at me and touched my arm. "You'll have to tell me later. That looks like Jack's turned up." She slipped off in the direction of the noise.

I stood wondering if she'd actually heard my words and decided she hadn't on the basis I still had all my limbs. I'd try again later.

I followed the source of the distraction. Jack burst through the undergrowth behind the set, tripped on a hidden wire and brought one of the lights down in the centre of the neatly cleared set. He wobbled for a moment, then collapsed in a heap on top of the light. Another man followed him out of the trees.

"Sorry," said Jack.

One of the technicians rushed to help him up.

"Damned trip wire under there." Jack pointed to the ground as he stood. "You want to be careful of that. The Kachin used to do the same thing in Myanmar. You ever been to Myanmar, son?"

"No, sir," said the tech.

"Best not, place is a bloody mess." He turned to the man who'd followed him from the woods. "Oh, this is my good friend, Gavin."

"Gawan," corrected the man.

"Really? I found him in The Smuggler's Arms." Jack pointed to the gap through which they'd just emerged. "He didn't believe I knew a shortcut up to here." He turned to Gawan. "You owe me five quid."

The tech helped Jack and Gawan out of the set area and then set about tidying the chaos.

Jenna faced Jack and grabbed his upper arm and I thought I saw him flinch.

"Are you going to be able to do this?" she demanded.

"Did I ever tell you about the time—"

"I don't want to hear about when you were in the Alamo or leading the Charge of the Light Brigade into the Valley of Death. I just want to hear that you can hold it together for however long this takes. You hear me?"

I now felt reassured that this probably wasn't the time to be telling Jenna about Scooter's bomb and that fortune had given me a narrow pass.

Jenna came back over to me while keeping an eye on Jack. "Why did I let Wayne talk me into Jack as a celebrity? Couldn't we have got a Hairy Biker? Oh, yes, you were telling me something? Something about Scooter?"

"What? Oh, not important. We need to be quiet; I think they're starting."

She flashed a suspicious glance at me, but then turned to watch what was going on.

A young man dabbed something on Jack's face and straightened his clothes, then guided him to the centre of the set. The lights flashed into life and immediately, Jack seemed a different man. In control, composed and genial.

He explained to the camera how he was going to cut nicks into selected branches, then pull them down to weave into a roof. He picked up a couple of the pre-cut branches and knotted them together to demonstrate.

He spoke for about five minutes, then the cameras cut and the lights switched off. Jack wandered off to talk with Gawan, and a couple of men in overalls walked onto the set. They set down a couple of toolboxes and one of them took an electric saw to some of the overhead branches. I watched as between them, they worked smoothly and efficiently to build a smart looking shelter from the growing wood and the pile of pre-cut branches. Surprisingly, I noticed a fair amount of nail-gunning and nylon twine being used. Although, by the time it was finished, none of it showed.

Jack reappeared at the end and showed how he had constructed the perfect shelter from the natural environment and how strong it was. The camera then turned to a man and a woman who were introduced as Tim and Tracey, who were going to replicate what they'd just seen in a different part of the woods.

"Well, that's not what I expected," Jenna said. "It's all a fake."

"Shame on them," I said.

~ * ~ * ~ * ~

I walked with Jenna back up The Yellow Brick Road with no real sense of where I was going. We stopped at the split which led one way to my cabin and the other to Jenna's house.

"I'd invite you in for supper," I said. "But I've used up all my Pot Noodles."

"You'd better come and have supper at mine then. But you're cooking, I did it last night."

"The egg and tomato sandwiches?"

"You complaining about my cooking?"

"No."

"That's okay then."

As it turned out, Jenna's food cupboard was in no better condition than my own. We phoned in for a pizza.

We sat on the sofa, balancing beer and pizza slices while watching some quiz show where contestants had to answer questions while negotiating an obstacle course.

"Oh, I contacted Eric, he says you can pop down to see him anytime," Jenna said.

"Thanks. Maybe in the morning?"

"If you like. You seem keen."

"I was talking with the guys this morning. We need some new ideas to boost this UFO thing. He might be able to help."

"From what I understand, he's been in hiding for quite a few years, so I doubt publicity stunts are really his area of expertise."

"I know, but he might have an idea or two," I said. "We just need a bit more of a boost and it will really catch. I know it will."

"Okay, I'll fix it up, but I need a favour in return. The bank are actually considering the expansion idea. I can't believe it, they must be mad. Problem is though, they want a business plan and I haven't the faintest idea how to do that."

"Sure, I can do that. I've done quite a few over the years."

"But didn't your business go pop?"

"Yes, but the banks always said how nice my business plans were."

We watched a bit more television, drank a few strange samples that various brewery reps had left behind, and somehow ended up in bed together again.

Jenna switched the light off as we settled for sleep, and I searched the dark for clues as to what we were doing. I tried to decide if this could conceivably be called a relationship or was it just two lonely people colliding occasionally? Two lost souls, as somebody once wrote.

The light burst back into life, startling my eyes. I squeezed them shut and waited while the colours exploded across the insides of my eyelids.

I heard Jenna say, "Did you say something about Scooter having a bomb?"

"No," I said, possibly a bit too quickly.

"That's okay then."

A click and the room returned to darkness. I let out a long breath as silently as I could.

Chapter Twenty-Two

WHILE JENNA DEALT WITH A food delivery in the morning, I spent an hour watching the two foils for Wilderness Jack's promo building their own version of the shelter. Jack was nowhere to be seen, but filming stopped at strategic points where I guessed his contributions would be edited in. The first attempt at the build seemed to be purposefully poor as one of them then leaned on it and it collapsed. Another cut away and rebuilding commenced. I assumed that was the comic relief part and Jack would insert suitably acerbic comments at that point.

My phone bleeped with a message from Jenna telling me to meet her at The Yellow Brick Road east shower block. She was just coming down the track when I arrived.

"Eric's cabin is down here," she said. "Lower Bermuda."

She led me through the maze of little paths between rows of cabins which, while all quite elegant and beautifully kept, all looked exactly the same. We stopped in front of one such innocuous home and she tapped on the door.

"Eric?" Jenna said. "It's me, Jenna."

I didn't hear the returning mumble but Jenna said, "I've got William with me, he's alright."

The door closed again, and I heard the rattling of a chain before it opened wide. Eric remained hidden behind the opened door and it wasn't until we were inside and he'd closed the door again that I first saw him. He stood a touch shorter than me, maybe about five ten or eleven and probably ten years younger. He was slightly built with a pallor to his skin which told of his preference for hiding.

"Lovely to meet you," I said. "I heard you'd disappeared?"

"Only from your perspective," he said.

"I saw William had your book on your stand his first day here," Jenna explained. "But I couldn't say anything."

I looked around the room. The walls strained under the array of bookshelves. A quick scan revealed an eclectic mix, including some of the same titles I carried, although most were leaning towards the Hard Sciences rather than New Age. Names such as Stephen Hawking, Neil deGrasse Tyson, Michio Kaku and Brian Cox dominated but popularists like Asimov also nestled in amongst Newton and even Plato.

Eric noticed my interest and said, "Ah, a fellow bibliophile. Jenna told me you deal in books."

"Not really," I said. "I used to have a bookshop before Atlas World Store came along and stole all my customers. But the liquidators were kind enough to leave me my stock of books. No value to the creditors, apparently. So now I sell them off one at a time."

Eric shrugged. "Sad, but ultimately, it's the information which is of value. The medium of the delivery is simply one of convenience or personal inclination."

I chose not to get into that discussion. "So, did you really run off with a bit of a space toilet belonging to the European Space Agency, or was that just a rumour put out?"

Eric studied me, then asked, "Did you read The God Machines?"

I knew I should have read his book before the meeting. "Well, not as in start to finish. It's one of those books which one dips in and out of. It's so full of information, too much to take in at once."

"So, no then?"

"I ran a bookshop. I didn't really have time to read."

"I see." He nodded slowly. "Well, in answer to your question, no, I didn't run off with a bit of a space toilet. I acquired a couple of bits of technology from an alien craft which crash landed at Rendlesham in 1980. They'd had it in the back of a cupboard for years, I thought nobody would miss it."

"What happened to it?"

His eyes scanned the room. "I think it's still here, somewhere. Would you like a cup of tea? I've just made a pot."

"Tea? What? Yes, tea? Sorry," I struggled to find the appropriate response. "You have a piece of a UFO here, somewhere, and we're talking about tea?" I sank into a nearby chair.

"To be honest, I don't tend to pay it much regard," Eric said. "After a while, the novelty wears off, a bit like a new pair of shoes. And, we usually referred to it as a CUO, a craft of unknown origin, rather than a UFO. The term UFO implies it's both unidentified and flying. And as the MOD knew perfectly well what it was, and it certainly wasn't flying when they found it, the term UFO was somewhat redundant."

"Have you ever met Gordon?" I asked.

"Briefly, why?"

"Never mind. And you said it's in here, a piece of an alien spacecraft? It's actually here?" I looked around the room.

"Hmm? Oh, yes." He waggled a carton of milk in my direction. "Milk?"

"Yes, milk. Thank you." I looked again at Eric. He looked like every office clerk I'd ever seen and should be in charge of the stationery cupboard in a planning office somewhere in Chipping Sodbury, not running around with bits of stolen ESA technology, or alien hardware. Or whatever it was he had.

"Do you think I could see it?" I asked.

"If I can find it." He handed me a mug with a science joke on it about the periodic table, which I didn't understand. "I hope I didn't put too much milk in."

"Not at all." I looked at the pale liquid in the mug.

He opened the fridge and handed Jenna a bottle of Budweiser. I felt a twinge of envy while I nursed my warm milk.

"Jenna's allergic to tea," he explained.

I glanced at Jenna and she gave me the narrowed eyes and thin smile which said, 'Say nothing'.

Eric stood in the centre of the room, put a finger to his chin and turned in a small circle as he contemplated. "That's odd," he said. "I was sure I'd put it on that cupboard." His finger flipped from chin to aim at the cupboard in question. "Maybe I put it under the bed? I do tend to put a lot of things under the bed." He inclined his head as if that would help see under the bed. "Maybe not."

I had visions of this going on for some time and dropped to my knees. The space under the bed confirmed that he tended to put a lot of things there. Mostly books and bundles of magazine, but nothing even vaguely resembling a space toilet. "Nothing here," I said.

"That's a nuisance."

I straightened up to the accompaniment of clicking noises in my knees. "How big is it?"

He rubbed at his head and pursed his lips. "Hmm, about the size of that box there." He pointed to a cardboard box perched on the top of the fridge.

"Could it *be* in that box?" I asked.

"It's a possibility." He took the box from the fridge and dumped it onto the floor. "Ah, yes. Here it is." He lifted a square, bronze coloured object clear of the box and set it on the sofa. It was a square shape, about the size of a small microwave oven, longer than it was high. Each face shone metallic bronze and silvery tubes formed the joins where the faces met. On the top sat a bright red semi-spheroid, looking a bit like half a bowling ball. Apart from that, it was featureless, with no obvious means of access or function.

"It doesn't look much like a space toilet," I said. "Do you mind?" I reached for the object.

"Go ahead," said Eric. "Just don't touch the phase-link couplings or it will eject the warp core."

My hands froze half an inch from the surface. "Huh?"

"Just kidding," Eric said. "It's my little Star Trek joke."

I let out my caught breath and said, "What does it do?"

"It makes omelettes," Eric said.

Jenna noticed my look of surprise and added, "Very nice omelettes though."

"Omelettes?" I hesitantly touched the cuboid, half expecting the warp coil, or whatever it was, to eject itself onto the carpet. It didn't. "Hardly a useful feature on a space toilet, omelettes."

"As I said, it's not a space toilet." Eric's voice tightened with irritation. "It came from that alien crash site."

I pushed at random panels on the object. "How does it work?"

Eric opened the fridge and passed me a box of eggs. "Just rest your hand on the round bit on the top."

"Shouldn't you plug it in first or something?"

"No, just do what I say."

I very slowly placed the palm of my hand over the red sphere, as I was told. I felt a slight tingle under my hand and then nothing. I snatched my hand away thinking I'd lost sensation but immediately noticed the red semi-sphere had opened up and was now just a narrow ring encircling a hole. "Okay," I said. "What now?"

"Chuck a couple of eggs in the top," said Eric.

I picked an egg out of the box. "You got something I can crack it in?"

"No need, just drop it in the top."

"Shell and all?"

"Shell and all."

I did as instructed and followed it with a second. "Now what?"

"Wait a moment."

After a few seconds, the front of the box slid open and ejected what looked like a small omelette out onto the sofa. The gap closed and went back to being a plain bronze panel.

I touched the omelette. It felt cold. "That's weird," I said.

"Yes, I haven't figured out if there's a temperature setting or something yet," Eric said. "Try it."

"Really?"

"Yes, it won't hurt you, it's only an omelette."

I broke a corner off, sniffed it, then popped it into my mouth. It tasted vaguely omelettey but then, it was so bland it could just as easily have been tofu or even polystyrene.

"And that's all it does?" I asked. "It makes omelettes?"

"Very nice omelettes," Jenna reminded me.

"Yes, you mentioned that. Why would aliens, if that's what they really are, lug an omelette machine around the galaxy? Haven't they heard of frying pans?"

"Because we don't know that's what they used it for." Eric took the machine and placed it back in its box. "You see, it could quite conceivably be a space toilet. Just not one of ours."

"I don't understand?"

"Well, I demonstrated with eggs and it produced a passable omelette. The reality is, it doesn't matter what you put in, as long as it has a biological base, it comes out the same. You could just as easily have put in potatoes or leaf mulch. It always comes out the same. Human waste even."

"Then why did you give me eggs to put in?"

"Just so the end product would be acceptable to you. If I'd taken a handful of three-day-old food scraps from the rubbish bin, would you have eaten it?"

"No."

"There you are then. It's the ultimate recycling machine."

"What do you plan on doing with it?" I asked.

"Jenna told me you always have lots of questions." He smiled. "What

~ 234 ~

can I do? I took it as proof of alien technology. But if I try to do anything with it, both it, and I, will disappear faster than an election promise. Very naively, I wanted to show the world what's being kept from them. Unfortunately, I didn't think through what to do with it once I'd taken it. As far as the world is concerned, I've stolen a prototype space toilet and the moment I show my face, I'm going to disappear and so is this. On the other hand, what good was it doing hidden in the back of a cupboard?"

"What about presenting it to a university or something? Publicly like, so they could investigate properly and prove what it is?"

"An idea, but ignoring the obvious problem of finding a university who would take it without contacting the D.O.D., what do you think they would actually do with it? Give a cat to a scientist and ask him to figure out how it works and the first thing you get, is a dead cat. They'd take it apart, and if they didn't destroy it in the process, the government would sequester the technology, firstly for any military advantage, and secondly, for profit."

"So you're just going to keep it in a box and carry on hiding?"

"For the time being." He lifted the box back on top of the fridge. "Jenna tells me you need some advice?"

I explained the situation to Eric and how if we didn't come up with a way of generating more customers, then Rose Well Holiday Park was going to close.

"Oh, dear," he said. "That will never do. This is my main hideaway. No, no, no, we can't let that happen. What help can I be? Observing of course, my continuing need for anonymity."

I shifted on my seat while I tried to work out how to explain about our fake UFO show to the man, who until a few years ago, had been head of the MOD's UFO debunking team.

Jenna noticed my discomfort. "He does know about the fake UFO show, so it's okay."

"Really?" I asked. "You told him?"

Jenna shook her head.

"No," confirmed Eric. "She kept your secret safe. But, despite my exile,

I do of course retain an interest in all things UFO related. And when I saw Rose Well Park come up in the news in relation to a sighting, well of course my interest was piqued. Not for long, I hasten to add, it was clear to me from the off what you were doing. Although of course, at the time, I had no idea why. It's one of the reasons I came back here now. Good show by the way. It seemed to have the media going."

"Thank you," I said. "Although, to be honest, I do feel a bit... uncomfortable about it. I know it's a bit iffy, deceiving people into believing the UFOs are real when of course they're not."

His look reminded me of a maths teacher I'd once had when I'd argued that algebra had no basis in the real world, so what was the point of learning it.

"Or you could look at it like this," he said. "What's more disingenuous? Tricking a handful of people that a fake UFO is real, or tricking the world that real UFOs are fakes? A career to which I devoted a significant part of my life. I would suggest that the latter is, by far and away, the more significant lie. For if that truth were known, it would change the reality of every human on the planet. All you are doing, is leading a handful of people into believing a greater truth."

"Okay, let's say I go with that. If you wanted to set up a realistic UFO sighting, one which would be really convincing, how would you do it?"

"Hmm, well contrary to what one might think, big is not best. Huge special effects or complicated models are usually quite easily exposed. Your balloons, for instance, they just don't move through the air the way a heavier-than-air vehicle would. Balloons vibrate in the micro-turbulence of air. Not difficult to spot when one knows where to look. No, it's the oddities which are the most convincing. Those little conundrums which defy logic. Have you ever seen Ghirlandaio's Madonna with Saint Giovannino? It's a fifteenth century painting with a UFO clearly in the background. Even people pointing at it."

"How does that help?" I asked. "We can't do anything like that."

"Because it's a puzzle, and puzzles persist. Take the Rendlesham incident. That little trace of radioactivity that somebody found after the clean-up team were supposed to have done their job. That's what turned it from an everyday story of somebody seeing something weird into a major conspiracy theory. How about Robert Taylor's torn trousers in the Livingston Incident? That one even ended up in a police crime report. Then we have anachronisms, they're always good for stirring up intrigue. Like the Swiss watch in the Chinese tomb? Or the Antikythera device? Things which are clearly out of their time and shouldn't exist, yet there they are."

"So we create something odd and out of place. How do we get people to notice?"

"Ay, there's the rub. You'll need to come up with an attention getter to point the curious eyes in the right direction."

"An attention getter? What would you suggest?"

"Oh, I haven't the faintest idea. I'm afraid I will have to leave that one in your hands. Attracting attention is something to which I devote a good deal of my time to avoiding."

We chatted a bit more about Rose Well Park, Jejune Water and craft beers, then Jenna said we should be going as she still needed to work on her business plan for the bank.

We twisted through the little paths leading out of Lower Bermuda and onto The Yellow Brick Road. I stopped at the crossroads with Route 67.

"I'm going to find Scooter and Wayne," I said. "I need to run some ideas past them."

"Why do I worry every time you talk about ideas?" she asked.

"I don't know, it must be something deep in your subconscious, a leftover from your childhood. These things usually are."

"Or it could be that you seem to get most of your ideas out of a Road Runner cartoon?"

"Ah, Wile E. Coyote, my role model." I smiled. "Catch you later." I took a couple of steps down Route 67, then stopped and turned. "Oh, about last night—"

"Oh, here we go." She turned square on and frowned. "You didn't have to, you know. Nobody forced you, you could have said no."

"No, not that. That was… well, maybe we'll talk about that later. What I meant was, when you asked me if Scooter had a bomb…"

"Yeeess?"

"I might have got a bit confused when I said he didn't have one."

Chapter Twenty-Three

I HAD TROUBLE KEEPING UP with Jenna as she marched with the determination of an invading army. I was actually beginning to fear for Scooter's safety.

"I wasn't going to say anything," I said. "I was worried you might over-react."

She stopped so abruptly I nearly collided with her. "You think? And just how was I supposed to react to the information that a misanthropic ex-squaddie with PTSD and an attitude problem is sitting on a bomb in my holiday park?"

"Well, to be fair, he's not actually sitting on it. Well not anymore. I think they've buried it now."

"Not helping." She spun one-eighty and continued her march.

I hurried behind her while trying to explain the story behind the bomb.

As we approached Scooter's headquarters, Jenna yelled, "Scooter? I want a word with you."

By the time we entered the building, both Scooter and Wayne were pressed with their backs against the far wall, looking for all the world like a pair of victims lined up for the firing squad.

Brian stood and said, "I think I should be going. I think I left the gas on."

Jenna glared at him. "Stay put." Then without looking, she pointed to her left, directly at Gordon who seemed to be getting ready to make a break for it. "Where are you going?"

I approached Jenna with the intent of trying to calm her. She made a noise which sounded distinctly like a snarl. I retreated again.

"Where's the bomb?" Her eyes skewered Scooter in position.

"What b—" Scooter started.

"Don't even *try* that on me. I didn't get breakfast and I'm running on coffee."

"It's gone," Scooter said. "We buried it."

"Oh, good. So basically, you've turned it into a landmine and somehow you think that's a better idea?"

Scooter shrugged. "It's too big to be a landmine. They only use..." he paused as he realised where that was going. "We can dig it up again?"

For a moment, Jenna seemed lost for words.

I chose the moment to speak. "We have a plan for it."

Jenna spun round to stare at me. "You do?"

"We do?" I heard Scooter ask.

"Yes." In truth, at that moment, my ideas were only in a fledgling state, but I needed to say something quick to prevent bloodshed.

"After earlier." I tried to wink at Jenna, but she just looked angrier. "When we talked with... you know." I pointed in the direction of Eric's cabin. "About the..." I waited.

"Oh, you mean..." Jenna pointed in a direction about forty-five degrees off where I had aimed.

"Really?"

"Uh-huh." Jenna nodded. "So, let's hear it?" Her eyes challenged me.

"Well," my brain raced, trying to slot together a series of disparate ideas that were nebulous at best. "We just need one more bump to stimulate interest and the intrigue will roll along. Like 9/11."

"9/11?" Jenna looked at me. "I ask you for ideas as to how to get rid of a bomb and you use 9/11 as the basis for your idea?"

"Ah, yes, I can see how that might have come across. Bad example. I meant the conspiracy theories surrounding it. How they keep popping up, like whack-a-mole. I wasn't meaning the explosion part. Say, like the Kennedy assassination?"

"More death and mayhem?" Jenna asked. "Just get on with your idea. Heaven help us."

"Right, so rather than trying to create a single, unexplainable event, like we did before, we need a series of little puzzles. They're much harder to debunk. Like the Moon Landings. As soon as somebody debunks one element of that conspiracy theory, another pops up. What about the boot print? What about the waving flag? Or the wrong shadows? It just goes round. That's what we need. There's a shelf full of books on that one alone."

"We're going to fake another moon landing?" Wayne asked.

"What? No," I said. "Just an example of building small elements."

"Probably best if we bypass the examples and proceed along with your idea?" suggested Brian.

"That's what I've been trying to do. Anachronisms, things out of time. We can do that." I drew a deep breath and looked at Jenna. "Now, just bear with me. Firstly, we use the bomb to create an explosion then—"

"And just how do you propose doing that?" Jenna interrupted.

"That's one of the more nebulous parts of my plan. But we can work it out."

Jenna walked in a tight circle. Like a tight whirlwind building to a massive twister readying to destroy everything nearby.

I tried to ignore her and continued, "So, explosion. The police send in somebody to investigate, as they are bound to, and what do they find?"

"Bits of a bomb and a big hole in the ground," suggested Scooter.

"Yes, but they also find things which shouldn't be there. Anachronisms which can't be explained."

"Like mutant tarantulas," suggested Wayne.

"What?" I turned to look at him.

"Mutant tarantulas, they'd be anachronis… whatsits which couldn't be explained."

"No, they'd be arachnoids. I'm talking about anachronisms. Something like finding a stone age axe down the back of your sofa."

The room turned to silence and everybody looked at me.

"What?" I asked.

"Where are we going to get a stone age axe?" asked Scooter.

"Down the back of William's sofa, apparently," suggested Jenna. She gave a mischievous smile and looked at me. "Go on, it's your idea, heaven help us. What do you propose?"

I raced through the conversation with Eric, grasping at twigs of ideas. "Scooter mentioned there's some old spare parts of World War Two planes down in one of the tunnels." I looked at Scooter for support.

Scooter shrugged. "Yeah, loads of junk down there. So what?"

"What if there's an explosion—"

"Here we go again," said Jenna.

"No, stay with me. There's an explosion in the middle of West Field. The police come to investigate and they find a hole with bits of a World War Two plane and traces of a wartime bomb."

Silence again.

Gordon finally spoke. "There's something in that," he said. "They're new parts, it could look like a newish plane had crashed. A new World War Two plane crashing would certainly raise a few eyebrows."

I smiled and held my hand towards Gordon. "There we go. That. What he said."

"But that, on its own wouldn't do it," Gordon continued.

"How about radiation," I said, remembering the conversation with Eric about Rendlesham. "How do we make radiation?"

"You're not exploding an atomic bomb," said Jenna. "We're going to call that a hard limit."

"Cool," said Scooter. Jenna glared at him.

"That's not too difficult," said Gordon. "Dolly's got some old-style paraffin pressure lanterns in her shop. They used thorium in the mantles until quite recently." Gordon's eyes trawled the blank stares. "Thorium, it's a radioactive material."

"In paraffin lamps?" I queried.

"Yes, you can still buy them, although most are different now. I'll bet she's got enough of the old type in there to make a significant reading on a Geiger Counter."

"Radioactive material in my camp shop?" asked Jenna.

"Yes," said Gordon. "It'll be in most of the smoke detectors you have in the cabins as well. But it wouldn't be as easy to get at there. And bananas."

Jenna shook her head. "I always knew this place was heading for being a disaster area, but I didn't expect it to turn into another Chernobyl quite so quickly."

"It's only traces," Gordon said. "Nothing to worry about... Mostly."

"Okay," I said, trying to get focus back. "We have an explosion, an anachronism, and a radioactive trace. I think we have a plan."

"How do we make sure it gets noticed?" asked Brian.

"We need some credible witnesses."

"What about Jack?" Wayne said. "Ain't he got his book promo filming thing soon? He'll have a whole load o' people tromping around then. Betcha."

I waited for alternatives. None appeared. "That's it then, we do this on the day of filming of Jack's book promo video. He'll be so pleased."

Jenna and I left the others to work out their bits, and we headed back to Downtown.

"I can't believe I let you me talk me into this," Jenna said as we picked our way back along the path. "I thought we were going to work on my business plan, and the next thing I know, you lot are planning on exploding an atomic bomb."

"It's not an atomic bomb. Just traces. Gordon said so. And we do the business plan now so when the bank get it, they can see Rose Well Holiday Park is already on the up."

"Hmm, and how are they going to explode the bomb?"

"I don't know. Scooter will figure something out." Even as I said the words, I didn't like the sound of it.

That evening, Jenna was on duty in the Pirates Bay, so I chose to eat there rather than trying to work out how to create a meal from a tin of peas, a packet of Jammy Dodgers and a tub of margarine. Which was all I had in my food cupboard. The chalkboard behind the bar announced the menu of the day as Chicken Stroganoff and salad, which seemed far more appetising. I took my wooden spoon to a table and settled to watch the band setting up their gear for the evening's entertainment. A poster on the side of the stage advertised them as The Spartanites, so I guessed they were a tribute band to Jim Sullivan's Spartans. This was probably going to get noisy fairly shortly. By the time my Chicken Stroganoff arrived, the place was already filling up with ageing rockers and the band were on their sound check. I took my food and moved as far back into the bar as I could. For a while, the sounds emanating from the stage faded into the distance, but I knew things were going to deteriorate when someone grabbed a microphone and yelled, "Can ya hear me at the back?"

I looked up from my plate and called, "Yes, unfortunately." But it was lost in the general hubbub.

I tried to ignore the world outside my table and focused on eating and leaving as quickly as possible. That went well until I was just about to leave when Gordon plopped himself into the seat opposite me and pushed a beer in my direction.

"Brought you one of these," he said. "Looked like you needed it."

I resisted the temptation to tell him that what I *really* needed was to get out of here as quickly as possible but instead, just said, "Thanks."

"I've been playing with the ideas you came up with." Gordon

rummaged in a brown leather satchel he carried. "What do you think of this?" He planted a large black-and-white photograph on the table.

I studied it as I ate. A row of RAF personnel posed in front of a World War Two plane. It looked like a bomber but my knowledge of these things was entirely based on the Dambusters movie and it didn't look like one of those.

I pushed the photo back to him. "Picture of a bomber crew from the war?"

Gordon looked excited, like a cheap quiz show host, itching to tell the contestant the easy answer. "Look more closely."

I took another fork of stroganoff and pulled the photo back. It looked like hundreds of these things. The air crew, the techie guys and an aeroplane. I guessed these were de rigueur before a mission in those days.

"What am I supposed to be seeing?"

"Look at the surroundings."

I studied the background. A couple of reinforced hangars in an area of flat ground with a rising hill in the distance. Then it dawned. "Is that here? Carter's Field?"

Gordon brightened. "Yes, the airfield in the war."

"Okay, interesting historical picture. But why?"

"Now look at the people. The faces."

I took the last of the stroganoff and pushed the plate to one side, replacing it with the photograph. Young men, some moustachioed, all with serious expressions.

"I'm not sure what you want me to see." I squinted at it more closely. "Although…" I homed in on one face. "That guy looks a bit like David Cameron. Is it his father or something? Is that what I'm supposed to be seeing?"

Gordon smiled. "Exactly, except…" he paused to build anticipation during which time the band decided to run another sound check. This time on the drums.

We waited while they finished, then I said, "You were saying?"

"It *is* David Cameron." He sat back with a self-satisfied smile on his face.

I stared at the picture again. "But that's impossible. It must be a relation. Although, it really does look like him."

"That's because it *is* him."

"That's ridiculous. How could he be in a World War Two aircrew photo? He hasn't even aged?"

"You wanted an anachronism, well, there it is."

I pondered this, then looked at the photo again, turned it over. "Is this a copy of an original?"

"No, I just mocked this up this afternoon. It's only a rush job. Amazing what computers can do."

"It's certainly impressive. It would have me fooled."

"It needs to be better though. I can use older paper and then age it a bit using coffee."

"Coffee?"

"Yes, smear the paper in coffee, then bake it a few minutes. It would take an expert to spot it's a fake."

I turned the paper over a few times and squinted at the image of David Cameron in his RAF uniform. "But what happens when the expert delivers his verdict?"

"By that time, the conspiracy theory will be unstoppable. Having an expert denounce it only adds fuel to the theory. Look how many times 9/11 theories have been denounced by experts."

I noticed Jenna heading in our direction. "Shush, here comes Jenna, don't mention 9/11. I did once, but I think I got away with it."

Gordon grinned at the reference and I tried to suppress mine.

"So, what are you two finding so amusing?" Jenna asked as she sat down.

I pushed the photograph to her.

She picked it up and gave it a quick scan. "What the... that's Carter's field." Her eyes widened and she looked up at us. "How..." She studied the photo again. "And... no, it can't be... That's David Cameron! What the hell is David Cameron doing in a picture of a Second World War bomber crew?"

"There you go," said Gordon.

~ * ~ * ~ * ~

On Jenna's promise of cake, I went back to her house to help with the business plan.

"So, how come you know so much about drawing up business plans?" She leaned over my shoulder as I tapped numbers into a spreadsheet.

"Practice," I said. "You got any more of that cake? It's really unusual."

"It's got Cointreau and whisky in it. It's a fiftieth anniversary cake we baked for a couple on holiday. Apparently they're their favourite drinks."

"How come we're eating it?"

"They fell out big time last night." Jenna dropped a plate with more cake in front of me. "She bought him a gold eternity ring, he bought her a spice rack."

"Ah, I can see how that would do it. When did you take over this place?"

"Umm, 1992. How many of these business plans have you done?"

"I don't know, lost count. A least one every six months all the time I had the bookshop."

"I'm guessing your bank didn't like them. Which begs the question, why am I allowing you to do mine?"

"On the contrary." I pushed back from the screen and rubbed the numbers from my eyes. "They loved them, they kept lending me more money."

"So how come you went bankrupt?" Jenna licked sticky cake from her fingers.

"Because they kept lending me more money." I picked up the last bit of cake and tried, without success, to eat it without making a mess. "Getting banks to lend you money is easy, that's their raison d'être. It's the paying it back which is tricky."

"Why do I listen to you?"

"Funny, that's what Edward used to say. He was my personal business manager at the bank. You and he would get on. Mind you, I think he's flipping burgers in McDonald's now."

"Are you sure persuading the bank to lend me more money is altogether wise? I mean, isn't that basically what Icarus Airlines did before they left their passengers scattered all over the world?"

"This is different. This is a Planned Programme of Expansion." I pointed to the title at the top of the spreadsheet. "See? It says so there. Anyway, it was your idea to expand into Water Tourism, I just progressed your basic idea a bit."

She leaned over and studied the screen. "But this says I'm planning on buying West Field from Jejune? I never said that. That's insane."

"We have to show the bank you're planning to acquire assets. Banks like assets. It makes them feel secure."

"But I'll never be able to afford that. Jejune paid a fortune for that."

"Don't worry so much." I turned away from the computer to face her. "Once you've got the money, you don't necessarily have to buy the field. You can use the money for advertising and doing up the site."

"So why don't we tell the bank that's what I want the money for?"

"Don't be daft," I said. "They'll never lend you money for that. You have to do big and bold, that's how to get banks to lend money. Look at Arcadia."

"Didn't they go pop as well?"

"Quite spectacularly, but they did get the loans." I closed the lid on the laptop. "Anyway, I've just submitted that business plan for you. You can thank me later. Or now, if you like?"

Chapter Twenty-Four

JENNA HAD HER USUAL BREAKFAST of two coffees and a shout at the radio news, while, in the absence of any more substantial breakfast items in her kitchen, I braved a '*Breakfast-in-a-bun*' from Big Moo Burger. The runny egg and fat from the bacon soaked into the bread roll and the whole thing fell apart in my lap. On the upside, the squirrels did okay.

I needed to find out from Jack when he was doing his book promo filming and, after a search of Rose Well Park came up empty, I finally tracked him down in The Smuggler's Arms in the village.

"Ah, William," he greeted as I approached his table. Despite the early hour, he had already managed to accumulate a sizable audience and a fair selection of empty glasses. "Come and join me, good boy." He waved his hand to point me at an empty seat. "Everybody, this is William, he's okay. William is a book expert, and he's helping me. Sit yourself down and join me in a jar of ale."

"No thanks, bit early for me." I sat, and a beer appeared in front of me. "I only stopped by to find out if you had a fixed date for your book launch."

"Yes, my agent called last night. All sorted. Where's that chap with my pastie?"

"So, when is it?" I persisted.

"What?"

"Your promo filming."

"Ah, yes. We had to change it as I'm off to host the new series of Celebrity Deathcamp. This one's in the Congo. Only country who'd allow it after last year's little contretemps, apparently."

"That will be nice. So when is it, your book launch?"

Jack thought for a moment. "Tuesday."

"Tuesday when?" I asked.

"Next Tuesday. Ah, here's the man with the pastie. Do you know they serve the best pasties in Cornwall here?" he addressed his fan club.

"But that's… That's Tuesday," I said. "We can't possibly get ready by Tuesday."

Jack patted my arm. "No worries. You don't have to do anything. My agent's got it all in hand. You just have to turn up for the drinks at the end."

"But you don't understand." I stood, took a token sip of the beer, and said, "I've got to go. Sorry, all. Catch you later, Jack."

~ * ~ * ~ * ~

I'd hoped to find our full UFO crew at Scooter's headquarters. As it turned out, Scooter and Wayne were the only ones there. Scooter was busy taking pot-shots at beer cans with his paintball rifle. Wayne, showing remarkable confidence in Scooter's marksmanship, stood close by and re-stood the cans each time they fell.

"Tuesday," I said as I approached. "It's Tuesday."

"Saturday," said Wayne. "Easily done. I once confused the whole of September for July. I still don't know what happened to August."

"No, I didn't mean today's Tuesday. I meant Jack's promo filming is on Tuesday. That only gives us a couple of days to set up our stuff."

"Alright," said Scooter, splatting another can. "I'm on it."

"What do you mean?" I asked.

"Getting in my aim." He waggled his gun in the air.

"For what? Who are you planning on shooting?"

"The bomb," he said. "I'm gonna shoot the nose plug. That's the bit which makes it go bang."

"With your paintball gun?"

"Yup. Unless you fancy belting it with a hammer. But I wouldn't recommend that unless you can run *really* quickly."

I studied the collection of paint spattered cans, then looked at Wayne. He had a matching pair of splats on his camouflage jacket. "And you can hit it from far enough away to be safe?"

Scooter shrugged. "Dunno, I'm gonna give it a go."

"Will the impact be enough to set it off?"

"Dunno."

"How far away do we have to be to be safe?"

"I'm gonna say… dunno."

"Can't you set up some sort of detonator wire?"

"Who'd ya' think I am? MacGyver?" He fired another couple of shots sending two newly painted cans spinning in the air, then blew imaginary smoke from the barrel. A big grin spread across his face. "You feelin' lucky, punk?"

"Not especially," I said. "What about your mate, Bangy, can't you talk to him? He might at least be able to suggest a slightly safer way to detonate it."

"He won't talk to me. Though, I think it's his missus won't let him." He swung round, dropped to his knee and fired two quick shots at a tree. "She thinks I'm a bad influence." He straightened up and shouldered the gun. "Tuesday, huh? We'd best get crackin'. No good standin' around here yapping, come and give us a hand to bring up some of these aircraft parts."

I followed Scooter and Wayne down into the tunnels. We came to an archway to a side tunnel which in turn led to a concrete bunker about the size of a double car garage. Old wooden cases, most of them with their lids prised off, lay randomly around the room. A quick glance showed they contained what looked like engine parts packed in wood shavings. Larger lumps of metal lying around seemed to be bits of fuselage panels or wings. Not that I knew that for any reason other than they were painted in the sort of aircraft camouflage pattern I'd seen in movies. *This lot must be worth a fortune to a collector.*

Scooter dragged a couple of objects from one of the packing crates. "Come on then, grab what you can and let's get some of this stuff up topside." He headed off with his load.

I picked up a couple of interesting bits of metal and looked at Wayne. "Do you think you could have a word with him? Persuade him to talk nicely to Bangy?"

Wayne shook his head. "I'm not getting involved. When he gets his mission-head on, there ain't no shifting him." He dragged a piece of equipment out of a crate and dusted off the wood shavings. "This looks like a speedo or something. Cool. I wonder if I can fix it to my moped?"

"Do you think you could get hold of Bangy's number? I could try to talk with him."

"Easy, Scooter leaves his phone in his bag. I'll get the number of it. But don't ell 'im it were me."

We headed upstairs with an armful of aircraft bits and found Gordon waiting outside when we emerged into the sunlight.

"Date's moved," I said. "Jack's filming is Tuesday now."

"This Tuesday?" Gordon asked.

I nodded. "Yes, they brought it forward. Apparently, he's been booked in for some reality TV show in the DRC."

"That doesn't leave us much time." He looked at my armful of aircraft oddments. "That lot for the explosion?"

"Yes, I'm taking it up to the hole."

Wayne emerged from the building and I felt a hand going into my shirt pocket.

"That's the phone number," he said. "Don't say nothing."

I put my finger to my lips.

"Have a look at this." Gordon handed me an ageing leather wallet.

I turned it over and opened it. A section in the back held a few notes, and a couple of other sections held bits of paper or photographs. "Where did you find that?"

"Have a closer look," Gordon said.

There's something strange and voyeuristic about going through somebody else's personal possessions. I felt oddly uncomfortable as I pulled the money from the wallet. That was odd. A couple of ten-shilling notes, a one-pound note and a five-pound note. Old currency notes, yet in surprisingly good condition. I pulled the photo out and unfolded it. That's when I when understood. It was a smaller, and much older looking, version of the picture Gordon had shown me yesterday. David Cameron sitting in the middle of the flight crew of a World War Two bomber plane.

I closed the wallet and tapped it in my hand. "That's seriously convincing. How?"

"Visit to the local junk shop. I doubt it would pass the Antiques Roadshow, but hopefully, it won't need to. Just enough to start the conspiracy theories going."

I handed it back to him. "That should certainly get them going."

"I also thought we could get somebody to turn up, all official looking like, and take something away. Maybe Scooter, doing his Men in Black routine again. Nothing stirs up rumours like something that disappears."

"I like the idea, but not convinced it should be Scooter. He's a bit... unpredictable."

Gordon's eyes widened, and he looked straight at me with a slight grin.

I realised what was going through his mind. "No, not a chance. You can count me *right* out of that one. I'll find somebody else."

Gordon shrugged. "Okay, whatever."

"What are you planning on making disappear?" I asked.

"Hadn't thought about that yet. It's never going to be seen close up, so I guess it's not critical." He looked at the junk I was holding. "Maybe something from that parts bunker."

I persuaded Gordon to grab a handful of bits and pieces from the crates downstairs, then we headed up to where the newbies had dug the hole for Scooter's bomb.

Scooter and Wayne were placing their aircraft bits in a small trench around a pile of rocks.

"Where's the bomb?" I asked.

"Under there." Scooter pointed at the rocks. "It's mostly buried, just the nose poking out so's I can shoot it later."

I took a few steps backwards. "Why all the rocks?"

"Don't want nobody finding it by accident, do we? Couple of hikers going bang will bollox everything up a treat. We'll move 'em before the off."

I looked at my watch in my best Am-Dram overacting. "I've got to go, I promised Jenna a hand with some accounts."

As soon as I was far enough away to not be seen, I pulled out the slip of paper Wayne had slipped me and called the number.

"Lee Bangrove," said the voice.

"Hi, Lee, or is it Bangy? We met the other day... with Scooter? I'm William."

"Oh, yeah, I remember. Can you hold a second? I just need to... there now I've completely forgotten, was it the green wire or the red one I was about to cut?"

"What?" I immediately visualised him deep inside the workings of a bomb and I'd just disturbed his train of thought.

"Just kidding," he said. "Bomb Squad humour. Yeah, I remember, what's Scooter gone and done now?"

"Nothing, well, not yet. It's what he's planning is why I'm ringing you."

"Don't tell me he's planning on carting that bomb of his up to the Houses of Parliament?"

"Close, he's going to try to set it off by shooting it with a paintball gun."

Silence for a moment, then, "He is? That'll be worth me coming down just for the shits and giggles."

"I was hoping you could stop him," I said.

"You don't know Scooter very well, do you? Once he gets an idea in his head, there ain't no turning him."

"So I've been told. Is there a safer way of exploding it then?"

"No, there's no safe way, short of putting an official call in and getting the local OED boys out." The line went quiet, and I thought he'd hung up on me, then I heard a sigh, followed by, "You do know he's going to blow himself up? Look, I reckon I owe Scooter one. Okay, I'll come down and detonate it. I'm not going to be messing around trying to make it safe for him to keep as a toy, or whatever he wants the damn thing for. I'm just going to detonate it, then piss off, right? Nothing fancy, so it doesn't look like a professional dem job. Just bang and go."

"Great, but could I ask you just one other little favour?"

I could hear the gritted teeth through the phone. "I'm not bringing him a box of grenades, if he's trying that one again."

"No, nothing like that. Can you keep a secret?"

"The Queen seems to think so, I signed her bit of paper."

I explained, as briefly as I could, the problem with Rose Well Holiday Park and the UFO project.

"So, what we need…" I paused to summon up the courage to ask, "… is for a couple of guys to turn up and take some artefact away. All secretive and mysterious."

"You mean like Tommy Lee Jones and Will Smith?"

"Yes, sort of."

"Well, why didn't you say that from the off? *Now* this is starting to sound like a party. You just tell Scooter to get the beer on ice."

Bangy ended the call, and I continued on down the slope and back along the track to Route 67.

"Ah, just the man I need." Charlie straightened up from leaning over a manhole in the path. "Grab 'a hold of this will ya?" She handed me the end of a drain rod which disappeared into the hole and off to who knew where.

I did as instructed and she wiped her hands on her overalls. "When I yell, waggle it to and fro, alright?"

"Um, yes, okay."

She disappeared around a corner and I held on to the end of the rod.

"Right? Waggle…. Are you waggling it?"

"Yes."

"What? I can't hear you; did you waggle it?"

"Yes," I yelled.

"Well waggle it again. To and fro."

I waggled it to and fro.

"Ah, thought it was you," a voice said from behind me.

I turned to see that Brian had crept up on me while I'd been busy waggling. "Oh, hi, I was coming over to find you."

"You still waggling?" Charlie's voice from round the corner yelled.

"Yes." I waggled more furiously and turned back to Brian. "The timetable's been moved up. Everything's happening Tuesday now."

"Yes, Jack told us," said Brian. "He's got to fly off to Africa somewhere for one of his specials. It's all very exciting."

"We've always wanted to go to Africa," said Brianna. "All the wild animals."

"We did go to Longleat last year," said Brian. "Not quite the same, but they do have lions and monkeys. Funny story, we were driving through the park and one of those monkeys with the bright red bottom climbed—"

"You stopped waggling?" Charlie's piercing yell interrupted.

"Oh, sorry. How's that?"

"Pathetic. Waggle harder."

I waggled harder and said to Brian, "Sorry, this doesn't leave us much time to get ready. We're going to do a UFO flight, then an explosion during the filming of Jack's promo."

Brianna's eyes brightened. "Ooh, that sounds dangerous. Do you think that's wise?"

"No, not entirely. But on the upside, we do have somebody who knows what they're doing looking after the explosion. Does Jack still want you both to do your foraging bit for his promo video?"

"Oh, yes," said Brianna. "We're going to be on Telly. Brian's going to wear his Countdown pully."

"We're not *actually* doing the foraging though, dearest," said Brian. "Just showing things which have already been foraged."

"Here's one we foraged earlier," Brianna said and giggled.

"Why've you stopped waggling?"

I pulled at the rod violently and it suddenly went slack. I pulled, a bit more gently, and it came towards me with no resistance. I continued pulling, and it came free from the hole at the same time as Charlie emerged from round the corner. She held the other end of the drain rod in her hand. "What you go and do that for?" she demanded.

I looked at the broken rod in my hand. "I only waggled it like you said."

She snatched it away from me. "You didn't have to break it. I'm going to have to explain this now to her Ladyship. Lord knows the aggravation I'm going to get over this." She marched off with the broken parts.

I turned back to Brian. "We'll give you a signal during filming and then you've both got to look over to West Field and point out the UFO."

"What sort of signal?" asked Brianna.

"What? Oh, I don't know, hadn't thought of that yet."

"You could raise a flag," suggested Brian.

"Or it could be a rocket," said Brianna. "Like on sinking ships."

"No, that wouldn't work," Brian said. "We'd probably have the Coastguard out."

"No, no flags or rockets. Somebody will signal to you," I said. "Just a wave or something. We've got to keep it subtle, casual."

"Okey-dokey," said Brian. "Roger that."

"Well, I must be off." I looked at my watch to reinforce my words.

"Are you sure you wouldn't like to join us for an apéritif?" Brian asked. "We're going to sample the first of this year's Birch Sap wine."

"We've been looking forward to it," added Brianna.

"Made with Scooter's special water."

"That sounds lovely," I lied. "But I really have to be…" I struggled and pointed randomly to a small path behind me, "… over there, to… meet somebody about some stuff. Sorry."

"Next time, then," Brian said.

"Yes, next time." I gave a little smile, a small wave, and slipped away down the random path.

As soon as I was out of sight, I paused and breathed while listening to see if I'd been followed. All seemed quiet, so I looked around to see where I'd ended up. The little chapel sat in the background and the small water fountain bubbled into its ornately decorated trough. The Rose Well Spring. Two men stood next to the spring. I thought for a moment they were locals come to fill up their water bottles, but their clothes said no. Smart trousers and neatly pressed shirts generally indicated either tourists on their first day here, or officials. These two were not tourists, their briefcases and clipboards gave that away.

One of them planted his briefcase on the edge of the basin, opened it and removed a tall glass jar. He held it under the running water until it filled to some line I couldn't see, then held it up to the light. He seemed happy with the result and poured a measure into a different jar and gave it a shake. Once more up to the light then handed it to his colleague who applied a little sticky label to the jar.

I moved closer. "Taking in the waters?" I asked.

Both men started and turned.

"Huh? Oh yes," said briefcase man. "We understand it's quite special."

"You on holiday?" I asked.

"Not exactly. Sort of a working, exploratory trip. Well, nice meeting you. We must be off now." He clicked the catches secure on his briefcase and I noticed the double, interlinked letter J of the Jejune logo on the lid.

"Jejune Water?" I said. "Checking out the competition?"

"Ah, yes." He looked at his briefcase. "Good catch. Well, as I said, we really must be going."

"Did you get permission from the owner to take water?" I'd never been good with confrontation, and a part of my sensible brain tapped at the door of the lizard part of my brain demanding to know what the hell I thought I was doing.

The man squared his stance. "But this is open to the public," he said.

"Only if you've registered at the front office," I bluffed. "It's to do with health and safety, all visitors have to report to the front office." I'd read that on a sign on a building site and it sounded nicely official.

"Oh, we didn't realise."

He looked off guard now, and I was beginning to feel emboldened. "That's okay. But you'll have to put the water back, then register. I know it's a pain, but it's the EU and all that." I was now wading into this way beyond the tops of my boots.

The two men shuffled and glanced at each other, then briefcase man smiled curtly, opened his case and emptied the jar in the basin. "We wouldn't want to upset the EU now, would we?"

He clicked his case shut, and they disappeared along the track.

My legs managed to hold on until the men were out of sight, then gave out, forcing me to perch on the edge of the basin. I felt the damp of the splashed water soaking into my trousers but could do nothing about it.

I surveyed the view for a moment, and until my legs decided the danger had passed, then lunch called and set I off for the Pirates Bay. On the way up, I noticed that Codden Ships was now open for the first time during the day, and I stepped inside. The aroma of fresh fried fish and chips and the noises of the frying and shouted orders brought a sense of familiarity and comfort.

"Large cod and chips, please," I said as I approached the counter.

"Coming right up," said the man behind the fryers.

"Not seen you open in the daytime before."

"First day of the season. Still very quiet but gives a chance to get our hand in before the grockles arrive. Salt 'n vinegar?"

"Yes, thanks."

He wrapped up my order in fake, but no doubt hygienic, newspaper, and I took it outside to sit at one of the wooden tables. The fish and chips were every bit as good as they promised to be, although the tiny wooden fork was a complete waste of timber and I resorted to fingers.

I tossed a couple of bits of chips for the squirrels and watched as a handful of starlings swooped and stole them. A figure approached from the path between the office and Pirates Bay. The dark jeans and black shirt identified Jenna long before I could make out her features.

"Might have guessed you'd be the first in there when it opened," she said, and planted herself opposite me.

"I queued all day," I said. "I was hoping I'd catch you."

"Oh yes?" She helped herself to a chip. "Don't tell me, you have a new plan?"

"No, did you know Jack's moved the date of his filming up? It's Tuesday now."

"This Tuesday?"

"Yes, he's off to the Congo to do a reality celebrity show."

"I'm guessing that means the UFO crash is off then?" She licked salt from her fingers, then took another chip.

"No, just the opposite. The guys are getting set to do it on Tuesday."

"Okay, well, we'll just have to hope for the best."

"There's another thing," I said.

Her eyes looked up from under dark eyebrows. "What?"

"I saw a couple of men earlier, down by the spring. They were taking samples of the water."

"That's not unusual." She studied a chip in her fingers. "You should have asked for extra vinegar, they're always a bit tight with it in there."

"I'll remember next time. They were from Jejune, and they looked like they were taking samples for testing."

Her hand froze mid chip-delivery. For a moment she stayed silent in thought, then said, "Right, we'll see about that." She stood upright so fast the table and bench vibrated.

"What are you going to do?" I asked.

"I'm going to cancel all negotiations regarding this place. That's downright sneaky. They've blown it, I'm fighting them every step now." She started walking away, then stopped and spun back to face me. "All of them, whoever tries to stand in my way," she added, then marched off.

Chapter Twenty-Five

MY PHONE BLEEPED. A MESSAGE from Jenna telling me that Eric Scringle wanted to meet with me again.

After only a couple of wrong turns, I managed to find my way back to his cabin. A feat with which I was well pleased, considering the tangle of paths, cabins and static caravans which would have taxed Theseus and his little ball of string.

I tapped on the door. "Hello, Eric? It's me, William? Jenna said you wanted to see me."

The door cracked open, and I assumed a pair of eyes lurked in the gloom somewhere weighing me up.

The door swung wider and Eric's hand appeared, flapping at me. "Come in, come in. Anybody see you?"

"No, I was careful." I slid inside and the door snapped shut behind me.

He shooed me over to the little built-sofa. "Tea?"

I recalled the last cup of tea. "No thanks, I've just had one, and too much caffeine in the afternoon and I'll be up all night."

"I know, I'm the same. I could make it weaker if you like?"

I wanted to ask him if that was actually possible, but instead said, "Perhaps a beer, if you have one?"

"Of course. I always keep a couple in for Jenna. She can't drink tea at all, you know." He took a bottle of Budweiser from the fridge and handed it to me. "How are you getting on with your show?"

"Well, to be honest, I'm beginning to think this might not be completely viable. We have to put up a convincing UFO in broad daylight and rely on one of Scooter's mates to detonate a very dodgy World War Two bomb while convincing the world that David Cameron was part of the flight crew of a 1941 Wellington bomber." I sipped slowly at my beer. "Not to mention, of course, dealing with the authorities afterwards."

"I see. But apart from that?"

"Apart from that, I'd say we're good to go."

"Jolly good." He headed to a large wardrobe. "I have something I'd rather like you to include in your, what shall we say... your Show and Tell box?"

He dragged a couple of cardboard boxes out and dropped them on the bed. "No. That's not it." He pulled an old Atari console from the box.

"I've not seen one of those in quite a while," I said.

"What? Oh that, yes. It's actually what got me started on hunting down UFOs. Ah... here we go." He dragged another box free of the wardrobe and sat with it on his lap as he dived into its contents. He pulled out a disk-shaped object, about the size and appearance of a clay pigeon. He blew dust from its surface and wiped it on his sleeve.

"What is it?" I asked.

"It's a Flux Capacitor. Or is it a Sonic Screwdriver? No, I think that's in a different box."

"Huh?"

"Just pulling your leg." He tossed the object across to me. "I haven't the faintest idea what it is."

I caught it and it felt heavy. The surface shone like a black mirror but oddly, reflected nothing. "Where did it come from?"

"The same place as the omelette machine," Eric said. "The crash site at Rendlesham. There were seventeen of them. All identical."

"What does it do?"

"Did you hear the bit where I said I hadn't the faintest idea?"

"It looks like a sort of frisbee," I said.

"If you like, we can call it a Space Frisbee. I've been calling it a thingamajig, but I think Space Frisbee is a touch more inventive, so I'm inclined to go with that."

"What do you want me to do with it?" I turned it round in my hands in search of some marking or secret opening. Nothing.

"I thought you could just pop it in the hole along with your photograph and aeroplane bits."

"Because...?"

"Well, it's made of something the science bods at Cheltenham were never able to figure out. So if they see another bit, that's going to upset them. Which is good for you as it's another pointer that your little effort here is for real."

"And for you?" I asked.

"For me? I spent thirty years chasing claims of UFOs and debunking them. Which, I was quite happy about as most of them were complete nonsense anyway. Dodgy Photoshopped images, endless sightings of Venus and idiots who get drunk and are convinced they've been anally probed by Martians. But then one day, something falls out of the sky over Rendlesham and all of a sudden we have incontrovertible proof of life outside of our understanding. And what do they order me to do?"

"I don't—" I started.

"They ordered me to debunk that as well," he said. "And then, I'm instructed to bury the reports in a filing system so dense it makes the British Citizenship legislation look like Dr. Seuss. So that," he pointed to the Space Frisbee. "... is now finally going to come out. If you get your publicity, they can't bury this a second time round and they'll finally have to own up to knowing about hiding this stuff."

"So that means..." I thought for a moment to gather the threads of an idea. "That although I'm actually involved in creating a fake UFO sighting, it's turning out to be…" I paused to gather a few more elusive threads. "It's really a real sighting… only not from now… but from before when…" My threads disappeared like a half-forgotten dream making its final exit. "No, sorry. What was I saying?"

"It means, that your conscience is clear. You are not conning people into believing an untruth, you are convincing people into believing a prior truth."

"Yes, that. Only…"

He wagged a finger at me. "Don't overthink it. Just take the Space Frisbee and blow it up along with the rest of your bits."

"Won't they know it's come from you?"

"They don't know I have it. They miscounted how many there were in the first place, then entered a totally different number in a spreadsheet which they accidentally deleted. After that, they mislabelled the box and put them all in the MOD deep storage facility at Porton Down. Hint, if you ever want to dispose of a murder weapon, give it to the MOD archivists and tell them it's important."

~ * ~ * ~ * ~

The following morning, I took the Space Frisbee to show Gordon.

"Where did you get this?" He weighed it in his hand.

"I can't tell you."

"Ah, I see. Eric's back then. How is he? Did you manage to avoid his tea?"

"No. How did you know?"

"He showed me this a couple of years ago. Has he shown you the light sabre yet?"

"Light sabre?"

"Well, that's what it looks like. It's really just a plasticky rod which glows when you get near it."

"No, I've not seen that. What does it do?"

"It glows when you get near it. So, what are you planning on doing with this?" He held up the Space Frisbee.

"I'm going to put it in the hole as a bit more of a convincer. Apparently, it's some weird material that'll drive the forensics' lab, nuts when they try to work out what it is. How are you getting on with coming up with something which will work in daylight?"

"I managed to get hold of this." He held up a huge, yet to be inflated, balloon. "It's a weather balloon, and this time, it's going to be filled with hydrogen—"

"But isn't that explosive?"

"Exactly. They used it in the Hindenburg. Now, inside that, is an LED light set, an electronic igniter and a packet of Potassium Chloride. Once up in the air, the igniter triggers, the hydrogen goes up and sets fire to the Potassium Chloride. The effect will be a glowing orange ball of light suddenly exploding outwards in a spectacular violet coloured explosion."

"That sounds dangerous. Where on Earth are you going to find this potassium stuff?"

He held up a clear plastic bag of white powder, which I assumed was probably the powder in question and not half a kilo of Colombia's finest Marching Powder.

"Atlas World Store," he said with a grin. "The everything shop. And just as a nice piece of synchronicity, Jejune Water use this as an additive in their bottled water."

"Why would they do that?"

"It's good for the heart. Small doses, of course. In larger doses, it's what the American government uses to kill their black criminals."

"That fills me with confidence."

"You've got an unstable, borderline paranoid schizophrenic, wandering around with an even more unstable World War Two bomb and *you're* getting the willies about a bag of mineral salts?"

"Oh, okay, we'll go with mineral salts. How long before this is ready to go?"

"It's pretty much there. Just need to tweak the trigger and we're all set."

After leaving Gordon, I headed up to Scooter's headquarters to see how things were coming together there.

They seemed to be engaged in another of Scooter's exercises. Two figures, who I guessed to be Scooter and Wayne, were wearing rubber Donald Trump masks and dressed in camouflage gear while Grayson and Theo wore orange jump suits and were securely duck-taped to their chairs.

"Kidnap and escape?" I asked.

Rubber Donald Trump number one shook his head. "Just kidnap," Scooter's voice said.

"How long are you going to keep us here?" Theo asked.

"Can you see that rock up there?" Scooter pointed to a granite lump towards the top of the rise.

"Sure."

"Okay, that was the escape word." Scooter took a ridiculously fierce knife from his belt and sliced through the tape holding Theo.

"The escape word was *'sure'*?" asked Theo as he shrugged himself free.

"Yes. We rotate codewords. Keeps them secure," Scooter explained. "It's a random codeword generator algorithm app."

"So, which is it? Do you rotate the codewords or randomly generate them?" Theo asked.

Scooter waved the knife at Theo. "Sit back in the chair."

Theo dropped back into the chair and Scooter wound fresh tape around him. "And that was the codeword for tie me up again," Scooter said. He finished off with a piece across Theo's mouth.

Scooter clearly caught my look of disapproval and snapped, "What?"

"Nothing," I said. "I wasn't going to say anything."

"That's alright then." He dragged the mask from his head. "It's like havin' yer head up a donkey's arse in that thing."

"I just came up to see if everything's okay for tomorrow?"

"All RTM."

"RTM?" I queried.

"Ready to move," answered Grayson.

Scooter looked at Grayson. "You were in?"

"No, Call of Duty." He looked at Scooter's puzzled expression and added. "Play Station. You know… phew-phew-kaboom!"

Scooter slipped behind Grayson and wound another piece of tape around Grayson's head, covering his mouth.

"Bangy's here," Scooter continued. "He changed his mind, I knew he would. He's going to…" Scooter looked down at Grayson then held his hands over the man's ears. "He's going to do… the wotsit, with the thing. Know what I mean?"

Grayson's eyes craned upwards as if trying to see what Scooter was doing behind him.

"I think so," I said.

Scooter looked at Wayne, who still wore his rubber Donald Trump mask. "Take William up the 'ill to where Bangy is. And take that thing of yer 'ead. We've done with that for now."

I walked with Wayne up the gentle hill towards where the trainees had dug the hole a few days ago.

"What's with Theo and Grayson?" I asked.

"Nothing," said Wayne. "Just an exercise like. Kidnapping and seeing how much someone can see once they've been kidnapped."

"Seems like an odd sort of exercise?"

"Dunno. He's not going to kidnap anybody."

I stopped and turned to face Wayne. "Who's he not going to kidnap, Wayne?"

"Nobody. He said to tell you."

"I thought we'd agreed, no kidnapping. I distinctly remember that conversation."

"No kidnapping the mayor. That's what you said."

"Sorry, should I have provided a list of people not to kidnap?"

"Will you two pipe down?" a voice called from the top of the slope and

~ 268 ~

Bangy's head appeared from behind a pile of earth. "I'm up to my ears in eighty-year-old TNT up here and I could do without your yapping." The head disappeared again.

"We'll finish this conversation later," I said.

We covered the last hundred metres in silence and found Bangy in the hole. He was patting fresh earth into a mound inside the bottom of the hole. Some wires trailed from the side of the mound and led out of the hole and onto a large reel.

He slid backwards out of the hole as we arrived and sat up, blinking into our faces as his eyes adjusted to the sunlight.

He clapped dirt from his hands. "Where's Plod with his 'Keep Out' tape when you need him?"

"Sorry," I said.

"I need to concentrate. It's bad enough I have to do this in the first place without you pair of idiots plonking around here like it's Clapham Common on a Bank Holiday."

"How's it going?" I asked, hoping to divert his annoyance.

"Pretty much done. Primer set and ready to go. Just got to put your trinkets in now and cover it over." He upended a khaki kitbag and the Space Frisbee and aircraft parts tumbled to the ground. He lay them gently over the mound, then spread more earth on top.

"What about the photo?" I asked.

He reached into an inside pocket of his black bomber jacket and pulled out the photo. "Don't worry." He lay that on the fresh earth and squashed more around it. "Need to insulate that a bit more from the main bang or all you're going to be left with, is dust."

He opened a pocket on the side of the kitbag and removed a plastic bag full of a rough-cut, ash coloured mixture.

"What's that?" I asked.

"Your mate Gordon's special potpourri. Ground up gas mantles, who'd have thought? It's certainly kicking this thing off a treat." He picked up what looked like an oversized yellow walkie talkie with attached wand. He pushed a button on the side and aimed the wand at the bag. Coloured lights ran across a little screen and a sound like a demented cicada tore at my ears.

"Is that a Geiger counter?" I asked. Then without waiting for the obvious answer added, "That seems scary. How much radiation is there?"

"Nothing to worry about. Unless you eat it. It's around 500 millirem. About the same as an X-ray. But it's certainly enough to wind up the CSI guys."

Bangy emptied the bag in a wide circle around the central mound. "Well, don't just stand there like a pair of tent poles, give me a hand to cover this over." He gently pushed earth over the mound.

Wayne and I knelt on the ground and pushed dirt. Very gently and as much at arm's length as my arms would allow.

"Careful," said Bangy. "It should be stable, but we don't want any surprises."

"So it's all set?" I asked as I stood and brushed dirt from my knees.

"Just need the switch, and I ain't attaching that till the last minute. Now, where can I get a beer and something to eat?"

"I'm heading that way, I'll show you."

I led Bangy to the Pirates Bay.

"Is this place for real?" His eyes scraped the surroundings. "It looks like something out of the nineteen sixties."

"Yup, pretty much. But they do know thirty-five different ways to do chicken and the beer's cheap."

"Sounds like my favourite place already." He slapped my arm. "Join me for a quickie?"

"Maybe later. I just need to check on the promo shoot for Wilderness Jack's book tomorrow."

"Good man." He slapped my shoulder. "Can't beat the Seven Ps."

"Huh?"

"Proper prior preparation prevents piss poor performance." He looked like he was about to slap me again.

I stepped back out of slapping reach. "Yes, that. I'll catch you later." I slipped away, curtailing the chances of any more manly bonhomie.

I made my way down to Tinker's Wood to find a surreal scene awaiting me at the site of the filming for Jack's promo. An array of tubular chrome stanchions formed an arc encompassing the front of the site. I guessed this to be the barrier separating crew from spectators. Beyond that, a collection of cantilevered tripod arrangements supported lights, reflective shields, microphone booms and a couple of umbrellas which sheltered the more delicate electronics from the chance of inclement weather. The area had been flattened and cleared of natural flora while the zone destined to appear on screen had been laid with artificial grass. The whole thing gave the impression of a grotesque, sanitised imitation of the very patch of nature in which it lay.

A couple of seemingly lashed together benches held some cooking utensils, a couple of hunting knives and some stripped-wood boards. A more scrutinous look at the benches revealed that, rather than being constructed by cut wood straights and twine, they were actually wicker garden tables cleverly disguised with artificial foliage.

"Ah, William."

I turned to identify the source of the voice. Lionel, the producer, disengaged himself from a pair of technicians and walked over to me.

"Just the man," he said. "I have a small favour to ask."

"Sure."

"Jack seems to have vanished again. I'm not overly worried as I'm beginning to understand his little ways. However, I wondered if you could keep a watching eye on him, so to speak. Just to make sure he gets here on time tomorrow. He seems to pay more attention to you than anybody else."

That actually gelled with my plans, so I said, "Well, I can try. But I'm not sure I'll have much influence."

Having a good reason to observe the filming suited me, although I would still need to duck out to see how things were going on in West Field.

"We just need him to be here, and if it's not too much of an ask, sober would be helpful."

"You might be pushing your luck on that one," I said.

"Okay, well, can we at least say upright?"

"I'll do my best. Apart from Jack's vagaries, is everything else all set?"

"Just waiting on a fresh delivery of the plants and stuff he'll be demonstrating and a truckload of firewood. Oh, while you're here, you don't happen to have any firelighters? Giles forgot to get them." He gave the evil eye to a young man wearing a cornflower blue sweater draped over his shoulders, whom I assumed to be Giles.

"Firelighters? I thought Jack would use a couple of sticks or a flint stone or something?"

"Really? Oh bless. This is an advertising film. Not Blue Peter. We leave nothing to chance."

"I'll drop a pack by."

"There's a good chap." He headed over to the table and rearranged the knives.

I surveyed the site again, taking in the careful reconstruction of a supposed make-shift camp. A perfect satire of the reality in which it was set, only sanitised and reformed to ensure it worked perfectly in a way that reality never quite manages. The make-shift table was sturdy, the knives sharp, the firewood dry, and the edibles cleaned and wholesome looking. Even the weather was under control with bright lights and canopies if needed.

"Thought I'd find you here," I heard Jenna's voice from behind me.

I turned, and she came alongside me. A family pack of cheese and onion crisps in her hand.

"Oh, hi," I said. "Lunch?"

"Lunch is for wimps." She held the packet towards me to help myself. "How's it going?"

"I think it's all okay." I took a crisp. "They're certainly leaving nothing to chance. They've got the firewood coming from IKEA and the freshly foraged stinging nettles from Sainsbury's. And as for the weather..." I looked at the lamps and canopies. "I think that's being piped in from Jamaica."

"But apart from all that?"

"Apart from all that, this little show bears slightly less connection to reality than our flying saucers." I took another crisp. "How did you get on with Jejune Water? You were going to give them their marching orders?"

Her gaze fixed ahead, but a smile spread across her face. "I told them we'd caught their people here nosing about without my permission and that I wouldn't do business with anybody who works in such a dishonest way."

"How did they take that?"

"Grovelly grovelly. They ended up saying they might consider raising the offer."

"What did you say?"

"I said they could raise the offer up their arse but they still weren't going to get their hands on my water."

"That was very... um, brave of you."

"All in or nowt, as my grandfather used to say. So, over to you now. The fate of my life's work and all I hold dear is in your hands. Crisp?" She held out the packet.

"No pressure then." I dipped into the bag. "Perhaps we should have a slap-up meal to mark the occasion."

"Brilliant idea. Where are you taking me?"

"I was thinking the Pirates Bay, I hear they do a good chicken."

"I'm not eating there, I've seen the kitchen. I was thinking a Harvester at the very least."

"A Harvester it is then."

~ * ~ * ~ * ~

"Have you been to a Harvester before?" the waitress asked.

Jenna and I both made noises of affirmation, but that didn't stop the waitress who had her script to get through. "We have the salad island over there and the carvery with today's selection of choice roasts including beef, pork, lamb and chicken…"

I zoned out as she explained more about salad islands, dessert peninsulas and beverage rocky-outcrops.

Once we'd settled with our meals, I held my glass up and said, "To the new adventure."

Jenna chinked glasses. "You do know I wasn't really looking for adventure? I've always been more of a keeping-my-head down type of person."

I noticed she'd put on a touch of eye makeup for the occasion. I felt honoured. Even her black shirt had little sparkles of silver thread highlights. She tucked a serviette across her jeans and broke a bread roll onto her side plate.

"Some are called to adventure and some have adventure thrust upon them," I said.

"You seem quite confident all this is going to work out," she said.

"Do I? Thank you, I work hard at giving that appearance. Years of dealing with Her Majesty's Inspectorate of Taxes, it's my super power."

"You know if this doesn't work out, I'm running out of options? I can't go crawling back to Jejune, not having just blown them off. They'd skin me."

"Have faith, we have Wayne and Scooter on our side, what could possibly go wrong?"

"Not helping."

I reached across the table and took her hand. I felt her flinch slightly at the public display of affection. "Sometimes, all we can do is give something our very best shot then hope." I lightly squeezed her hand, then broke contact as I sensed her discomfort. "I've been sacked, had my business destroyed by internet behemoths and been made insolvent."

"Still not helping. Am I supposed to be finding some comfort in that?"

"It's what I was going for, but I don't have any huge success stories to relate as examples, so I tend to go for pathos instead."

She smiled and started work on her meal. "I guess there comes a point where keeping my head down turns into burying it in the sand. Besides, I could always hitch up one of the caravans and go off and live on Bodmin Moor." She raised her glass again. "Sod them all, huh?"

"Sounds perfect. Sod them all." We chinked again.

She speared a potato, then paused just before biting. "Um, just refresh me, how's all this going to work tomorrow?"

"Well, Gordon has a larger balloon, it's actually a weather balloon and those things are often mistaken for UFOs anyway. It's dressed up a bit, lights and stuff to make it visible in daylight. That's going up on some really thin fishing line. Brian and Brianna are going to notice it on my signal and make sure the crew filming Jack's promo spot it. It's a safe bet they'll turn their camera to it. That's when Gordon triggers it to explode. Big, colourful flash of some chemical he's got in there. That's Bangy's signal to detonate the bomb with all the Easter eggs—"

"Easter eggs?"

"Hidden prizes. So, huge bang, hole in the ground and bits of World War Two plane and Space Frisbees scattered around. People rush to see, find the Easter Eggs, and we leave the rest to the selfie brigade to spread it all over social media. Job done."

"Sounds simple."

"Foolproof." As I said the word, I knew it was a mistake.

Chapter Twenty-Six

DESPITE THE LATE HOUR OF our eventual bedtime, and the ensuing groping and clawing at each other's bodies, we both awoke before the sparrows.

I sat with my coffee, and bacon and egg sandwich at Jenna's kitchen table. The sky beyond the window drew orange smudges across the sky and gradually replaced them with blue. It looked like being a fine day.

I mentally ticked through the points of the plan again. Most of my plans never actually reached the starting gates, let alone fruition, so there was a strange mix of satisfaction at having got one through this far tinged with the knowledge of past experience that this was probably going to end in spectacular disaster. I just couldn't quite work out how yet.

There were certainly enough variables to ensure the inevitable. An unstable and unpredictable bomb. Trusting Wayne and Scooter to clean the explosion site of the wrong kind of evidence before the authorities descend. Jack doing one of his usual disappearances. The Brians messing up their cues. The balloon failing to explode or even heading off in the wrong direction and landing on the roof of the Little Didney police station. My ability to conjure up visions of breathtaking failure had never disappointed, and today was going to be a humdinger.

I felt an arm slip round my shoulder and Jenna slid into the seat next to me. "Ready to conquer the world?" she asked.

"Not so sure. Though, I might well annoy it a little."

"What time are you meeting Jack?"

"His taxi is dropping him off at Main Building at ten, or thereabouts. That's assuming he gets into it in the first place. Or even if he went to bed in his hotel last night. Knowing Jack, he's probably in a pub in Aberystwyth about now." I turned to look directly at Jenna. "You do realise this is all going to go horribly wrong, don't you? And that I might have been overstating my confidence a bit. Or maybe bit more than a bit."

"You mean your dogged, yet completely unsubstantiated eternal belief in a better tomorrow?"

"It shows, huh?"

"Just a little. But hey-ho," She patted my shoulder and stood. "Even Wiley Coyote's plans worked out sometimes."

~ * ~ * ~ * ~

The taxi pulled up in the gravel car park outside Main Building and Jack tumbled out. I ran to help, expecting to be greeted with drunken ramblings or curses, instead, I found he had simply caught his foot in the seatbelt.

He straightened up and brushed car park dust from his trousers. "Damned seatbelts. Always knew they were dangerous."

"You okay?" I asked. "Can't have any injuries today."

"Not a bit of it." He pulled a silver hip flask from his pocket and took a quick drink. "Did I ever tell you about the time I was in Angola? Damned Chinook went down and my harness jammed. The rebels were closing fast and I had to cut the bloody thing off on a piece of torn metal." He took another drink and dropped the flask back in his pocket. "We got time for a quick half before this thing kicks off?"

"Afraid not," I said. "We're on a tight schedule. I mean, *they* are on a tight schedule. I just have to watch."

"Lead on then, Macduff." He flapped his hand at me.

We headed down to Tinker's Wood and found the site was already a hubbub of activity.

"Ah, Jack," greeted Lionel. "Just in time, your makeup chair is ready. Coffee?"

"With a drop of brandy in it?" Jack said. "Cold mornings aggravate my chilblains. In fact… hold the coffee. No point in diluting the medicine."

"Absolutely, I know exactly what you mean." Lionel guided Jack to the makeup area and as he went, he called, "Wendy, organise a coffee for Jack, will you? There's a love."

I watched as one of the technicians laid out the produce on the pretend makeshift table. A pile of what looked like rocket salad leaves, some garlic, kale, mushrooms, onions, chestnuts. and much other greenery some of which defied identification.

"Some of this isn't even in season," I heard Brian's voice from behind me.

I turned to see both Brians. "Did you get this?" I asked.

"No, I saw a Sainsbury's van arrive earlier, so I assume they ordered it."

"I thought you were doing the foraging?"

"No," said Brianna. "They just want us here as sort of technical advisers."

"But when we told them most of this stuff wasn't in season, they just ignored us," said Brian. "Look, not only are the hazelnuts not in season, but they're still in the plastic bags. And the apples, they're not even an English variety."

"But blackberries are local." I dipped into the little plastic box of blackberries and popped one in my mouth. "I used to pick those as a kid."

"Not in June you didn't," scolded Brianna.

I looked at my watch. It had only moved two minutes since the last time I'd looked. "They should be starting soon, shouldn't they?" I asked nobody in particular.

A steady flow of onlookers gathered around the barriers. Most just stood patiently but others had come more prepared and set up folding chairs and picnic tables.

"Where's Jack?" I heard somebody call.

I looked over to the makeup chair, but he wasn't there. A quick scan of the rest of the area confirmed his absence. I slipped round the back of the cordoned area to see if he was just taking a nature break somewhere. Nothing.

"I thought you were keeping an eye on him?" Lionel strode towards me.

"I thought he was having his makeup done," I said.

"He did that. It only took a minute, he refuses to allow anybody to touch his hair or beard so basically, a bit of primer and a quick dab with the bronzer is about all we can do before he gets uppity. You'd best find him quickly."

I did another circuit of the site and came up empty, so I took off up the track towards the Pirates Bay. I found him leaning against the bar with a pint in his hand. I had to give him credit, that was quite an achievement in such a short time.

"Ah, there you are. I thought you wouldn't be able to resist a quick half while we endure the interminable wait for that lot to organise themselves."

"But we only got there twenty minutes ago," I said.

"Really? Feels like an absolute lifetime." He turned towards Ray behind the bar. "Barman, another of these for my good friend here." He held his arm out towards me.

"We haven't got time," I protested. "They're waiting to start filming." A pint appeared in front of me.

"That's the problem with the world. Everything has to be in such a hurry. Fast food, Polaroid cameras, supersonic passenger planes. No wonder nobody knows how to live in harmony with nature anymore, they're all there waiting for the pizza delivery man instead of watching the animal spoor."

"Well, just this one then." I drank about a third of the glass in one and winced. This was too much, too early, even for me.

Jenna appeared from the kitchen door behind the bar. "What on Earth are you two doing here?" she greeted. "Don't you both have somewhere else you're supposed to be?"

"Mea culpa," said Jack. "But a man can only suffer so many trials of the media focus without a little extra fortitude."

Jenna looked at me. "Aren't you on some sort of schedule with all this?"

"Not my fault. He's very quick."

She gave me the fierce look, and I turned to Jack. "Come on. We've got to get back."

He sank the rest of his drink and turned towards the door. "Forward to battle."

I risked another quick sip of my beer, for a little extra fortitude, then caught up with Jack.

"We can't have you being late for your own promo," I said.

"Indeed. Have you read any of my books?" he asked.

"Sorry, no. Never seemed to find the time."

"Hmm, me neither. I'm not even sure what this latest one's about."

"Surviving Climate Armageddon," I said. "Well, that's the title anyway."

Jack stopped and said, "Good title. I might give this one a go."

We arrived back at the filming set to be greeted by a very flustered Lionel. "There you are." He gave me a black look then guided Jack to the pre-set campfire. "We're waiting to film you lighting this, here," he handed Jack a fire-lighting bow.

Jack flapped his hand at the offering. "I'm not messing around with that. Have you any idea how long it takes to get one of those working?"

"It's just for show. We have a gas igniter hidden in the kindling. Just make it look good."

Jack took the bow and Lionel stepped out of camera shot and said, "And roll."

Jack pretended to roll the stick in the bow and the fire sprang into life. Just a little too conveniently I felt, but I guessed there'd be a lot of editing later.

We then had a scene with Jack sorting through the 'Freshly Foraged' Sainsbury's produce on the table and trimming it with his knife. I checked my watch again. It was close to the time we'd set. I turned to scan the sky over West Field. No sign of the balloon yet but it would be any moment now. I looked for Brian and Brianna to make sure they were watching me for the signal.

No sign of the Brians.

I felt a brick settle in my stomach. I moved alongside Lionel and said, as innocently as I could, "Have you seen the Brians?"

"Who?" he whispered without taking his eyes from Jack.

"The foraging people. Brian and Brianna?"

"Oh, Tweedledum and Tweedledee. We needed some poisonous mushrooms so Jack could show what to be aware of." He risked a glance behind himself. "They should be back by now. How long does it take find a handful of dodgy fungi?" He returned to the action. "No, no. Let's do that bit again."

I scanned the sky again. Still no balloon but still no Brians. At this rate, I was going to have to do the alert myself. Not ideal as I'd wanted to keep myself back from scrutiny.

A noise broke from the far end in amongst the group of people behind the stanchions. A woman broke through the barriers and tumbled into the filming area. She wore a brown coat and brown felt hat with a yellow flower in the band.

"Cut," yelled Lionel.

The woman picked herself up and stared, wide-eyed at the people. She opened her mouth, silently at first, and then from her very soul, yelled, "Aliens. They're here."

Lionel shouted, "Giles? Deal with this."

Giles rushed to the woman's side and fluffed sympathetically around her. "That was a nasty trip. Are you alright?"

"When I said deal with this, I meant get her out of my shoot."

Giles put his arm out for the woman to hold. She slapped it and said,

"I'm old, young man, not decrepit. Get the police I've been kidnapped by aliens."

"Madam," said Lionel. "I assure you, we are not aliens and we have no desire to kidnap you or anybody else."

"Not you, you imbecile," yelled the woman. "I'm talking about the aliens with the big orange heads. They tied me up."

"Mrs Pomfrey?" somebody called. I turned to see Brianna emerging from the woods. She held an armful of very colourful toadstools.

The woman, who I assumed to be Mrs Pomfrey, turned towards Brianna. "Aliens. They kidnapped me."

Jack turned at the commotion. "What the devil's going on?" Flames flickered from the end of his fire-lighting bow.

"Look out," I called, pointing at Jack's burning bow.

"Was that the signal?" Brianna stage-whispered in my direction.

"No, it's Jack, he's on fire," I pointed.

Jack turned around at the sound of his name, trailing the burning bow behind him. Flames caught at the produce table.

"Oh, I say, what's that strange thing in the sky?" Brian stepped forward, aiming a finger at some random point in the sky.

"Not yet," I hissed.

Brianna bustled her way into the set and took Mrs Pomfrey's hands in her own. "What happened, Mrs Pomfrey?"

"I've been kidnapped," wailed Mrs Pomfrey again. "Pushed me off my bike and put a bag over my head. Not human, monsters with huge orange heads. I managed to escape when I broke my umbrella over one of the rascals. He won't be kidnapping any more defenceless old ladies, he won't."

"There it is," repeated Brian. "That strange thing flying in the sky."

I scanned the sky over West Field but there was no sign of our flying saucer. I flapped my hand at Brian, but he didn't see.

A woompf sound from my right caught my attention, and I turned to see the produce stand erupt in flames, right next to Jack. For a moment, he just watched it then looked at the burning bow in his hand. He gave a decidedly girl-like squeal, threw the burning bow across the set and ran in the opposite direction. The burning bow landed in the pile of freshly bought kindling where it immediately caught.

Brianna led Mrs Pomfrey from the centre of the chaos while Lionel hurled his coffee-to-go paper cup at the building flames to zero effect. Giles grabbed a long stick and beat at the spreading fire but only succeeded in spreading it further. I grabbed the cooking pot and emptied the water and here's-some-we-prepared-earlier vegetables over the flames. It damped the fire a bit but not enough and I searched the area for more water.

All the time, the cameraman kept panning the scene, completely lost in his own world of apertures and frame-speeds and seemingly oblivious to the mounting danger.

"I wonder what that strange thing is in the sky," Brian repeated but nobody was listening.

"Oh, hell," I heard a new voice from behind me and turned to see Wayne. He appeared to be trying to conceal something behind his back.

I was just about to approach him when another new arrival rushed onto the scene. This time it was Jenna. She carried a fire extinguisher in each hand. "Here," she said and pushed one at me.

I took a moment to understand how it worked, never having actually used one before, but it proved to be fairly instinctual and within a couple of seconds I had a face-full of carbon dioxide. As soon as my eyes cleared, I tried again and this time the campfire disappeared behind a white cloud. I checked Jenna. She stood watching me from besides the now extinguished flames of the produce table.

I was about to say something in my defence when the ground under us rumbled and the clap of a huge explosion filled my ears. As my ears cleared, all I could hear was Brian saying, "I wonder what that thing up in the sky is."

Wayne looked at me and said, "I was about to tell you about..." He gave an exaggerated wink and nodded his head in the direction of Mrs Pomfrey.

I caught a glimpse of the object he seemed so keen to hide from view. It was one of the Donald Trump masks they'd been using in the kidnapping exercise. I'm not always the fastest in assembling disparate pieces of information but the wheels finally started to click into place.

"Didn't we have a deal about no kidnapping?" I asked him. I kept my voice low but needn't have bothered as the chaos around me would have drowned out an invading medieval army in full armour.

"No," Wayne said, flatly.

"I'm fairly sure we did, I distinctly remember."

"You said no kidnapping the mayor. You didn't say nothing about Mrs Pomfrey."

"I'm sorry, I didn't realise I was supposed to give you a full list of people *not* to kidnap."

"You wanted somebody important you said. Somebody important to see the UFO."

"Mrs Pomfrey?"

"She runs the Little Didney Fudge Emporium. Can't get much more important than that, well, apart from old man Goodenough who runs The Smuggler's, but he gave us the slip."

I noticed a huddle gathering around the cameraman. "Don't go away," I told Wayne and headed over to see what was happening.

The cameraman held his camera at arm's length with the preview screen rerunning a video of the events of the last few minutes. "Here, look," he said. "You can just see it over the trees."

I pushed my way into the group and strained to see the little screen.

"There it is, see?" the cameraman said. "Just for a moment then it's gone."

The squashed group went ooh, then aah as a tiny dot on the screen suddenly turned into a purple flash then disappeared.

"What was it?"

"Some sort of aircraft."

"But it stood still in the sky."

"Is that what the explosion was?"

"I was kidnapped by alien monsters."

"Come and have a sit down, Mrs Pomfrey."

"They were going to probe me."

"Has somebody called the police?"

"We should go and see what's going on."

The group started to disperse and I approached the cameraman. "Can you make it any clearer?" I asked.

"Maybe in the studio," he said. "But to be honest, I didn't have time to focus, I was just panning across the fire when I caught sight of it. It was gone before I could get the right settings."

I grabbed Wayne and hissed, "Get rid of that thing."

"What this?" He held up the mask for me to see.

I snatched it out of his hand and scrunched it up into my pocket. "Come on, we need to get to the field before this lot."

Chapter Twenty-Seven

WAYNE AND I HAD A slight edge on the charging herd. We knew exactly where to go and we knew the shortcuts. Even so, we only arrived just ahead of the throng of excited onlookers.

I ran up the slope to where the bomb had been set. Gordon and Scooter were already there and poking around in the debris. Clods of earth and bits of metal lay scattered around the hole. Gordon was busy sprinkling more of the ground-up gas mantles around the area while Scooter desperately dragged Bangy's trigger wire from under a pile of dirt which had covered it.

The jabbering voices closed on our position, and I signalled everybody to pull back a bit to make it look like we'd just arrived.

Just as the group crested the brow of the slope, I heard a loud engine approaching. I turned to see a black van bouncing up the slope. Blue lights flashed from the roof and dirt threw up from the wheels as it sped across the field. Apart from the lights, there were no identifying features at all. No signs, no number plates, even the windscreen was blackened.

"Oh hell," I muttered. "Who's that?"

"Don't worry," said Scooter. "Just help us keep everybody back for a moment."

The van slid to a halt between the bomb crater and the approaching, and growing, crowd. Two men jumped out. They wore black jump suits, again with no markings, balaclavas and carried weapons slung across their shoulders. One of them carried what appeared to be a rolled-up field stretcher.

"Bangy?" I whispered to Scooter.

"Who'd ya think it was? The bleedin' Pope?" He headed to the approaching crowd and held his hand up. "Stay back," he yelled above the noise. "It might be dangerous."

The crowd paused in confusion. Their hesitancy sent clear signals that the pauses were only going to be very temporary at best. I turned to watch Bangy and whoever it was with him. They ran to the hole and disappeared below the mound of thrown earth in front of it. The crowd murmured as their bravado increased in direct proportion to their growing numbers. They started pressing forwards again.

A moment later, Bangy and his companion popped up from the dip. They carried the now unrolled field stretcher between them, and on top of which sat an orange globe. They trotted across to the van and slid the stretcher into the back. One of the men jumped in with it and the doors slammed shut. The other man ran to the driver's door and within seconds, they were speeding back down the slope to the collected dropped jaws and wide eyes of the still growing crowd.

Emboldened by numbers, people began to push forwards to the crater. One or two at first, then more as it became apparent the vanguard hadn't been zapped by alien death ray machines.

"Need to try to keep them back until the police arrive," said Scooter as he interposed himself as much as possible between crowd and crater.

I was still trying to process what had just happened, but did as instructed. Scooter suddenly seemed in his natural environment. He was taking charge of a chaotic and potentially dangerous situation with a relaxed confidence I'd never seen in him before.

The four of us flapped arms and repositioned ourselves constantly as the onlookers pressed forwards. It felt like we were trying to hold back a plague of locusts with a can of fly spray.

I found myself next to Gordon and risked a snatched exchange. "What was that?"

"That was Bangy and his mate doing their Men in Black routine. And the thing on the stretcher was my prize bowling ball with a fresh coat of paint. And I want it back when all this is over."

I dodged to the left to distract a young man who looked like he was preparing himself for a run at the crater. Cameras and phones thrust forwards, and sometimes backwards in selfie mode as people were already counting their forthcoming 'Likes' and 'Shares' on social media.

"And the van?" I asked as we came within speaking range again.

"Yeah, impressive huh? Apparently it's a military hearse. For when they need to be discreet. Bangy wouldn't tell me how he got hold of it, but I'm guessing he didn't sign it out."

Another push by the crowd. We were now in physical contact with them and nobody was interested in our pleas that this might be a dangerous area. Our main concern was not the photos or selfies, or even people poking at our evidence. We just needed them not to start dragging stuff off as souvenirs before it had been seen by some credible witnesses. And a flash mob dedicated to gaining more social media likes than their virtual friends was hardly credible.

The cavalry arrived remarkably quickly. Faint sirens drifted through the air and then a set of blue lights appeared over the rise attached to a police Landrover. A couple more, not quite so agile, police cars struggled up the mud behind it. Within a couple of minutes, a circle of blue tape surrounded the area and several burly policemen pushed at the crowd.

As we slid into the anonymity of numbers, I noticed the cameraman from Jack's promo shoot filming the scene. I wondered how long he'd been here. Before long, a large white van arrived, it bore the legend, 'Royal Logistic Corps - Bomb Disposal'. Several men in army uniform jumped out and the circle of onlookers was pushed back even further. Another van arrived shortly after, this one, Devon and Cornwall Police - Forensic Investigation. A white tent was rapidly constructed over the crater, and people in white overalls scurried around with pieces of equipment while one of the army guys walked a Belgian Shepherd dog around the area.

All gradually fell quiet as the calm efficiency of these professionals went about their work as if they did this every day.

I took the opportunity to slide away and headed back to Rose Well Park Downtown. I felt a cold beer in the Pirates Bay calling loudly.

The Pirates Bay offered the sanctuary of its own unique, but now comfortably familiar, version of normality. A puppeteer entertained a group of children who sat on the floor in front of the stage while their parents drank wine, ate the kids' party food and chatted at tables just behind them.

Further into the bar area, a scattering of individuals sat at table with beer or snacks, reading papers or watching the silent big-screen sports showing at the far end. I guessed it wouldn't be too long before the excitement at West Field reached this far.

"Isn't there somewhere else you're supposed to be?" Jenna greeted as I settled on a stool at the bar.

"Nope, my work here is done." I took the beer Jenna slid towards me. "The police are up there now, so it's all out of my hands." I felt strangely calm.

"Do you think we should go up there and tell them it was all a joke? You know, before they find out for themselves?"

"We just need to keep calm now. There's nothing they can trace back to us."

"Seriously? You fancy our chances once they get Wayne handcuffed to an iron table in the police station and start with their grilling."

"You've been watching CSI again, haven't you?"

"Just because I like detective thrillers, doesn't mean they're not real."

I took her hand. "Don't worry. Just savour the moment of one of my plans actually working."

"I think we'll hold judgement on the whole *working* part until we see if you still have your freedom and I still have a business."

"Cynic."

Jenna went off to serve a small girl in a party frock who knelt on one of the barstools, surveying the row of pretty coloured liqueurs behind the bar. As Jenna approached her, the child pointed to a bottle of Blue Curacao.

I sat there with my beer, watching the increasingly confused ebb and flow of people. Somebody would rush in and talk excitedly with another already there then they would both rush out. This happened several times and with increasing frequency. On the other hand, other people would wander in looking confused. Stare around for a moment, then exit again. Sometimes they stopped to talk to somebody, at which point they would then both run out.

I figured word was getting around.

"What is it with this place and UFOs?" a loud voice complained as a silhouette entered from the bright sunlit door.

I squinted at the person as he materialised in the internal lighting. Jack pushed his way through the growing numbers and arrived at the bar.

"Every time I come to this place I get upstaged by Martians, or whatever the hell they are."

"Maybe it's you they're coming to visit," I suggested.

"Wouldn't mind if that was it." He spotted Jenna and called, "A large whisky, my dear. Better make it a double."

"Is that a large whisky or a double, or a double large, sir?" Jenna tried to conceal her distaste for Jack but failed.

"Just leave the bottle, my agent will sort it out with you." He turned back to me. "Ruined my book promotion. Months of work and then not only does ET turn up in the middle of it and steal my publicity, *my* publicity, but then he blows up his flying saucer all over the shop and everybody buggers off and leaves me standing there looking as sorry as a carrot in a McDonalds."

"Is that what it was, do you think?" I asked. "An alien spacecraft?"

"They filmed the damned thing. They were supposed to be filming me and they wasted all their film on that nonsense." He filled his glass with whisky, then took a drink straight from the bottle. "If they think they're getting paid for this, they're on the wrong bus."

"Well, I think they should give you any profits they make from the film."

He stopped and looked at me in silence for a moment, then, "You know what? You're right. Have a drink with me." He pushed the bottle in my direction.

"Maybe later, I have to see a man about a hole."

I slipped through the pressing crowd and into the sunlight.

As I reached West Field, the whole place was beginning to look like Glastonbury Festival. Crowds milled around, trying to gain a glimpse of what was going on in the police tent. Several food vendors had already set up stands to take advantage, one man wandered the crowds with an armful of hats with pictures of an alien on and a balloon seller seemed to be doing a grand business with helium balloons printed to resemble the Star Wars Death Star. That was a bit too close for comfort. Through it all, a variety of police and men in white jump suits flowed in and out of the tent.

I slipped through the people, tuning my ear to snippets of conversation as I went.

"Did you see the crash? It must have been a huge spaceship."

"Somebody said the Men in Black arrived and took away the quantum drive."

"A guy over there said there are bits of old, World War Two planes there. Like they came through a time vortex."

"I heard they've captured a live alien."

"Like to see them try to cover this one up."

A rise in noise came from the crater and the crowd started squashing backwards. We were being pushed down the slope. I strained to see or hear what was going on, but couldn't make anything out.

The movement away from the centre became more urgent, and I began to catch a few shouts. People were shouting about radiation and maybe more explosions. Clearly somebody had detected Gordon's trail of radioactive dust and the police were widening their cordon. I kept up with the backwards movement until I decided I'd seen enough and broke free of the mass.

I returned to my cabin. It looked lonely, having not been occupied for a while. I could have gone to Jenna's house, but I felt the need to be on home ground for a moment. Home ground? When had I decided this place was home?

I switched the television on and tuned to the local news. As expected, the events here were the main item. It looked like they had a crew on-site, although I hadn't noticed them. The newscaster was being careful with her words and just talked about a strange explosion and the police were investigating some debris. Reassurances were given that it wasn't terrorist related, and the police had no reason to believe it was deliberate.

My smartphone gave a flurry of beeps from various social media outlets who were all less circumspect with their assessments. Much jabber about aliens and the Men in Black. Wild speculation about the source of the radiation occupied a lot of space, and several threads were already well under way about the nature of the aircraft wreckage.

I sat back on the sofa and breathed slowly to quell a rising panic. I told myself it was too late to panic now, the train had left the station and whatever happened next was totally beyond my control.

A gentle tap at the door demanded my attention. "Come in," I called. I didn't feel up to moving just yet.

The door swung open and Jenna stepped inside. "I thought I'd find you here," she said.

She settled alongside me on the little sofa.

"Just catching up with…" I waved my arm in the general direction of the television. "… all this."

"Is that Mrs Pomfrey?" Jenna pointed to the screen where a woman in a brown felt hat with a yellow flower in the band was being interviewed.

"You know her?" I asked.

"Everybody knows Mrs Pomfrey. She makes the local fudge, Little Didney Fudge, it's famous. Turn up the volume a bit."

I turned it up and listened to Mrs Pomfrey explaining to the reporter how she'd been kidnapped by aliens.

"Oh, dear," said Jenna. "I think she's lost the plot entirely. I always worried about her."

"Hmm, perhaps I should explain something here."

She fidgeted around in the small space to face me and locked eyes with me. "Go on." It sounded like a threat.

"Well, Wayne and Scooter—"

"Wayne and Scooter?" she interrupted. "I might have known."

"No, wait, they came up with this plan. They wanted to kidnap somebody important to witness the crash." I looked at Jenna, hoping that would be sufficient. Her silence confirmed it wasn't, so I continued, "They wanted to kidnap the mayor but—"

"The mayor?"

"Yes, but I stopped them. I said definitely *no* to kidnapping the mayor."

"But somehow, kidnapping Mrs Pomfrey seemed like a good idea?"

"No, not at all. But they did it without me knowing. Then she escaped."

"Hmm, well good for Mrs Pomfrey. I wouldn't want to try to kidnap her."

We turned back to watch more of the interview.

"And they had giant orange heads and they were going to probe me with their probing thing and…"

Jenna looked at me again. "Giant orange heads?"

"Yes, they got hold of some rubber Donald Trump masks," I said.

"Donald Trump masks? Good grief, this gets worse. We're all going to prison."

We sat and watched more of the various news items and kept a watching eye on social media. The main thread appeared to be that something, possibly alien or possibly government top secret, had crashed and the powers were moving to cover it up. Rumours were already flying around about World War Two planes coming back through a time vortex and crashing and nuclear leakage from some alien craft.

"I'd offer to cook," I said after the news became too repetitive. "But I've only got one packet of Pot Noodles."

"I've got some birthday cake and cucumber sandwiches with the crusts off back at mine," Jenna said.

"Who could resist a temptation like that?"

We went back to her house, ate crustless cucumber sandwiches and pink birthday cake then finished off a bottle of wine. When we eventually tumbled into bed, I reached to hold Jenna's hand, then sleep closed over me like a warm black fog.

Chapter Twenty-Eight

A FARAWAY WARBLING COASTED INTO my dreams and I awoke entwined in Jenna's arms. I listened, but the sound went away.

I had a faint recollection of stirring a few times in the night, finding we were either holding or snuggled into each other. I put it down to the fact we were both savouring our last night of freedom before the forces of outrage descended and carted us off to do fifty years' hard labour for causing a public nuisance.

I untangled myself and stumbled to the coffee making area. I had to pause for a moment, leaning against the worktop, while I gathered enough brain power to work out what happened next. I turned taps, boiled water and dispensed into mugs while my mind replayed bits of the day before. Mrs Pomfrey, Jack on fire, police everywhere. I might have misjudged this one.

"You're up early," a sleepy voice drifted from the bedroom.

"I have a lot of coffee to get through."

There was the warbling sound again. This time I recognised it as my phone. I picked it up and wedged it between shoulder and ear while I finished making the coffee.

"Hello?" I said into the unknown.

"William? It's Keeley."

"Huh?"

"Keeley Trevellick. From the Sentinel."

"Sorry, yes I recognised your voice." I put Jenna's coffee on the bedside table. "The grunt was my attempt to say hello, how are you this bright morning?"

"Okay, heavy night?"

"Heavy few months. What can I do for you?"

"Nothing really, just got Lucas all over me demanding to know what the hell's going on at Rose Well Park and why I'm not covering it."

"I see." I sat on the edge of the bed and sipped at my coffee.

"You see?" Keeley challenged. "ET's crashed his spaceship in your garden, after colliding with what looks like a World War Two bomber and all you can say is, I see?"

"I'm sure there's a rational explanation." I felt Jenna stroking my back.

"I'm sure there is, and I wouldn't mind betting you know more than you're letting on."

"You think I arranged for a UFO to crash here?"

"Oh, no. I know your wild schemes from past days. This is way too out there, even for you. I just want the story. You owe me."

"What can I tell you?" I smiled at Jenna to let her know I had this. She pursed her lips and frowned to let me know she didn't believe me.

"You can tell me what you know."

"Well, it all started forty billion years ago with a big bang and when things started to cool—"

"William," Keeley snapped down the phone. "Cut the bullshit, come on, for an old friend."

"I tell you what, persuade Lucas to run an advertising feature on Rose Well Holiday Park and you get the exclusive. How's that?"

"What makes you think he'll go for that?"

"I know how you can wrap him round your little finger, especially if it might sell copy. Deal?"

The phone stayed silent for a moment, then I heard Keeley draw a deep breath. "Deal," she said. "Get dressed, I'll be down in an hour."

I met Keeley at the seating area outside Big Moo Burger. She wore a shortish, dark blue, button through dress. I guessed she was aiming at social rather than business.

"Coffee?" I asked.

"Do they do latte macchiato?" She peered towards the counter area, trying to see the coffee menu.

"I'll find out."

I went inside and collected a latte macchiato for Keeley and a white coffee with extra caffeine for me.

"Apparently it's the same thing as a latte, but upside down," I said as I put the cardboard cups down. "I never knew that."

"Well, there we go," she said. "You've learned something new and now you tell me something." She smiled.

"What do you want to know?"

"You can start with what you saw yesterday. I understand you were one of the first on the scene."

We chatted for about an hour or so. I gave her the censored version but added in a few details which I doubted she'd got from whoever else she'd been talking with. I told her about the old aircraft parts I'd seen lying around and about the radiation traces the police had found. I guessed she knew that, but it gave her confirmation. I told her about the mysterious men who appeared and collected a strange orb from the site.

She asked me if I'd heard anything about a kidnapping, so I gave her my slightly modified version about the kidnapping of Mrs Pomfrey. I figured it was Public Domain by now anyway, so why not?

I also said I'd seen a wallet on the ground by the site, but a policeman had taken it away in a plastic bag. I hadn't actually seen that, but I guessed it must have happened. She seemed particularly interested in that.

"So," she said as she switched off her recorder. "Tell me, do you believe the things they collected show real evidence of extra-terrestrial life?"

Her eyes searched mine. We'd never had a relationship other than that of colleagues, but we knew each other well enough to read the truth when we heard it.

"I can honestly say that I've seen stuff here that I believe came from something not made on Earth."

"That's a very circumspect answer." She studied me carefully. "I think I'm going to take it at face value."

"Thank you," I said.

"I'm not quite sure what's going on here, but you'll get your feature piece."

We chatted for a while longer about the old days and then parted with a handshake and a promise to keep in touch.

~ * ~ * ~ * ~

For the rest of the day, Jenna and I fielded a constant stream of phone calls from various branches of the media. We gave them all the same answer, the Daily Sentinel had the exclusive and all questions should be aimed in that direction.

A day later, the Sentinel ran a huge piece about the event, complete with a reproduction of the photograph of David Cameron as part of the flight crew of a Second World War bomber crew. I guessed the police must have owned up to it under pressure from the Sentinel. Much speculation followed about its authenticity, and I had no doubt it would be proved fake before long. But by then, the conspiracy theorists would be all over it, and it would live on forever alongside the faked moon landings, the twin towers false flag, the JFK shooting and a dozen other zombie conspiracies which refused to die. However, the paper did suggest that, according to sources within the MOD, certain other items were found which were currently being studied by scientists at Porton Down. I guessed they weren't going to be able to keep the Space Frisbees secret for much longer. At least Eric would be pleased.

Interestingly, the Sentinel actually linked this story with the Rendlesham event and several other sightings which have always proved problematical to the debunkers.

As soon as the Sentinel printed their story, Jenna's booking line exploded into life and within two days, all accommodation was fully booked for the next two weeks.

A couple of days later, we had our feature spread in the paper as promised and the forward bookings extended into months instead of weeks.

The waves pushed at the rocks below. Steadily and persistently, as they had done for millennia. The late afternoon sun clipped at the horizon and, for a moment, painted a golden path across the water to the beach below us.

Jenna leaned into me. I didn't know if it was affection or if she was just shifting to a more comfortable position on the hard wooden bench.

"I had a phone call this morning from Jejune Water," she said.

"Oh, what did they want?" I asked.

"They want shot of West Field and did I want to buy it. Apparently, owning a plot of radioactive land is bad for their image."

"Bit of a climb down for them?"

"Indeed, they already tried selling it back to old Tom Pengelly, the farmer who sold it to them in the first place, but he told them to sling their hook. Seems they're a bit stuck."

"Well, now the bank are falling over themselves to invest in Rose Well

Park, why not? You've been thinking about expanding the accommodation capacity. Here's your chance, you'll get it for a fraction of its worth. There's no one else they can sell it to."

"Scooter will have to move his headquarters. He doesn't take easily to change, you know what he's like. Sandwich?" Jenna took the clingfilm from a paper party plate full of sandwiches and placed it on her lap. "Egg and cucumber, I think."

I took one and studied it. Bite sized with the crusts cut off. "Scooter'll go along with it. He's getting so much interest in his Prepping Courses now, it's time he upgraded."

Jenna's phone warbled, and she pulled it from her pocket. She squinted at the screen. "Zero one? That's America, isn't it?"

"Yes."

She answered the call and stood. Her facial expression showed puzzlement, but I couldn't make out what was happening as her end of the conversation consisted mostly of monosyllables. She paced up and down while talking. Eventually, she closed the call and returned the phone to her pocket then settled back on the wooden bench.

"Well, that was an odd call," she said.

"Go on."

"American, somebody called Sam Wilkes. Says he's the mayor of Roswell, New Mexico. That's the place you kept on about, isn't it? With the alien stuff and all the tourists?"

"The mayor of Roswell? *The* Roswell? What did he want?"

"He wants to twin with us. He says, can he bring a delegation over for an official ceremony? Hands across the Atlantic sort of thing."

I munched thoughtfully on an egg and cucumber sandwich. "Cool."

"Cool? Is that the official response from my Head of Publicity?"

"Yes, I've been meaning to discuss that with you. With all this extra responsibility, and now the twinning thing, I think I should be a director at least."

"A director, huh?" Jenna raised an eyebrow and watched me.

"Yes, I was thinking Director of Public Relations. Or, *International* Public Relations now, given this latest development."

"I'll put it to the board. Meanwhile, you're cooking tonight." She covered the sandwiches again. "I did lunch."

The End

Author Note
I do hope you enjoyed this tale, if so, I would be grateful for a few words as a review on your favourite book buying website or Goodreads. Reviews are very important to us authors and I always appreciate them.

Many thanks.
David

~ *Find my books and sign up for the newsletter* ~

If you would like to subscribe to my Newsletter, just enter your details below. I promise not to sell your email address to a Nigerian Prince or send you adverts for various biological enhancements.

I will however, at entirely random moments, send you a newsletter containing my writing updates, competitions, give-aways, general meanderings and thoughts on the latest Big Thing.

luddington.com/newsletter

Or to find out more about the author

To Follow On Facebook: facebook.com/DavidLuddingtonAuthor

The Website: www.luddington.com

Twitter: @d_luddington

Other Books From This Best Selling Author

Tony Ryan is bemused. He thought he understood the way the world worked, but now, as a sacrificial lamb of the credit crunch he finds himself drifting... drifting into the clutches of the ever resourceful Pete who could find the angle in a Fairy Liquid bubble... and into the arms of the enigmatic hippy girl, Astrid, who's about to introduce Tony to rabbits, magic caves and the joys of mushrooms.

Charles Tremayne is a spy out of his time. After a long career spent rescuing prisoners from the KGB or helping defectors across the Berlin Wall the world has changed. The Wall has gone and no longer is there a need for a Russian speaking, ice-cold killer. The bad guys now all speak Arabic and state secrets are transmitted via satellite using blowfish algorithms impenetrable to anybody over the age of twelve. Counting down the days to his retirement by babysitting drunken visiting politicos he is seconded by MI6 for one last case. £250,000,000 of government money destined as a payoff for the dictator of a strategic African nation goes missing on its way to a remote Cornish airfield.

Tremayne is dispatched to retrieve the money and nothing is going to stand in his way. Armed with an IQ of 165 and a bewildering array of weaponry and gadgets he is not about to be outmanoeuvred by the inhabitants of a small Cornish fishing village. Or is he?

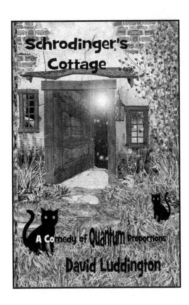

Tinker's Cottage nestles in a forgotten corner of deepest Somerset. It also happens to sit on a weak point in the space time continuum. Which is somewhat unfortunate for Ian Faulkener, a graphic novelist from London, who was hoping for some peace and quiet in which to recuperate following a very messy breakdown.

It was the cats that first alerted Ian to the fact that something was not quite right with Tinker's Cottage. Not only was he never sure just how many of them there actually were, but the mysterious way they seemed to disappear and reappear defied logic. The cats, and of course the Pope, disappearing literary agents, mislaid handymen and the insanity of Cherie Blair World.

As Ian tries to untangle the mystery of the doors of Tinker's cottage he risks becoming lost forever in the myriad alternate universes predicted by Schrodinger. Not to mention his cats.

Schrodinger's Cottage is a playful romp through a variety of alternate worlds peopled by an array of wonderful comic characters that are the trademark of David Luddington's novels.

For fans of the sadly missed Douglas Adams, Schrodinger's Cottage will be a welcome addition to their library. A heart-warming comedy with touches of inspired lunacy that pays homage to The Hitchhiker's Guide whilst firmly treading its own path.

"...And there will be a corner of some foreign field that will be forever England."

Only these days it's more likely to be a half finished villa overlooking a championship golf course somewhere on one of The Costas.

Following an unfortunate encounter with Spanish gin measures and an enthusiastic estate agent, retired special effects engineer Terry England is the proud owner of a nearly completed villa in a new urbanisation in Southern Spain.

Not quite how he'd intended to spend his enforced early retirement Terry nevertheless tries to make the best of his new life. If only the local council can work out which house he's actually bought and the leaf blowers would please stop.

Terry finds himself being sucked in to the English Expat community with their endless garden parties and quests for real bacon and Tetley's Tea Bags. Of course, if it all gets too much he can always relax in the local English Bar with a nice pint of Guinness, a roast beef lunch and the Mail on Sunday.

With a growing feeling that he might have moved to the 'Wrong Spain', Terry sets out to explore and finds himself tangled in the affairs of a small rustic village in the Alpujarras. It is here where he finds a different Spain. A Spain of loves and passions, a Spain of new hopes and a simpler way of life. A place where a moped is an acceptable means of family transport and a place where if you let your guard down for just a moment this land will never let you go again.

Forever England is the tale of one man trying to redefine who he is and how he wants to live. It is a story of hope and humour with an array of eccentric characters and comic situations for which David Luddington is so well known and loved.

"Overall, this is a very warm and funny book. It is filled with wonderful characters and many laugh out loud moments." book-reviewer.com

"Genuinely funny, with many laugh out loud moment..." Matt Rothwell - author of Drunk In Charge Of A Foreign Language

"Always at the heart of it, that deadpan wit" — Nigel Planer

Whose Reality is this Anyway?

David Luddington

Author of the Best Selling comedy, 'Forever England'

Reading David Luddington is like *"Like reading your favourite sitcom." – Nigel Planer*

Retired stage magician turned professional mystic debunker, John Barker, finds his sceptical beliefs under fire when he encounters a strange man who claims to be Merlin. After several unsuccessful attempts to rid himself of his increasingly unpredictable companion, John finally relents and agrees to assist in the man's crazy mission, to find the true grave of the mythical King Arthur.

Following a hidden code contained within the text of a soft porn novel, they gather a growing entourage of hippies, mystic seekers and alien hunters as they leave a trail of chaos across the south west of England. When the group comes to the attention of a TV Reality Show producer looking to make a fast profit out of harmless eccentrics and fading celebrities, John decides it's time to take charge and prove one way or the other, the identity of this mysterious person who claims to be a fictional wizard.

"Whose reality is this anyway?" is a warm-hearted tale of what it means to be an individual and to follow one's dreams. With his trademark cast of oddball characters and absurd situations, David Luddington once more transports us into a world where who you are is more important than what you are.

"David Luddington epitomizes the elusive quality of writing that he perpetuates - the British Comedy." – Grady Harp

"Like reading your favourite sitcom"
Nigel Planer

CAMP
SCOUNDREL
Doing what it takes to survive paradise

DAVID LUDDINGTON
Author of the Best Seller - 'Forever England'

When ex-SAS soldier, Michael Purdy, comes in front of the judge for hacking the bank account belonging to the Minister for Invalidity Benefits and wiping out his personal wealth, he braces himself for a prison sentence.

What Michael doesn't expect, is to be put in charge of a group of offenders and sent to a remote location in the Sierra Nevada Mountains in Spain to teach them survival skills as part of their rehabilitation programme.

But Michael knows nothing at all about survival skills. He was sort of in the SAS, yes, but his shining record on the "Escape and Evasion" courses was more a testament to his computer skills than his ability to catch wildlife and barbecue it over an impromptu fire. Basically, he was the SAS's techy nerd and only achieved that position as a result of a bet with a fellow hacker.

Facing a stark choice between starvation or returning home to serve out their sentences, the group of offenders under Michael's supervision soon realise that the only way to survive is to use their own unique set of skills – the kind of skills that got them arrested in the first place.

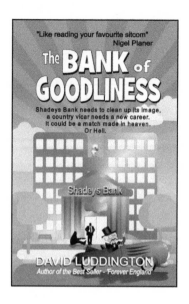

When Shadeys Bank loses yet another C.E.O. to a major scandal, they are desperate to show they've reformed. Who better to present their redemption to the world than a country vicar with a reputation for being annoyingly good?

Reverend Tom Goodman is ousted from his job as a country vicar for allowing a homeless family to stay in the church hall. Meanwhile, a major bank is trying to rescue its image after the latest in a long string of financial scandals.

It seems like the perfect match and Goodman is hastily appointed as the bank's new C.E.O. All they have to do now, is promote him as the new face of Shadeys Bank whilst at the same time, keeping him away from the day-to-day business of dubious banking.

However, Tom Goodman has other ideas. He's not going to be satisfied with being used as an empty puppet for a PR stunt. Unfortunately for Shadeys, Tom is planning on actually making a difference.

And so begins an epic battle of wills. The might of a multi-billion pound bank versus a seemingly naïve country vicar.

No contest.

"Yes Minister meets The Vicar of Dibley."

Lightning Source UK Ltd.
Milton Keynes UK
UKHW010240090223
416650UK00001B/48

9 781913 833978